BULLET IN THE CHAMBER

By

John DeDakis

Published in the United States of America by:

Strategic Media Books, Inc.
782 Wofford St., Rock Hill, SC 29730.
www.strategicmediabooks.com

Manufactured in the United States of America.

ISBN-10: 1-939521-63-7

ISBN-13: 978-1-939521-63-7

Requests for permission should be directed to:
strategicmediabooks@gmail.com

or mailed to:

Permissions
Strategic Media Books, Inc.
782 Wofford St.
Rock Hill, SC 29730

Distributed to the trade by:

Cardinal Publishers Group
2402 North Shadeland Ave., Suite A
Indianapolis, IN 46219

Cover design by Christine Ganas

DEDICATION

For
Stephen John DeDakis
Beloved Son
July 25, 1989 – August 21, 2011
Too young. Too soon.

ADVANCE PRAISE

Bullet in the Chamber is two stories — an intensely personal one wrapped inside a thriller that moves at high-speed. They collide at 1600 Pennsylvania Avenue. DeDakis combines the heart-stopping and heartbreaking in a story of drugs, drones, corruption and politics. Lark's latest adventure is entertaining and harrowing. And always riveting.

> ~ *Henry Schuster, CBS News "60 Minutes" Producer*

There are a lot of novels about White House correspondents. There are only a few by folks who have actually been there. Washington journalist John DeDakis writes about an AP correspondent on her first day on the job – when disaster strikes. What follows will keep you turning the pages.

> ~ *Susan Page, Washington Bureau Chief, USA TODAY*
> *Past President, White House Correspondents' Association*

I've been there. So has John DeDakis. Lark Chadwick's first days as a White House correspondent are spot-on. DeDakis kept me turning pages well past two o'clock in the morning. His writing is so real I couldn't put down *Bullet in the Chamber* for the last fifty pages, then woke up the next morning worrying about how I would advance the story.

> ~ *Carolyn Presutti, Voice of America (VOA) TV Correspondent*

DeDakis effectively lures us into his professional and personal world, yet from the perspective of a young female protagonist whose strength we can all admire.

> ~ *Carine McCandless -*
> *Author of the New York Times Best Seller "The Wild Truth"*

Finally! A man who understands women — and the human condition. *Bullet in the Chamber* is a good ride: entertaining, informative, and reassuring. John DeDakis created a woman I wish was my best friend. Lark Chadwick has courage, deals with life head-on, and isn't a victim. In spite of her fears, she faces a world of turmoil and confusion with integrity and mindfulness — a great role model for all of us.

> ~ *Joyce B. Wilde, Psychologist and Author*
> *Former Crisis Intervention Trainer, Ventura County, California Law*
> *Enforcement*

Realistic and moving, an absorbing novel.

> ~*Michelle Stanley, ReadersFavorite.com*

ACKNOWLEDGMENTS
&
AUTHOR'S NOTE

Bullet in the Chamber is personal. The story explores, in part, the issues surrounding the death of my 22-year-old son Stephen.

I came up with the title and began making notes for the manuscript on August 24, 2011 – three days after Stephen went missing. He was gone for a week, but was eventually found dead in my car parked next to a *Neighborhood Watch* sign in a quiet residential area near my home in Washington, D.C.

Eight months later, I began writing the first draft, but I was only able to write six chapters before I had to stop. It was too soon.

I set the project aside for nearly two years – until September 2014. Over the next seven months, I wrote the first full draft. Portions of the original, agonizing chapters survive here. So, a lot of this novel is autobiographical, yet heavily fictionalized, too.

My wife Cindy and I are indebted to and grateful for the thousands of people who have supported us with their prayers, encouragement, and kindness. When Stephen went missing, our friend Julie Chen set up a *Find Stephen DeDakis* page on Facebook that galvanized a groundswell of support on social media during our desperate search. My CNN colleague Wolf Blitzer spread the word to his 500,000+ followers on Twitter. Later, in the spring of 2012, Julie kept Stephen's memory alive in a lovely art installation she titled "Whirlwind: What's Left Behind" – a creative display of Stephen's clothing at the Massachusetts College of Art and Design in Boston. (www.juliechen.net/stephen).

I'm eternally grateful to my wife Cindy for her companionship and love. If there's one thing she and I have learned about surviving the death of a child, it's that grief is personal. There's no *one* way or *right* way to grieve. Consequently, I needed to write this book, but Cindy may choose never to read it. And that's okay. Even so, and in spite of her own excruciating pain, she has been a constant and comforting companion during the writing process, offering a helpful description or turn-of-phrase every now and then at just the right time.

Many people have played an important role in my life during this time and in the creation of this book. I'm especially grateful to my grief counselor, Adrienne Kraft. Adrienne listened attentively and actively as I navigated the shoals of grief. She helped me gain clarity and understanding about myself as a writer – and as a human being.

For more than two years, Adrienne and I met regularly at The Wendt Center for Loss and Healing – an organization I first became aware of when I was at the D.C. morgue identifying Stephen's body. I strongly urge you to support the Wendt Center in its desire to make grief-counseling services affordable for all who mourn. (www.wendtcenter.org)

I created my protagonist, Lark Chadwick, in 1994 when I began writing my first novel, *Fast Track* – long before I met my friend Jillian Harding in 2008 when she was a CNN intern. Jill's now a producer at CNBC in New York, but her acquaintance with Stephen and her friendship with me have given me valuable insights into what makes Lark tick. Jill's influence permeates *Bullet in the Chamber,* and *Troubled Water* before it. Thank you, Jill for being such a great friend and sounding board (without sounding bored).

Jenna Bourne is another former CNN intern who has gone on to have a successful career in journalism (she's now a television reporter at WJAX in Jacksonville, Florida). She's also deigned to be my friend – and collaborateur. Jenna and I are now working together to make my novels into a TV series – and I credit her with providing me with many astute observations that added much substance to *Bullet in the Chamber.*

My "Hollywood" agent, Garry Dinnerman of Beverly Grant Associates (BGA), has been an unflagging encouragement and guide. Thank you, Garry, for being Lark's champion.

It was my privilege to be a White House correspondent for CBN News during the last three years of Ronald Reagan's administration. I'm particularly proud of a piece I produced in 1986 showing the adversarial relationship between the press and the presidency.

"Sometimes, it seems to be less of a hunt for news than to see if they can't catch ya," Reagan told me when his press secretary, Larry Speakes, ushered my camera crew and me into the Oval Office to shoot some video of him conferring with the president. I've tried to capture a bit of that press-versus-the-prez friction in these pages as reporters persistently try to find out what's really going on behind the spin. You can see the piece for yourself on YouTube:

https://www.youtube.com/watch?v=0il1MJdklUs

Paula Cruickshank of Commerce Clearinghouse, the late Forrest Boyd of Mutual Radio, and Helen Thomas of UPI were kind to me during my White House years. Helen graciously came to speak to a journalism class I taught one summer at American University in Washington.

Josh Lederman of the Associated Press now regularly occupies Helen Thomas' front-row center seat in the White House briefing room. Josh, yet another former CNN intern, took the broadcast news writing class I taught in CNN's D.C. bureau. I'm indebted to Josh for reading the *Bullet in the Chamber* manuscript and giving me his invaluable comments, corrections, and insights on covering the White House in the digital age. Thanks, Josh, for being so generous with your time.

For the record: I know that the annual White House Correspondents' Dinner is traditionally held at the end of April. In this book, I moved the date up to the end of February because, for the sake of the plot, it needed to be close to Valentine's Day.

As is the case with all my novels, I've gotten extremely helpful *critical* feedback from beta readers who are faithful in telling me what *isn't* working in early drafts. In alphabetical order they are: Jenna Bourne, Karen Hallacy, Jillian Harding, Carine McCandless, Lauren Phillips, Carolyn Presutti, Treva Thrush, and Joyce Wilde.

Learning to be a better writer is a two-way street. These students in my "From Novice to Novelist" writing workshops at The Writer's Center in Bethesda, Maryland and the Politics and Prose Bookstore in Washington, D.C. read portions of the manuscript and gave me helpful feedback: Tracy Balarezo, Sheryvonn Burrell, Kimberly Connolly, Dawn Hardgrave, Barbara Hurwitz, Sheila Khatri, Betsy Mirel, Lauren Phillips, Ted Seale, Susan Shapiro, Mike Smigocki, and Elizabeth Smiroldo.

I'm also indebted to my University of Maryland journalism students Nicole Ebanks, Meghan Moriarty and Treva Thrush for their feedback. Treva, by the way, is a rock-solid copy editor.

Many thanks to former medical examiner Steele Lipe for once again giving me his helpful feedback.

I credit my graphic designer cousin Christine Ganas for her splendid work visualizing my book cover idea of a bullet in a syringe – a powerful way to show just how Russian-roulette deadly even one hit of heroin can be.

Maryglenn McCombs in Nashville has been instrumental and effective in getting the word out about my novels, and my publicist Lisa Strickland of the Brava Creative Group in San Diego plays a key role in helping arrange my speaking events.

Finally, yet another big hug to my agent Barbara Casey. Barbara's been my champion since 2004 when we met at the Harriette Austin Writers Conference in Athens, Georgia. Thank you, Barbara, for your support, encouragement, and for always being able to find a home for Lark.

John DeDakis
Washington, D.C.

CB BO

CHAPTER 1

Have you ever tried to fake confidence? That's what I was doing as I stood in Lafayette Square looking at the White House. It was my first day on the job as the newest White House Correspondent for The Associated Press, the nation's leading wire service.

Up close, the White House seemed smaller than I expected, but no less magnificent. Perhaps it's a subtle magnificence. Elegant.

Intimidating.

I was about to go inside for the first time. And I felt like I didn't belong. Felt like I was an impostor. Just three years earlier I was a college dropout trying to find out what caused the car accident that orphaned me as an infant. I could've cared less about politics. But that was then.

You have to be smart to cover the president, but smart is not the way I felt on this Monday morning – Valentine's Day. Nor did I feel particularly loved. The guy I'd been "dating" hadn't answered my last text in more than forty-eight hours – the entire freaking weekend.

The eleven o'clock briefing was going to start in twenty minutes, and I was running late. I revved up Aretha Franklin's "Respect" in my head to give myself the psychological boost I needed to cross the Pennsylvania Avenue pedestrian mall and approach the Northwest gate.

By the time I got to the formidable black-barred fence blocking the way to the guard shack, my knees were weak and wobbly and I was shivering in my down jacket. It was a cold-crisp day. I wore tights, but they weren't doing any good.

R-e-s-p-e-c-t...

"Where's your ID?" commanded a metallic voice coming from a speaker. Sunlight reflected off the bullet-proof glass so I couldn't see inside.

"Oh. Sorry." I fumbled in my messenger bag. "Here it is," I called through the bars as I held up my newly-issued, laminated, press pass – white block lettering against a bright red backdrop:

CHADWICK
Lark E.
AP
PRESS

I heard a *click* come from the doorknob, so I stuffed my pass back in my bag, opened the spear-topped gateway and strode more confidently than I felt to the guard shack.

"ID!" The Voice barked.

"I just showed it to you."

"I need to see it up close."

I sighed, pulled it out again, untangled the lanyard and pressed it against the window, my reflection an angry scowl masking the terror I still felt.

The door next to the window buzzed and The Voice said, "Enter!"

Inside, the guard shack was claustrophobic, but at least it was toasty warm. The Voice sat behind a counter that separated us. He was mid-thirties – young, cute, and wore a crisp white shirt and narrow black tie. His badge announced he was a member of the *Secret Service Uniformed Division*. Two other uniformed Secret Service guards stood off to the side.

A radio newscast was on in the background. "More tough talk from China this morning," the announcer read.

"Put your bag up here on the counter," The Voice said.

I did. And so began several minutes of being searched, wanded, magnetometered, and scrutinized that made going through airport security feel like a breeze. Finally, The Voice handed me off to a tall African-American man in his fifties with salt and pepper hair.

"Good morning, ma'am." His comforting brown eyes were alive with interest and caring.

"Hi," I said brightly, grateful for his friendliness.

The nametag on his tunic read *Crandall.* "You're new here," he said gently.

"Uh huh. First day." I bit my lower lip. "Is it that obvious?"

He simply smiled. At *me.*

"Do you know how I can get to the press room?" I asked as I squeezed through a turnstile, clearing the final hurdle.

"Sure," he said, putting on his uniform cap. He opened the back door and let in a fourth guard who'd just arrived from the White House. "Now that my relief is here, I can *show* you. I'm heading that way."

"Thanks."

Officer Crandall spoke to The Voice. "I'll be on break inside, Jim."

"Okay, Ernie. Thanks for your help."

Ernie Crandall touched me lightly on the elbow as we stepped out the back door of the guard shack and onto the White House driveway.

I was *inside* the black bars of the perimeter fence.

I stopped to look at the iconic alabaster building. It looked bigger from here.

"First time, huh?" he asked.

I nodded, my mouth slightly agape. I felt like a rube from Wisconsin. Oh, wait. I am!

"It never fails to impress me, either," he said.

"How long have you been here, Officer Crandall?"

"Ernie. The name's Ernie." He tipped his hat. "Twenty years. Been here twenty years. Retiring soon."

"How soon?"

"Friday," he beamed.

"Wow. And then what?"

"Fishin'. A *whole* lotta fishin'." He chuckled.

I smiled. "I'm sorry you'll be leaving. I miss you already. Thanks for being so nice to me."

He smiled. "You'll like it here. Lots of history in the making. And you'll have a front-row seat. Press, right?"

I nodded. "A.P."

The driveway where we stood bifurcated. The left fork curved up toward the imposing north portico of the White House. The president's front door. Another asphalt driveway headed straight toward the one-story West Wing and a low-slung doorway beneath a porch held up by several white columns.

"Press room's this way." Ernie Crandall guided me along the drive-way toward the West Wing. We walked slowly, like old friends.

"Who was president when you started here?" I asked.

"Clinton."

"Was he as much of a player as they say?" I asked.

"My lips are sealed," Ernie smiled, pretending to zip them.

"What were you doing before here?"

"D.C. Metro Police," he said. "A cop on the beat."

"Family?" I asked.

He nodded, but a shadow crossed his face. "A son in Michigan. A daughter in California." He paused and swallowed. "Wife passed a year ago. Year ago today, as a matter of fact."

"Oh no! Valentine's Day. That's so sad." I touched the sleeve of his coat. "I'm sorry," I said.

I'm only twenty-eight, but I know pain and loss far better than most people my age: I found the body of the aunt who raised me after my parents were killed; my boyfriend, Jason, was murdered just as our re-lationship was about to take off; and I was sexually assaulted by an English professor I idolized. And all of this happened just within the past few years.

Ernie smiled faintly. "Life goes on," he said. "Life goes on."

As we walked up the driveway, we passed to the left of a long row of about a dozen television cameras, each beneath its own awning-covered workspace crammed with power cables, equipment boxes, and light stands. I found out later the camera positions – affectionately nicknamed "Pebble Beach" – are where network reporters do their standups and live shots with the White House in the background.

"This is my stop," Ernie said. We had come to where the asphalt driveway went around a grassy circle and passed beneath the porch in front of the entrance to the West Wing where a Marine in dress blues stood at attention.

Ernie pointed toward the White House.   "The press room's that way down this sidewalk. See the double doors right there?"

I looked. He was pointing at a spot halfway down the sidewalk on the right, an entrance to the West Wing that was far less imposing than the one where we stood – no elegant portico, and no handsome young Marine guard.

"I see it," I said. "Thank you, Officer...um...Ernie," I said. "Glad we met." I held out my hand.

He shook it and bowed slightly. "I am, too. Maybe our paths will cross a few more times before I move on."

As I watched him turn toward the West Wing entrance, my phone went off. I fished it from my messenger bag.

"This is Lark," I said.

"It's Grigsby."

Rochelle Grigsby is my nemesis. She's about forty, single, and good looking – *way* better looking than me. She's also the deputy bureau chief at the A.P. – my immediate supervisor.

"What's up?" I tried to sound cheerful but, based on my experience of the past seven months as one of her general assignment reporters, I'd come to accept that she saw her job as trying to trip me up at every turn.

"Heads up, Lark." I could hear Grigsby's gum snap. "Ridgeway's out today. You're in the front row."

Stallings Ridgeway is the long-time and legendary White House Correspondent for A.P. He's been there at least thirty years. Maybe more.

Grigsby plowed on. "I know it's your first day on the beat, but if you're the golden girl all the higher-ups think you are, then you'll be fine. Me? I have my doubts."

"Thanks for the vote of confidence," I replied.

Grigsby merely grunted and hung up.

R-E-S-P-E-C-T! Sing it, Aretha! A little louder, please, babe.

I turned toward the briefing room. Doug Mitchell stood at the double doors, Nikon at the ready, and flashed me his trademark neon smile that contrasted sharply with his ruddy complexion, dark eyes, thick black hair, and stubble beard. He's six-two and was looking fine in a navy pea coat, jeans and work boots.

I hadn't seen him in a week and my heart did an involuntary flip-flop.

Doug is ten years older than I am. We'd worked together at the *Sun-Gazette* in Columbia, Georgia, where he was a staff photographer. We had a thing for each other then, but it never got off the ground because the police were, shall we say, "very interested" in him for awhile, so I backed off. But, when the police lost interest, mine picked up. And so did Doug's interest in me.

We both got jobs at A.P. when the *Sun-Gazette* folded, but right away he was on the road covering Will Gannon's successful presidential campaign, so we only saw each other off and on. Mostly off.

Now, after not hearing from him all weekend (okay, forty-eight hours, sixteen minutes, and thirty seconds, give or take – but who's counting?), there he was thirty yards ahead of me, hatless in the cold, his dark, wavy hair parted down the middle and curling slightly over his ears and collar.

Doug raised the camera to his face and began shooting pictures of me. He wore fingerless gloves and I could hear the rapid-fire *chick-koo, chick-koo* of the shutter as he squeezed off shot after shot.

My cell phone bleeped again. The display read *Lionel Stone.* Lionel is my friend, mentor, and the guy who got me started in journalism. He earned his Pulitzer decades ago while covering the White House for *The New York Times.* Since his "retirement," he's been the publisher of his hometown newspaper, *The Pine Bluff Standard* in Pine Bluff, Wisconsin, and he teaches journalism as an adjunct professor at the University of Wisconsin-Madison.

Normally, I'd be glad to take Lionel's call, but lately he'd been blowing up my phone with all kinds of mansplain texts and links to various online articles. It all started when I told him I'd gotten the White House gig.

Now Lionel's living vicariously through me. And it's getting old. But I haven't had the heart to tell him. Yet.

"Hey there," I said into the phone. "I've only got a second. I've just been told I'm in Ridgeway's front row seat for the daily briefing."

"Outstanding!" Lionel roared. "Front row seat on your first day. That's awesome, kid."

I winced. I hate it when he calls me kid. I'd told him that when we first met. It was when I learned from a *Pine Bluff Standard* newspaper clipping about the car accident I survived as an infant. The crash killed my parents. I convinced Lionel to let me look into the accident. What I came up with almost got Lionel and me killed, but instead landed me my first job in journalism with Lionel as my boss.

Gradually, I'd let "kid" creep back into his lexicon. But now it was grating.

"Yeah," I said. "We'll see just how awesome it really is. Rochelle Grigsby made it real clear she doesn't think I'm up to the job." I sighed. "Maybe she's right."

"It's a tough job. No doubt about it," he said, "but you're tough, too, kid."

I sighed again, unconvinced. "At least they let me through the Northwest gate."

"Put me on FaceTime," Lionel ordered. "Lemme relive the experience of the ole place."

I took the phone away from my ear and pushed the *FaceTime* button. My wide, terrified eyes stared back at me.

Lionel noticed immediately. "I see that deer-in-the-headlights look. Stop it, Lark. You're gonna be fine."

"So you say. I almost turned around and went back home to throw up, but one of the uniformed Secret Service agents was nice to me, so I think I'll keep going."

Lionel's face came on the screen. He wore a white shirt, tie loosened – and, to my surprise, he had a white beard.

"Whoa. Lionel! When'd you grow the beard?"

He stroked it and preened. "You like?"

"Very distinguished. What does Muriel think?"

He frowned. "She thinks I should shave it. Says it makes me look old."

"Lionel. I hate to tell you this: You *are* old."

"Nonsense. Seventy-five is the new thirty-five."

"Yeah. Right."

"Geez, I wish I was thirty-five again," he said wistfully, then cleared his throat. "Age is all in your head. It's just a number. Did I ever tell you about the time–"

I cut him off. "Yeah. Probably. Look, Lionel, the briefing's gonna start any minute and I'm late, so let's get on with this little tour."

I turned the camera around so Lionel could see, but Doug filled the screen. He was now about ten feet from me, camera at his face, clicking off more shots and adding his own narration.

"Here's the famous Lark Chadwick about to enter the White House briefing room for the first time. She's taken her iPhone from her ear and is pointing it in my general direction."

I was annoyed. He gives me nothing but radio silence all weekend, has the nerve to turn up, all jovial, acting as if everything's wonderful, and then he makes a point of trying to embarrass me. But I couldn't afford to make a scene. Not here. Not now.

I put on my best tight smile and gave his lens a laser stare. "Good morning to you, *too*, Mister Mitchell." I hoped he felt the chill from the ice in my voice. "What you're looking at, Lionel, is my *so-called friend* and colleague Doug Mitchell. Doug is in the process of being exception-ally obnoxious."

I brushed past him, pulled open the door and stepped into the briefing room. Doug followed.

"Here it is, Lionel." I held the phone in front of me and panned the scene, left to right. In front of me, a sea of about fifty blue leather fold-ing seats faced to the right. To my left, at the back of the room, TV cam-eras sat atop tripods and pointed toward the podium at the front of the room.

As I panned right, I noticed that many of the seats were empty, but some reporters were strolling from the back of the room to take their places for the briefing. The room was much smaller than I expected – barely the size of a swimming pool. Actually, according to one of the links Lionel sent me, I learned that the James S. Brady Press Briefing Room is built right above the old White House swimming pool where President Kennedy used to cavort with "Fiddle" and "Faddle," two of his many mistresses.

"Wow. The place looks great since the facelift," Lionel exclaimed.

I made a right turn and walked slowly down the side aisle that went along the windows. When I came to the front row I stopped and turned around. Doug nearly bumped into me.

"Chadwick has stopped now," Doug narrated. "It looks as though she's about to use her phone to get a wide shot of the entire briefing room."

I pointed the camera toward the back of the room.

"Yes," Doug proclaimed. "That's exactly what she's doing, folks." He continued to take more pictures. I continued trying to ignore him.

"Show me the plaque on Helen Thomas's chair," Lionel said.

"Which chair's that?"

"Front row center," Lionel said. "I miss that old broad."

I found the seat and put my phone close enough to the plaque so Lionel could read her name on it.

"She sat there for nearly sixty years. Covered ten presidents. She's a legend, Lark. I wish you could have known her. She would've loved you."

"Thanks, Lionel."

Just then a voice came out of a speaker in the ceiling above me. "Attention, everyone. The briefing will start in exactly two minutes. President Gannon and National Security Adviser Nathan Mann will be conducting the briefing. This is your two-minute warning. The President will be in the briefing room in two minutes."

"Holy crap. Did you hear that, Lionel?"

"Yup. Better take your seat."

"Which one is it?"

"Front row center."

"Helen Thomas's old seat?"

"The very same."

I gulped.

The sudden announcement that President Gannon would be giving the briefing caused a stampede as dozens of people came running – thundering – into the room, the sound echoing on the hollow floor above the old swimming pool.

Everyone was piling into the room through a narrow hallway in the back. I pointed my iPhone toward the commotion so that Lionel could see.

In the row just behind me the correspondents for Fox and CNN were hastily getting wired up to do their live reports. Each of them faced the cameras at the back of the room. The guy from CNN awkwardly slung himself into his suitcoat while inserting an earbud into his ear. The perfectly coifed blonde reporter for Fox stood stoically, hand to her ear, waiting for her cue.

The room buzzed with expectation.

"Better sit down, kid," Lionel urged.

I sat, my pulse quickening. The lectern towered in front of me.

Suddenly, an older, bald man wearing black-rimmed glasses and carrying a long, narrow reporter's notebook darted toward me from my left. "You!" He yelled at me and jabbed his thick forefinger dangerously close to my nostrils. "You're in my chair."

From the phone in my hand Lionel said, "Stallings? Stallings Ridgeway? Is that you, you old fart? It's Lionel Stone. How are ya, man?" Lionel's voice was giddy with nostalgia.

For a moment, Ridgeway's face lost its intensity as his eyes searched in confusion for who'd called his name, but then he focused on the phone in my hand.

"Lionel," Ridgeway said gruffly, "whoever this is you're talking to is sitting in my seat."

"Oh, c'mon, Stallings. Let the kid have your chair just this once."

Embarrassed, I stood. "I'm sorry, Mister Ridgeway. Rochelle Grigsby told me you were off."

Suddenly, I became aware of a deathly silence. I looked around. The room was full to overflowing, everyone was standing, and all eyes were on me.

I turned around. Stallings Ridgeway, hands on his hips, glowered at me. Standing at the podium, an amused look on his face stood the imposing presence of Will Gannon, the forty-ninth President of the United States.

"Oh, my God," I blurted.

The entire press corps erupted in laughter.

The president spoke. "That's okay, Miss Chadwick. I'll wait until you and Mister Ridgeway get things straightened out."

"I'm so sorry, Mister President." I slid away from the front row seat and Ridgeway eased into it. "I'll call you back," I rasped into the phone and scurried to the side aisle and toward the back of the room.

I kept my head down, but could hear some clapping and sniggering as the reporters took their seats.

I'd only gotten past the second row when I heard the president say, "I suppose this is as good a time as any to introduce you to Lark Chadwick. Today marks her first day as a White House Correspondent for the Associated Press. I met Lark when I was Governor of Georgia campaigning for this job. Lark is an impressive young woman who wasn't afraid to ask me some tough questions. So, welcome, Lark."

By this time I was in the back of the room, as far from the president and the blinding spotlight as I could possibly get. Fortunately, it was next to Doug. He gently touched my shoulder to comfort me.

"Thank you, Mister President," I hollered.

There was a bit more chuckling and then the room became silent again as reporters turned their attention to President Gannon. He'd only been in office a few weeks, but I noticed that the pronounced southern drawl he'd had as a candidate was already beginning to fade.

Behind and to the president's right stood a nervous, diffident man wearing a dark suit – Nathan Mann, the president's newly-appointed National Security Adviser.

The president cleared his throat, eyed the TV cameras just behind me, and began to speak. "During my campaign, I was asked many questions about what my policy as president would be on the commercialization of drones. As you know, my consistent answer has been that I want to study the issue before coming up with a plan. I'm announcing today my administration's position on the subject, and I'm announcing our legislative plan to put it into place. I'll give you the broad outline of the legislation, then Nathan will stay behind to take your questions.

"First and foremost, as your President, it's my responsibility to–"

Just then the door to the president's right rear burst open and a torrent of Secret Service agents swarmed into the room. Ernie Crandall was one of them.

"EVERYONE OUT. NOW!" shouted one of them. "OUT. NOW. SIDE DOORS. MOVE! MOVE! MOVE!"

Two agents grabbed the president and hustled him out of the room.

❧

CHAPTER 2

The briefing room erupted in bedlam. Everyone jumped to their feet. Some scrambled toward the side door while others pressed closer to the lectern where the president had been speaking.

I craned my neck to see what was happening up front. One agent had grasped the president firmly around the shoulders and steered him toward the door behind the lectern while the other agent gripped Gannon's upper arm. In a matter of seconds, Gannon was gone. Ernie Crandall slid the pocket door closed, then turned around and stood against it.

Doug, all grim seriousness now, steadily snapped pictures – one right after the other, almost randomly, yet he seemed to be pausing just an instant to compose the shot before pressing the shutter.

"Everyone out of the building! Keep moving!"

A phalanx of uniformed Secret Service agents – a sea of white and black, batons drawn – pushed reporters to the side doors.

"Where are they taking the president?" I shouted, but my voice was drowned out in the commotion.

Doug and I tried to make our way to the aisle on the far side of the room, opposite the double doors, but the way to the front was blocked by more white uniforms.

"What's happening?" I asked one of the guards.

"I don't know, ma'am." His young face was worried, brow furrowed. "Our orders are to clear the building. Keep moving, please. And hurry."

Doug and I turned toward the double doors where the last stragglers among the press corps were leaving. Doug continued to steadily snap pictures. Before I left, I glanced back toward the front of the room. Stallings Ridgeway was on his feet trying to push past Ernie Crandall, whose outstretched arm was keeping Stallings from charging after President Gannon.

"Keep moving! Keep moving!" The uniformed agent behind me kept urging Doug, me, and the others. "All the way out the Northwest gate. Keep moving, everyone."

As we trotted down the sidewalk that hugged the north side of the West Wing, I fished my phone from my messenger bag and speed-dialed the desk. Ever since my first day at A.P. several months ago, it had been drummed into me that "every minute is a deadline," so I called the Mother Ship.

"It's Chadwick at the White House," I said to the voice that answered the phone.

"Yep. Just saw the turmoil there on CNN," the guy said. "I'm switching you to radio. We'll transcribe your bulletins while you're on the air with them."

I didn't have time to be nervous. I was running now on instinct and adrenaline.

I heard some clicking, then another voice. "A.P. Radio."

"It's Lark Chadwick at the White House," I said breathlessly. Doug and I were now running down the driveway past Pebble Beach toward the gate that opened onto Pennsylvania Avenue.

"Okay, Lark. You'll be on the air live with James Macateere in just a sec."

There was another pause on the line. Doug and I got to the gate. It was open just a crack to let everyone out, but several guards, guns drawn, were positioned to keep people on the outside from getting back in.

Another voice in my ear said, "Live now from the White House is A.P.'s Lark Chadwick. Lark, what's happening?"

If I'd been talking with Lionel, he would have gotten the full force of my agitation, but, because I was on live radio, I needed to talk calmly and authoritatively to the entire country. I took a deep breath and swallowed the bile I felt clawing its way up my throat.

"The White House is being evacuated." I said the words with a steely steadiness I most certainly did not feel. "President Gannon was just beginning to brief reporters on his drone policy when Secret Service agents swarmed into the briefing room. I saw two agents hustle the president away. The rest of us were ordered to leave. Right now I'm at the Northwest gate of the White House."

I turned to look back. "I can see numerous armed guards who have fanned out all along the fence in front of the White House. Their weapons are drawn, but it appears to be a precaution. No one is aiming at anything."

I paused just long enough to collect my thoughts and to give Macateere a chance to interject a question. All he said was, "Go on."

"I'm not able to get a head count on the number of armed men – I don't see any women. They are guarding the front perimeter of the White House. The show of force is massive. It appears there are several dozen armed guards. Some are in military fatigues. Others are members of the Uniformed Secret Service. Some look like Ninjas – wearing black, the word *police* emblazoned on their backs. All of them have their weapons drawn."

Macateere jumped in. "Has anyone told you the reason for the evacuation?"

"No. I asked one uniformed Secret Service agent that question and he merely said he has orders to clear the building."

"Is there a sense of panic there at the White House?"

"I wouldn't call it panic, but there's a definite sense of urgency here."

The guard who'd been urging us along, prodded me once more. "You must leave the grounds, ma'am. *Now.*" He pushed me firmly on the arm with his baton.

"Why? Can you tell me why?" I held the phone out to him like a microphone.

"No, ma'am. Get as far away from the building as possible."

As Doug and I were about to exit the White House grounds, I put the phone back to my ear. "There. You heard it yourself from one of the uniformed Secret Service agents. For some reason, they want everyone out of the complex and far away from the White House."

I passed through the gate, but couldn't bring myself to walk any farther away from the president it was my job to cover. Doug and I pressed ourselves against the fence and inched our way down the sidewalk so we could get a better look at the North Portico.

"Stand back. Back away from the fence." A helmeted soldier in combat fatigues, holding a rifle across his chest with both hands, stepped toward us menacingly from the other side of the black bars of the White House fence. "BACK!" he shouted.

Doug snapped the shutter yet again and in that instant I knew he had just taken what photogs call "the money shot" – in this case, a snarling soldier, rifle at the ready with a fixed bayonet, and the White House in the background.

I backed away from the fence. So did Doug, but he kept on taking pictures.

Continuing to narrate the scene, I said, "I'm now directly in front of the White House, outside the fence, looking at the North Portico. From where I'm standing, there does not appear to be an intruder or any fence jumpers trying to make it toward the build–"

Just then, a deafening burst of rocket fire let loose from the roof of the White House.

"Oh!" Instinctively I crouched, but managed to hold tight to the phone. "It looks as though an anti-aircraft battery on the roof of the White House is firing a furious fusillade into the sky."

Really? Did I just say "firing a furious fusillade"? In my head, I could hear half the country chortling at me, led by Rochelle Grigsby. But those were the words I blurted out of my mouth without thinking – the dangers of live reporting on the radio.

Ignoring the cringe-worthy description, I plunged ahead, now nearly breathless again. "The anti-aircraft battery is shooting into the sky in the general direction of the Potomac River and the Pentagon to the West." My voice was now no longer steely and steady. I was shouting. "I can't tell what's being shot at."

"Get back," the soldier behind the fence yelled at me. "Get back." His expression changed from menacing to worried.

An instant later, Doug and I were thrown to the ground by a bone-jarring explosion. When I looked up, I saw an orange fireball roiling toward the sky above what had been the White House briefing room.

CB ᗛᎾ

CHAPTER 3

The fireball churned upward and elongated, a combination of fire and dark black smoke. It looked like a towering, angry, orange and ebony exclamation point.

I heard screams coming from behind me in Lafayette Square. In the distance, I heard the swell of approaching sirens and the blaring Klaxons of desperately-in-a-hurry fire trucks.

The force of the explosion had knocked the phone from my hand. I picked it up and held it to my ear.

"Lark! Lark! Are you still there?" Macateere's voice was nearly frantic.

"I'm here," I gasped.

"We just saw the explosion live on CNN – taken from the camera atop the Chamber of Commerce building on H Street a block from the White House. If you're just joining us, this is James Macateere in New York. I'm speaking live with Lark Chadwick, A.P.'s correspondent at the White House where there's just been a massive explosion. Lark, pick it up from there."

"James, just moments ago I was in that White House press room with about seventy-five other reporters. President Gannon and his newly-appointed National Security Adviser Nathan Mann were just beginning to brief reporters. Suddenly Secret Service agents burst into the room, whisked away the president, and ordered everyone else out of the building and off the White House grounds.

"Just a few seconds ago, an anti-aircraft battery atop the White House began firing into the sky. Then a massive explosion threw us to the ground. It appears the explosion was in the pressroom in the West

Wing of the White House where the president's office is located, but from my vantage point, I'm not able to see if the Oval Office was hit."

"Can you tell if anyone's been hurt? Are you okay?" Macateere asked.

"I'm fine." I looked around. "I can see several people on the ground near me. They appear to be tourists, knocked onto the pavement by the force of the explosion, but they're getting up now."

I walked up to one of them. "I'm with the Associated Press reporting live on A.P. Radio. Can you tell me what you saw?" I held my phone out toward a blonde middle-aged woman with black-rimmed glasses. She looked dazed and frightened, her eyes were wide and she was having trouble catching her breath as she spoke rapidly.

"My husband and I were walking past the White House when all of a sudden there was this major commotion and people started streaming out of the building, through the gate, and onto the street. Then the guns on the roof started firing into the sky."

"Could you see what they were shooting at?"

"No. It looked like they were just shooting randomly into the sky. Then there was this big explosion coming from over there." She pointed behind me toward the West Wing. "It knocked me to the ground. Scared the hell outta me." Suddenly, she looked stricken. "Sorry. Can I say hell on the radio?"

I pulled the phone back and gave her a tight smile. "Thank you, ma'am."

I caught Doug's eye and pointed toward the gate. He gave me a thumbs up.

"James, I'm going to make my way back to the Northwest gate with my photographer Doug Mitchell. We'll see if we can get a better look from there."

Doug and I inched our way along the fence as I continued my narrative. "I can see flames rising from the West Wing," I reported.

"Are you able to tell if the Oval Office has been hit?" Macateere asked.

"I can't. The Oval Office is on the other side of the West Wing." I glanced to my left to check out the main residence. "It doesn't appear as if the White House itself was hit or is damaged, although I can see the reflection of the flames on the side wall and windows of the executive mansion. The flames are clearly visible now shooting through the roof of the West Wing."

As Doug and I neared the gate, I saw a fire engine – siren blaring – stopped at the 17th Street end of the Pennsylvania Avenue pedestrian mall waiting for the retractable metal posts to finish being lowered. Once the bollards were level with the pavement, the fire truck made its way slowly toward us, scattering the clots of people – tourists, reporters, and White House staffers – who were mingling helplessly outside the White House compound in front of the Eisenhower Executive Office Building.

"A fire truck is now making its way to the Northwest Gate," I said. "The noise is going to drown out anything else I have to say, so let's listen for a moment."

I held my phone out toward the fire engine as it got to the gate. The noise was deafening. I put a finger in one ear and tilted my head toward my shoulder to muffle the cacophony. Armed guards, their guns drawn, surrounded the side and rear of the vehicle as the gate swung open to let the truck in.

I felt the phone vibrate in my hand – an incoming call. I looked at the display. *Lionel.* In my head I screamed, *NOT NOW, LIONEL. I'M WORKING!* I hit the *ignore* button and exiled him to voicemail.

The gate closed behind the fire engine and it charged up the driveway toward the Marine still guarding the official West Wing entrance, but now the man was armed with an M-16 rifle.

The fire engine's siren went silent, so I could talk again. "A fire engine, red lights flashing, has now entered the White House compound through the Northwest Gate. It's approaching the West Wing where a Marine brandishing an M-16 continues to guard the door.

"I'm now in a position where I can see the briefing room area better. It looks like it's entirely engulfed in flames."

Suddenly something caught my eye. "Oh my God!"

"What is it?" Macateere asked, his voice matching the alarm in mine.

"A man is running from the direction of the briefing room. He's on fire. Oh my God!"

I wanted to look away, but couldn't. I tried to say more, but I gagged on the words. They stayed trapped in my throat. In my head, I prayed, *Oh, Dear Lord. Help him. Please help him!*

Finally, my voice returned. "The man is staggering toward the fire engine." My voice broke. "He's just now collapsed onto the sidewalk. A fireman carrying a fire extinguisher is rushing toward the burning man."

A cloud of white *whooshed* from the nozzle of the fire extinguisher, engulfing the man. Another fireman, carrying what looked like a tackle box, ran to the man's side.

"Two firemen are now tending to the person who's on fire as other firefighters are frantically working now to unspool hoses from the truck."

Then, I held the phone as far away from my mouth as I could, and vomited.

ೞ ೲ

CHAPTER 4

Ten hours later, Doug and I sat slumped next to each other on the plush theater seats of an auditorium in the Eisenhower Executive Office Building, better known in D.C. geek-speak as the EEOB. Long-timers refer to it as the OEOB before Ike's last name replaced O for "old."

The building is the big, ornate gray building next to the White House that looks like a multi-tiered wedding cake. Built in 1888, it once housed the departments of state, war, and the navy. But, as the government's bureaucracy began to bloat, those departments took on lives – and buildings – of their own. Now the EEOB is home to most of the White House staff, except for the privileged elite whose desks are actually in the White House proper – or, more accurately, the East and West wings.

Doug and I had been working steadily all day since that morning's briefing room explosion. We were now waiting with the rest of the press corps in the auditorium for White House Press Secretary Lucia Lopez to update us.

During our all-day vigil just outside the Northwest gate, Doug and I saw several ambulances carry away people who had been killed or wounded in the explosion. But we had few hard details – no names, no numbers. We hoped the Lopez briefing would nail things down. But the biggest question of all remained unanswered: What happened to President Gannon?

I'd hectored Lopez all day – by phone, and in the two impromptu briefings she held in Lafayette Square – but all she'd say is "the president is alive."

"But is he wounded?" I'd persisted.

"That's all I can say at this time," was the Lopez refrain.

As Doug and I waited, we scoured the Internet on our phones, trying to get a sense of how the rest of the country was reacting to the explosion at the White House.

Doug nudged me.

My eyes blinked open. "What?" I sat up abruptly. Apparently, I'd been dozing.

"Listen to this," he said, then read from the screen on his phone. "'Someone should get a medal for trying to take out the lame-stream media.'"

"Who wrote that?" I asked indignantly.

"Some moron posted it on Facebook." He poked and scrolled, then added, "Oh! You're famous again."

"What do you mean?"

"Here. Take a look." He turned his phone so that I could see it, then hit the *play* button that launched a YouTube clip. The scene started with President Gannon entering the briefing room with Nathan Mann. Stallings Ridgeway and I were in the middle of our stare-down. The president paused, an amused look on his face, then smiled broadly when I turned toward him as he stood at the podium.

The shot from the back of the briefing room switched to a shot from one of the cameras in the front corner. It caught the utter shock and embarrassment on my face when I saw the president. The reporters behind me laughed uproariously. Some poked each other and pointed at me. The scene switched again to a wide shot from the back as I slinked, head down, along the side aisle.

Missing from the clip were the president's generous and gracious remarks about me.

I put my hand over my face and buried my head in Doug's shoulder. "Please. Make it stop."

"And have you seen this?" Doug asked.

"You mean there's more?"

"You saw the atta-boy email that upper management sent around earlier congratulating us – and especially you – about the good job today, right?"

"Uh huh. It was nice." And unexpected.

"But now there's this," Doug said, once again turning his phone screen to me.

It was a reply-to-all email from Rochelle Grigsby: *Sorry. I can't buy in to the accolades for Lark. Her embarrassing attempt at usurping Stalling's front-row seat at the briefing, and her "firing a furious fusillade" gaffe continue to reinforce my belief that The Famous Fusilier is in over her head and is as useless as Kim Kardashian.*

I noticed that my name was missing from the addresses at the top of her email. She'd deliberately kept me out of the loop so she could lie with impunity about why I was in Ridgeway's seat.

"Why does she hate me so much, Doug?" I fumed.

"She's jealous."

"Really?"

"Sure. She's a news nun."

"A what?"

"A news nun. She gave up on romance and on having a life because she poured herself into her career. Now, at forty-five, life has passed her by. Then you come along, and everything you touch turns to gold. She hates you because she wanted to be you, but it didn't happen for her."

I was about to ask Doug how he gained this deep insight into Grigsby's character, but then Lucia Lopez entered the auditorium from a side door on the stage.

"Gotta go." Doug picked up his camera from the seat next to him, shot to his feet, and then began shooting pictures of Lopez.

Lucia Lopez is an extremely attractive thirty-eight-year-old Latina with long black hair clasped together at the back of her head and hanging just below her shoulders. She insists that we reporters pronounce her first name LOO-shah instead of loo-CHEE-ah or loo-SEE-ah. Lopez had been Gannon's chief campaign spokeswoman where she developed a well-earned reputation for scrupulous honesty – and rabid loyalty to the candidate who would become president.

As the president's spokeswoman walked to the podium at the center of the stage, I studied her countenance for any evidence of grief. She'd been stonewalling us about the president's condition, but would her face betray the truth?

It didn't. It only hinted. Her expression was grim, her make-up was intact, but her eyes were bloodshot as if she'd been crying. I braced myself to hear some ominously bad news.

Lopez put her briefing book onto the podium. A cacophonous clatter of shutter clicks erupted from the dozens of still photographers at the back of the room and along the side aisles. Lopez blinked uncomfortably as she faced the blinding strobes of their cameras.

She opened the briefing book, took a deep breath, and looked up at us. "First, a couple quick housekeeping issues. Until the briefing room is repaired, the new press office will be at 726 Jackson Place." She gestured vaguely in the direction of Blair House directly across the street from the EEOB. "Some of you may remember it. It's where press operations were headquartered adjacent to Lafayette Square when the James Brady briefing room was being remodeled in 2007 during President George W. Bush's administration."

As I scribbled the address in my notebook, someone asked, "How long is the repair operation supposed to last?"

"I don't have that for you," Lopez sighed.

I looked around, wondering where my colleague Stallings Ridgeway was. I hadn't seen him all day.

"Here's what we know now," Lopez continued. "It took about an hour for firefighters to bring the West Wing fire under control, and another few hours to put it out completely. Damage was confined to the briefing room. There's smoke damage throughout the West Wing, but the Oval Office was not physically damaged.

"There are a lot of numbers flying around, so let me try to put some of the misinformation to rest.

"Ten people were injured in the explosion," Lopez said. "Their names, pictures, and conditions are listed on our website: w-w-w-dot-white-house-dot-gov.

"Three people were killed in the blast. Their next-of-kin have been notified, so I can now release their names. The dead are..." she paused, then went on. "Ernest Crandall..." Her voice cracked.

I let out an involuntary gasp. My new friend at the front gate!

Lopez continued, "...age fifty-five, of the Uniformed Secret Service Division. Stallings Ridgeway of the Associated Press..."

"Oh, no!" several reporters cried out in unison.

"...age sixty-four. And Charles McGlaughlan, age forty, a videographer for CBS News." Lopez looked up from her notes and looked directly into the TV cameras at the back of the room. "The administration's thoughts and prayers are with the families of the victims."

"What about the president, Lucia?" I asked. "You say 'the *administration's* thoughts and prayers.' What about the president's?"

"The president is alive and is at an undisclosed location," she said, tersely.

"Is he wounded? Is he conscious? Is that '*undisclosed location*' a hospital?" I pressed.

"Where's the vice president?" someone shouted.

"The location of both the president and vice president are undisclosed for national security reasons," Lopez said, unhelpfully. Her comments were raising more questions than answers and I could feel the tension building among my press corps colleagues in the room.

Someone hollered from the back of the room, "Can we at least get a picture of the president taken since this morning?"

Lopez ignored the question, looked down at her notes and continued. "We have determined that the explosion at the White House was caused by a rogue drone under the control of the U.S. Air Force."

There was a collective gasp.

"Friendly fire?" someone exclaimed.

"Is anyone under arrest?" I asked.

"An investigation is underway," she replied. "So far, no charges have been filed, but the person who was in control of the drone is being questioned."

"What's the person's name?" someone yelled.

"We're not releasing that at this time," she said. "Not until the investigation is complete."

"What happened to the drone?" someone asked.

Lopez shuffled a few pages of her briefing book, then said, "I don't have anything on that for you."

From the CNN correspondent behind me came another question: "The president was about to announce his position on the commercialization of drones. What was he going to say?"

"What he was going to say is under reconsideration at this time," Lopez answered.

"Would you call the explosion an attack?" I asked.

"I don't want to label it that way at this time," she said.

"When you say 'rogue,' that implies that somehow the drone strayed off-course and fired accidently. Is that what you're saying?" asked another reporter.

"Let's wait until the investigation is complete before we parse words. For now, I'm saying the drone was not where it was supposed to be."

"Are you saying it was an accident?" the reporter persisted.

"At this point, I'm suggesting it *might* have been an accident. Yes," she said.

"Which leaves open the possibility that it could also have been a deliberate attack." The comment came from the correspondent for *The New York Times.*

"I don't want to speculate or get ahead of the facts," Lopez dodged.

"Was this an assassination attempt, Lucia?" I asked.

She ignored my question and pointed to a person near the back of the room.

"Was this an assassination attempt?" I raised my voice to be heard above the person she'd called on.

She gave me a look of annoyance, then turned her attention again to the person in back.

"Wait a minute," I pressed. "How can you *'suggest'* – your word – that it's an innocent accident when a military drone fires at the exact spot where the President of the United States just happens to be standing? I'll repeat my question: Was this an assassination attempt?"

That's all I have for you," Lopez said. She slammed her briefing book shut, pivoted, and bolted for the exit, pursued by a chorus of shouted questions.

CB BO

CHAPTER 5

A few hours later, Doug and I were sitting next to each other on barstools at Shotzie's Pub, a cozy watering hole at the corner of 17th and H Streets, just down the street and around the corner from the White House. The place was teeming, mostly with decompressing reporters. The energy in the room was palpable.

To say it had been a long and eventful day is the biggest understatement imaginable. Shell-shocked after filing several stories, we sipped our beers in silence.

Two hours earlier, before Lopez had even left the EEOB briefing room, reporters began writing their stories. The newspaper correspondents were on a tight deadline for their morning papers. The reporters for CBS, ABC, NBC, CNBC, MSNBC, Fox, and CNN immediately stood and faced their respective cameras in the back of the room, preparing to go live. Even though they stood just a few feet from each other, their Herculean powers of concentration kept them from being distracted by their competitors.

I'd been on a moment-to-moment deadline all day. The power nap I'd taken against Doug's shoulder was just what I needed to sustain me as I made a final push to file the latest update from Lopez.

Shortly after Lopez left the podium, a press office underling announced over the auditorium's P.A. system, "We have a full lid. We have a full lid." That meant the press office was shutting down for the night. There would be no more news released until the next morning.

As I sipped my brew, Doug struck up a conversation with the bartender, a handsome blond guy with spiked hair. He looked to be about thirty. I really wasn't interested in their conversation. They mostly seemed to be swapping war stories from their days in the service.

My mind had been on overload all day and I was trying as best I could to decompress. The Lopez briefing had been intense. My lead for the write-through was:

The whereabouts and condition of President Will Gannon are still unknown. White House press secretary Lucia Lopez said the president is "alive and at an undisclosed location."

Lopez cited "national security" concerns for not revealing where the president was taken after he was hustled from the White House briefing room moments before it was struck by what she called a "rogue drone" late Monday morning.

I also did a profile piece on Ernie Crandall, the nice man who'd welcomed me to the White House and pointed me toward the briefing room. Rochelle Grigsby wrote a profile of Stallings Ridgeway because, as she condescendingly pointed out to me, "I knew him better than you did." True enough.

Accompanying the Ridgeway and Crandall obits was a picture of them Doug had managed to squeeze off just as we were being shoved out of the briefing room. The shot, once it was cropped and enlarged, showed Ernie and Stallings in an intense confrontation in front of the closed door through which the president had been hustled seconds earlier. Ernie Crandall, a stern look on his face, held out an arm as he tried to keep Ridgeway from pushing past him to follow after the president. Each man died doing his job. I began to wonder if Stallings was the man Doug and I saw who was on fire and staggering from the burning building.

Also, with my help, Doug wrote the obit for Charles McGlaughlan, the CBS photog who'd been killed in the attack. Turns out, McGlaughlan's nickname was "Boom Boom" because he'd lost a hand in a Fourth of July fireworks accident when he was a teenager, yet amazingly, he overcame his disability to become an Emmy Award-winning photographer Doug had known when he was stationed in Iraq as a combat photographer in the Army and Boom Boom was on assignment for CBS.

As I sat exhausted at the bar next to Doug, my mind circled back to the drone angle, and as it did, I became aware through the din that that's what Doug and the bartender were discussing.

I tuned in.

"How can a drone go rogue?" Doug asked the bartender.

"There are all kinds of ways," the guy answered as he toweled down the bar.

"Excuse me," I butted in. "Sorry to be late to this conversation. How do you know about drones?" I asked the guy.

Before he could answer, Doug said to me, "Let me introduce you two. Shotzie is the owner of this place. Our paths crossed briefly when we were serving in Iraq." He turned to look at Shotzie, but gestured at me. "Shotzie, this is my friend and colleague Lark Chadwick."

My heart sank. I wished he'd used the word "girlfriend." The omission made me realize we hadn't yet clarified if we were in an exclusive relationship – or not.

Shotzie put down his bar rag, wiped his hand on his jeans and grasped my outstretched hand in a firm grip. "Hiya, Lark," he smiled.

"Lemme guess. Shotzie's not your real name, is it?" I teased.

He laughed. "You're good. It's Horst. Horst Wehnke. German name. So, Shotzie seems just right for a guy who sells shots – and other adult beverages."

I laughed, then turned serious. "What's your connection to drones?"

"I used to work with them when I was in the Air Force."

"Work with them how?"

"Told them where to go and what to shoot."

I pulled my reporter's notebook out of my messenger bag, opened to a fresh page, slid a ballpoint from its place inside the top of the notebook's metal spirals, and clicked the pen into ready mode.

"Whoa. No names," Shotzie said, scissoring his hands across each other over my notebook like a football ref signaling illegal procedure.

"Why not?" I asked.

"Let's just say the Air Force and I didn't get along."

"How so?"

"Ever hear of Edward Snowden?"

"The guy who leaked all those National Security Agency secrets? Sure."

"The Air Force thought I had Snowden tendencies."

"Were they right?"

"Oh yeah. I think a lot of what the government is doing to spy on Americans is dangerous and criminal."

"Did you ever leak secrets?"

"Nope. But thought about it."

"What happened?"

"It was in the wake of the Snowden affair, so the military was being hyper vigilant. They felt I was a loose cannon."

"Were you?"

He nodded. "I probably woulda leaked some things if I'd known who to contact."

"What happened?"

"They caught me with some confidential documents. Nothing top secret, but it was enough for them to give me the boot. Got a dishonorable discharge." He spread out his hands in front of him to highlight the bar. "But I landed on my feet. I'd saved my money and was able to open this place four years ago."

"So, how can a drone go rogue?" I asked.

"No names, right?"

"No names," I agreed. "But help me understand and, if you wouldn't mind, maybe point me toward someone who can confirm what you're telling me."

He paused. "Okay," he said finally.

"A minute ago you were telling Doug that there are several ways a drone can go rogue," I said. "What are they?"

"One way," he said, "is if incorrect targeting information is entered accidently into the system. Garbage in, garbage out. Bad information, wrong target."

I wrote down the gist of what he said. "What are some other ways?"

"A rogue *operator*."

"Meaning the drone's not rogue, but the person in charge of it is?"

"Bingo."

"Is it possible that a drone can fire at a target if the drone's accidently been fed incorrect target coordinates?"

"No. Somebody has to pull the trigger. It's not something that's done automatically."

"So, what you're telling me is that the so-called 'rogue drone' story the White House is putting out is bogus?"

"*I'm* not telling you anything."

"Right. No names. Got it. But is that the upshot of what you're saying – that someone deliberately piloted the drone over the White House and shot a missile at the briefing room where the president had been speaking?"

He gave me a stern glare and nodded soberly.

"How can I check this out with someone on the record?"

Shotzie shrugged. "Ya got me."

"What's your cell phone number, just in case I need your, um, guidance in the future?" I asked.

He reached for a napkin, took the pen from my hand, and scrawled his number for me. When he finished, he looked up at Doug. "Are you two an item?"

Doug frowned and looked at me.

I shrugged and gave Shotzie a *beats-me* look.

"Not sure yet," Doug said, "but hold that thought."

"Well, then, if you're not sure yet..." Shotzie turned to me grinning, "what's *your* cell?"

In the next nanosecond, these thoughts crackled through my head:

If I give him my cell, Doug will interpret it as a major diss.

But maybe keeping Doug off balance will keep him on his toes and teach him a lesson that going off the grid on me is a big risk.

But, on the other hand, if I don't give Shotzie my cell, he might not be helpful to me if I need to check out something with him in the future.

But if I do give him my cell, he might think I'm signaling that I'm interested in him – which I'm not, plus it wouldn't be ethical to date a source.

I took my pen back from him and snatched another napkin off the pile on the counter. As I wrote down my number, I said to Shotzie, "I'll call you first. This way you'll know it's me."

I shot Doug a look. A thunderstorm seemed to be forming on his brow.

"It's thinning out a little in here. Let's take these to a table so we can talk." Doug slid off his barstool, beer glass in hand. He reached across the bar and shook Shotzie's hand. "Good talkin' to you, man."

"Same here, dude," Shotzie said.

I followed Doug back to a table in a dark, quieter corner of the pub, wondering – and worrying – if what I'd just done had landed me in big trouble.

ൠ ൠ

CHAPTER 6

I've been conflicted about Doug from the moment I met him a year ago. My first impression: smart-ass. I'd been the new reporter at the paper in Georgia and Doug was assigned to be my photog for an interview I hoped to get with the parents of a girl who'd been strangled to death.

I'd talked with him on the phone as he vectored in on where I was parked outside the parents' doublewide trailer home. He had a sexy voice, but then he shattered the mood by sneaking up on me as I sat waiting for him in my car. He suddenly appeared at my window making a grotesquely maniacal face.

But that scare, which annoyed me, was followed almost immediately by the realization that he was an attractive hunk. Yes. I'm sorry to say, just as I don't like it when men objectify me, that's exactly what I did to Doug Mitchell when I met him. He was wearing a tight-fitting T-shirt and form-fitting jeans and I was immediately turned on by how confident he was in his own skin.

As we worked together, I'd admired his professionalism. He was personable and sensitive toward the grieving couple and his work was stellar. But he was also cheeky toward me. I'm used to guys coming on to me and usually I can tell in the first few seconds if I'm interested. I almost never am. But I was interested in Doug then – and now.

He sat with his back to the pub wall, and scowled at the candle on the center of the table. I chose the chair on the opposite side. My desire was to slide up next to him, but instinct told me to keep my distance.

The two people at the table next to us were sucking face like there was no tomorrow. Come to think of it, they might be on to something.

When I couldn't stand the silence between us any longer, I broke it. "Are you pissed at me?"

Crickets.

I sighed and took a sip of my beer.

He continued frowning as he traced the edge of his coaster with a forefinger.

"C'mon, Doug. I gave Shotzie my number because he might be a good source."

"It's not that," he said softly.

"Then what is it?"

"Boom Boom," he said.

"The photog who died?"

He nodded. "He was a good man. A great shooter. Fearless."

The gloomy mood didn't surprise me, even though I hadn't seen it in him before. Doug lost the lower portion of his right leg when an improvised explosive device blew up his Humvee in Iraq. He'd enlisted in the Army after his big brother was killed in the collapse of the Twin Towers on 9/11. Pain and loss, I was coming to realize, are permanently embedded in Doug Mitchell's psyche.

I reached across the table and put my hand on top of his. "I'm sorry," I said, gently.

His thumb caressed the side of my hand briefly, then he broke the spell and reached for his beer.

"Thanks." He took a swig.

I decided it would be petty of me to grill him about why he'd suddenly gone off the grid on me all weekend.

Shotzie appeared next to the table. "Last call. Can I get you two another round?"

Doug looked at me.

I knew I should stop at one, but it had been an exceedingly rough day. Plus, I liked being with Doug and wanted the time with him to last.

"Works for me," I said.

"Okay. Make it two, Shotzie. Thanks."

When Shotzie retreated to the bar, Doug stood and brought his chair to the side of the table nearest to me.

"I owe you an apology," he said as he sat down.

"Oh?"

"Yeah. I've been a little scarce."

"Ya think?"

He nodded.

"How come?" I tried to sound casual.

He shrugged, then chugged what was left in his glass.

I started to say something, but just then Shotzie returned with our two beers. And the bill. He collected our empty glasses and went away.

"I really like you, Lark," Doug said.

"I like you, too."

"No. I mean I *reeeeally* like you."

I tossed my hair teasingly. "Yes. I've been known to have that effect on all my gentlemen callers."

Instead of chuckling, he pursed his lips, glanced toward Shotzie, pulled his chair even closer to mine, then spoke. "I think I've been scarce because, to be   honest . . ." he paused, looked at the floor, then continued hesitantly, "I'm a little intimidated by you." He gave me a shy glance, then looked down again.

I let out an involuntary laugh. "You're kidding, right?"

He shook his head slowly. "I probably shouldn't have told you that," he mumbled.

"Why not?"

"It isn't manly."

Our eyes locked.

"But it's true," he added.

"Why do I intimidate you?" I was serious now. And honestly curious. I saw myself as a bundle of needy, fearful emotions. In my heart, I knew that the Lark Chadwick everyone saw on the outside was all false bravado.

"You know I've been with a lot of women, right?" he asked.

"Duh. I've seen all those nude portraits you've painted, remember?"

"But you're different, Lark. You scare the shit outta me. I've never met anyone like you. Frankly, I don't think I'm good enough for you." He took a swig, leaned back and looked at me sheepishly, waiting for me to make the next conversational move.

"I don't know what to say," I said.

"Don't say anything." He leaned forward to kiss me.

Involuntarily, I leaned back.

He winced.

I took his hand. "I need to go slow, Doug. I told you that when I first let you kiss me in Georgia."

"Yeah," he said, gripping my hand, "but that was a long time ago. We've been going slow for months. That's too slow, if you ask me."

He leaned in.

I leaned back.

"One reason we've been going slow is that we've hardly seen each other since then." I needed a shield and reached for my beer glass.

"But we've been talking." He continued to hold my hand.

"Texting isn't the same as talking. It's nice, but it's not the same."

"We're talking now."

"Yes. And that's a start."

"So, what do you want to talk about?" he asked.

"Let's talk about you."

He let go of my hand and took a swallow of beer.

"Tell me about yourself, Doug Mitchell."

"We're back to the job interview, are we?" It's the line he used when I interviewed him when he was a suspect in a murder investigation.

I nodded. "But to be fair, I'm willing to tell you about myself, too."

"Okay, then. Why is it so important to you that we go slow?"

"A fair question. And, even though I asked you first, you deserve an answer." I took a gulp of beer and gathered my thoughts, deciding how much I would tell him. "Let's just say I've had my heart broken a few times."

"Haven't we all?"

"Actually," I said, "I get the impression you've *never* had your heart broken." It was only a hunch, but I wanted to turn the tables on him as soon as possible.

"Busted," he said.

"Really?"

He nodded. "I won't lie. I'm used to getting what I want."

"You mean you've never been turned down?"

"Oh, sure. But that's not the same as having your heart broken. If six out of ten chicks turn me down, that's still a .400 average. In baseball, that's slugger territory."

"I should call you slugger."

He scowled.

"But I won't."

"Thank you." He took a sip and went on. "The point is, the reason I haven't had my heart broken is that I've never really fallen for anyone before. I protect myself by playing catch and release."

"Catch and release?" My brow furrowed.

"Right. The thrill is in the hunt – and in the subsequent conquest. Once that's done, the thrill is gone. We have some fun and then I toss her back into the lake before things get messy." He made a motion of brushing off the palms of his hands.

"Jesus, Doug. I appreciate your honesty, but, God, that's so predatory. Just think of the hearts you've broken."

"I know." He looked down.

"But you keep doing it anyway?"

He raised his head and looked at me. "No. That's my point."

"What's your point? What am I missing here?"

"My point is . . ." he paused to take a swig, a vexed look on his face. Clearly, he'd never talked about this before. "My point is that since I've met you . . . ." He stopped and suddenly stood.

"What's wrong?"

"I've gotta take a leak. I'll be right back. Save my place."

He strode to the men's room, limping slightly, leaving me alone with my beer. And my thoughts.

Unlike Doug, I'd done my share of falling. And it never seemed to turn out well. It hadn't even been two years since Jason died. They say time heals. But I'm not so sure.

Just then, my phone triple-chimed, signaling that I had a text. I fished it out of my messenger bag. The text came from a phone number I didn't recognize.

I saw you on TV 2nite. Good questions about drones. You're on to something. Wanna know more?

I turned to look at the bar. Shotzie was at the cash register ringing up someone. I checked the phone number he'd given me against the one on the text. They didn't match.

Who is this? I typed.

I got an almost immediate response. *Not important.*

How do you know about drones, and how can I trust that what you "know" is reliable? I wrote.

Open your laptop, the anonymous texter commanded.

Intrigued, I set my phone on the table, dug out my computer and opened it. To my surprise, I was already logged on. And my cursor was moving all by itself. It opened a Word document and then typed these words onto my screen: *Now do you believe me?*

ରେ ଫେ

CHAPTER 7

I was staring in astonishment at my computer when Doug returned from the bathroom where he was allegedly "taking a leak," but I believed him to be in a cowardly retreat from intimacy and vulnerability.

"What's wrong?" he asked looking back and forth between me and my laptop.

"You won't believe this." I told him about what had just happened and showed him the text exchange with the anonymous tipster and the note in my commandeered computer.

"Do you think it's Shotzie?" Doug asked, his voice a stage whisper. He turned toward the bar to make sure Shotzie wasn't hovering within earshot.

"That's what I thought, too, but I don't think so."

"Why not?"

"I looked over there as soon as I got the text, but he was busy with a customer." I gestured at my phone on the table. "And the phone number of the text doesn't match the one he gave me."

Doug pulled his chair around so that it was side by side with mine, then sat down so we could both look at my computer screen.

"Now what?" he asked.

"Good question," I said. "Let's see where this goes." I started typing a reply. *This only proves you know how to hack my computer – which I deeply resent,* I wrote. *It does NOT prove you know ANYTHING about drones.*

I sat back in my chair waiting to see if the Tipster had a response.

If you want to know more about drones, you need to contact Dolph Rogan, my cursor typed all by itself. Then, on the next line, the cursor magically inserted a link to a website.

"Don't click–" Doug said.

I clicked.

"…on it." He sighed.

I held my breath, realizing too late I'd already impulsively clicked on the link without thinking.

Fortunately, the link didn't take me to some shady backroom in China, but to Dolph Rogan's bio on the website of Applied Electronics, a high-tech firm located in Reston, Virginia, near Dulles International Airport just northwest of Washington. Rogan's picture showed a swashbuckling guy with a shaved head, bulging biceps, and a cocky smile.

Quickly, I skimmed the copy beneath his picture. According to his bio, Rogan, 37, made his millions on Wall Street as a derivatives trader, then got his Masters and Ph.D. in physics at MIT. His company manufactured "drones for the common man – or woman – once the current F.A.A. restrictions are lifted." His motto: *A Drone in Every Garage.*

Are you Rogan? I typed.

No, came the curt reply. *Call him. He knows a LOT.*

A lot about the attack? I asked.

Call him, the tipster repeated, placing a phone number on the next line – a number that differed from the mysterious texter's.

By this time it was almost one o'clock in the morning, but I called anyway. The sultry voice of a woman answered – a recording. Her accent sounded Swedish:

"You have reached Applied Electronics. Our office hours are eight a.m. to five p.m. Monday through Friday, or by appointment. Please leave a message after the beep."

Beep.

"This is Lark Chadwick of the Associated Press calling for Mr. Rogan." I paused, trying to decide if I should say more. Less is more, I concluded. I left my cell number and hung up.

"Uh oh," Doug said. He was fumbling with his wallet.

"What?"

"I'm out of cash, and I must've left my credit card at home. Would you mind picking up the tab?" He gave me a bashful look.

I scowled. This wasn't the first time. I dug a hand into my messenger bag and brought out my wallet. "Okay, but this is becoming a habit. You pick up the tab next time. Deal?"

"Deal," he said eagerly. "Thanks, Lark. I'm really sorry."

I left Shotzie a five-dollar tip on a twenty-dollar bar bill. Outside, the night air was crisp and cold and H Street was quiet.

"My turn to say 'uh oh,'" I said, looking at my watch, my heart sinking.

"The Metro?"

I nodded. "I bet I missed the last train to Silver Spring."

"That's okay," he said. "You can crash at my place. I owe you. And I promise – no funny business."

"You don't mind?"

"Not at all. My Jeep's in the parking garage over there," he pointed across 17th Street, "and I live just up Florida Avenue a little ways."

"Thank you."

We didn't talk much on the short drive to his place, mostly small talk about the weather. He lives in a two-story brownstone with a bay window. He parked his Wrangler out front and we walked up the dozen or so stone steps to his front door. He unlocked it, then stepped inside ahead of me and switched on a light.

"I'll sleep there on the couch," he said. "You can have my bed. But I need to change the sheets first."

"No. That's okay. You're beat. I'm beat. I don't mind collapsing here, Doug. Thank you."

"You sure?"

"Uh huh."

He gave me a quick tour – half bath downstairs, kitchen at the rear, his bedroom on the second floor, a den, and a full bath. I noticed he kept it reasonably clean – for a single guy – pretty much the way he kept his apartment in Columbia, Georgia, when I'd interviewed him the previous spring.

When he was showing me the upstairs, he fished a gray sweatshirt and sweat pants out of his bottom dresser drawer and tossed them to me. "Your jammies," he smiled.

There was a moment of awkwardness, but he quickly dealt with it by giving me a goodnight fist-bump. "Sleep well," he said, then went into his room and closed the door.

I went back downstairs, turned off the floor lamp, stripped by the light of the streetlight on Florida, and put on the "jammies" Doug gave me. They were enormous. The sleeves extended at least six inches beyond my fingertips, and I had to pull the waist tie-string super tight. The ensemble smelled of detergent and fabric softener.

I lay awake for a few minutes acutely aware that I felt like I was falling asleep in Doug's cottony embrace. And I liked it.

ↈ ↈ

CHAPTER 8

I'd set the alarm on my phone for six, but my eyes popped open Tuesday morning at 5:55. I needed to get an early jump on the day because the Drone Attack story – not to mention the President Missing story – would fully occupy my time, possibly for weeks to come.

Reluctantly, I got out from under the toasty afghan on Doug's couch, folded his sweat suit neatly after I'd dressed, and placed everything on the couch. I ripped a page from my reporter's notebook, scribbled a message, and placed it atop what had been my jammies for the evening.

Doug – Thanks for letting me crash here last night. I'm going to dash home, shower, and change. I expect to be in the Jackson Place press room by 8. See you later!

I thought about putting a string of Xs and Os, but decided a smiley face would be wiser. I didn't want to send a mixed signal of being more available to him than I actually felt.

I tiptoed out the door, closing it quietly behind me. It was still dark outside. I walked briskly down R Street to the Dupont Circle Metro a few blocks away on Connecticut Avenue. I usually read the papers online, but cell service is spotty on the Metro, plus yesterday's story was momentous, so I impulsively bought a *Washington Post, New York Times,* and *USA Today* at the station and read all three by the time I'd gotten to my stop in Silver Spring.

Doug's picture of the snarling soldier in front of the White House was on the front page of the *Post*. The coverage all three papers gave to the story was almost identical, stressing the attack, but also noting the absence from view of President Gannon. I took particular comfort that the *Times* picked up on my pointed questions:

When asked if the drone attack was an assassination attempt, White House press secretary Lucia Lopez had no comment and abruptly ended her briefing of reporters.

The lead *Post* editorial scolded the White House for "obfuscation" by not at least providing the public with a photograph of the president "to assure that he's alright. Not doing so," the *Post* argued, "makes the world wonder just who's in charge over there."

On an inside page, *USA Today* ran a truncated version of my profile of Ernie Crandall, Rochelle Grigsby's obit on Stallings Ridgeway, and Doug's tribute to Boom Boom. Accompanying the write-ups was the dramatic shot Doug took of the Ridgeway-Crandall face-off at the front of the briefing room just before the two men died.

When I got home, I showered, put on some comfortable clothes, and headed back to the Metro. I was able to find a seat and browsed social media (Twitter, Facebook, Instagram, the blogs) during my commute back downtown. Fortunately, there's an unspoken rule that no one talks to each other on the D.C. Metro in the morning, so I could concentrate on getting a sense of what people were saying about the attack online.

Frankly, if I hadn't been getting paid to know what's going on, I'd give social media a wide berth because I rarely come across anything useful. More often than not, it's the ravings of sometimes articulate (but mostly not) conspiracy theorists or simply the pooled ignorance of people spouting opinions, conclusions, or speculations based on few facts, but much emotional intensity – most of it fear or downright paranoia. I consider it to be my job – my *mission* – to provide the public with reliable *facts*. All too often, it feels like I'm fighting an uphill battle.

I will say, however, that Twitter is a helpful tip service, assuming I'm following the right newsmakers at the right time. But keeping an eye on Twitter can be a full-time job requiring a second computer monitor.

I got off the Metro at the Farragut North station and walked the two blocks to Jackson Place. Along the way, I checked in with Rochelle Grigsby.

"Nice piece on Stallings," I said when she answered my phone call. "I saw it in *USA Today*."

She grunted.

I knew she hated me, but months earlier I'd decided that I would be kind to her no matter what so that it would be obvious that whatever rancor existed between us would be coming from her, not me.

But on this morning it was hard to muster the requisite kindness.

"I do have a quick question, Rochelle."

"What's that?" She sounded wary.

"I'm confused about one thing. As I remember, you explicitly told me Stallings was off yesterday. You specifically assigned me to his seat. But then he showed up which led to that embarrassing scene in front of the president."

She didn't miss a beat. "Stallings must've changed his mind but didn't tell me."

"Uh huh. But then, in an email reply to upper management, you specifically accused me of – quote – 'usurping' his position. How can you have it both ways? If Stallings didn't tell you he'd changed his mind and you assigned me to his chair, how can you then turn around and accuse me of being a usurper?" I decided that bluntly calling her a liar – which she is – would have been too confrontational.

Rochelle was silent, but only for a second or two, then said, "I'd love to chat with you more about this, Lark, but – in case you haven't noticed – there's a lot going on. We're moving Paul Stone over from the Capitol to replace Stallings. Where are you now?"

I sighed and let her win. This time. "A block from the temporary press center on Jackson Place."

"*He's* already there." A rebuke. "You'll be showing him the ropes today."

"Okay." I decided not to tell her about the tip I'd gotten last night about contacting Dolph Rogan, the drone expert.

Grigsby hung up without saying goodbye, which would have been yet another lie.

I pocketed my phone, but then thought better of it, took it out and dialed Lionel.

"Did I wake you?" I asked when he picked up. "I know it isn't even seven there in Wisconsin yet."

"Muriel and I are just beginning to stir," he said sleepily. "Good job yesterday, by the way. I didn't realize you were doing radio when I called."

"Thanks."

"I'm glad you're okay," he said, his voice husky.

"Me too. I've got a news flash for you."

"Yeah?"

"Your son Paul is replacing Stallings. And it's my job to train him."

"Paul will be *thrilled.*"

"I know. That's what worries me."

"What do you mean?"

"In case you haven't noticed, Lionel, Paul has a serious crush on me."

"Yeah. I've noticed. You'd make a great daughter-in-law."

"Stop it, Lionel. You know he's not my type. He's smart and handsome, but the sparks just aren't there."

"Give it time."

"Lionel, please don't encourage this. You'll only set him up for heartbreak."

"Yeah, yeah."

"I've gotta go. I'm almost at the press center. Big day today."

"Okay, you be strong, kid."

I pocketed my phone and bit my lip, worried about my upcoming encounter with Paul Stone. He's A.P.'s Capitol Hill correspondent. I'd met him a few times, but the chemistry just wasn't there. His family was still reeling from the sudden death of his sister Holly – Lionel and Muriel's daughter – a few years earlier along the Inca Trail to Machu Picchu in Peru. Holly had been my age, but I'd never met her. Now Lionel seemed to cling to me emotionally as his surrogate daughter. And Paul couldn't help wearing his emotions on his sleeve for me. It was suffocating.

Lafayette Square was to my left as I approached the temporary press center from the north. Straight ahead, down Jackson Place, yellow police tape cordoned off Pennsylvania Avenue in front of the White House. H Street at Jackson Place was lined on both sides by live trucks from various televsion stations and networks, their microwave masts sticking high into the sky. Electric generators groaned as they supplied juice to rows of high-intensity lights that lit up clusters of TV reporters.

About a dozen of them were getting ready to do their top-of-the-hour live shots from in front of the White House. Apparently, access to Pebble Beach on the White House grounds was restricted.

I scampered up the stone steps, pulled open the tall wooden door, and stepped into a room aswirl with activity. Standing just inside the door to greet me stood Lionel's son, Paul Stone. He's a tall, lanky guy of about thirty – maybe a little older. He was impeccably dressed in a charcoal suit Ryan Gosling would wear.

Paul's grin was ear to ear. "Lark! Hello! Dad just texted to tell me you were almost here! It's good to see you again!"

Yes, he speaks in exclamation marks.

He leaned down to give me a hug, but I took a step back and offered him my hand.

"Hi, Paul! It's good to see you, too!" I tried to match him exclamation point for exclamation point. "Looks like we'll finally be working together!"

All this smiling was hurting my face.

"I know! I'm *so* excited!"

"Where's our cubicle?" I asked, trying to break the hyperglycemic mood. I looked around.

"It's right over here!" He turned and began walking. "Follow me," he said over his shoulder.

He led me to a cramped space just off the entrance. Thank God it had a window overlooking Lafayette Square, but barely enough room for the two of us to sit at the same time. It had a phone, a TV, and plenty of electrical hook-ups for our laptops. His was already open on the desk. I set my messenger bag down on the desk, pulled out my laptop and opened it. We'd be facing each other.

We chit-chatted a bit, then each of us burrowed into our respective computers. About 8:30 my phone went off.

"Lark Chadwick," I said.

"Miss Chadwick, this is Dolph Rogan returning your call." His voice sounded European-precise.

"Hi, Mr. Rogan. Thanks for calling back."

"What can I do for you?"

"As you may know, sir, the drone attack story is big news right now."

"Yes. A pity."

"I'd like to pick your brain and get a better understanding about drones and how the attack on the White House could have happened."

"Of course."

"Do you buy the White House story that the attack was caused by a so-called rogue drone?"

"No. Not at all."

"Why not?" I was surprised at his candor.

"Drones don't just fire automatically."

"How do you know?"

"I've spent most of my adult life studying and then developing the technology."

"Have you had any military experience?"

"No. I've never been in the service."

"Does your company have any military contracts?"

"No. None. I'm purely a peacenik. I'm developing drones for peaceful, private, and commercial uses."

"But right now, there are a lot of restrictions on that, aren't there?"

"Yes, but I'm also an optimist. I'm fairly certain that will change soon."

"Before the attack, President Gannon was about to announce his policy on drones. Any idea what he was going to say?"

"I read this morning in the *Wall Street Journal* that he was about to introduce legislation that would have opened the skies to private drones, but that now he's reconsidering his position."

I hadn't seen that yet, but didn't want to signal my ignorance to Rogan.

"Does that concern you?" I asked.

"It does, but it's understandable, under the circumstances."

"Is it possible to weaponize commercial drones?"

"I suppose it's *technically* possible, but that's certainly not something that I would advocate. Say," he said, as if just getting a bright idea. "Why don't you come on out and I'll give you a personal demonstration? I can show you the future."

"That would be great. I can't come right now, though. I'm stuck downtown until the White House press office tells us not to expect any more news today. Can I call you back later?"

"Sure," he said. "You can line it up with Anne-Marie, my executive assistant. In the meantime, let me email you some background information."

"Okay. Thanks." I gave him my work email address and we hung up. I then went to *The Wall Street Journal* website and read the story Rogan had mentioned. The *Journal* cited "a senior White House official" as its source for the tidbit that President Gannon was about to come out in favor of the commercialization of drones.

"Hey, Paul."

"Yes, Lark?" He looked up from his screen.

"You've been covering Congress for a long time now, right?"

"Five years."

"Did you see the *Wall Street Journal* piece?"

"Which one?"

"The one that says Gannon was about to come out in favor of drones?"

"Missed it," he said, frowning.

"I'll send you the link." I copied the link into an email to Paul and hit *send.* "Maybe you can check with your sources to see if they can confirm this and if they have any specifics of what Gannon was about to propose."

"On it!"

"Let's see if we can advance that angle of the story before the briefing at eleven."

"Okay! Good idea!"

My email inbox chimed. Dolph Rogan had sent me several links to articles he'd written for various high-tech publications about the benefits and possibilities of having your own private drone. Each story featured a flattering photo of him handling one of his drone creations.

As I read through the material Rogan sent, I could hear Paul on the phone talking with a source – actually, several sources, because he made at least six calls in half an hour. He was clearly an experienced reporter – *way* more experienced and capable than me, I felt, yet I was technically the more "senior" person on the White House beat, if only by a day. But Paul certainly had way more A.P. experience. *Good thing he's such a positive person*, I thought to myself. *Less likely he'll be a backstabber.*

The eleven o'clock briefing, held in a fairly comfortable, but dingy theater down the hall, was nearly as contentious as the one twelve hours earlier in the EEOB. Lucia Lopez was bombarded by questions – and not just from me. Most centered around the president's whereabouts and condition.

"I can tell you unequivocally that President Gannon is alive and well, but still in an undisclosed location." Despite all of our attempts, she didn't budge beyond that, yet she'd added one word to her report from last night: the word "well." The inference – President Gannon had not been seriously wounded.

But had he been *slightly* wounded?

Others picked up on the nuance, too. "When can we see him?" clamored a television reporter. "Can you at least release a photo?"

"I might have something even better than that for you," Lopez said, smiling for the first time since the attack. "The in-town pool will assemble at the front door immediately after the briefing."

A.P. is a regular member of the pool, along with the other wire services – Bloomberg News (the business and financial wire) and Reuters. The pool is also comprised of reporters representing radio, print, and a major television network. Those positions rotate daily among the dozens of news organizations with White House credentials. Rounding out the pool are wire photographers from A.P. and the French news service *Agence France-Presse* (AFP), plus a still photog from the *New York Times*.

The press pool is necessary because it's often too cumbersome for all 250 accredited members of the White House Press corps to cover an event in a cramped space like the Oval Office or the Cabinet Room. Being a member of the small press pool means that the print and broadcast reporters have to report back to the rest of the White House press corps before they're allowed to file with their own news organizations.

The wires and still photogs can file their stuff immediately – to the colossal annoyance of everyone else.

About 11:45, after the briefing ended, I stood at the front door of 726 Jackson Place next to Doug, waiting with the rest of the pool to be escorted to who knows where by Lucia Lopez – and/or one or two of her underlings.

"Where do you think we're going?" I asked Doug. It was the first time I'd seen him that morning. He looked exhausted.

"Dunno," he shrugged. "Maybe the 'undisclosed location.'"

"Or not," I added.

Lucia Lopez came to the front door and led us down the steps and toward the White House.

"Thanks again for letting me use your couch," I said to Doug as we crossed the Pennsylvania Avenue pedestrian mall.

"Sure. Not a problem. How come you left so early? Afraid of my cooking?" he smirked. "I make mean scrambled eggs. And bacon."

I laughed, but didn't have a chance to answer because by this time we'd entered the White House compound via the Northwest gate and were being led toward the ruined briefing room.

Doug immediately began snapping still pictures of the damage, as did the photographer for Voice of America (VOA), the TV network with rotating pool duty today.

Part of the outside wall of the briefing room had collapsed. All the windows were broken, and the portion of the white wall still standing was soot-blackened from the fire that had raged here. The roof was missing, letting in plenty of sunlight. We could easily see the rubble inside.

The poignancy of the moment was interrupted when the door to the West Wing entrance opened, the Marine standing guard saluted, and out strode President Will Gannon.

We swarmed him.

ೞ ಐ

CHAPTER 9

As soon as I saw the president, flanked by two Secret Service agents, I speed-dialed the desk. "It's Chadwick at the White House," I said, as soon as someone picked up. "I need to dictate a news alert. President Gannon is alive and speaking to reporters right now at the White House. Listen and take down what he says."

The two other wire reporters in the pool were still fumbling for their phones. I had them beat by at least a minute.

I positioned myself immediately in front of the president and held my phone out toward him. Several of us shouted questions at him at the same time: "How are you, Mr. President? Where have you been?"

Gannon smiled broadly and held up both hands. "Hold on. Hold on, everyone. I'm fine. I'm fine."

The VOA photog switched on the light atop his camera, instantly eliminating the shadows that obscured part of the president's face. Gannon wore a dark suit, light blue shirt, and a muted purple tie. I scanned his face and hands, but saw no obvious injuries.

"I'll take your questions in just a moment," the president said, "but first I want to offer my condolences to the families of the men who were killed here yesterday. Ernie Crandall, Stallings Ridgeway, and Charles McGlaughlan were good men who died doing what they loved most." He paused.

"Where were you taken, Mr. President, and were you hurt in any way?" I asked.

"The Secret Service performed admirably," the president said. "They rushed me to safety. They don't want me to tell you where, but no, Lark, I wasn't injured."

The VOA correspondent, a handsome brunette, piped up. "So, why have you been incommunicado? Why all the secrecy?"

Gannon smiled indulgently. "For the time being, we're going to be a bit vague on my whereabouts, but I can assure you that my people will be keeping you folks updated on a more regular basis."

"What can you tell us about the attack, Mr. President?" I asked. "I'm hearing that there's no way a rogue drone can fire accidentally."

"The investigation is still ongoing," he replied, "so, I'm not going to get into the particulars of that."

"What about your drone policy?" the pool's print reporter asked. "There are reports you were about to come out in favor of lifting the restrictions on the commercialization of drones. Were you?"

"In light of the current situation, we're reviewing our stance and should have something for you shortly," Gannon answered.

"But–" the reporter tried.

Gannon held up his hands again. "I really have to go. Thank you, everyone." He then turned on his heel, and retreated past the Marine's salute and back into the West Wing, trailed by the two agents.

As soon as the president was out of sight, we all broke into a dead run to get back to the filing center on Jackson Place.

"Did you get that?" I shouted into the phone as I ran.

"Yep. Your bulletin's already moved. Plus a couple leads."

"Okay," I hollered. "I'll have a write-through for you in just a couple minutes."

When I dashed into the press center, it seemed as though the walls were bulging because of all the commotion stirred up by the returning press pool.

"I saw your bulletin," Paul said as I dove into my chair across the desk from him, logged onto my laptop, and began banging the keys.

"Thanks," is all I could muster.

It took me a few scant minutes to pound out the five-paragraph story and hit *send.* The desk had already given it a slug: *Gannon Resurfaces.* The story was updated throughout the day as additional details were added to it, but the byline was mine. By the end of the day the story included the names at the bottom of the write-through of the reporters from other A.P. beats who contributed – a true team effort. Just about every major news organization is a subscriber to A.P., so our reporting formed the basis of the rest of the world's coverage.

"Whew! That was fun!" I let out a breath and leaned back in my chair.

"Dad'll be proud," Paul said. "And I'm honored to be working with you, Lark Chadwick."

"Thank you. I think we're gonna be a good team, Paul Stone."

Paul beamed at me from across the desk.

ↄ ᗰ

CHAPTER 10

Once the president had resurfaced, it felt as though much of the tension in the press room was siphoned off and we could get back to covering the Gannon Administration, not the Gannon Assassination. But the attack on the West Wing – rogue, or otherwise – remained our sole focus for the rest of the day.

Paul and I worked our sources – as did A.P. reporters at the Pentagon, Capitol Hill, and the Justice and State Departments – trying to get a handle on the bigger story: Who pushed the button that sent a missile streaking into the West Wing briefing room? Why? And what effect will the attack have on the Gannon Administration's policy on the commercialization of drones?

A city filled with reporters representing news organizations from around the world trying to get answers to the same questions is a daunting process to behold. And, it can be downright terrifying if you happen to be a press secretary inside a government agency trying to fend off wave after wave of questions – most of them prosecutorial.

By the end of the second day after the attack, we reporters had only eked out a few factual nuggets, but the government prevailed and the bigger truth behind the facts remained hidden.

One of our Pentagon correspondents learned that the drone had been shot down, but, because all the wreckage landed on the south lawn of the White House, it was hidden from public view.

Our Justice Department correspondent, quoting "a senior government official close to the investigation," reported that the F.B.I. was questioning an Asian-American lieutenant in the U.S. Air Force about his role in the attack, but so far no charges had been filed, so no name would be released.

Paul learned from his sources that bipartisan sentiment on the Hill was building to stave off the privatization of drones. There were rumors that several members of Congress, fearing the havoc a sky full of drones could cause, were beginning to draft bills designed to stall the commercial drone industry.

I spent the day watching cable news, mostly CNN, Fox, and MSNBC. For the most part, it was sensational, speculative, and repetitive blather, but occasionally I was able to pull a quote from a member of Congress, or an expert on drones, and drop it into the *Gannon Resurfaces* story. I also did a lot of background reading on drones – enough to see both their possibilities and dangers.

By four o'clock – even earlier than when the press office usually announces a travel and photo lid – Lopez herself announced the full lid. So, not only would there be no more paper coming from the press office, but no more pictures would be released, nor would the president be traveling anywhere.

But the re-emergence of President Gannon was a huge story that would keep the chatterverse talking for the rest of the day.

"Wanna get a drink and then maybe dinner?" Paul asked as soon as the lid was announced.

"Gee, Paul, I'd love to," I lied, "but I need to work on something. Rain check?"

"Sure." He tried to say it brightly, but there was no exclamation point and his megawatt smile lost some of its luster.

I *hate* saying no. And I knew that soon I would need to placate him, if, for no other reason than to be nice – and to cement our working rapport. But my wheels were already turning as I began strategizing about how I was going to keep our relationship platonic and professional, not romantic.

"Have a good night, Lark." Paul put on his overcoat and trudged toward the door.

"You too," I called after him as brightly as I could. After he left, I sighed.

I was just about to call Doug when his blues piano ringtone went off. His picture on the display was a shot of him I'd taken several months earlier. He sat in front of an easel, the end of a small paintbrush clenched between his teeth. The jovial pose had reminded me of a classic picture of FDR – ebullient, with a cigarette holder tilted up at a jaunty angle.

"Hey, what's up?" I asked. "I was just gonna give you a call, but you beat me to the punch."

"I've been spending the better part of the day playing cards with the network photogs back here. I just won the last round and can now afford to buy you a drink."

"I'll take that offer under advisement," I said. "In the meantime, do you want to take a drive out to Reston?"

"With you?"

"Uh huh."

"Of course. What's up?"

"I'm gonna see if I can line up an interview with Dolph Rogan, that drone mogul last night's tipster turned us onto."

"I like the 'us' part. I'll get my gear and swing by."

I called Rogan's office.

"Applied Electronics," came the sultry, Swedish-sounding voice that had been on the answering machine the night before. "This is Anne-Marie."

"Hi, Anne-Marie. This is Lark Chadwick at the Associated Press. I spoke with Mr. Rogan this morning and he invited me to come out there to interview him later today. He suggested I talk with you about lining it up once I knew when I'd be free."

"Yes," she said. "He briefed me on that. I've been expecting your call." Her voice had a huskiness that sounded like it had had a long and intimate relationship with cigarettes and whiskey.

We set up the interview for five o'clock "depending on traffic" and she made sure I had the correct address. Doug came by just as I was hanging up and we walked the few short blocks to retrieve his Jeep Wrangler from a nearby parking garage.

I'm glad I'd hedged my arrival time at Applied Electronics because Doug and I were stuck in D.C.'s formidable rush-hour traffic. We had plenty of time to talk.

I got the ball rolling by holding a pretend microphone to my mouth: "If you're just joining us, let's rejoin the conversation between Doug Mitchell and Lark Chadwick where we left it last night at Shotzie's Pub.

As you may remember, Doug has just told Lark that he reeeally likes her. But then he conveniently – and indelicately – wussed out of the conversation because he had to – in his words – 'take a leak.' Let's pick things up from there, shall we?" I turned to Doug and held the "micro-phone" out to him.

His jaw tightened and he gripped the steering wheel in both hands at the ten and two position – even though we were at a dead stop in bumper-to-bumper traffic.

"Mr. Mitchell? You were saying?"

"I forget," he mumbled.

"No you don't, you liar." I poked him playfully on the shoulder.

His face remained sphinx-like as he glowered out the windshield and studied the writing on the back of a panel truck advertising plumb-ing services.

"Alright," I sighed. "Let me prime the pump a little. For the record, I reeeally like you, too, Mr. Mitchell."

His features relaxed and he took his eyes off the back of the panel truck long enough to throw me a furtive glance. "What? Am I supposed to say more?"

I nodded. "Yes, sir."

"I've already said my piece."

"Okay. Then let me ask a follow-up, Mr. President. You were telling me about the charming practice of 'catch and release' and how the thrill of the hunt and conquest protects you from having your heart broken."

"Geez." He scratched his head. "Did I say that?"

"Yes. But you'd been drinking, which explains your plea of tempo-rary amnesia."

He chuckled.

"However," I continued, "if I remember correctly, you said that I'm different and that you're no longer interested in playing that chivalrous – or should I say childish – little game anymore. Could you elaborate, please?"

At last Doug relaxed and seemed to begin to warm to my approach. He coughed self-consciously. "Of course, Lark." He turned to look at me. "May I call you 'Lark'?"

"I'll allow it."

"As I was saying. I've grown tired of the Catch-and-Release game because I've come to realize that it's shallow and selfish. Since I met you, I've simply lost interest in anyone else."

"And why is that?" I asked, tossing my hair coquettishly and batting my eyes. "Use both sides of the page, if necessary."

He turned serious for a moment. "I think it's because you're so..." he paused, groping for the right word. "You're so smart. You're brave. And you're, just, well, *fun* to be around. Hearing you laugh gives me a contact high."

I felt myself blush.

"Shall I go on?"

"Please do. Take as much time and as many words as you'd like."

"Nah. I think I'll leave it there." He grinned impishly.

"Noooooo!" I whined.

He laughed. "Nope. My turn. Let me ask you: why do you reeeally like *me?*"

I scowled, not wanting to be put on the spot when being on the pedestal felt so much better.

"Okay," I sighed. "First," I opened my left hand and with the forefinger of my other hand began ticking off his positive attributes. "You're easy on the eyes. But, yes, I know, that's superficial and it shouldn't count. But it does. Whatever."

I was feeling flustered. And when I feel flustered, I yammer. And when I yammer, I feel like a fool – which makes me keep yammering. Pathetic.

"Two," I said, "you're good at what you do and you're smart."

"That's two and *three,*" he corrected.

"Whatever. Four - I like being with you." I paused. "And..."

"Go on," he prompted.

"As I remember, you're a pretty good kisser."

"It needn't stop there," he said, eyebrows bouncing suggestively.

"But–"

"Uh oh," he interrupted. "Here comes 'on the other hand.'" He sat back and drummed the fingers of his right hand impatiently on the top of the steering wheel.

"Yes," I admitted, "there *is* the other hand."

He took a deep breath, held it for a moment, then exhaled powerfully. "Okay. Bring it. I can take it."

"You sure?"

"Yes'm," he said, subdued and wary.

"Okay. You asked for it. On the other hand." I switched hands and repeated finger-ticking. "To be honest, I still don't know if I can trust you."

He turned serious, his brow furrowed, and he scowled. "Really?"

"Yes. Really. You've been short of cash on more than one occasion, and you have a tendency to disappear for extended periods of time for no apparent reason."

His face flushed and he seemed to slump in the seat.

"Should I go on?"

"There's more?"

"Yes."

"Shit. I'm toast."

"Not necessarily. But there is one more thing."

"What's that?" he asked, turning to look at me.

"You've had a *lot* of partners. I, um, haven't."

"What do you mean you 'haven't'?"

I bit my lip.

"Are you okay?" He reached for my hand and smothered it with his big warm one. But just for an all-too-brief moment.

I nodded, curtly. "Yeah. I'm fine." Tears suddenly and involuntarily spurted into my eyes, but my voice remained strong. "I've never told this to anyone before, but even though we live in a libertine world, I'm still a virgin."

I looked at him for a reaction.

Doug cinched his eyebrows. "Really?"

I nodded.

"Wh-why?"

"It's not because I'm a prude. It's because on some fundamental gut level, I don't trust men. I had a serious crush on my English professor in college, but he took advantage of me."

Doug's voice became gentle. "Do you mind telling me how?" He reached toward my arm and grazed it with his fingertips. "You don't have to tell me."

I took a deep breath. "He tried to rape me."

"Oh, man. Lark, I'm so sorry. I didn't know."

"He's in prison now. But the point is, I don't give away my heart easily, Doug. For me, giving myself physically to another person is intimately intertwined with giving myself to another person *emotionally*. It's just who I am."

"I see." He was silent a moment, brushing his left forefinger back and forth against his lower lip in thought. Finally he spoke. "Last night, you also mentioned that you've had your heart broken."

"Yes. Partly it's because of the sexual assault, but then there was Jason."

"The reporter you knew back in Wisconsin?"

"Uh huh. We were right on the cusp of something special when he–" My voice cracked. "When he died." A tear leaked out of my eye and I swiped at it as it trickled down my cheek.

Doug gently placed his hand over the tear-track. "I'm so sorry, Lark." He turned, took my face in both his hands and looked me deeply in the eyes. "I promise you this: I will *never* hurt you."

I put my hands on his. . . and wept.

03 80

CHAPTER 11

By the time we pulled into the parking lot of Applied Electronics, I'd managed to compose myself. It was after five o'clock, but I'd called to let them know we'd be running late. Dolph Rogan's assistant, Anne-Marie, assured me that she and Rogan would be there when we arrived and said we shouldn't worry about the time.

Applied Electronics is located in an industrial park near Dulles International Airport in a nondescript three-story, bland-beige building. Frankly, given the swaggering image presented on his website, I'd expected Dolph Rogan's digs to be a little more impressive.

A stunning strawberry blonde bombshell, mid-to-late thirties, sat behind the semi-circular reception desk. When she stood, I thought Doug's eyes would pop out of their sockets. She wore a white, low-cut blouse that was at least one size too small and left very little to the imagination.

"You must be Lark Chadwick," The Bombshell beamed, pronouncing the W in Chadwick like a V. She reached out to shake my hand. "I'm Anne-Marie Gustofsen, Mr. Rogan's assistant."

"Hi," I said cleverly, taking her hand. "And this is my photographer Doug Mitchell."

As they shook hands, I stifled a grin as I watched Doug try with all his strength to keep his eyes locked on Anne-Marie's. While he was still struggling to keep himself from ogling her chest, I'd already fully assessed her threat level: DEFCON 1 – red-alert severe. It was Anne-Marie who gave Doug the once-over, rather than vice-versa.

"May I get you anything?" she asked.

"No, thanks. We're fine," I replied.

She picked up the phone from its cradle on her desk, punched a button, and said into the receiver, "Miss Chadvick and her photographer are here."

"Have you worked here long?" I asked her when she hung up, trying to make small talk while we waited.

"I've been Mr. Rogan's assistant for the past five years – ever since he opened up shop here."

"How did you meet?"

"I'd just come to the United States from Sweden where I grew up. We were Ph.D. students together at MIT. "

"Oh, my," I said. "What's it like to be smart?"

She didn't laugh. "It's a burden."

Just then, a door off to my left opened and out stepped Dolph Rogan, the spitting image of Mr. Clean himself: shaved head and an impressive physique that made it look like any minute he'd rip the seams of his ocean-blue dress shirt like the Incredible Hulk.

"Hello, Ms. Chadwick," he gushed. "I'm so glad you could make it."

"Call me Lark," I smiled, shaking his massive hand.

After I introduced him to Doug and they shook hands, Rogan said, "How about we go on a field trip to the hangar?"

"Great!" I said, channeling Paul Stone.

Rogan ducked into his office for a moment, re-emerging wearing a down jacket. While he was gone, Anne-Marie slipped on a down jacket of her own.

"Anne-Marie will be joining us, if you don't mind," Rogan said.

"Works for me," Doug said, a little too eagerly for my taste.

Once we got outside, Rogan said, "We can take my SUV. Lark, you ride shotgun."

The black Lincoln Navigator looked like something Donald Trump would drive: tinted windows and distinctive gold wheel rims.

When we'd all strapped in, Rogan propelled the Navigator out of its parking place and rocketed us down a side road that led to a row of hangars at a far end of Dulles. The drive took just a few minutes. Rogan talked the entire way, a veritable stream of consciousness about the weather, the sunset, the buildings we passed, the traffic – but nothing news or quote-worthy. My reporter's notebook rested uselessly on my lap, the fresh page still empty at the end of our ride.

The hangar was so cavernous and cold we could see our breath.

"Have you ever seen a drone, Miss Chadwick?" Rogan asked.

"Lark."

"Sorry. Lark."

"Not in person."

"That changes today," Rogan said. "I want to show you what I consider to be the Model-T of drones."

"And that would make you the Henry Ford of drones?"

"Exactly. I like the way you think, Lark."

"And, let me guess: you want the drone to be as ubiquitous as the Model-T was more than a hundred years ago."

"Yes."

I finally had something I could scribble into my notebook.

As he talked he walked us to a corner of the hangar where a tarp covered something.

"Okay to take pictures of everything here?" Doug asked Rogan.

"That's fine. I'll let you know when to stop if we get to anything that's still top secret." Rogan winked at me.

Doug unslung his Nikon, made some adjustments, then readied himself for whatever looked interesting. He found it as soon as Rogan got to the tarp. Before Rogan even removed the tarp from what it was covering, the *chick-koo* of Doug's shutter clicks began echoing off the metal walls.

Rogan swept away the tarp and handed it to Anne-Marie in a maneuver so smooth that it reminded me of well-rehearsed choreography between magician and assistant. Beneath the tarp sat what looked like a metallic spider with four legs, propellers atop each of them. A Plexiglas dome containing a camera sat in the center of the contraption.

"This is the Model-D," Rogan said proudly.

"D for drone, right?" I asked.

"You're good," he said. "Shall we take it for a spin?" He didn't wait for my answer – which would have been, "You bet!"

Rogan bent down, reached under the dome and easily lifted the Model-D off the hangar's cement floor.

"How much does it weigh?" I asked.

"Just a few pounds. Here." He handed it to me.

"Wow. It's light," I said, hefting it, pen in one hand, notebook in the other.

Rogan took it back from me and walked us to the door of the hangar. Anne-Marie followed carrying what looked like an elaborate TV remote the size of an iPad with an array of switches, toggles, and a TV screen.

When we got outside the hangar, Rogan put the drone on the ground while Doug circled us, taking pictures from every angle.

"To show you how easy it is to fly, I'll have Anne-Marie do the honors," Rogan said.

So easy even a girl can fly it, I thought cynically.

But Anne-Marie seemed unperturbed and unoffended. She immediately began flipping switches and toggling the joystick as if she'd done this choreographed demonstration hundreds of times.

The metallic spider seemed to come alive. The propellers began spinning and in no time the Model-D slowly lifted off the ground, the propellers producing merely a whisper.

For nearly half an hour, Anne-Marie skillfully ran the Model-D through its paces as Rogan kept up a steady narration about the potential for drones in the daily life of Americans.

"I really can see a day when the drone will be just as ubiquitous as the cell phone, the laptop, and the automobile," he gushed.

At one point, after having Anne-Marie demonstrate how the controls operated, Rogan let me give it a try. I quickly discovered that the Model-D isn't as easy to fly as Anne-Marie made it seem. Rogan, who'd been hovering over me as I toggled the joystick, had to intervene suddenly when I came dangerously close to crashing it.

"How much does one of these cost?" I asked after Rogan had safely retaken control.

"This one retails for about seven-hundred dollars," he said.

I chuckled. "I can see why you stayed so close to me while I was trying to fly it."

"Well, that was certainly *one* of the reasons," he laughed and winked.

I knew where he was going: not where I was going. I let the remark pass.

Fifteen minutes later the four of us were back at Rogan's office for what I told Rogan would be a brief "sit-down interview." Doug snapped stills of Rogan and Anne-Marie as they sat next to each other on a camel-colored settee in Rogan's office, my iPhone on the coffee table in front of them, recording the conversation with their permission.

Even though Anne-Marie is Rogan's assistant, he dominated the conversation, often stealing the ball from her mid-answer after I'd deliberately directed questions at her, yet I picked up no hint of annoyance on her face or in her demeanor when he did so.

During our twenty-minute interview, I kept asking myself why the anonymous tipster had pointed me to Rogan. He certainly knew a lot about drones, as the tipster had said. In fact, Rogan had an almost evangelical zeal in trying to promote them. But did he know more about the attack itself? I decided to ask.

"As you know, Mr. Rogan, the Gannon Administration alleges the attack on the White House–"

Rogan held up both hands like a traffic cop and cut me off. "Yes. You asked me about that on the phone. And, as you remember, I told you I'm skeptical of their explanation. But I don't want to talk politics. I'd much rather we discuss the future of drones."

"Fair enough," I said, "but drones won't *have* a future if the current anti-drone sentiments on Capitol Hill come to fruition."

Rogan frowned. "Yes. That's troubling."

"In what way?"

"I'd hate for a culture of fear to pervade the nation's thinking about drones."

"Because if it did, you'd stand to lose a lot of money?" I pressed.

He nodded and smiled ruefully. "Yes. Certainly that's a consideration. But I think it's best to look at it as a win-win."

"How so?"

"If President Gannon throws his considerable clout behind lifting the current restrictions on drones, it's not only a win for the free enterprise system that makes this country the economic envy of the world, it also is good for society because we'll have at our disposal one more tool that will make our lives easier."

"But there are downsides to drones, as well, aren't there?"

"Of course." He leaned forward placing his elbows on his thighs and gestured earnestly. "Look at the automobile, for example. It's true that many people die in traffic accidents every day, but that's not a reason to ban the car. It just means that efforts should and are being taken every day to make driving as safe as possible."

"How does that logic translate to drones?" I asked.

"I feel a balance can be struck between making drones widely available to the general public, yet regulating them so they are operated safely."

"What kind of limits do you believe should be placed on the operation of drones?"

"First," Rogan began, "a person should have to have a license to operate a drone, just like a driver's license. Next, I feel that drones should not be allowed to operate near airports. I think that the current four-hundred-foot ceiling should be relaxed but that drones shouldn't be allowed to fly higher than, say, five-thousand feet off the ground."

"Should there be restrictions on *how* they're used?"

He paused. "Not sure. Haven't thought about that."

I was scribbling rapidly.

"Am I going too fast for you?"

I looked up. "No." I nodded at my iPhone on the coffee table in front of him. "My iPhone's getting it. These notes are just a back-up. Please, go on."

"Very well," he said. "I do think it's imperative that there be strong sanctions against the weaponization of drones. And I suppose there should be some way to guard against drones being used as vehicles for voyeurism."

As I wrote *vehicles for voyeurism* into my notebook, I said, "I would think that last caveat might be the most difficult to enforce."

"Perhaps. But not impossible."

"What do you propose?"

"Hmmmm," he said, sitting back and crossing his legs. "I'd have to think more about that. I don't want to blurt out something I haven't thought through and then have to eat my words." He chuckled and smiled. His teeth were whiter-than-white perfect. "Besides," he added, "that's way outside my area of expertise. I'm an inventor and an entrepreneur. I'll leave policy to the wonks."

"So," I said, shifting gears, "tell me more about you two." I fixed my gaze on Anne-Marie, hoping she'd take my cue and pick up where we'd left off when I was making small talk with her before Rogan emerged from his office.

"We met at MIT," Rogan said, not bothering to even see if Anne-Marie had anything to say. "I was very impressed with her intelligence. It became immediately obvious to me that we were on the same page in our vision about drones."

"Anne-Marie?" I said, still looking at her. "What can you add to that?"

She smiled shyly and pulled uncomfortably at the hem of her pencil skirt as if tugging it an eighth of an inch closer to her knee would make any difference – her hem was already mid-thigh.

"Not much, really," she said. "Dolph's explanation is exactly right."

My next question was a calculated risk. "Was the relationship ever romantic?"

Anne-Marie immediately blushed.

Rogan said, "It's always been purely professional. A business relationship. A partnership, actually."

"You're business partners?" I asked, once again turning to Anne-Marie.

"Yes. That's correct," she nodded, avoiding my eyes.

Not long after that, I wrapped up the interview. Anne-Marie bolted from the office. Doug wasn't far behind. I was about to follow Doug to the reception area where he'd left his camera case when Rogan touched me gently on the arm. I turned to look at him.

"Before you leave, Ms. Chadwick – Lark. Do you have a business card?"

"Sure." I pulled one from a pocket in my messenger bag and handed it to him.

As he looked at it he said, "I'd like to invite you to dinner sometime – *without* your photographer."

Now it was my turn to blush. Rogan was definitely an imposing Alpha Male, but I had feelings for Doug. And they needed exploring.

"Okay," I said, "but you should know up front that I'm seeing someone."

"Of course," he said without missing a beat. "I appreciate your candor. This would be purely platonic. A chance for me to better understand *your* profession."

As Doug and I left the offices of Applied Electronics, I still wasn't sure how I'd respond if – but probably when – Dolph Rogan called to set up a dinner date.

CB 80

CHAPTER 12

"Well *that* was interesting," I said when Doug and I were back in his Wrangler and he was easing us into the tail end of rush-hour traffic on the congealed Beltway.

"Indeed," he said.

"Did you notice that blouse Anne-Marie was *almost* wearing?" I asked.

"I'm aware."

"And I'm not buying for a minute that they're just business partners."

"Me neither," Doug said, reaching into the breast pocket of his shirt. "But if they *were* involved, they might not be any more." He pulled a business card out of his pocket and handed it to me.

"What's this?"

"It's Anne-Marie's business card. She gave it to me after the interview when you and Rogan were talking in his office. She put her personal cell number on the back and said I should give her a call sometime."

"And Rogan invited me to dinner," I said. "He made it clear it's just him and me, *not* my photographer." I handed him Anne-Marie's card. "So, are you gonna call her?"

Doug took the card back. "Nope." He ripped the card in two and handed it back to me. "How 'bout you?"

"I haven't decided yet."

"Really? I just tore up her card. The least you can do is tell him no."

"I might. But I made it clear that I'm seeing someone."

"Oh? Who?" He shot me a side glance.

"You, I guess."

"You *guess*?"

"Well, yeah. But all I know for sure is that you reeeeally like me."

He fished in the pocket of his jeans and pulled out a key and held it up.

"What's that?" I asked.

"It's a key to my apartment."

"Doug, don't you think it's a little early for this?"

"I'm not asking you to move in."

"Then what *are* you asking?"

"I'm letting you know of my new 'open door' policy. You're welcome to crash at my place any time. And I promise: No funny business."

I took the key and turned it over in my hand.

"Just so you know: this is a big deal for me, Lark. I've never given my key to anyone else. Ever. You're special."

I pocketed the key without comment.

08 80

CHAPTER 13

"This traffic is terrible," Doug snarled. He checked his rearview and side mirror, then swerved onto the shoulder of the Beltway.

"What are you *doing?*" I asked, alarmed.

"Finding a place where we can eat, file, and wait for the traffic to thin out." He wasn't asking, he was telling.

As we careened along the side of the road, I checked to make sure my seat belt was tightly fastened. Fortunately, an exit was only a few hundred feet ahead. Doug took it. He found a diner nearby, parked, and we brought in our stuff.

After only a brief wait, we were seated at a booth. We each ordered coffee. Doug had a burger and I ordered a Caesar salad. While we waited for the food to arrive, we opened up our laptops, their raised covers touching at the center of the table.

While Doug began uploading and studying all the pictures he took, I scowled at the blank page staring back at me. But it didn't stay blank for long – almost immediately I got the keys clattering as I began constructing the first draft of my piece on Rogan.

Originally, I'd intended my piece to merely be a profile of Rogan – which it still would be, but I had the added and unexpected benefit of him giving me a stronger "newsie" lead:

Drone entrepreneur Dolph Rogan called on President Gannon Tuesday to lift restrictions on the private operation of drones.

Doug and I barely talked for an hour as we worked steadily, picking at our food only when pausing to collect our thoughts. He showed me what he called "the top ten" pictures he'd taken. We agreed on five, which he sent in with the piece I filed about eight o'clock – plenty of time for the desk to edit and move it on the wire for the morning papers.

"So," I said to Doug as we turned our full attention to the remainder of our meals, "why do you think the tipster pointed us in Dolph Rogan's direction?"

"I think the tipster *is* Dolph Rogan," Doug said before taking a hungry bite out of his burger.

"Yeah. I've thought of that too. The guy is quite the self-promoter." I shoved a piece of Romaine lettuce around my salad bowl. "He certainly has some interesting things to say, but it seems his not-so-hidden agenda is to get Gannon to lift the restrictions on drones – something that's been threatened by the drone attack on the White House."

"Uh huh," Doug nodded, his full attention on his half-eaten burger.

"Rogan's a good story." I stabbed a crouton with my fork. "And so are drones. But I hate the feeling that I'm being used."

"I hear ya," Doug mumbled, his mouth full.

An hour later, he dropped me off at my place – The Liberty Apartments in downtown Silver Spring. He'd suggested we hang out and watch TV – "or something" – but I was wiped out and told him I needed some time to decompress. He seemed cool with that.

When I got inside my seventh floor, one-bedroom place, I immediately poured myself a glass of wine and was about to switch on the TV when Lionel called.

"Hey," I said, flopping onto the sofa. "What's up?"

"Just calling to check in. How you doing?"

"I'm exhausted. As you can imagine, it's been a long day."

"Tell me everything."

I chuckled. And sighed. "That could take awhile. Be more specific."

"Well, if I know you, you're like a dog with a bone when something's bothering you. My guess is you're bugged about the so-called 'rogue drone' story the White House is spinning."

"Yup. You got it. It smells. What do *you* think?"

"I think it's time to make an end run. Do your own digging. Find out all you can about drones."

"I'm already doing that."

"No surprise there. Tell me more."

"Last night, after the attack and the Lopez briefing, I got an anonymous tip that pointed me in the direction of Dolph Rogan, an entrepreneur who's trying to put a drone in everyone's garage."

"Yeah. I've heard of him. Sounds like he's doing a modern-day spin of Herbert Hoover's 1928 campaign slogan 'a chicken in every pot.'"

I laughed. "You read my mind, Lionel. That's almost word-for-word what I used in the profile piece about Rogan that I filed tonight. I got it from that book you sent me on presidential history. My piece hasn't moved on the wire yet, but keep an eye open for it. Maybe you can find a place for it in the next edition of The Pine Bluff Standard."

"No fair lobbying the editor," he grumped. "Plus, I need more of a local angle."

"Hey, a drone in every garage, remember? They've got garages in Wisconsin, don't they?" I took a deep drink of my Pinot Noir.

"So, what else is new?" Lionel asked.

"Oh, Lionel." I stood and walked to the window and looked down onto the always-busy Georgia Avenue. It doubles as U.S. 29. "It's too late and I'm too tired to give you chapter and verse on my life."

"What's his name?"

I laughed – and sighed again. "It's more like what are *their* names."

"*Now* you've got me intrigued."

"It's waaay tooo complicated." I pushed myself away from the window and turned toward the bedroom. Suddenly I felt like crying myself to sleep.

"That's because you haven't taken the opportunity to talk things through with dear old Lionel. C'mon, kid. What's goin' on?"

Maybe it was because my emotional buffer was gone, but I snapped. "*You* c'mon, Lionel. I'm not a kid. Would you quit calling me that?"

"Geez, kid. And I do mean *kid*. Lighten up."

I felt myself quickly losing my temper. When that happens, I become the impulsive and petulant Lark Chadwick that I loathe.

"I already told you I'm exhausted, Lionel, but you keep pushing. And you keep condescending. Please stop."

For a moment, he was silent, but then he said softly and slowly, emphasizing every word for maximum effect, "You're *being* a *kid.*"

"Lionel!" I exploded. "I'm twenty-eight years old. I'm *not* a *kid.*"

Before he could say anything else, I hung up.

He called right back, but I immediately sent him to voicemail. Yes, I was being a sixteen-year-old brat – and I didn't care.

When he called again, I turned off my phone and went to bed. I *tried* to sleep, but mostly I cried.

CZ 80

CHAPTER 14

I dragged myself out of bed Wednesday morning before six feeling as if I'd been run over by a train. I felt lousy and was in a crummy mood.

This was the second time Lionel and I had been on the outs. I didn't like it then. And I didn't like it now. But now I was in the phase that always seems to come after I've been impulsive and petulant – proud and stubborn. He'd be getting no apology from me, I resolved.

I was at the Jackson Place press room before seven, just in time for the gaggle with Lucia Lopez.

The gaggle is a small, informal meeting of mostly wire reporters in Lucia's office where she gives us a hint of what's on the president's agenda for the day so that we can file look-ahead pieces or let our desks know what to expect – or not to expect – that day.

"I'll tell you up-front," Lucia said to the five of us sitting in her office, "it's gonna be a slow news day here. The president has no public events scheduled."

"Where is he?" I asked.

"Still at an undisclosed location," she said.

"How much longer will that be going on?" the Bloomberg reporter wanted to know.

Lopez gave the guy a look over her reading glasses. "Really? Do you really think I know?"

The rest of us chuckled.

"Will you at least let us see him again, or release a picture that shows the country they still have a working, living, breathing president?" I asked.

"I'll look into it," Lopez scowled. She looked as tired and frazzled as I felt.

The meeting broke up shortly after that. I gave Rochelle Grigsby a call to let her know what little had transpired in the gaggle.

"This is Grigsby," she said when I called.

"It's Lark."

"Oh. Hi." I could tell I'd just gotten *her* day off to a great start.

"There won't be much coming out of here today, except maybe a White House photo of the prez working at the undisclosed location."

"Okay."

"Did you see the piece I filed last night on Dolph Rogan, the drone mogul?"

"I saw it."

"What'd you think?"

"You really want to know?"

"Hmmm. Maybe I don't."

"I spiked it."

"You what?"

"I killed it."

"Why? He made news."

"Jesus, Lark, it was a puff piece. The only thing missing was a tag line saying, 'buy your drone *today.*'"

"Rochelle, that's so unfair. Why are you being like this to me?"

"Because it's my job."

I sighed. "What can I do to salvage it?"

"Nothing that I see right now unless you can find a way to give it some balance."

"What do you mean?"

"If you don't know what balance is by now, then it's a little late to give you a crash course in Journalism 101. Didn't Lionel Stone teach you *any*thing?"

I winced. Lionel is like the father I never had, but I'd pushed him away. Guilt and anger began competing inside me for my attention.

"Okay, I'll–"

"Gotta go." Grigsby hung up.

Paul Stone, sitting across from me, looked concerned. "What's wrong?"

"Grigsby. *She's* what's wrong. She hates me, Paul. She honest-to-God hates me."

Just then my text chime pinged. I didn't recognize the number. The message read, *So, did you check out Dolph Rogan like I suggested?"*

I did, I typed.

And?

And he's an interesting guy.

Are you going to do a story about him?

Is this what you want?

I want you to understand what's going on.

About what?

Drones.

I think I understand a lot. I felt myself getting annoyed – and defensive.

No you don't, the tipster challenged.

How do you know what I do or don't know?

Because if you knew what was going on with drones you'd write about it.

My job is not to carry water for Dolph Rogan.

I never said that it was.

Then why'd you point me to him? I was so frustrated, I couldn't type fast enough.

Because there's a bigger story there.

Bigger than drones?

Yes.

Gimme a hint.

I just did.

No you didn't. Point me in the right direction, or leave me alone.

There was a pause, then the texter-tipster sent me a link, adding, *Look into Rogan's associates.*

I clicked on the link. It was a Google digest of images showing Dolph Rogan with scads of people, mostly at parties, but also at speaking events, plus there was the swashbuckling shot of him that graced his own Applied Electronics website.

I scrolled through the pictures. There was a shot of Rogan with a smiling (this time!) Anne-Marie Gustofsen at a cocktail party. They each held champagne glasses. He wore a tux with a red bow tie. She wore a tight and revealing sequined cocktail dress.

Several shots showed Rogan at various parties with several – how can I say this kindly? – babes on his arm. But other images showed the more serious side of Rogan: in one picture, he was giving a speech – it looked like a commencement address. I clicked on it. Sure enough – the MIT graduation keynote two years earlier. A few more clicks and I was able to find a transcript of his speech. It was full of the usual platitudes.

In another picture, he was a panelist at some sort of high-tech symposium in Tysons Corner, Virginia, just across the Potomac River from D.C. I clicked. It was at an event sponsored by NASA. Also appearing on the same panel with Rogan were Hiram Aldridge, the head of NASA, and Nathan Mann, the then-head of the Federal Aviation Administration.

A similar photo showed Rogan and Aldridge testifying before Congress. I clicked and found the date – a year ago. After a few more minutes of digging, I found the transcript of Rogan's remarks before the Senate Science and Technology Committee. His sanguine comments about drones were almost word-for-word what he'd told me a day earlier. But Aldridge, the NASA administrator, had numerous misgivings, most revolving around safety and privacy issues.

After more than an hour of this, I sat back in my chair. I was getting cross-eyed. And frustrated. Obviously, Rogan had a *ton* of associates.

I picked up my cell and typed a reply to the Tipster.

Help me out here. Rogan's got a lot of associates. Be more specific, please.

But when I hit *send* I got an error message telling me that the phone number I was trying to reach did not exist.

Just then my cell rang: *Applied Electronics.*

"This is Lark," I answered.

"Lark. It's Dolph Rogan."

"Good morning. Thanks again for showing us around yesterday." I didn't have the heart to tell him the story had been spiked.

"I enjoyed it. Any idea when your piece will run?"

"None. Once I file, it's out of my control. But, because the drone story still has legs, I'll probably drop a quote or two from you in any follow-up stories I do."

"I see," he said, then paused before adding, "Are you free for dinner tonight?"

"Tonight? Let me check."

Of course I was free, but I didn't want him to know that right away – any more than I wanted him to know that I was being stonewalled by Grigsby.

"Yes," I said after a tasteful pause. "You're in luck. I'm free."

"I'm in luck indeed," he replied.

We made arrangements to meet at seven that evening at a nice place, The Hamilton, just a few blocks from the White House at 14th and F. I felt that by accepting his invitation, it would give me one last stab at finding out if there was anything more newsworthy here than Rogan simply wanting to spin me – and bang me.

CB EO

CHAPTER 15

The rest of the day was, indeed, uneventful. Paul and I continued to work the drone attack story, but had little luck doing much to advance it. And Lucia Lopez was no help. Her eleven o'clock briefing was devoid of anything solid and petered out by eleven-thirty.

I saw Doug at the briefing – he looked haggard – but our paths didn't really cross, so we exchanged no words. He gave me a half-hearted wave from across the room, but later, when I went looking for him, he was doing another one of his disappearing acts.

After the briefing, Paul invited me to lunch, so I took him up on it. We got sandwiches at a bistro around the corner on 17th Street. It would have been a pleasant conversation except at one point he tried to pump me for information about my spat the night before with Lionel.

"So, what's up between you and my dad?" He tried to sound nonchalant.

"We're taking a break. A friend break." The phrase just popped into my head. But it sounded good and felt accurate. Never mind that Lionel had never agreed to it.

"Why?"

"Oh, Paul. I know what you're doing, and I'm not going to play."

"What? What am I doing?"

"You're doing your dad's bidding, trying to find out why I'm mad."

"You mean a lot to him."

I gave him a look. "Nice try."

"Well, I hope the two of you can work this out."

"Me too. I just need some space."

"Okay. But he told me he misses you."

"Did he tell you to tell that to me?"

"Maybe. What should I tell him?"

"Don't tell him anything. I think it's unfair of him to put you in the middle and make you some sort of go-between emissary."

"I don't mind."

"Well, I do. I'm a big girl and can work out my own problems. I don't need his – or your – 'help.'"

Paul turned sullen.

"Sorry," I said softly. "Obviously, I'm still upset with your dad, but I shouldn't be taking out my anger on you."

"It's okay," he said. He smiled bravely, but it looked tight and forced.

I like Paul. He's a nice guy. But, I guess that's the problem: he's nice. I like a little more mystery in my men. Doug has plenty of mystery, yet I also know deep in my gut that Doug can be a little dangerous, whereas Paul is safe – and predictable. Yes, it's counterintuitive. I suppose I should be attracted to the nice guys who put me on a pedestal and tell me I'm wonderful and beautiful. But it's the confident bad boys like Doug who hold a special allure for me. Hard to explain. Even harder to understand. But there it is.

That night I timed my arrival at the restaurant for a tastefully late 7:05. Dolph Rogan was waiting for me just inside the door when I walked in. He wore a perfectly tailored, snazzy gray suit with a purple and white polka dot tie and matching handkerchief in the breast pocket. I felt underdressed in flats, black tights, a dark skirt that hit just above the knee and a bulky wool sweater.

Rogan shook my hand by taking it in both of his, then he gently guided me by the elbow as the hostess led us to our table – a semi-circular booth in a darkened corner. Most of the clientele consisted of older men with classy, much younger women. I wondered how many of the ladies were mistresses, or hookers, then scolded myself for being so judgmental.

Rogan, not to my surprise, took the initiative and ordered us a bottle of an expensive Malbec. He probably thought he was impressing me with how suave and in control he was, but I found his pretentiousness amusing. If I'd been the least bit attracted to him, I would have found his presumptuousness to be off-putting. Instead, I saw it as a learning experience and a reminder that I'm much more attracted to the down-to-earth Doug Mitchell types who like to drink beer in dive bars.

True to his word, Rogan threw the spotlight onto me and, rather than dominate the discussion, really seemed eager to learn as much as he could about me.

I'm pretty good at making a person feel I'm telling them a lot, when I'm actually being guarded about the personal stuff I lock deep inside. So, Rogan never learned from me the story of how I was orphaned as an infant when my parents were killed in a car accident. He never got me to open up about the death of Annie, the aunt who'd raised me and whose body I found after I came home from my waitressing job three years ago. And Rogan never got me to tell him about the death of Jason Jordan, the only man I ever really loved.

But I was more than willing to regale Rogan with stories about Lionel Stone. Rogan didn't need to know that my friendship with Lionel was in jeopardy after I'd hung up on him. Rogan didn't need to know how much I was agonizing inside about the self-inflicted loss of my best friend and mentor.

Instead, Rogan got me talking about my job and how I liked being a reporter. He must have been a more skilled questioner than I'd given him credit for because I found myself discussing my misgivings about journalism and my interest in psychology.

"Tell me more," Rogan said, pouring wine into my half-full glass that I'd barely touched. We'd already eaten.

"Only if you pour some for yourself, too," I said.

"Very well." He topped off his glass and, without asking me, signaled our server to bring another bottle. Rogan was already on his fourth glass and was beginning to slur his words. "You were telling me that you're beginning to have misgivings about journalism. Serious misgivings?"

"I'm not sure yet."

"What kind of mish- misgivings do you have?"

"I like a lot of things about journalism – don't get me wrong. I like the high-energy adrenaline buzz I get from a breaking news situation. And I love to learn, but. . ." I paused, groping for the right word.

"Go on."

"I don't know. I always feel as if there's something missing."

"Like what?"

"Something deeper. Something more *personal.*"

"Personal?"

"Yeah. Maybe psychological is a better word."

"How do you mean?"

"I guess I'm incredibly intrigued by what it is that makes people tick – that makes a person do what it is that he or she does."

"And journalism doesn't fulfill that need?"

I shook my head. "Not completely. Lately I've been wondering if maybe I should get an advanced degree in psychology. Maybe go into counseling, or something."

"Really? That's fascinating." He skootched an inch or two closer to me in our cozy booth.

"Why do you think it's fascinating?" I asked. "I would think you science guys are more into your gizmos and gadgets, and not so much interested in people."

"Oh, quite the contrary. I mean, sure, a lot of what I do revolves around science and technology, but the entrepreneur side of my brain is very people oriented."

"And my guess is *high-powered* people?"

"Indeed." He'd finished his wine and took a sample sip from the next bottle our server poured for him to approve.

"Like who?" I coaxed. "Humor me. Drop some high-powered names."

As he gave a quick thumbs-up to the waiter, Rogan blushed. He actually blushed. Perhaps much of it had to do with all the wine he'd consumed. I was trying to stay clear-headed, so I'd managed to daintily sip not even two glasses. Yet it also seemed as if he really did want to drop some names to impress me.

"Let's just say I've got friends in high places," he said.

"How high?"

He took a sip and tried to stifle a self-satisfied grin. "As high as you can get."

"The president?"

Rogan just gave me a Cheshire-cat smile.

"And who's your gateway to the prez?"

Rogan chuckled, but shook his head. "Not so fast."

Before I knew it, he'd leaned in and was kissing me on the lips. He'd taken me by surprise, although I should have realized that he was going to make a move sooner or later. I'd just expected it would be later.

I politely returned his kiss, but then pulled back sooner than he would have liked.

"So, if *I* kiss, do *you* tell?" I smiled.

"Maybe." He leaned in again.

This time I placed my hand gently on his chest.

"Remember, I'm seeing someone," I said.

"I think you should consider trading up," he said, still pressing against my hand and trying to invade my personal space.

In a flash, Ross Christopher, my English professor was pressing me hard against the sofa of his Madison, Wisconsin apartment.

I couldn't breathe.

"Um, Mr. Rogan." I pushed firmly against his chest. "This is my stop. I need to get off here."

Reluctantly, he leaned back. "But we haven't had dessert."

"You're free to have as much as you like, but I'm a working girl and have to be up early tomorrow." I stood. "Thank you for the wonderful evening. Goodnight."

I nearly sprinted out the door and began walking briskly toward Metro Center. My heart was racing and I was still having trouble catching my breath. On impulse, I pulled out my cell and called Doug.

"Hey," he said.

"Hi. I just need to hear a familiar voice."

"Why?"

"I was having dinner with Rogan tonight."

"Oh?"

"Yeah."

"How'd it go?"

"Not as well as he hoped."

Doug laughed. "That's a relief. Where are you now?"

"Trying to get to Metro Center before Rogan pays the bill and tries to come after me." I shot a worried glance behind me as I crossed 13th Street and darted to the Metro entrance. I was relieved that Rogan wasn't already on the street looking for me.

"Why don't you stop off here for a nightcap on your way home."

"Okay, but just a quick one. I've got to be up early."

"Something's better than nothing. I'll see you soon."

It was after 8:30 when I ran up the front stairs of Doug's place on Florida Avenue. He must've been watching for me because he opened the door just as I was getting ready to ring the doorbell.

"You could've used your key, you know."

"I know. Maybe someday."

He stood aside and I entered.

"What's your pleasure? Beer? Wine? Something stronger?" He closed the door and followed me into the living room.

"I'll have what you're having – which means a beer. Am I right?"

"Oh yeah." He walked to the kitchen, opened the fridge and pulled out two Coronas. I followed him.

"So tell me more about your big date." He twisted off the caps and handed me one of the bottles. "You look lovely, by the way."

"Thank you. The 'date,' as you call it, was awful. Geez, the guy is so full of himself." I turned and walked back to the living room and sat in one of the easy chairs that faced the street.

Doug sat in the chair next to me, but inched it a little closer to mine first.

"To your health," I said, tipping my bottle toward his. They met with a clink.

He took a thirsty gulp, but then stood suddenly. "Did I ever tell you I used to do standup?"

"Whoa. Where did *that* come from?"

90

"You had a lousy night. I'm trying to lighten the mood. Help me out here, Lark."

I leaned back and relaxed. "Lighten away." The beginning of a grin curved my lips.

He smiled, too, warming to the moment. He placed his beer bottle on a table, mussed his hair, put his feet apart, and stuffed his fists into the pockets of his hoodie. For a moment, I thought he was about to channel Elvis.

As he loosened up, he started his patter. "Awhile back, I had a job as a cook at a restaurant in Georgia." His voice adopted a kind of Elvis drawl. "One of the guys I used to work with was a jive hipster who fancied himself to be something of a ladies' man." He flicked the edge of an imaginary bow tie.

The more Doug talked, the more his voice resonated deep inside me. It was smooth. Velvety. His words – but more importantly, their tempo and timbre – wormed their way past my defenses in a way that seemed to fuse my soul to his.

"Now, this jive hipster..." Doug let the word *jive* play out sensually, "had what let's say was a *limited* vocabulary. So, when he'd be tellin' the rest of us about his latest exploits with..." his voice swooped down an octave, "the *ladies,* the story would sound something like this–"

"Wait!" I said. I pulled out my iPhone, switched to the video function, aimed it at him, and pressed the red dot. "Okay. Go!"

Doug mussed his hair a little more so that it looked like he'd just gotten out of bed. Then he began swaying back and forth. When he resumed speaking, he had the same drawl, but his voice seemed to take on a more guttural tone.

"Heh. Yeah. So, like I'll be hangin' out and, y'know, this chick's real cool, and, y'know, sometimes she'll say somethin' real cool, and then I'll say somethin' real cool, and then ever'thing'll be reeeeal coooool."

As he repeated the words *real cool,* he'd bend his knees then bounce up so that by the time he got to the last *real cool* his body was simultaneously bending, bouncing, and swaying, and his head was bobbing so enthusiastically it seemed as though his bones had turned to rubber.

On the final *real cool* he took his hands out of his pockets and swept them smoothly to his right in a sort of "and-away-we-go" gesture. Then he turned to me, smiled impishly, thrust his fists back into his pockets and said, "It's kinda like that, man, y'know?" He let out a hollow "heh heh" then dipped deeply, concluding with a simple, "Yeah," drawing it out to two syllables. At the end of *yeah* he popped up and gave me a self-satisfied smile.

The humor wasn't so much *what* Doug said, but *how* he'd so effectively transformed himself into an entirely different person. It was all I could do to keep from laughing out loud, but I can still hear a few of my stifled snickers whenever I play back the video – which is often.

I stopped the recording, howled with laughter, set down the phone, and applauded.

There's something I like about a man who has a sense of humor and can make me laugh. In the space of a few short minutes Doug had gone from making me feel beautiful, to making me feel safe and welcome, to making me feel relaxed and at ease. He was comfortable in his skin and I felt the magnetic pull of his self-confidence.

I retrieved my phone, got up and stood beside him.

"Wanna take a look?" I held my iPhone between us so we could both watch the playback.

"Sure," he said, edging close to me.

As I watched him on the screen dodge, bob, and weave his way through his short, *real cool* routine, I became acutely aware of everything about him as he stood next to me: the intense heat that seemed to emanate from him, the sweet, but understated scent of his cologne, and the light touch of his rock-solid bicep against my shoulder. I *wanted* him. The feeling came out of nowhere – and wouldn't let go.

I was sorry when the clip ended. I didn't want to break the spell. So I didn't. I remained rooted in place and let my head tilt so that it rested gently against his arm.

We stood like that, suspended in time, both of us, it seemed, holding our breath. I was definitely holding mine.

After a moment, he put his arm around my shoulder, then turned to face me. As I looked up at him, he leaned in and kissed me, first gently, but then with more purpose as I urgently returned his kiss.

Nothing else mattered at that moment.

But then, instead of taking me into his arms, he leaned back.

I opened my eyes, surprised.

He was looking at me admiringly, a crooked smile playing at his lips.

"Doctor?" he asked. "Whose assistance should I seek for an erection lasting more than four *months?*"

I threw my head back and laughed. "Mine!" I said, throwing my arms around his neck and kissing him. "Mine!"

CB BO

CHAPTER 16

My body was still tingling in the afterglow of our unrushed carnal detour. I'd fantasized about what Doug might be like as a lover, but the reality was even better. He was generous, gentle, and patient. His smooth fingers, soft lips, and probing tongue slowly and steadily brought me to a kaleidoscopic climax twice before he would even allow me to explore his body and return the favor.

At one point, I was startled when my naked leg bumped against his prosthesis.

"Oh! Iraq! I'd forgotten," I said.

"Does it matter?" he asked, his face grim.

"Nope. Never," I smiled and nuzzled against his chest.

After we made love, I cried softly as he held me in his arms, my heart bursting with gratitude. I was grateful that my first sexual experience had been such a good one. Yes, there was a sharp pain at first, but that discomfort was quickly set aside by the feeling that I was loved, really loved, by such a caring, giving, gentle, strong man who could make me laugh, yet comfort me when I was frightened.

Our lovemaking lasted an unrushed hour. Afterward, as we lay in bed talking, I must have said something funny because he laughed. But then his laugh turned into a wheeze. Then another. And another.

"Doug? Are you all right?" I sat up, alarmed.

The wheezes became a series of gasps. He clutched at his throat and his eyes bugged out in panic.

"Doug!"

"I, I, I c-can't breathe. C-c-call an ambulance," he managed to croak.

I lunged at the phone on the bedside table. My fingers trembled as I poked the numbers. Doug was writhing on the bed, trying unsuccessfully to take a deep breath.

"Nine-one-one. State your emergency," came the all-business voice of a woman.

"My friend is having trouble breathing. He needs an ambulance."

"Is he choking?"

"No! He can't breathe. I don't know why." I gave her Doug's address. "It's an emergency. Hurry!"

I slammed down the phone and jumped onto the bed where Doug was still struggling for breath. His face was red, but his lips weren't blue. He was getting *some* air but not enough.

"I can't—I can't–" he rasped. Beads of sweat glistened on his forehead.

"Shhhh. Don't try to talk." I cradled his head in my hands. "An ambulance is on the way, so just try to calm down. Don't panic. It's gonna be alright, Doug. It's gonna be alright."

Amazingly, his body seemed to relax. And, as it did, he was able to take one or two deeper breaths. But it was still a struggle.

In a few minutes, I heard a siren getting closer. Doug was holding his own, so I quickly threw on my clothes and tossed Doug's boxers and jeans at him.

"Are you able to put these on?" I asked.

He sat up, chest heaving, and managed to put on his undershorts, but the effort caused him to start wheezing again. He was struggling to put on his jeans when the ambulance pulled up in front of the place.

I ran to the door and let in the two EMTs – a middle-aged African-American man and a much younger white woman.

"He's upstairs," I shouted, leading the way.

When we got to him, Doug was gasping for air, his face ashen, struggling to button his jeans.

"Sir, you need to sit down," the female EMT said, easing Doug into a sitting position on the bed.

The other EMT carried an oxygen canister into the room. He slid a mask over Doug's head. "Take deep breaths, sir."

Doug obeyed. His eyes were wide with terror.

As Doug struggled to catch his breath, the female EMT took Doug's blood pressure and put a stethoscope to his chest while I stroked Doug's back in an effort to calm him. Soon he was taking deep, greedy gulps of the pure oxygen.

After a few minutes, she took the oxygen mask off Doug. "Sir, are you able to breathe on your own now?"

Doug inhaled and coughed. "Yeah. I think so." His voice sounded husky.

"What happened?" the black EMT asked.

"Lark and I were talking. I laughed and then all of a sudden I couldn't seem to catch my breath," Doug explained.

"Do you have a history of asthma?"

"No. Not at all." He was pale, but some color was returning to his cheeks.

The woman said, "Your blood pressure is high and your heart rate is elevated. Let's wait a few minutes until you're more stable."

Doug looked up at me, his expression devoid of confidence. He was still panting. Before he placed the oxygen mask over his mouth and nose he asked, "Am I going to die, Lark?"

I kept rubbing his back and said reassuringly. "No. No, Doug. You're not going to die."

But the frightened look in his eyes made me realize I'd failed to comfort or reassure him – and that frightened *me*.

Doug poked me. Through the oxygen mask came his muffled voice: "I can't feel my arm, Lark."

"What?"

"I can't feel my arm." He was rubbing his left forearm with his right hand. "It's numb. I can't feel anything below my elbow."

The female EMT stepped forward and pulled a penlight from a pocket and shined it into each of Doug's eyes.

"Maybe you slept on it funny and it just went to sleep," I said.

"That's what it feels like," he said, "but it actually started getting numb an hour ago and the numbness hasn't gone away. I'm worried, Lark."

"Is it a stroke?" I asked the woman.

She shook her head. "Dunno." Then, to her partner: "Let's roll. *Now!*"

"Is it okay if I ride with you to the hospital?" I asked.

The man looked at the woman, then shook his head. "We'd prefer if you follow behind. It's a liability issue."

"You can follow the ambulance in my Wrangler," Doug said to me. "The keys are in the right pocket of my jacket. It's hanging on a peg by the front door."

While the EMTs placed Doug on a gurney and rolled him to the ambulance, its red lights still flashing outside on Florida Avenue, I got behind the wheel of Doug's Jeep. I had to make a U-turn in the middle of the street, then stayed as close as I could to the ambulance because I'd forgotten to ask them where they were taking Doug.

At one point, the ambulance went through a red light, but I stayed right on its tail and blew through the light, too. To my surprise, the ambulance pulled over to the curb and the female EMT came out of the back and ran up to my window waving her arms.

"Ma'am, you can't follow us that closely. It's too dangerous." She turned and hustled back toward the waiting ambulance.

"Where are you taking him?" I hollered.

"G-W," she called over her shoulder. She pulled herself up and inside before closing the door.

Once again, the ambulance, siren wailing, took off down the street. I followed at a discreet distance this time, but when I got stopped at another red light, I took out my iPhone and found George Washington University Hospital on the map app. The hospital's not too far from Dupont Circle in a nice part of Northwest D.C. on 23rd Street just south of Washington Circle and K Street.

By the time I got there, the ambulance had already unloaded Doug and was pulling away from the emergency entrance. I parked the Wrangler and rushed to the emergency room. Amazingly, no one tried to stop me – I just walked in boldly like I belonged.

When I got to the curtained-off area where Doug was, an ER nurse wearing a light blue smock was examining Doug. She took several blood samples, then left us alone for a few minutes.

Neither of us talked. Doug, the oxygen mask pulled over his still-pale face, nodded off.

In a few minutes, the nurse was back, a concerned look on her face. "We want to do an MRI to see what's going on in your brain," she said to Doug, "but we can't do that right now."

"Why not?" Doug asked.

"Your potassium levels are too high and it'll affect what we're able to see on the MRI, so we need to wait until the levels come down." The nurse looked at me. "Are you his wife or his sister?" she asked.

"Girlfriend," I said. Until that instant, I'd never used that word – even in my head – to define our relationship. It's funny how one's mind works in the middle of a crisis.

"I need you to wait in the hall a minute while I talk with Mr. Mitchell privately," she said.

Doug and I exchanged confused looks, then he said, "I don't mind if she stays."

"I'm sorry," the nurse said. "She's not an immediate member of the family."

"She's close enough," Doug said.

"That's okay," I said. "I'll wait in the hall." I got up and stepped out of the room.

While I waited for the nurse to finish talking privately with Doug, I paced the hall. After a few minutes, the nurse left Doug's room. When she saw me, she walked toward me quickly, took me by the arm and walked me down the hall.

"I'm sorry I wasn't allowed to let you stay," she said, apologetically. She had a kind, motherly face.

"That's okay," I said. "What's wrong with him?"

"We still don't know. But I want to tell you that I'm *extremely* worried about him."

Warning bells started jangling in my head. "Why?" I asked.

"I can't tell you. *He* has to."

"What do you mean?"

"The blood test revealed a very serious issue, but I'm not allowed to share it with you without his permission."

"Did you tell him what you found?"

"Yes."

"And does he want me to know?"

She shook her head, sadly. "No."

I nearly doubled over. "Oh, God. Does he have AIDS?" I nearly screamed.

"I'm sorry. I'm not allowed to tell you. But I feel strongly that if you're his girlfriend, you need to know. But only *he* can tell you. Maybe you can get him to change his mind." She took me by the hand and looked deep into my eyes. "I'm *very* worried about him." There were tears in her eyes.

"Okay," I sighed. "Maybe I can get him to tell me what's going on."

"I hope so." She squeezed my hand. "I'll be praying for you."

"What happens next?" I asked.

"He still has to have an MRI, but we have to wait a little longer until his potassium levels come down. We're concerned about his liver, too."

"How much longer do we have to wait?"

"At least an hour – maybe two," she said. "Maybe you can talk some sense into him."

I went back into Doug's room. He was dozing. I shook him and his eyes opened. He looked weak.

"We need to talk."

"About what?"

"You tell me."

He shrugged and closed his eyes.

"Doug!" I said sharply.

His eyes flew open.

"The nurse told me she's concerned. She said she told you what she's concerned about, but I'm in the dark. I can't help you unless you tell me what's going on."

Doug shrugged and closed his eyes again.

"Doug, I'm your girlfriend. I'm the one you said you reeeeally like. Remember? And I'm the one who . . ." I started to cry.

He took my hand and squeezed it.

"I love you," I said, snuffling.

"I l-love you, too," he stammered. "I feel–"

"Those aren't just words, Doug."

"I kno–" he started to say, defensively.

"They *mean* something. They mean something to *me.*"

"I know," he whispered. "I feel–"

"This isn't about feelings, Doug. Love isn't a warm fuzzy feeling. It's a choice. It's a decision. I consider this moment to be a test. If you love me, if you care at all about me, then you'll tell me what's going on with you. Now. I love you," I said, taking his hand in both of mine and looking him straight in the eye. "I love you, and I can take the truth. But I can't give you the support you need, unless you tell me."

He closed his eyes again.

"Are you going to tell me?"

"I'm thinking about it."

I gently placed his hand back in his lap and walked out of the room. But not out of the building. I found a quiet corner. And prayed.

When I came back, he was dozing again. About ten-fifteen the nurse came in and took another vial of blood from his arm. Shortly after that he was finally cleared to get the MRI. They wheeled him down the hall to another area. I was able to go with him, but then had to cool my heels in a waiting room for about fifteen minutes while he had the brain scan.

The results were in by the time they'd wheeled him back to his room in the ER. The nurse and doctor – her nametag read Preeya Singh – looked it over.

"The results are negative," Dr. Singh said. "He didn't have a stroke."

"So what's the problem?" I asked.

"He's free to go home now," the doctor said. "How's your arm, Mr. Mitchell?"

"Still a little numb, but not nearly as bad as it was." He rubbed his arm and wiggled his fingers.

"By tomorrow you should be fine." Dr. Singh handed Doug some papers. "This explains everything we did today," she said.

Doug looked at the pages, then handed them to me, a scowl on his face.

I scanned the pages. At the very bottom were the words that made the blood in my veins turn to ice: *heroin abuse.*

ᑕ ᔓ

CHAPTER 17

I can only imagine the look on my face when I finally tore my eyes from the page and glared at Doug. I'm sure my mouth hung open and my eyes had never been wider.

When Doug saw the look on my face, he winced, pursed his lips and nodded slowly, as if to say, *Now you know the absolute worst about me. Do you STILL love me?*

Slowly, I shook my head in disbelief. So many thoughts and feelings were rushing through me that I couldn't latch onto just one. I stood mute, looking back and forth between Doug, Dr. Singh, and the nurse. Finally, my mind settled on a single, simple question:

"How? How can this be?"

Doug shrugged.

I lost it.

"Don't just shrug this off, Doug Mitchell, like this is no big deal," I shouted. "This is heroin we're talking about. Fucking *heroin!*"

"I know what it is," Doug said, his voice rising to keep up with mine. "This is why I didn't want to tell you." He jabbed a finger at me. "I knew you'd lose it. That you wouldn't understand."

I took a deep breath and tried to calm myself, but my heart was galloping and my ears were ringing. Hot tears spurted into my eyes.

Doctor Singh stepped in. "As near as we can tell, Mr. Mitchell may have nicked a nerve with a needle. No permanent damage has been done. In fact, he's regaining feeling. I suspect that by this time tomorrow, he'll have full feeling in his arm."

"B-but what about the heroin *usage*, Doctor Singh? That's the bigger problem, wouldn't you agree?"

"It is, indeed," she said. "I've talked about that with Mr. Mitchell and, as you can see on that sheet," she nodded at the discharge papers trembling in my hands, "there are several suggestions on what he can do to deal with that."

Doug held out his hand to the doctor and flashed her a big smile that I knew masked his extreme discomfort.

"Thanks for everything, doc," he said.

They shook hands and the doctor and nurse left the room.

When we were alone, Doug asked, "Would you mind driving? My arm's still a little numb."

"Let's go." I turned on my heel and stormed toward the parking lot, not looking, or caring, if Doug kept up.

I maintained an icy silence during the ten-minute drive back to Doug's place. I spoke only once and that was when he tried to explain.

"Lark, I–"

"Shut up," I snarled. "Just shut up. I'm so angry I can barely see straight."

Heroin! My boyfriend's a fucking heroin addict! You really know how to choose 'em, Lark Chadwick.

Doug sighed and looked moodily out the window for the rest of the drive.

It was nearly eleven at night by the time we got back to Doug's place. Car and pedestrian traffic on Florida Avenue was thin.

"You hungry?" Doug asked as he swung himself from his side of the Jeep.

"I'm too pissed to eat," I said. "I'm going home." I locked the driver's side door and tossed the keys to him over the top.

"I haven't eaten anything substantial all day," he said, "and you haven't eaten for hours. I'll order a pizza."

"I really want to be alone right now."

"It'll be just like our first date," he smiled.

"No," I said as firmly as I could, but I could feel myself melting at the memory.

Our first "date" was actually me interviewing him for a story I was doing during the hunt for a serial killer in Georgia. Doug was one of the suspects. I got to know him as we ate pizza and talked. I came away convinced that he was innocent. I didn't realize it at the time – because I was too caught up in trying to be objective and pushing my personal feelings aside – but that meal was when I first felt myself falling for him.

"C'mon, Lark. We need to talk."

Whenever he looked at me like that, with his crooked grin, I knew I was a gonner.

"Yes. You're right. We most *definitely* need to talk. And I am famished, so if you're treating, I'll be eating."

"Deal," he said.

He put his arm around me as we walked up the steps to his apartment building, but I reached up and gently pushed his arm away.

"Not so fast, Johnson."

He laughed, but I could tell he knew that the punch line of our little inside joke masked steely seriousness on my part.

While Doug phoned in the pizza order, I busied myself in his kitchen, getting out plates, napkins, forks, and I opened a beer for each of us. But I was still keyed up.

"Here," I said, handing him a Corona as he hung up the phone.

"Thanks." He took a big gulp and wiped his mouth with the back of his hand. "That. Tastes. Great." He smacked his lips extravagantly. "Have a seat," he said, patting the sofa cushion next to him.

"I'm too agitated to sit. You sit. I'll pace."

"C'mon, Lark. It's not as bad as you think."

"No. *You* c'mon, Doug." I stood over him, hands on my hips. "You're shooting *heroin.*" Suddenly, I began to cry again.

He stood and made a move to embrace me.

"Do *not* touch me. Do. NOT." I straight-armed him and he sat down again.

"I can explain," he said weakly.

"This I've gotta hear. Ex-PLAIN." I knew I sounded sarcastic, but I didn't care.

"I've only done it a couple times," he began. "I'm managing it."

"Yeah. Right. Managing it so well you stuck a nerve with a needle. A *needle*, Doug. A *needle!*" I was almost shrieking.

"Now calm down."

"I will *not* calm down. Don't you realize how serious this is?"

"I know it's serious," he said. "Today was a wake-up call. I'm going to quit."

I snapped my fingers. "Just like that?"

"Sure."

"Heroin is extremely addictive, Doug." I began to pace. "I've heard that the first high is so amazing that people spend the rest of their lives – their very *short* lives – chasing that first high, trying to repeat it. And they never do."

"I know. I've heard the same thing. But it's not going to be that way with me. I'm not letting it. I haven't gotten hooked, so I don't think it's too late to turn it around."

I stopped pacing and looked at him. "But do you *want* to turn it around?"

He nodded soberly. "I do, Lark. I really do." He maintained steady eye contact with me.

I gave him a very long, penetrating look. It really seemed like he meant it.

I sighed.

"Do you believe me?" he asked, still holding my gaze.

I nodded. "I do. God help me, but I really do," I said softly.

For the first time all day, he visibly relaxed.

"It didn't just begin with heroin," I said, taking a seat next to him on the sofa. "How'd you get started on it?"

"It goes way back to when I lost part of my leg in that bombing in Iraq. I got addicted to morphine. Got weaned from that onto painkillers. But painkillers are expensive. It might surprise you, but heroin's pretty cheap."

"How cheap?"

He shrugged. "I was able to get high on just twenty bucks. Pills cost four or five times more than that."

I shook my head. "But why? It's been years since you were in Iraq. Surely you're not still in pain."

"No. I'm not. That's why I think I can beat this."

"But why were you using at all? That's what I don't get."

Just then the doorbell rang. Our discussion paused while Doug paid the delivery guy and brought the steaming pizza box to the kitchen where we opened it, flopped two slices each onto our plates, and immediately began stuffing the delicious food into our mouths.

As we ate at the kitchen table, Doug picked up our conversation where we left off. "I think I'm depressed," he said, simply.

"Depressed?"

"Yeah. I think that's why I was using." A piece of pepperoni dangled precariously as he gestured with the slice. "Heroin was the ultimate pick-me-up, like the warmest hug you can imagine – an all-over embrace." He took a bite.

"But why are you depressed?" I asked, turning my attention to my second slice.

"I don't know."

"Sure you do. You just haven't had to put it into words."

"You sound like a shrink."

"I've seen my share." I took a swig of beer.

"Yeah?"

"Yeah. And they've been really helpful."

"How so?"

"Talking through my problems helped me to see things more clearly and understand myself better."

"Really?" He looked doubtful.

"Really and truly."

"Are you seeing a shrink now?"

I shook my head. "Not now. But I did after Annie died."

"She's the one who...?"

"Right. Annie's the aunt who raised me after my parents were killed when I was a baby. Losing her was when I *really* felt like an orphan. I had a lot of issues I needed to work through."

"Like what?"

"Actually, we're talking about you, so don't try to shift the focus. But one very relevant issue has to do with trusting men. And I've gotta tell ya, Doug. That trust thing is back. You've really done a number on me. All this time I trusted you so much that it was unbelievable when I learned today that you've been taking heroin. That's a mind-blower. In some ways, it's like being back at square one with you."

I got up and carried our empty plates to the sink.

"Are you breaking up with me?"

I shook my head as I tossed the crusts into the garbage disposal. "Not now. But if this heroin thing keeps going on, we're through." I turned on the garbage disposal to emphasize my point.

As the disposal groaned, Doug got the metaphor. He looked stunned, like I'd sucker punched him.

"I mean it, Doug." I turned off the garbage disposal. "I'm not gonna date a junkie. I'm just not."

"I'm not a junkie, Lark. You'll see. I will rebuild your trust. We're gonna get through this. Trust me."

I gave him a stern look. "I want to trust you, Doug. I really do. But you're gonna have to prove to me you're serious about this." I came back to the kitchen table and sat next to him. "And the way you're going to do that is, first thing tomorrow morning, you're going to make an appointment to see a therapist. I really want to see you taking positive steps to overcome your depression so that you'll never again be tempted to take heroin. Deal?"

"Deal," he said, eagerly. He held out his hand.

I looked at it for what felt like a very long time. Then I looked Doug deeply in the eyes.

When he smiled that smile of his at me, I took his hand in both of mine and squeezed hard. "Deal," I said.

There were tears in my eyes. And, when I kissed his hand, there were tears in his eyes, too.

ങ ൽ

CHAPTER 18

I had mixed feelings when Doug offered to let me stay the night at his place. I was exhausted – drained from an incredibly stressful day. But staying at Doug's would mean I'd have to get an extra-early start in the morning to go home, shower, and change before hustling to work for the morning gaggle at seven with Lucia Lopez.

Doug pointed out that if I'd leave at least one change of clothes at his place, I'd be able to stay on the nights I missed the last Metro train to Silver Spring. I pointed out that I need my space, plus I said I didn't want him to feel like I was being an untrusting mother hen.

In the end, he relented and drove me home.

As it turned out, I needn't have hurried to get to work Thursday morning because Lopez was nowhere to be found when a handful of us clustered around her door at seven. An hour later, I was back in my cubicle with Paul Stone when I got a text – again from an "unknown" number:

Have you been able to check into Rogan's associates? the Tipster wanted to know.

He's got a lot of associates. You're being too vague. I don't have time to chase wild gooses. I was typing fast and didn't proof read. No worries. The Tipster did it for me.

Geese, came the quick correction.

Whatever. Be more specific, or I won't play.

Okay. There's something unsavory going on in the president's inner circle.

C'mon. I don't have time to play around.

This is bigger than Watergate.

Yeah, that's what they all say, I replied. *But even Woodward and Bernstein knew the identity of Deep Throat. And they protected him for decades until he decided to reveal his identity. Right now, all I know for sure is Rogan needs the president's support to open the skies to private drones. And it doesn't look like the prez is gonna do that. Are you Rogan? Are you trying to use me to pressure, or possibly even blackmail the president?*

No answer.

I'd had enough. *I want a face-to-face with you. If I don't hear from you by tonight, I'm moving on.*

My text didn't bounce back as undeliverable, so I was pretty sure the Tipster got the message. I was becoming increasingly convinced that Rogan himself was the Tipster – and his narcissistic game playing was getting tiresome.

This was when I normally would have called Lionel to talk about my frustrations and suspicions. In fact, I nearly reached out, but then remembered we were in the middle of a spat. I had a legitimate beef with him, but also was grudgingly coming to accept that it was my petulance that led to the actual break.

I remembered back to our first big blow-up. It was in the newsroom of *The Pine Bluff Standard.* I'd just gotten a big scoop, but Lionel refused to run the story because I'd made the rookie mistake of going off the record prematurely. The screaming showdown between us ended with me calling Lionel a "bully" and storming out of the newsroom.

Later, after Lionel and I reconciled, his wife Muriel lovingly pointed out to me that "fight and flight" is how I tend to deal with conflict. I thought I'd gotten beyond it, but apparently not. Once again, I realized, that dynamic had gotten the best of me.

Just as I began to consider taking the first step toward burying the hatchet with Lionel, this bulletin from our Beijing bureau cleared the wire:

China's Defense Minister Tong Ji Hui declared himself president in an apparent bloodless coup Thursday.

In a written statement, Tong said Chinese President Lu Shing is under arrest, but the statement gave no reason for Lu's imprisonment and no further details.

The announcement came at the end of the business day in China.

Tong promised to give more details in an address to the country tomorrow morning.

This was a big story with international implications.

The deposed Lu Shing had been a thorn in the side of the United States even before Will Gannon became president. Lu had been in office for two years. During that time there'd been a steady increase in tensions as Lu became more and more erratic and unpredictable.

Pesky problems between the United States and China were rapidly becoming existential.

China's flagrant violations of U.S. copyright laws and incessant attempts to hack into the computer systems of major corporations and government agencies were giving way to threats from President Lu that he was going to call in the fourteen trillion dollars in debt the U.S. owed to China.

So, the sudden coup was not only big news but perhaps really good news.

At the regular eleven a.m. briefing, Lucia Lopez announced that President Gannon would be making a major address to the nation from the Oval Office at eight that night about the China situation.

Paul and I spent the rest of the day reading up on China and trying to find out what Gannon was going to say. The drone attack on the White House was no longer the lead story. And I quickly and easily forgot all about the Tipster. It suddenly became much easier to make good on my threat and actually move on.

ᘓ ᘔ

CHAPTER 19

Paul and I worked steadily all day on *China Coup*, the slug the A.P. desk in New York gave to the story. The byline went to the Beijing bureau chief who broke the story, but throughout the day, Paul, me, and other A.P. reporters made contributions to it.

I pestered Lucia Lopez all day for details of what the president was going to say in his nationally televised address. Lopez was mostly unavailable, but the few times I did see her, she was mum – a sphinx. The only quote I extracted from her was a terse, "An advance copy of the president's remarks will not be available. Nor will we be releasing selected excerpts. You're just going have to watch like everyone else to see what the president will say."

Long-time White House reporters told me that this was extremely uncharacteristic of past administrations. For decades, there was a tradition of the press office releasing at least excerpts of presidential remarks as a way to tease the speech. The tradition also included releasing the text of the president's speech just before delivery with a strict embargo forbidding its dissemination to the public until the president began speaking. To dispense with those two traditions "is highly unusual," to quote the reporter for *The New York Times*.

In the hours leading up to the speech, I read all I could about the U.S.-China relationship. There wasn't much online about the new president, Tong – he was mostly a mystery. President Lu, on the other hand, was as frightening as he'd been enigmatic. In the weeks leading up to the coup, he'd been making increasingly bombastic statements directed at the West in general, and the United States in particular.

Half an hour before the president's eight o'clock address – the press office ordered the pool to assemble at the front door of our Jackson Place filing center. At 7:40, two of Lopez's underlings escorted

Doug, me, the two other wire reporters, a network television crew and reporter, and a radio correspondent across the Pennsylvania Avenue pedestrian mall and through the Northwest gate. Because the Brady Briefing Room was still a shambles, the pool was led to the Oval Office via West Executive Avenue – the driveway between the EEOB and the West Wing.

Even though it was essentially just a photo-op, reporters always accompany the photographers into the room – a concession made only grudgingly by just about every administration, usually after at least one showdown.

The showdown usually goes like this:

The press office says only cameras will be allowed in for a photo op. News organizations then band together and refuse to send in their cameras if reporters aren't also allowed into the room with the president.

The press office argues, "This is just for pictures. The president won't be making remarks."

The White House Correspondents' Association then argues, "We refuse to be complicit in your attempt to stage manage the news by getting us to slavishly distribute flattering images of the president while protecting the president from our legitimate questions. He's accountable to the public. He doesn't have to answer, but we reserve the right to ask."

Both sides then stamp their feet and glower – usually for a day – before the press office capitulates because they need the news media to get their message out, especially pictures showing the president being presidential. The showdown between the White House Correspondents' Association and the Gannon Administration played out this way, as scripted, a few weeks earlier – a day or two after Will Gannon was sworn in as president.

I felt a nervous excitement as the pool approached the Oval Office. Of course I'd seen a gazillion pictures of it, but I'd never been inside. I remember reading a memoir written by President Reagan's former press secretary, Marlin Fitzwater. Fitzwater described the scene on Reagan's last day in office. Reagan, Fitzwater wrote, respected the office so much that he never worked in it with his suit jacket off – never in shirtsleeves. And, when Reagan left the Oval Office for the final time, he turned at the door for one last look, and snapped a smart salute to the hallowed room.

We of the press pool entered the Oval Office through the French doors at the end of the colonnade off the Rose Garden. My first impression was that the Oval Office is bigger than I'd imagined. It felt spacious. I was surprised that the ceiling is so high.

President Gannon sat behind the famous oak desk, his back to the Washington Monument. The desk had been cleared of everything but the text of his speech. CBS was the network pool. Two cameras were set up and a bank of lights shown down onto the president. The rest of the room was dark, quiet, and cold.

I was the first reporter through the door. As soon as I saw Gannon I said, "Good evening, Mr. President."

"Hello, Ms. Chadwick," he replied.

"What's the lead? What are you going to say tonight?"

He smiled coyly. "You'll just have to listen."

"How are you feeling, sir?" the Reuters correspondent asked.

"Pumped," the president said.

"Why are you pumped, sir?" I tried.

Gannon didn't answer and turned his attention to the text of his speech. He knew that image-craft is a big part of statecraft, so he studiously ignored us and shuffled his papers while the photogs snapped away.

I checked, but the TelePrompTer was blank – not even *Hello, My Fellow Americans.*

The constant shutter-clicks from Doug's and the others' still cameras echoed off the ceiling and yellow walls adding to the sense of the room's cavernousness. The photographers fanned out in front of the president, getting shots from every angle, including from behind the network pool television cameras.

After what seemed like a scant minute, one of the press aides called out, "Time's up. Everyone out through the French doors, please."

As we were being walked back to Jackson Place, I made a quick call to the desk in New York.

"It's Chadwick at the White House."

"Whatcha got?"

"The pool just left the Oval Office ahead of Gannon's address. The president says he's 'pumped.' That's a quote."

"Anything else?"

"He offered no details of his upcoming speech. All he'd say is – quote – "you'll just have to listen."

"Got it," the guy said. "We're moving an Urgent on it now."

Some reporters in the pool groused that the lack of an advanced text would slow down their ability to file. They weren't assuaged by Lucia Lopez's promise to release the transcript of the address as soon as the president had finished speaking.

Earlier in the day our bosses in New York decided that the national desk would run installments, called "leads," throughout the speech whenever Gannon said something quote-worthy. Paul and I were tasked with doing the write-through of the speech as a co-bylined story.

I got back to the A.P. cubicle at Jackson Place just as the president was about to begin his remarks. Paul had our TV tuned to CNN's coverage. Both of us switched on the voice memo app on our iPhones and placed them by the TV just before Gannon began to speak. We also had our laptops open and fingers poised.

Doug walked in just as Wolf Blitzer said, "And now, let's go live to the White House for remarks from President of the United States Will Gannon."

The blue and gold presidential seal filled the screen. It dissolved to a wide shot of the Oval Office, then switched to a close-up of President Gannon.

"Good evening, my fellow Americans," Gannon began solemnly.

"As you've no doubt heard by now, there has been a sudden change in the leadership of the Chinese government. China's President Shing Lu has been deposed by Defense Minister Tong Ji Hui. At this time, the United States of America formally recognizes President Tong's government."

"Whoa!" Paul and I said simultaneously as we began typing.

Similar exclamations of surprise were emerging from the cubicles of the other news organizations covering the White House.

Paul exclaimed, "The U.S. is giving its blessing to the overthrow of a sovereign government!"

Suddenly the television screen containing Gannon's image split in two with Gannon on the left and another man on the right. In the upper right hand portion of the screen came the words *Beijing, China.* On the upper left hand side of the screen – Gannon's side – *Washington, D.C.* dissolved onto the screen.

Gannon continued speaking. "My words to you tonight are also being broadcast into the People's Republic of China. And joining me right now, in an unprecedented joint address to our respective nations, is China's new president – and my friend – Tong Ji Hui."

This was stunning. Already we could hear computers throughout the press center emitting the jangling sound of the A.P. bulletin written by the national desk in New York. I glanced at my computer screen. *President Gannon formally recognizes new Chinese government.*

I looked back at the television. The screen remained split in two, but now the man on the right – China's new president, Tong Ji Hui, began to speak.

"Thank you, Mr. President Gannon. Good evening to our friends in the United States of America and good morning to my fellow citizens in China."

Doug blurted out, "Good *morning?*"

Paul said, "It's Friday morning in China. They're eleven hours ahead of us."

"Oh," Doug said. "Thanks."

"Shhh," I scolded.

As Tong Ji Hui began to speak, his name dissolved onto the lower third of the screen.

"Shouldn't Gannon be calling him President Hui instead of Tong?" I asked.

"The Chinese put the surname first," Paul said.

"Oh. Thanks."

"Shhh." Doug shushed me, then gave me a wink when I scowled at him.

President Tong said, "President Gannon has asked me to speak with you on a matter of the utmost urgency and solemnity."

I was struck immediately by how "Western" China's new president seemed to be. It wasn't only because of his dark suit, white shirt, and burgundy tie. It was also because he spoke impeccable English.

President Tong continued, "I want to explain the reason for the sudden change of government here in Beijing. As you may not realize, I have known your president, Will Gannon, for twenty years. We met when I was an exchange student at Vanderbilt University. We were both students of President Gannon's National Security Adviser Nathan Mann.

There were more exclamations of surprise in the filing center. The Gannon/Mann connection was common knowledge and part of both men's bios, but their connection to Tong was news.

"On Monday," Tong said, "just hours after the tragic attack on the White House, President Gannon and Nathan Mann presented me with irrefutable evidence that the attack was an assassination attempt on President Gannon carried out not by a rogue drone, but by a drone operated by a member of the United States Air Force acting on behalf of and under the orders of China's President Lu Shing."

"Holy shit!" I exclaimed as I my fingers flew across the keys of my laptop.

I'll admit it. As President Tong spoke, part of me felt a smug satisfaction that my initial hunch right after the attack was correct: the White House spin of a rogue drone was phony and lurking behind the story was the cover-up that the attack was a deliberate attempt to murder the President of the United States.

But how did it happen? And why? And how is it that Tong was now in power? The questions lined up in my mind hoping that Tong and Gannon would provide answers. I pulled my chair closer to the TV monitor and stared down President Tong, daring him to answer the questions screaming in my brain.

Another A.P. bulletin announced itself: *Monday's drone attack on the White House was an attempt by China to assassinate President Gannon, according to China's new President Tong Ji Hui.*

The Chinese leader continued. "When your president showed me the evidence, I took immediate action to remove and imprison our former leader. He and his co-conspirators will be tried for their crimes. President Gannon is to be commended for being a man of peace. Rather than going public with the evidence and escalating tensions between our two countries, President Gannon came to me privately and urged me to take peaceful action to rectify the situation."

The screen remained split. Obviously, this was a carefully choreographed announcement, designed to be a surprise for maximum effect in both China and the U.S., not to mention the rest of the world.

Gannon, his expression stern, spoke again. "President Tong is to be commended for taking decisive, but peaceful, actions that uphold the rule of law. And here in the United States, the Air Force officer who carried out the attack that killed three people and wounded ten others is in custody. My office will release his name when President Tong and I are finished making our joint statement. The individual has been charged with three counts of murder and attempted assassination."

More questions began competing in my head for attention: *Did the Tipster know about any of this? Was the tipster not Rogan but someone inside Gannon's administration?* Gannon's next words gave me what I thought was a clear indicator:

"Sometimes the truth needs to be surrounded by a bodyguard of lies. Because the information about the attack was so volatile, I wanted to avoid putting my highly ethical press secretary, Lucia Lopez, in the position of having to knowingly mislead the press. I want you to know that I take full responsibility for deliberately shielding her from the truth and giving her information about the drone attack that I knew to be false. In my eyes, she's a hero for doing her best to answer tough questions from a rightfully skeptical White House press corps. But Lucia has chosen to tender her resignation and it is with deep regret and sorrow that I have accepted it. Lucia Lopez is a trooper. Her service to me and to the country has been outstanding and I wish her all the success in the world."

The Chinese leader smiled and added, "The groundwork has now been laid for a process that deals systematically with a host of issues that have been a source of conflict between our two countries. China is now solidly on a path toward democracy that has been deferred for way too long.

"Mr. President," Tong said to Gannon, "I pledge to be your partner in peace."

"Thank you, President Tong. Thank you for your bold leadership. I look forward to working with you as we forge an alliance that I pray will result in stability, peace, and prosperity not only for our two nations, but for the rest of the world."

As soon as Tong and Gannon finished speaking, my phone pinged.

Okay, the Tipster texted, *I'm ready to meet.*

☙ ❧

CHAPTER 20

When? Where? I frantically texted the Tipster as soon as both presidents had finished speaking.

The Tipster set the time for three o'clock the next morning in a parking garage across the Potomac River in Rosslyn, Virginia. *Come alone.*

I tried to ask more questions – *Why there? Why then?* – but, as usual, the Tipster went silent and ditched the phone.

I was on deadline, anyway. Paul and I worked feverishly to craft our double-bylined story.

True to its word, the White House press office released not only the official transcript, but also the name of the Air Force officer charged with trying to assassinate President Gannon. He's 1st Lt. Joseph Fan, 24, a naturalized U.S. citizen from Hong Kong. According to the multiple-count indictment against him, Fan was a sleeper spy – secretly planted in the U.S. by China long ago, then recently activated to carry out the assassination. He would face the death penalty if convicted.

It was after eleven when we finished.

"Want to get a nightcap?" Paul asked, his face beaming with eager expectation.

Just then, Doug stuck his head into our cubicle. "You ready yet, Lark?" he asked.

I gave Paul a helpless shrug. "I've already got plans. Rain check?" I asked.

Paul's smile dimmed only a fraction. "Sure," he said. "Rain check." He stood, put on his overcoat and walked alone into the night.

"I'm such a bad person," I said to Doug, "but I'm just not feeling it with him and I don't want to lead him on by sending him the wrong signal and hurt his feelings."

"You're not a bad person, Lark," Doug replied. "You're the best person I know."

Earlier, after I'd made arrangements to meet with the Tipster, I'd told Doug about it. I'd planned to go alone, but he convinced me that it would be safer at that late hour if I let him drive me to the Rosslyn rendezvous location. We'd get a late-night bite to eat nearby, then he'd park on the street outside the parking garage and linger until my meeting ended. He would then drive me home.

We got to the location about eleven-thirty and scouted it out. It's a nondescript parking garage at North Nash Street and Wilson Boulevard. I laughed out loud when I read the historical marker that stands out front:

> Mark Felt, second in command at the FBI, met Washington Post reporter Bob Woodward here in this parking garage to discuss the Watergate scandal. Felt provided Woodward information that exposed the Nixon administration's obstruction of the FBI's Watergate investigation. He chose the garage as an anonymous secure location. They met at this garage six times between October 1972 and November 1973. The Watergate scandal resulted in President Nixon's resignation in 1974. Woodward's managing editor, Howard Simons, gave Felt the code name "Deep Throat." Woodward's promise not to reveal his source was kept until Felt announced his role as Deep Throat in 2005.

I was to meet my secret source at space 32D. Doug and I found it at the end of a long row of parking spaces in the lowest level next to an exit door to a secluded stairwell that leads up five flights to the street.

"Whoever you're meeting, sure knows their history," Doug said. "Take a look." He pointed to a makeshift marker taped to a pillar next to parking space 32D identifying it as the exact location of the clandestine Deep Throat meetings between Bob Woodward and Mark Felt.

"Well, the tipster did say this story is bigger than Watergate," I said.

"Who do you think you'll be meeting?" Doug asked, his voice reverberating off the concrete.

"I think the Tipster is Lucia Lopez," I said confidently. "She's a free agent now. Apparently, there's a lot more to this rogue drone attack story than we're being told."

"Like what?" Doug asked.

I shrugged. "Let's wait and see."

We got dinner and drinks at a place nearby, then, a little before three in the morning, I was back at stall 32D.

Alone.

Doug was parked on North Nash facing Wilson in a parking space with a perfect view of the entrance to the garage and the doorway to the stairwell leading all the way down to stall 32D.

Only a few cars were parked in the garage, otherwise the place was deserted, cavernous, and forlorn. But it was bright with fluorescent lighting, unlike the shadowy creepiness of the scene in the movie "All the President's Men."

I kept my iPhone at the ready, a prearranged emergency text to Doug already written that I could send instantly in case something went wrong, but, to be honest, I felt no fear. I was eager – and confident.

As three a.m. came and went, I paced back and forth in the empty parking space trying to keep warm – it must have been close to freezing. I was also trying to figure out what Lopez might know that the president wasn't telling the nation about drones. I planned to press her about Gannon's relationship with Dolph Rogan.

Just when I thought I'd been stood up, I heard the *click-click-click* of footsteps coming down the stairwell.

I turned to look.

As the door creaked open, my jaw dropped.

C8 80

CHAPTER 21

Anne-Marie Gustofsen looked terrified – stylish, but terrified. Dolph Rogan's executive assistant wore an ankle-length red coat, her strawberry blonde hair in an upsweep revealing the glint of two diamond ear studs.

Her hands trembled as she fished a pack of Virginia Slims and a lighter from her Louis Vuitton handbag. She uttered no words of greeting, but she held the pack out to me as an offering.

I shook my head.

Her eyes looked sunken and bloodshot when the flame flared to ignite the tobacco.

"Thank you for meeting with me," she said, her voice whiskey-smooth. She put away the lighter and pack. "My life is in danger." She took a drag and exhaled. A nimbus of frozen breath and cigarette smoke drifted over my head. "Now, your life is in danger, too."

"That's comforting."

More silence. She looked at me, seeming to size me up before she took another deep drag.

"Why is *my* life in danger?" I asked.

"*Our* lives."

"Why?"

"He's crazy man," her syntax a reminder that Swedish was her first language, not English.

"Rogan?"

She nodded.

"Crazy how?"

"He's become a monster. Not at all like he was when we met at MIT."

"What was he like then and how has he changed?"

She leaned against a pillar. A black *32* was stenciled on the concrete. From there she could look over my shoulder and have a clear view to see any approaching vehicles or people.

"Back then Dolph put me on a pedestal," she said, her voice flat. "He told me how my mind was so mesmerizing to him. He wasn't like the others. All they were mesmerized by was my body."

"Did you two become an item?"

She scowled. "An item? I'm not familiar with the term."

"Did you hook up? Were you lovers?"

"Yes. Of course. Technically, we still are, but, as I say – he's changed."

"In what way?"

"He's not so affectionate any more. Now, instead of praising me, he's more likely to belittle me."

"Is that why you've been contacting me?"

"It's not the reason, it's the catalyst."

"Why me and how did you get access to my computer and discover my cell phone number?"

She smiled for the first time. "That's easy. I'm a hacker. Breaking and entering is my specialty. I used my access to your computer only once to get your attention. Since then, I've used burner phones to text you."

"How'd you get my number? And why me?"

"Your cell number is not as private as you might think. As for why you? I've been aware of you since Dolph first saw your byline when you joined A.P. He thought your stories on homeland security were smart. When he began talking about you, I did my own searching because, quite frankly, I was jealous. But I became impressed with what I learned about you. I saw the YouTube clips. You seem to be a very brave person. A person of integrity."

I'd done a series of reports that highlighted technological short-comings in the U.S. effort to combat cyber terrorism. The YouTube clips show that I have a knack for being in the wrong place at the right time. Twice cameras had been rolling just as my life was in peril. The dramatic images went viral and I became something of a minor national celebrity.

"Thank you," I said. "But why do you want me to look at Rogan's associates? What am I supposed to find and why is that important?"

"You need to underst–" Suddenly, she stopped talking, pushed away from the pillar, a wild-eyed look on her face. "Did you hear that?"

I looked around, but saw nothing out of the ordinary. "Hear what? It's quiet as a tomb down here."

"I thought I heard something. You're alone, yes?"

"I'm alone." I gestured to emphasize the empty parking space where we stood. Yes, technically I was with Doug, but, I rationalized, he's not down here with me. He's just my ride.

"Dolph can't know I'm meeting with you," Gustofsen said. Her hand trembled as she brought the cigarette to her lips.

"Why not? What are you afraid of?"

"I'm afraid he'll kill me if he discovers – or even suspects – that I've been disloyal."

"Loyalty is a big deal with him?"

"Oh yes," she laughed mirthlessly. "He's very controlling."

"Is he capable of murder?"

She nodded curtly. "Yes. I think so."

"What's he afraid of?"

"Ah. A very good question, Ms. Chadvick. He's very afraid of poverty. Of being poor." She relaxed a little and leaned against the pillar again.

"What's threatening that?"

She took a drag and exhaled. "If President Gannon actively opposes opening the skies to private drones, Dolph would be financially ruined."

"Is he trying to blackmail the president?"

She shook her head. "He would if he could. He's already tried, but President Gannon is a highly moral person – a rarity in politics."

"So how is Rogan trying to influence the president?"

"Through Nathan Mann."

"The president's national security adviser?"

She nodded and took another drag, the filter tip now ringed in red with her lipstick.

"But, according to everything I've ever read about him, Mann's Mister Integrity," I said. "How's Rogan blackmailing Mann?"

"Mann *was* Mister Integrity. But only Dolph knows that."

"What is it that Rogan knows?"

Just then we both heard a car door slam. Anne-Marie's eyes got wide with terror. She instantly dropped her cigarette and ground it out with the sole of one of her six-inch spiked heels.

"I'll text you later," she stage-whispered to me. She dashed to the stairwell door, flung it open and disappeared, her footsteps echoing as she raced up the stairs.

ભ ∞

CHAPTER 22

A car engine started.

My heart began to beat faster. I ducked behind the pillar, worried that I, too, might be in immediate danger.

The engine revved and I heard a slight squeal of rubber on cement as the vehicle got rolling.

I peeked my head out from behind the pillar and caught a glimpse of a black Lincoln Navigator backing out of a parking space about fifty yards away. The windows were tinted so I couldn't see inside, but I became alarmed when I saw the distinctive glint of gold on the SUV's wheel rims.

The vehicle's rear end angled toward me, then the driver (Rogan?) shifted gears and the SUV chirped forward before making a right turn onto the ramp leading up to North Nash Street. The engine's throaty growl echoed throughout the garage.

I waited a few minutes behind the pillar until I couldn't hear the SUV any more. When I hadn't heard any other sounds for several minutes, I crept up the stairs and out of the garage.

Doug was parked just outside the stairwell on North Nash Street where he'd dropped me off.

"How'd it go?" he asked when I dove into the front seat.

"Drive. Just drive." I was out of breath from my long climb.

Doug put the Wrangler in gear and pulled away from the curb, then made a right onto Wilson.

"Where to?" he asked.

"I'm not sure yet. Just drive." I gnawed at a cuticle, thinking.

"I don't like not knowing where I'm going," he grumped, turning right again onto Quinn heading toward Lee Highway.

I ignored him and tried to capture and process the thoughts and questions percolating in my mind.

Doug sighed and kept driving. "So, who's the tipster?" he tried.

"I can't tell you."

"It's Anne-Marie Gustofsen, right?"

I gave him a look.

"I saw her walk into the stairwell of the garage shortly after I dropped you off." When I didn't reply, he continued. "Saw her skittering outta there like a scared cat a little bit ago."

"Did you see the SUV?"

"Yeah. Rogan's. Are they *both* the tipster?"

"Which way did he go?"

"Looks like I got my answer."

"It's not what you think."

"Then why not tell me?" He paused, adding softly, "Is it because I'm a junkie?"

"Whoa! Where did *that* come from? I won't even dignify it with a response. It's because I'm a journalist."

"So am I." He sounded defensive, testy – itching to pick a fight.

"Then, as a journalist, you understand why I can't tell you. It's a trust thing between the source and me."

He sighed.

"So," I said, trying to choose my words carefully, "was she – um, was the *woman* followed by. . .the SUV?"

He laughed. "You're not very good at keeping secrets, Lark."

I pursed my lips, angry with myself for being so transparent. But this was Doug. Even now, I felt I could tell him anything.

"Okay," I said, "but before I tell you, you need to know that your life will be in danger."

"Is yours?"

"It is."

"Since I'm with you – and we tend to hang – that puts my life at risk, anyway. You might as well tell me. At least I'll know who I should watch out for."

"You sure?"

He nodded decisively. "Yup."

"We're in the absolute cone of silence, right?"

"Yes."

"Rogan's not the tipster, but Anne-Marie is. And she's afraid for her life. She said he might kill her if he finds out she met with me. Did he follow her?"

"No."

"Whew. Good."

"She drove off with him."

"What?" I nearly yelled. "You're *kidding!*"

"Nope. When she came flying out the stairwell door, she bolted across the street toward the Hyatt just as Rogan drove out of the garage behind me and onto the street."

"Did she try to run away from him?"

Doug shook his head. "He came to a stop right alongside me and called to her. She was in the middle of the street. She turned around and they talked for a minute."

"What did they say?"

"I put my window down a couple inches, but she was on the other side of his Lincoln, so I couldn't hear. He must've sweet-talked her, though."

"Why do you say that?"

"Even though she looked scared and hesitant, she came around to the passenger side and got in. When she opened the door, that's when I saw Rogan at the wheel."

"Damn. That means he probably saw me talking with her. Did either of them see you?"

He shook his head. "I was hunkered down. But as she got in I saw that Rogan was smiling at her and had a silver flask in his hand. I heard him say something like, 'We'll have a drink and talk about it.' I also saw what might – *might* – have been a gun on the console between the front seats."

"Jesus! Did he point it at her?"

Doug shook his head. "Lark, I'm not even sure he had one. I just *thought* I saw one. Let's not jump to conclusions. Jeez."

He was starting to sound defensive and peevish. I decided to change the subject. "Which way did they go?"

"Around the corner onto Wilson – the way we went." Doug palmed the wheel and made another right.

I strained to look ahead, but Lee Highway going toward D.C. was deserted.

"He's got at least a five-minute head start on us, Lark. They could be anywhere by now."

"I know. This is not good, Doug. It's not good."

"What do you want to do?"

"Let's see if we can find them."

"Needle in a haystack."

"Yeah. I know. But we should try. Her life depends on it."

By this time it was almost 3:30 in the morning. Doug was driving over the Key Bridge into Georgetown. No one was on the road. D.C. looked spectacular as I gazed down the Potomac toward the Kennedy Center and Lincoln Memorial. Light from the Watergate complex sparkled on the water, but I was too preoccupied to appreciate it.

"Where to?" Doug asked.

Neither of us had slept in nearly twenty-four hours. I was running on fumes – and worries about Anne-Marie.

"We know where they work," I said, "so let's take the route Rogan might have taken to get to either their office or the hangar. It's a long-shot, but maybe we'll come across them."

"What if we do?"

"We keep an eye on them. If she's in trouble, we call the cops."

"And if we don't find them?"

"Then would you mind taking me home? You're welcome to crash there."

"I thought you'd never ask."

"You better behave yourself or I won't ask again."

Doug sighed and gripped the steering wheel tightly.

I studied the map app on my iPhone and came up with a plan. "Let's go back to the parking garage in Rosslyn. We can go west on Wilson, jump up to Fairfax Drive, get on I-66, then take the Dulles Toll Road to Applied Electronics."

"Really? Do you really think we're gonna find them?"

"I doubt it, but we should at least try. I'll never forgive myself if I don't."

Reluctantly, Doug made a U-turn on M Street in Georgetown and went back over the Key Bridge into Arlington. I navigated as he drove, constantly scanning side streets and parked cars anxiously looking for Rogan's Lincoln.

Throughout our search, my mind was churning about Anne-Marie's revelation that Rogan was blackmailing Nathan Mann. I couldn't imagine how I'd be able to confirm that, much less find out more, but I knew I wouldn't be able to wait for Anne-Marie to get back to me to arrange another meeting.

"I don't get it," I said at one point.

"Don't get what?"

"Anne-Marie was terrified of Rogan. Why would she get into the vehicle with him?"

"I told you: sweet talk."

"I'd ask 'how would *you* know?' but that would be unnecessary, right, Casanova?"

He laughed.

"Seriously, though," Doug said, "you hear about these things all the time. The battered woman keeps going back to her abuser because she thinks maybe *this* time he'll change."

I nodded. "Yeah. Even though she didn't mention physical abuse, it could be the same dynamic if a person's been psychologically abused."

"Maybe the promise of what was in the flask helped," Doug said. "Had she been drinking?"

"Not that I could tell, but her throaty voice leads me to believe that she loves to take a nip."

"Twisted. Sounds like a twisted relationship." Doug checked his mirrors and maneuvered his Wrangler onto the Dulles Toll Road.

"And *if* he had a gun, waggling it at her would sure get her attention – and cooperation," I said. "I'm worried, Doug."

There was no sign of Rogan's Lincoln along the route I'd chosen. And it wasn't at Applied Electronics or the nearby drone hangar, either.

"You're welcome to sleep in my bed. I don't mind using the couch," I said to Doug when we finally got to my apartment.

"Really?" He moved toward me. "Don't you want to...um..."

"Do I *want* to? Of *course*. But I don't think it's a good idea just now–"

"But–"

"...for a *lot* of reasons, not the least of which is–"

"...I'm a junkie."

"Will you stop! *You're* the one who keeps using that word."

"But that's what you're thinking, isn't it?"

"I'm *thinking* that it's after four-thirty in the morning and I need to get at least some undistracted sleep."

"So, now I'm a distraction?" He made a move toward the door.

"Look. Doug. Thank you for being my ride, my companion, my sounding board, and my protector tonight. I truly appreciate it. But neither of us have emotional buffers right now, so let's not have a fight when we're so tired and strung out."

He stood with his hand on the doorknob, a look of indecision on his face. "So, this has nothing to do with the heroin thing?"

"I won't lie. It does. At least a little."

"I knew it." He opened the door.

"Stop right there!" I commanded.

He stopped.

"Close the door."

He closed it.

"Come here."

134

He did.

I kissed him. "I love you."

"I love you, too."

He tried to take me into his arms, but tensed when I backed away.

"And, because I also respect myself," I said, "I need to take a step back from intimacy with you until I can be sure that you've really kicked it."

"C'mon, Lark. That's emotional blackmail."

I laughed.

"What's so funny?"

"That's the same argument I was going to use on you when you made a move to walk out that door because you weren't getting your way."

He looked stunned, then he smiled. "Touché." He paused and his body relaxed, then added, "Okay. I'm cool with the couch."

I really, *really* wanted to at least snuggle with Doug, but I was glad I held the line. And glad he respected it. Something deep inside kept warning me sternly that I needed to keep him at arm's length until I felt comfortable enough to trust that he was indeed making progress on his promise to kick heroin. But I wasn't sure how much longer I'd be able to hold out. As I drifted off to sleep, my last conscious thought was, *This guy is like catnip.*

I was up at six, showered and dressed by 6:30 and at the Jackson Place press center by seven. Doug was kind enough to drive me in and drop me off early even though he didn't need to be at work until later.

"Good morning, Lark!" Paul greeted me with his usual exclamation-point enthusiasm. "Looks like you had a late night!"

"Is it that obvious?"

He nodded and smiled wanly.

"Time for my morning Starbucks." I reached into my messenger bag and pulled out my trusty bottle of stay-awake caffeine pills – one is the equivalent of two cups of coffee, but without the mess, expense, or bad taste of java. I *hate* coffee.

I popped the pill, then got down to reading in. The overnight reaction on the editorial pages of the major newspapers to Gannon and Tong's stunning joint announcement was through-the-roof positive. It's like the world took a collective sigh of relief, daring to hope again for more stability and less strife in the world.

Granted, Gannon and Tong hadn't brought peace to the Middle East, nor had they stopped militant Islamic terrorism, but there was now some hope that enemies could become friends.

That got me wondering – and worrying – about Lionel and me. Could we ever be friends again? We usually talk or text every day – sometimes both. It was now almost three days since I'd hung up on him.

I looked at Paul. He was scowling at his computer screen, eyes rapidly scanning.

"Um, how's your dad?" I asked hesitantly.

He looked up, still scowling. "Hurt. Pissed. Thanks for asking." He turned his attention back to his computer screen.

Hmmm. Not good.

I'd hoped my friendship with Lionel could still be salvaged, but now I was beginning to have my doubts. Lionel and I are stubborn people. He's not used to me – or anyone, especially a woman – standing up to him. I was still annoyed at him for being presumptuous and controlling, but hanging up on him was certainly not very mature.

The almost-argument a few hours earlier between Doug and me was making me rethink my own role in the current spat with Lionel. Who would blink first? It might have to be me. But if I blink, will Lionel even be interested in being my friend anymore?

The morning gaggle was with Ron McClain – Lucia Lopez's number two, and in the collective opinion of my fellow reporters, her heir apparent. Ron's a geeky, affable guy. He smiled knowingly when we asked him if he'd be replacing Lucia.

"I think the president might have something to say about that later today," Ron said.

We also asked Ron when we could talk to the president to learn more about how he managed to engineer the rapprochement with China.

"I think it's safe to say the president will be available to the pool to talk about that later today, as well," Ron told us.

After the gaggle, I checked in with Rochelle Grigsby to tell her about the upcoming pool interview with Gannon, but was stunned, angry, and disappointed when she told me, "Paul will be the one representing A.P. in the pool interview."

"Why? I'm more senior." I probably sounded whiney and petulant, even though I was trying not to be.

"Sure. You're more senior at the White House...by a *nanosecond*," she said. "Paul's more senior at A.P. Plus we want to give him some personal exposure to the president."

"I only just now told you about the interview. Who exactly is the *'we'* making this decision? Are *you* the imperial *we?*" There was a clear edge to my voice because I was finding it harder and harder to be civil to Grigsby. The only thing holding me back from just losing it completely and going off on her is that I knew in my gut she was provoking me and would have liked nothing more than for me to go berserk, justifying her to get me reassigned at least, and fired at best.

"*We* made this decision in principle knowing that at some point there'd be just such an occasion," Grigsby said.

"Fine." I hung up and placed a call to Nathan Mann's office. By the end of the call, I'd managed to score an exclusive one-on-one interview with President Gannon's national security adviser – the man who was allegedly being blackmailed by Dolph Rogan to influence the president on drone policy.

CB 8O

CHAPTER 23

I have a very bad habit – actually, several, but that's another story. Whenever I'm worried about something, or I'm thinking things through, instead of biting my fingernails, I gnaw at the dry skin around my cuticles. It's sort of the poor person's manicure. While I nibble and bite, my subconscious is trying to work out whatever it is that's bothering me. Usually, I'm able to come up with a solution, but at the expense of the tips of my fingers, which end up looking like bloody nubs.

So, as I sat at my desk in the Associated Press cubicle in the Jackson Place press center, I was gnawing and thinking. First, I was worrying about Anne-Marie Gustofsen. Somehow I needed to reach out to her discreetly to at least make sure she was alright. Plus I kept trying to figure out what it is about Nathan Mann's character that makes Dolph Rogan think he can exploit it.

Because Anne-Marie feared that Rogan was trying to control her, I decided an email would be the best way to approach her. But I needed it to look innocent. I found her email address on the *Contact Us* page of the Applied Electronics website.

I wrote: *Hi, Ms. Gustofsen...I need to set up another interview. Possible?*

I hoped that if Rogan intercepted it, he'd merely assume I was going through her to arrange a follow-up interview with him.

Then, I turned my attention to figuring out just how Mann might be vulnerable to blackmail. He'd been a public figure for a long time, so there was a lot about him on the Internet. I'd been aware of him ever since I came to Washington, but our paths hadn't yet crossed on any stories.

His official bio on the WhiteHouse.gov website was a skimpy three paragraphs with no picture. It just listed the basics: born and raised in Nashville, married, two children. Prior to becoming the president's national security adviser, he'd been the administrator of the Federal Aviation Administration and before that, the head of the D.E.A – the nation's drug czar. He got his undergrad degree in political science at Vanderbilt, went to Harvard Law, then taught constitutional law at Vanderbilt.

I had better luck on Wikipedia. The picture of him was outdated by about ten years. He'd just turned 63 on January 7th. Under *Personal Life*, Wikipedia noted Mann was Roman Catholic, a marathon runner, and married his high school sweetheart forty-five years earlier. But apparently, they had children later in their marriage because his two daughters were both in college.

At the eleven o'clock briefing, Ron McClain revealed that the president would be meeting with the pool at three o'clock in the Oval Office to discuss in greater detail the renewal of friendly relations with China. The interview would last an hour – finishing just in time for it to lead all the major network newscasts and get plenty of play that night and the next morning on cable.

When we got back to our cubicle, Paul was clearly uncomfortable.

"What's wrong?" I asked.

"I just heard that Grigsby wants me to represent A.P. in the pool."

"I know. Why so glum? I would think you'd be pumped."

"I suppose I am, but it seems to be coming at your expense, Lark."

I made a dismissive wave. "Don't worry about it."

"But I feel bad for you. This is an obvious snub."

I shrugged.

Paul went on. "I tried to talk Rochelle out of it, but she said it's important for me to get face time with the prez."

"She's right."

"So, you don't mind?"

"Look. I'm happy for you, Paul. This is a great opportunity. And your dad will be very proud. Grigsby hates me – even though I have no idea why. I know that. I accept that. I've bent over backwards to be civil to her, but I can't change how she feels about me."

"You're an amazing person, Lark. That's just one more reason why I like you. And I *love* working with you!"

I smiled. "We *are* a good team, aren't we? Do you mind if I help you brainstorm some questions for the president?"

"Not at all! That would be great!"

We strategized for the next two hours. If the interview went according to protocol, A.P. would get the first question, followed by a network television reporter, then a newspaper reporter. After that, it would be fairly open ended. We knew that presidents tend to filibuster and give long-winded answers so they can control the content and direction of the conversation.

Paul and I were on the same page as we discussed all the problem areas threatening to undermine or stall progress in the new relationship with China. We saw it as our responsibility to extract every possible policy nuance from the president so that the public could see and understand Gannon's vision.

We also knew we were writing the first draft of history and that the president's remarks would be hyper-analyzed by world leaders as well as by the planet's financial markets – plus his words would be diced and sliced for decades in colleges and universities. We assumed that probably eighty percent of our questions would never be asked, but we wanted to be thoroughly prepared because there might be other opportunities to put the questions to Ron McClain and other administration officials, including my interview with Nathan Mann set for late in the day after the pool interview with the prez.

My hidden agenda in helping Paul was to try to find out more about the Mann/Rogan connection: how did it come about? When? And what influence, if any, was Mann having on President Gannon's thinking about drones? In fact, what *is* the president's thinking on drones? He was about to announce his plan to open the skies to private drones when a drone attacked the White House. Last we'd heard, Gannon was rethinking his position. But now that he knew the full scope of the attack, was he planning to go ahead with his original plan, or was it being redrawn?

"I like your drone questions, Lark," Paul said, "but I think the first question should go more to the tick-tock of his decision-making – the nuts and bolts of how things came down."

I scowled. "But that's boring process stuff."

"True. But I think that's where we are in the story. I'm not saying the drone issue shouldn't be right near the top – just not the first question."

I nodded and accepted defeat gracefully. "Based on our discussion, then, let's prioritize our questions," I said.

"Okay."

It took us half an hour to come up with about fifty questions, another half an hour to pare them down to ten, then put them in the order of importance, fully aware that if Paul was lucky, he might be able to ask five questions, but more likely three – and possibly only two. Plus we had no idea what the four other reporters in the room would ask. Chances are, our first questions would also be high on their lists, so we also wanted plenty of fallbacks that others hadn't thought about that could take the story in new and perhaps deeper directions.

We knew that Gannon's job would be to paint his own involvement in the most flatteringly positive light. Our role was, admittedly, to be used as the president's megaphone to announce the administration's positions. But we also saw it as our mission to find out what's really going on behind the scenes so that the electorate would be better – and more thoroughly – informed. By nature, the relationship between the press and the president is potentially adversarial, but it needn't be nasty.

And Paul Stone is an extremely affable guy. People like talking with him because he's not confrontational. He's smart, patient, and kind. He's generous to the person he's interviewing. And that earns him the right to push, nudge, cajole, and wheedle information out of a person – information that they might not have been intending to share. The longer we worked together, the more I could see how Paul's mind operated and I came away from the experience with an increased respect for Paul Stone.

I could see the influence of both his parents on him. From Lionel, Paul got the steel-trap mind that missed nothing and remembered everything as he brought formidable analytical powers to the table. Yet, from his mom, Muriel, Paul had inherited a gift for being able to read people and empathize with them. No doubt, Muriel had learned from decades of experience dealing with Lionel's irascibility that there are ways of communicating that don't involve frontal-assault confrontation, which is, all too often, my way of dealing with people.

The Oval Office interview with the president was made available live to all the networks, but only CNN, Fox, and MSNBC took it live. The president was seated in a chair in front of his desk facing the correspondents who were seated in a semi-circle in front of him on sofas and easy chairs. It was a setting that conveyed cozy intimacy – the president having an "informal" living room conversation – with a majestic backdrop of his desk and the Washington Monument.

Masterful.

I watched in our A.P. cubicle on a monitor tuned to the video feed supplied by NBC and its three cameras. The president began by making a brief introductory remark and then opened it up to questions.

Just as we expected, the president turned to the chair on his right. "Mr. Stone, the first question goes to you."

"Thank you, Mr. President," Paul began.

I could imagine Helen Thomas spinning in her grave. She *hated* it when reporters thanked the president for calling on them. "It's our *job* to ask him questions," Helen would've said. "He's not doing us any favors."

But Paul Stone is a nice guy. He would have smiled at her and said, "Yes, Helen, but I appreciate the opportunity to be invited to ask a question. There's no harm in being gracious."

And, true to form, Paul asked a nice question. "Sir, walk us through the events of last Monday, beginning with when the Secret Service agents whisked you out of the briefing room, up until you learned of the coup in China."

"Sure," the president began. He started by praising his personal protective detail. He had to pause to maintain his composure as he talked lovingly of Ernie Crandall. As I felt a lump form in my own throat, I thought to myself, this guy is *good!*

The president continued, describing a mad dash through the narrow warren of hallways and offices of the West Wing. He wasn't very specific about where he was taken other than to say, "My detail got me to a safe place just before we heard – and felt – the blast."

"What happened next?" interjected a hotshot reporter from NBC who had a reputation for being pushy and obnoxious. He'd broken protocol by injecting himself into the interview before his turn came, but the president didn't seem to mind, probably because the question followed the logical direction of the president's remarks and moved him along.

"During the next few hours I received regular briefings about the extent of the damage and also what we knew about the nature of the attack," Gannon said.

"Were you in the White House during this time?" the NBC reporter pressed.

A shadow of annoyance passed over the president's face and he basically ignored the question. "We learned early on that the attack came from one of our own weaponized stealth drones. It was shot down and the wreckage landed on the South lawn of the White House. It wasn't long before the person who'd been piloting it was identified and taken into custody and we quickly learned of his connection to China."

"How did–"

The president held up his hand and talked through the network reporter's next question. "Here's the point I want to stress," Gannon said. "It has to do with the power and importance of personal relationships. I met and got to know Tong when we were both taking constitutional law at Vanderbilt. Our professor was my current National Security Adviser Nathan Mann. Tong and I have always looked up to Nate and, as you know, Nate's been a long-time mentor of mine and source of solid advice and wisdom.

"Likewise," Gannon continued, "Tong and I stayed in touch with each other over the years. I was delighted when I learned a couple years ago that Tong had become the head of the Chinese military. So, after the attack, I picked up the phone, called him, and told him what we knew. He simply took things from there."

"Was – or is – Tong a U.S. spy?" the reporter asked.

Gannon grinned impishly. "Let's just say he was in the right place at the right time. We can *all* be thankful for that."

Because there were five reporters in the Oval Office with the president, the interview felt, to me, as if it lurched and swerved in a way it wouldn't have had it just been a conversation between two people. But such is the nature of covering the President of the United States. And journalism is competitive. Each news organization is looking for that unique angle that will distinguish it from the others. Each reporter is tempted to ask the most provocative question designed to get the quote or sound bite that will go viral and yield the most eyeballs.

Consequently, the drone issue was raised, but not explored in depth. That's partly because the NBC reporter was fixated on the spy angle and wouldn't let it go. But Paul was able to ask my drone question and – bless his heart – he asked it word-for-word the way I crafted it:

"Mr. President, just before the drone attack on the briefing room, you were about to unveil your administration's policy on the privatization of drones. What were you going to say and did the attack in any way cause you to alter your position?"

The president said, "Nathan Mann and the rest of my team are currently taking a second look at the issue."

"What were you about to announce?"

"Nice try, Mister Stone," Gannon smiled. "I might change my mind. Let's wait and see."

"When do you expect to make a decision and announce it?" Paul asked.

"I don't want to make a hasty decision," the president replied, "so I don't want to be held to a deadline."

"In your opinion, sir, what are the strongest arguments for and against private ownership of drones?" Paul asked.

"Oh, I think most people are familiar with the pros and cons. I'd rather take this time to focus more on the bigger issue of our new relationship with China and what that could mean, not just for our two countries, but also for the rest of the world."

Even though I was thrilled and grateful that Paul asked my questions about drones – and bummed that the president dodged answering them – I realized I could now follow up on the drone angle in my interview with Nathan Mann, which was scheduled for five p.m. in his office in the Eisenhower Executive Office Building. That is until I got a call from Mann's office immediately after the Oval Office interview with President Gannon ended.

"I'm sorry, Ms. Chadwick," Mann's secretary said, "but Mr. Mann has to cancel his interview with you. He has a meeting with the president."

"What time are you rescheduling me for?" I tried.

"Let's see," she said, sounding as if she was trying to be helpful. "He might have some time available on Monday. Let me check with him and get back to you."

"Thank you."

That reminded me. I still hadn't heard back from Anne-Marie Gustofsen. This time, I called the main number of Applied Electronics, but the person who picked up didn't sound at all like Anne-Marie.

"Applied Industries, may I help you?" The voice sounded like a Valley Girl, barely out of high school.

"Do you mean Applied *Electronics?*"

"Oh. Um, yeah. Right. Dang it. I've been getting it wrong all day."

"I'm calling to speak with Anne-Marie Gustofsen. Is she there?"

"She is so, like, *not* here?"

"Who are you?"

"I'm Jennifer? I'm, like, the temp?"

"Uh huh. Where's Anne-Marie?"

"Good question."

"What do you mean?"

"She's, like, missing?"

"Missing?" I echoed Jennifer's question.

"Yeah. And Mr. Rogan is, like, freaking *out.*"

"In what way is he freaking out?"

"I mean he's just, like, freaking out, y'know?"

I didn't, but I could tell Jennifer and her limited vocabulary wouldn't, like, be much help?

"Would you like to talk to Mr. Rogan? He's right here."

"No. Thank you."

"Who should I say called?"

"Never mind," I said, hanging up quickly, my whole body trembling.

I just barely made it to the bathroom before I threw up.

⋘ ⋙

CHAPTER 24

I didn't sleep well Friday night. I tossed and turned worrying about what might have happened to Anne-Marie Gustofsen – and debating what I should do.

I considered calling Lionel, but decided against it, figuring I'd burned one bridge too many with him. I was already feeling weak and vulnerable. Crawling back and apologizing to him for my part in our failed friendship, I reasoned, would only bring me lower at a time when I needed to be strong.

I distracted myself by getting ready for that night's "Nerd Prom." It's the annual rite of passage for the Washington power elite – a high-class, formal dinner sponsored by the White House Correspondents' Association at the Washington Hilton on Connecticut Avenue at T Street.

I spent much of Saturday getting my hair done – or as "done" as my wildly curly thicket would allow. I also practiced wearing false eyelashes. It felt like I was wearing windshield wipers on my eyelids.

And I tried to decide what to wear. Doug was going to be my date, so I needed a guy's reaction to my ensemble. Throughout the day I'd text Paul Stone pictures of myself in front of a full-length mirror wearing different outfits.

Not only did Paul have excellent fashion sense, but brainstorming questions with him the day before helped me feel closer to him as a friend. But I soon discovered that Paul wasn't as good a fashion editor as I'd hoped. In response to each getup, he'd exclaim variations on *Wow!* and *Gorgeous!* But when he got to *Whoa! Hot!* I knew I needed to dial it back a notch or two – or ten.

In the end, I opted for a tasteful, but tight-fitting fuchsia number that hit two inches above the knee, but covered my ample (too ample, for my taste) boobs. Frankly, I'm uncomfortable with my looks because they always seem to attract unwanted attention from creepy guys.

Doug showed up precisely on time – and even brought flowers. He wore a perfectly tailored tux with a handsome red bow tie. We didn't have to leave for at least an hour, so I invited him in for a drink.

Before stepping across the threshold he took my hand, kissed it, then eyed me up and down – and up again – before pronouncing me "beautiful."

I felt myself blush and nearly swooned, but I'd already had a stern, out-loud talk with myself. As I was getting dressed, I'd glared at my reflection in the mirror and snarled: "Do *not* do anything stupid tonight, Lark. If this really is love, then it will declare itself clearly over time by his *actions*, not your feelings."

"You clean up well yourself, sir," I said to Doug as he came inside.

Doug and I had yet to discuss if he'd taken concrete steps to kick heroin, and as much as I was tempted to ask, I desperately wanted not to be *that person* who becomes a nag. Yet, to my surprise, Doug brought it up immediately after we sat down with our respective glasses of wine.

"I called my H.M.O. to set up an appointment to talk about my depression," he said simply.

"Oh?"

"Yeah." He frowned. "All their counselors' schedules are full. I'm supposed to call back in two weeks when they begin making appointments for the next month."

"Are you okay with waiting?" I asked.

"I think so. As I said, I've got things under control."

I nodded. "Good." I was grateful for the update, but didn't want to dwell on it. I changed the subject. "I really need you to be my sounding board about something."

"Sure," he said, giving me his full attention.

"Anne-Marie Gustofsen is missing."

His eyes widened. "Really? What happened?"

I filled him in on my phone call the day before with the temp at Applied Electronics, then said, "I'm worried, Doug."

He must've seen my lips trembling because he got up from his chair and sat next to me on the sofa and put his hand gently on my shoulder.

I leaned against him.

He kissed the top of my head and murmured, "It's gonna be okay."

"I'm scared."

"I know."

"Do you think Rogan killed her?" I asked.

Doug didn't answer right away.

I sat up straight and looked at him.

He took his hand off my shoulder.

When the silence became deafening, I asked, "Are you looking for the diplomatic thing to say?"

"Kinda." He avoided my gaze.

"You think she's dead, don't you?" I whispered.

"I don't know." He looked down. "It's certainly possible. But it's also possible she made a break from him and is simply lying low." He looked me in the eye as he tried, lamely, to convey optimism.

"Yeah. Maybe." I began gnawing a cuticle.

"You don't sound convinced," he said.

"I'm not. Even if she's okay, I think we really need to be hyper-vigilant." I turned to him. "And I mean *we.*"

"That makes sense. Can't hurt." Doug nodded soberly.

The drive down Connecticut Avenue to the Washington Hilton was quiet. Doug and I were each lost in our own thoughts. At one point, I reached over and put my hand on top of Doug's as it rested on the gear-shift between us. He stroked the side of my hand with his thumb.

As we turned off Connecticut and onto T Street, I held an imaginary microphone to my mouth and became Doug's tour guide. "On your left, ladies and gentlemen, is the famous Washington Hilton Hotel. It's known to locals as the 'Hinckley Hilton' because it's where John Hinckley shot and nearly killed President Ronald Reagan in 1981. Reagan's press secretary, James Brady, was gravely wounded in the attack."

"And look over there," I said, pointing to my left. "See that small, boxy garage attached to the hotel?"

"Looks like a tacked-on appendage," Doug joked.

"Actually, it is."

"Really?"

"Uh huh. It's where Reagan was shot. After the shooting, the Secret Service built that little garage. It's just big enough to accommodate the presidential limousine so that the president can enter and leave the building without being exposed to the general public."

"Interesting."

Doug parked his Wrangler in the hotel's underground garage and we went inside. I absolutely hate these kinds of pretentious gatherings, but being here hobnobbing with bigwigs is part of my job. If Doug hadn't been with me, it would have been awful.

I'd never been to one of these galas before. I was a geek in high school and managed to avoid the proms, preferring, instead, to cuddle up alone with a good book. So, I was totally unnerved to have to run the gauntlet past a bank of TV cameras – just like at the Oscars – with reporters from *E!* and *Showbiz Tonight* screaming for the stars of Washington, D.C. to stop and say hello.

Fortunately, I'm not a star – or so I thought. Doug and I were able to skirt the cameras until someone from *The Daily Show* recognized me and invited me over.

I felt sure I was going to be asked about my cringe-worthy debut in the Brady briefing room on the morning of the drone attack. I braced myself.

"With me now is Lark Chadwick," the attractive blonde began. "She's the new White House Correspondent for the Associated Press, but you might know her better from her visit with us after that dramatic showdown with a gunman last year in Georgia. Lark, how does it feel to be here?"

I put on my biggest smile and proceeded to lie through my teeth. "It's great. This is an amazing experience."

"And who are you wearing?"

"Excuse me?"

"Your gown. Who designed it?"

"Um, I think it's Old Navy?" I laughed and winked.

The reporter chuckled. "And who's your date?"

I pulled Doug next to me. "This is my colleague and friend Doug Mitchell."

"Hi, Doug."

"Hi."

"What do you do at A.P.?" the reporter asked him.

"I'm a photographer. I make Lark look good. It's a full-time job." He gave me a playful sock on the shoulder.

The woman laughed. "Enjoy the evening, you two."

"Thanks," we said.

"Could've been worse," I whispered to Doug as we wound our way to the magnetometers.

We had to go through security because the president would be in attendance and speaking later. Fortunately, Doug, Paul, and I didn't have to work – the A.P.'s weekend team would be in the travel pool when the president and first lady arrived.

The place was magnificent with plenty of crystal, glass, and spacious hallways. The banquet hall was crammed with at least a hundred big, round tables covered in white. People were milling about. Some had already taken their seats. Waiters circulated throughout the room pouring wine and carrying *hors d'oeuvres* as a classy jazz combo played "Satin Doll" in the background.

I'd never seen so many famous faces in one room at the same time. The hunky actor George Clooney was there with his journalist father Nick. So were Angelina Jolie and Brad Pitt. I felt myself blush deeply when he actually winked at me when we passed in a hallway.

The Associated Press table was down near the front. Paul was already there looking spiffy in a tux with a classic black bow tie. He was in an animated conversation with another guy, but looked crestfallen when he saw me with my arm linked through Doug's.

Part of the tradition of these dinners is for news organizations to invite public figures to join them at their table. It's an unsubtle competition to see which company can attract the most famous, or sought after, or newsworthy guest. I was pleased that the A.P. powers-that-be had invited Nathan Mann, the president's new national security adviser.

When I saw Mann, he was standing behind a chair talking with one of A.P.'s top executives from New York. The chair next to Mann was vacant, so I sidled up to it and stood, waiting for Mann to turn around and notice me.

As Mann talked, I watched him. He's shorter than me and slender, almost fragile with thinning gray hair on the sides, but bald on top. He wore gold wire rim glasses. When he gestured, I noticed that his hands were delicate, almost birdlike. He seemed deferential, doing more listening than talking. He blinked a lot, too, spasmodically like a nervous tic. I was finding it hard to believe he's one of the most powerful men in the country, if not the world.

After a moment, Mann turned to me and smiled. His teeth were a brownish yellow making me think instantly of coffee and nicotine. He held out his hand and I shook it.

"Hi, Mr. Mann. I'm Lark Chadwick. I'm sorry our interview fell through yesterday, but I'm hoping we can sit down and talk on Monday."

"Yes," he said, his alive eyes twitching nervously. "Duty called. Thank you for being so understanding. But we can at least talk a little bit tonight and then do the more formal sit-down on Monday. I'll have my secretary finalize the arrangements with you first thing."

"That would be wonderful. Thank you." I turned to my left to introduce Mann to Doug, but my date was deep in conversation with the woman standing behind the chair to his left. It was none other than Rochelle Grigsby. I nearly gagged.

Rochelle was slightly flushed as if she'd already had too much to drink. She wore her dark hair up, a black dress with a plunging – and revealing – neckline, a diamond necklace, and a stunning rust and yellow shawl over her shoulders, but low and to the sides so that her bodacious cleavage would be the center of attention. And it was. Several times during the evening I caught the exec from NYC sneaking admiring glances at the view.

Rochelle seemed to literally bask being on the receiving end of Doug's attention. He was telling her a funny story about going through the magnetometer. She glanced my way, but pretended not to see me. Instead, she gripped Doug's bicep greedily and laughed as he delivered the punch line of his story. She then looked past him at me and, without releasing her grasp of Doug's arm, reached her left hand out to me magnanimously.

"Lark. Hello," Grigsby said cheerily. "You never told me you and Doug are an item."

I reached out my hand and she took it lightly by the fingers and gave them a perfunctory squeeze.

I didn't know what to say, other than something snarky, so I said nothing, gave her a tight smile, and took Doug possessively by his right bicep. When he turned to look at me, I planted a huge kiss right on his mouth.

I surprised myself at just how boldly and spontaneously I moved to mark my territory. I still had serious questions about whether or not my relationship with Doug would work, but dammit, there was no way I was going to lose him to *her* – cougar that she obviously was. She was probably ten years older than him, but she still had her looks and I already knew her to be nothing less than a ruthless, lying bitch – not to put too fine a point on it.

Just then, the jazz combo played a slightly hip, swing version of "Hail to the Chief" and in swept Rose and Will Gannon, accompanied by the travel pool – a handful of reporters and photographers who got into position briefly in front of the head table to record the arrival.

I was struck by how perfect the Gannons looked as a couple. He wore a black tux and a white bow tie. Rose's gown was royal blue. They stood behind their chairs on the dais, about thirty yards in front of our A.P. table. President Gannon acknowledged the applause with a wave, then the cheering intensified when he gestured dramatically at his wife who stood to his right.

I hadn't seen Rose Gannon in person since we'd met the previous spring in Columbia, Georgia, during the campaign. On that day, she was bronzed and sculpted. Today she looked a tad pallid, but she smiled gamely and waved.

Soon the applause died down, the first couple took their seats, the pool was shooed out of the way to the back of the room, the jazz combo segued into an up-tempo tune I didn't recognize, and the crowd's pre-dinner conversational buzz resumed.

As we took our seats, Nathan Mann pulled out my chair for me and scooted it under my fanny when I sat.

Nice move, I thought.

Waiters hustled through the room delivering steaming plates. Our choices were fish, chicken, or beef. I chose fish; Doug, no surprise, had beef. He's such a dude.

The mood was festive.

Mann talked more with the A.P. exec from New York, but when the conversation flagged, he turned his attention to me. At first it was small-talk chitchat, but I decided to try to build some rapport by asking biographical questions that would seem like idle, polite conversation. In reality, I was desperately trying to figure out what it was about Mann that Rogan was trying to exploit.

The only hint I had was one of Anne-Marie's first tips to look at Rogan's associates. I now knew that Mann was the associate she wanted me to discover. So, I took a stab at trying to get a better understanding of the Rogan/Mann relationship.

"I interviewed a friend of yours the other day," I said.

"Oh? Who?"

"Dolph Rogan."

I watched Mann's face closely for the slightest shadow.

Mann's eyebrows went up in surprise and his eyes widened in recognition, but I detected no fear.

"Oh, yes. Dolph. How is he? And what did you talk about? Drones, I'll bet."

"He's fine. And, yes, drones. He gave me a demonstration. How do *you* know him?"

"We go back a ways. I think I met him when I was the head of the F.A.A."

"He feels very strongly about the privatization of drones."

"That he does."

"Is he lobbying you?"

Mann laughed. "It seems like *everyone* is lobbying me."

"And the president," I said. "He was one of your students?"

As soon as I asked the question, I regretted it. It was weak and ineffective. I'd unwittingly thrown the conversation away from the direction I'd wanted it to go.

"Yes. One of my best students," Mann answered. "A standout from day one."

The inertia of his answer prompted me to make an addled follow up: "You must be surprised and pleased at the way things turned out with your other student who now just happens to be the head of China."

Mann laughed again. "Not too shabby having two of my former students go from the top of the class to the top of their respective, and very powerful, governments. I'm quite pleased – and I'm very proud of them."

I wasn't really getting anywhere, and it was my own fault, yet I was determined to keep trying, but before I could bring the conversation back to probing Mann's personal life, he turned the tables on me and tried to get me talking about myself. Clearly, he didn't seem to know anything about my background, so he asked basic job interview stuff about where I was from (Madison, Wisconsin) and what I studied in college (English).

The table was so large and the room so loud that it was only possible to talk with the people on either side of me and on either side of them. Doug and Rochelle were deep in conversation. Paul was to Rochelle's left. Even though I still worried Paul might have an unrequited crush on me, I was relieved to see him clearly enjoying the company of the young man sitting next to him, an A.P. intern, I found out later.

I dug into my salmon plate and tried another tack with Mann. "As I was researching our interview, I read that you're a marathon runner. How did that come about?"

Mann took a sip of coffee and smiled revealing, again, his stained teeth. "I used to be a heavy smoker," he said. "My doctor said it would kill me if I didn't stop. I decided to take up running, instead. In time," he laughed, "I traded in one addiction for another."

I chuckled. "Got any big marathons coming up?"

"Right now I'm training for the next one – a 5-K – in April."

Our talk was cut short when the wait-staff cleared the tables, began distributing dessert and the formal program started.

Doug leaned over and whispered to me, "I need to use the latrine."

"You mean take a leak, right?" I smiled. "How charming."

"Okay. How's this?" he said, "I have to check the Hilton's plumbing."

"Much better. I'll allow it."

He stood and gave my shoulder a gentle, affectionate squeeze. "I'll be right back. Save my place."

"Okay."

He limped almost imperceptibly as he headed out of the banquet hall. As I watched him, I remember whispering a quick prayer of thanks that he was beginning to take the first steps toward kicking heroin.

There were announcements and awards during dessert, and then Jimmy Fallon took the podium to tell some jokes and introduce the president.

When Doug wasn't back in time for Fallon, I began to get worried. I dug my phone out of my purse.

Where are you? You're missing Fallon! I texted.

No answer.

Paul saw the worried look on my face. "What's wrong?" he mouthed.

I pointed at Doug's empty chair and gave Paul a WTF-shrug. Then I got up and walked behind Doug and Grigsby's chairs to whisper in Paul's ear so that Grigsby wouldn't be able to hear.

"Doug went to the men's room, but that was at least twenty minutes ago. Would you mind checking to see if he's okay?" I asked.

"Sure," Paul whispered and darted from the room.

I took my seat, but I was no longer listening to Jimmy Fallon. I craned my neck and looked all around the room at the laughing faces of D.C. and Hollywood glitterati, hoping to get a glimpse of Doug. But he'd disappeared, his vanilla ice cream now nothing more than a white puddle in a glass goblet.

He was still missing when Fallon introduced President Gannon.

Everyone stood and clapped as Gannon kissed Rose, shook Fallon's hand, then grasped both sides of the podium.

"Thank you, everyone. Thank you."

The applause died down and everyone sat, but I delayed so I could look around the room once more for Doug. There was still no sign of him. Or of Paul Stone. Reluctantly, I took my seat, stewing. My worries about Doug were intensifying.

"It's good to be here at the so-called 'nerd prom,'" the president began as the crowd chuckled. "Thank you for looking up here, especially when there's not one, but two Clooneys in the room."

More laughter as people turned to look at George and Nick Clooney smiling as they sat at a table near the center of the banquet hall.

"I was just telling Rose on the way over here–" the president continued, but then he stopped suddenly when we all heard a thud. It came from the side of the head table in front of me where Gannon had been sitting with his wife during dinner.

"Get a doctor," someone at the head table shouted, "she's collapsed!"

The room let out a collective gasp.

President Gannon turned to his right to look in the direction of the commotion. The smile on his face morphed to horror. "Rose!" he shouted, and dashed toward where his wife had been sitting.

03 80

CHAPTER 25

Rose Gannon had apparently fallen from her chair and was now on the floor obscured from view by the white tablecloth that hung down in front.

I shot to my feet and dashed to the stage, still clutching my phone. Two Secret Service agents sprinted onto the dais. They nudged a couple of the dignitaries aside to clear the area around where Rose lay.

President Gannon got to her and knelt down, out of my view, but I could hear him over the commotion continuing to call her name.

"Rose! Rose!"

I speed-dialed the desk. Someone picked up on the first ring.

"It's Chadwick with the president, dictating a news alert."

"Go ahead, Lark."

"First Lady Rose Gannon has collapsed at the White House Correspondents' Dinner in Washington. President Gannon, who had just begun speaking, rushed to her side."

"Got it. Thanks, Lark. You beat the pool. They're just calling it in now."

A Secret Service agent spoke into one of his French cuffs and, moments later, two EMTs rushed into the room through a side door pushing a gurney.

Meanwhile, a phalanx of Secret Service agents, their faces tense, formed a protective cordon around the front and side of the stage to keep me – and the rest of the crowd – from pressing any closer.

Clearly, the evening was a shambles. The people in the room buzzed and murmured while the EMTs attended to the first lady.

After what seemed like a long time, the president stood as the EMTs began to push the gurney to the end of the raised platform.

President Gannon looked distraught and his bow tie was askew. He was oblivious to everyone else in the room, his focus on the still-out-of-view gurney where his wife lay.

I worked my way toward the end of the head table to get a better look, but a Secret Service agent prevented me from getting any closer than about ten or fifteen yards. I had a death grip on my cell phone and quickly began taking still shots of the scene as a TV cameraman from the White House travel pool crowded next to me shooting video.

As soon as the gurney was lowered from the stage onto the main floor, I craned to get my first look at Rose Gannon. She appeared to be unconscious. Her eyes were closed. Her face was ashen. Her head lolled to the side. An oxygen mask covered her nose and mouth.

The president, flanked by two Secret Service agents, quickly caught up with the gurney and trotted alongside. He reached out to Rose and, in that moment, I knew I'd snapped the money shot of the president grasping his wife's hand and looking down at her worriedly.

"Where are you taking her?" I shouted at the EMTs.

The trailing EMT doing the pushing, obviously not a fan of the press, replied, "Go fuck yourself" just as the dispatcher's voice on the medic's two-way radio blurted, "G.W. Hospital has been alerted that Dancer is enroute."

"Thank you!" I hollered.

I called the desk. "It's Chadwick again."

"Go."

"First Lady Rose Gannon is being rushed to George Washington University Hospital. She appears to be unconscious. An oxygen mask covered her face as she was wheeled on a gurney from the ballroom of the Washington Hilton. President Gannon, clearly worried, held her hand as she was being taken to an ambulance."

"Got it. You beat the pool again, Lark."

Just as I was hanging up, Paul tapped me on the shoulder. He looked distressed.

"I checked all the men's rooms on this floor and the ones on the next level up. No Doug. Anywhere. I can't find him, Lark. I'm sorry."

"Thanks, Paul. I'm gonna head to the hospital. You stay here and keep an eye open. They're gonna be treating this place as if it's a crime scene."

"Okay," he said.

I called Doug. When he didn't pick up, I left a voicemail.

"Where *are* you? I've gotta tell ya, Doug: I'm pissed. The first lady's collapsed. They're taking her to G.W. Hospital. That's where I'm going now. *Call me!*" I nearly shouted those last two words.

I managed to flag down a cab a block away at Connecticut and Florida. From the cab, I sent New York the pictures I'd taken of Rose Gannon being wheeled from the ballroom, the distraught president holding her hand.

G.W. Hospital was a madhouse. I counted at least a dozen live trucks parked in a tangled jumble at the front entrance, their masts transforming the area into a metallic forest. Reporters were directed to an auditorium where we were told that Ron McClain would be briefing us "in a few minutes."

I called Paul. "What's happening there?"

"It's a crime scene alright. They have yellow police tape around the head table and a C.S.I. unit's been going over everything."

"Has anyone been arrested?"

"Not that I've seen, but it looks like they've been interviewing the wait-staff."

"Did you call it in?"

"Yep. We're covered here at the hotel. Anything new there?" Paul asked.

"McClain's just entered the room. I'll know in a minute."

I hung up and called the desk.

"It's Chadwick," I said to the person who picked up. "Are you watching?"

"Yep. CNN's carrying McClain's presser live."

Ron McClain, looking grim, grasped the sides of the lectern and began to speak.

"First Lady Rose Gannon was rushed here to George Washington University Hospital this evening after collapsing during the White

House Correspondents' Association Dinner at the Washington Hilton. The first lady regained consciousness in the ambulance and is now alert and in good spirits. She will remain in the hospital overnight so that doctors can observe her condition and run further tests." McClain paused. "I'll take questions now."

The first came from a network correspondent: "Was she poisoned?"

"Not as far as we know." McClain smiled inanely. "Maybe it was just something she ate."

"Like, um, *poison*?" someone behind me said under his breath.

Several of us tittered.

"Did the president accompany her in the ambulance?" I asked.

"Yes," McClain said. "He insisted."

"What were her first words when she regained consciousness?" someone asked.

McClain said, "The president told me she looked at him and joked, "It's *Will*, right?"

Several reporters laughed – and for the first time, the tension that had been gripping us, relaxed a tad.

"When will the president be returning to the White House?" I asked.

"At this point, I believe he intends to spend the night here, Lark."

Another reporter asked, "If the president's staying here overnight, what should we read into that?"

McClain didn't miss a beat. "You can read into it that the President of the United States loves his wife very, *very* much."

The reporter for the *New York Times* asked for and received the names of the doctors treating Rose Gannon.

A few minutes later, before McClain left the podium, he told us the lid was on and not to expect any more news tonight.

For the next half hour, I worked with the A.P. pool reporter to craft the story. New York gave me the byline because I filed first, but Paul and the pool reporter also got honorable mention.

As soon as we filed, I called Doug again.

Still no answer.

This time, I didn't bother to leave a message because I felt I'd lose it and, in my anger and anguish, say something I'd regret.

I caught a cab to Shotzie's Pub where I knew Doug liked to hang out. The place was packed and stuffy. I looked around, didn't see Doug anywhere, but found Shotzie wiping the bar.

"Has Doug been in here at all tonight, Shotzie?" I asked.

"Nope. Haven't seen him in a couple days, actually."

"Thanks." I headed for the door.

"You're looking very fetching tonight, Lark," Shotzie called after me. "Got a hot date?"

"Something like that," I muttered.

I left Shotzie's, ran down H Street and around the corner to the Jackson Place press center, but Doug wasn't there, either.

I hailed another cab, this time to Doug's apartment on Florida Avenue. His Jeep wasn't parked out front and no lights were on inside, but I used the spare key he'd given me to unlock the door.

"Yo! Doug! I'm coming in," I hollered as I entered.

I stood for a moment on the threshold, pausing to listen.

Nothing.

I flipped on a light and stepped into the living room. He always kept his place clean. Other than a couple back issues of the *Washington Post* splayed on the sofa by the bay window overlooking the street, the place was immaculate.

And way too quiet.

"Doug? Are you here?"

Crickets.

I bounded up the stairs to his bedroom.

"Doug! Ready or not, here I come. If you're naked, *tough.*"

The door to his bedroom was ajar. I pushed it open.

☙ ❧

CHAPTER 26

Doug's bedroom door squeaked on its hinges when I pushed it open. I hoped I would see him sprawled on the bed, asleep, entangled in the covers. I feared I'd find him in bed with someone – or dead.

When I switched on the light, I found none of the above.

His bed was empty and neatly made. Ever since I'd met him, he'd been a neat freak, probably from his three-year stint as a combat photographer in the Army, including two tours in Iraq. He told me the military is big on neatness and order or, as Doug put it, "having your shit together."

I let out a disappointed sigh and leaned against the wall of his bedroom, trying to figure out where he could be – and what to do next.

Where is he? I asked myself, then out loud, I hollered, "Doug! I mean it, man. Are you here?"

My voice echoed throughout his obviously empty apartment.

Slowly I walked through the place, absentmindedly checking the bathroom, kitchen, and the other rooms, my worries intensifying with each step.

Has Doug been kidnapped by Rogan? Or killed? It was certainly possible, but the more I kept thinking about it, the less likely it seemed that Rogan would go after Doug.

I said to myself, Doug's not a threat to Rogan. I am.

My mind kept looping back to heroin.

Admittedly, I knew very little about illicit drugs of any kind, least of all heroin. As far as I was concerned, heroin was a drug of desperation, used primarily by low-life losers. It certainly was not the drug of choice in my social circle. A few of my friends used marijuana recreationally, but I'd never even been curious about trying pot. An artificial high holds no allure for me. I've always been a realist, preferring to face life straight on – and sober.

What seemed more likely to me is that heroin's siren call compelled Doug to leave the hotel, hoping to score a quick hit. Even though I knew he might have overdosed and died, I wasn't ready to dwell on that possibility – yet. Instead, I preferred to believe that he'd gotten super stoned and passed out at some crack house and was now too ashamed to face me, so he'd decided to stay off the grid until he could think clearly.

I decided to go back to the hotel to see if Doug's Wrangler was in the garage where we parked. If it was there, I reasoned, then he might still be in or near the hotel and, perhaps, easier to find.

I pulled up the Uber app on my phone and, within five minutes, I was in a private vehicle-for-hire being ferried down Florida Avenue to the Hilton. I asked the driver to wait while I dashed into the hotel's pay-to-park garage, but Doug's Wrangler wasn't where we'd left it when we arrived for the dinner.

My funk deepening, I asked the Uber driver to take me back to Doug's.

By the time I got there, I was annoyed and angry at Doug for the way he so cavalierly seemed to be throwing away such a promising relationship. It just didn't make sense that he would so irresponsibly walk away.

I'm not an alarmist, but I couldn't shake the sick feeling that something was dangerously wrong.

I dialed 911.

"Nine-one-one. State your emergency."

"I'm not sure this is an emergency," I began, "but I want to report a missing person."

The woman on the other end of the phone was kind, but no nonsense. She took down the basic information about Doug and then said she'd dispatch someone to meet me at his apartment.

By this time the false eyelashes I'd been wearing no longer felt like windshield wipers, they felt like brooms. While I waited for a cop to arrive, I pried them off.

Soon a white patrol car pulled into the spot where Doug normally parked in front of the building. A gigantic African-American man emerged and lumbered up the steps.

I met him at the door.

"Evening, ma'am. I'm Officer Gwynn," he said, shaking my hand. "Are you Lark Chadwick, the person who called in the report?"

"I am. Come on in."

He closed the door after stepping inside.

"Thanks for getting here so quickly," I said. "Can I get you some coffee, water, anything?"

"No, thank you." He took a notebook out of the breast pocket of his uniform and opened it.

"Have a seat." I gestured to one of the two easy chairs that faced out the bay window.

He sat down and I sat in the chair next to him.

"What's your relationship to the person who's missing?" he asked, pen poised.

"Friend. *Girl*friend, I guess. And co-worker."

"Tell me more about him."

I brought the cop up to speed, ending the story with the search I conducted after Doug had excused himself to go to the bathroom at the dinner.

"Can you think of any reason why he disappeared? Did you two have a fight?" Gwynn asked.

"No. This is not like him at all. He's very conscientious."

"Is he on any medications like antidepressants?"

"None that I know of."

"Does he own a weapon?"

"No. He hates guns."

"Do you have any reason to believe he might be a danger to himself or others?"

The question threw me. Threw me all the way back to the carbon monoxide death of Annie, the aunt who'd raised me from infancy when my parents were killed in a car accident. I hadn't thought Doug was suicidal. But I hadn't thought Annie was, either, until I'd found her body sprawled on the floor of our house back in Wisconsin. That had been three years ago.

"N-no," I managed to stammer. "I can't imagine that Doug would kill himself."

"Does he have any enemies?"

I hesitated. I thought about Dolph Rogan again, but heard myself say, "No. None."

The cop picked up on my pause. "You *sure* about that?" He raised his eyebrows and gave me a skeptical look. "Was he in an altercation with anyone recently?"

"No. It's not that."

"What is it, then?"

I debated telling him about Rogan and realized I had conflicted feelings. As a reporter, my deep-seated instinct is to protect my confidential source and keep the story under wraps until I have enough confirmed facts that justify going public. But, in this case, my source herself was missing and I feared she was dead. Even though I thought I was more at risk from Rogan than Doug was, I decided to tip my hand, at least a little.

"I'm not sure this is related, but it might be," I began.

"Go on."

"I'm a reporter. I'm working on an investigation. I have a confidential source who's now missing. Before I lost touch with her, she told me she was afraid for her life."

"Has she been reported missing?"

"I don't know, but that's something you'd be able to find out."

"What's her name?"

I told him, spelled it out, and he wrote it down.

"How might her disappearance be connected to Mr. Mitchell's?" the cop asked.

"It might not be."

"But if it is?"

"If it is, the common denominator might be a guy named Dolph Rogan."

"Who's he?"

I gave him a quick thumbnail explanation and Officer Gwynn jotted down a few more notes.

I decided to leave out the part about Anne-Marie's allegation that Rogan is blackmailing the president's national security adviser, Nathan Mann, because, I felt, not only is it irrelevant to Doug's disappearance, but it also opens a whole other can of worms based on explosive, but unsubstantiated, accusations.

"So, why do you think this guy, Rogan, might be connected to Mr. Mitchell's disappearance?"

I told Officer Gwynn about my three a.m. meeting with Anne-Marie and how it was cut short when she saw what Doug confirmed to me was Rogan's SUV leaving the garage.

"Did Rogan see Mr. Mitchell?" Officer Gwynn asked.

"Doug said he didn't, but Rogan probably saw me talking with Anne-Marie in the garage. That's why I'm not certain that Rogan's involved with Doug's disappearance. Rogan probably considers *me* to be more of a threat."

"I see." The cop thought a minute, then said, "But making a move against Mr. Mitchell could be Rogan's way of sending a warning to you, yes?"

"Yes," I nodded slowly. "True."

Officer Gwynn made a few more notes. "We can look into that. Do you have Rogan's contact information?"

"I do, but before I give it to you, can you assure me that he won't be told who pointed you toward him?"

"Yes," Gwynn said.

I wasn't so sure, but I liked Officer Gwynn. He seemed smart and sensitive. I decided to take a risk and, against my better judgment, gave him Rogan's contact information.

When I did, I felt myself relax. I realized I might be closer to getting some answers, not only about Doug, but maybe about Anne-Marie, too. Plus, I thought, if the cops came sniffing around Rogan, he'd be less likely to make a move against me because he'd know the police have him on their radar.

"Is there anything else I should know?" Gwynn asked, "*Anything* that might give me the lead I need to help you find your friend?"

I bit my lip. "Um, there might be."

The cop gave me a penetrating look.

I did my best to avoid his eyes. As I did, I considered my options. And the high stakes. Doug was missing. The longer that time went by, the more at risk he might be. The cops, I reasoned, needed to know everything – even the bad – because that might help them find Doug before it was too late.

"There's one more thing you should know," I said slowly.

"Go on," the cop prompted.

"I don't know if this is relevant or not, but it might be." I paused.

"It might be, ma'am. Especially since you seem reluctant to tell me. You do want us to find him, don't you?"

The lump in my throat nearly strangled me. "Y-yes," I managed to croak. "Yes I really do."

"Then, whatever it is, I think you'd better tell me."

I took a deep breath and told him about the emergency room visit to G.W. Hospital which revealed that Doug had been using heroin.

"Is he still using?" Gywnn asked as he made another notation.

I shook my head. "I don't think so. I haven't seen any evidence of it. He did tell me that he'd been depressed."

"Has he started seeing a therapist?"

I frowned. "He told me this evening he tried to make an appointment, but they said he should call back in two weeks."

"How did he seem tonight?"

"Fine. Normal. Jovial."

Gwynn shook his head sadly. "Okay," he sighed. "What can you tell me about his vehicle? Make, model, year, license number."

"He drives a forest green Jeep Wrangler. I don't know the year or the license number, but I think I can find that out for you. I'll be right back."

On a hunch, I left Gwynn sitting in the living room and dashed upstairs to Doug's office where I'd seen an accordion file on his desk. The file had a slot marked *Auto* and inside I found papers that had the Wrangler's vehicle identification and license numbers. I brought the info to Officer Gwynn and he copied it all down.

"Okay," he said when he'd finished writing, "Let's see if anything turns up."

He unclipped the microphone attached to his shoulder and keyed it. "This is thirty-two."

"Go ahead, thirty-two," came the disembodied voice of the dispatcher.

"I've got a missing person to report."

"Go ahead."

Gwynn flipped back a few pages in his notebook and read from it. "The missing person is a Douglas Grant Mitchell, age 38, white male, six-two, 200 pounds. No tattoos or other markings, but the person lost his right leg below the knee in Iraq and wears a titanium prosthesis. He was last seen at the Washington Hilton Hotel about seven o'clock tonight wearing a tuxedo with a red bow tie. He drives a forest green Jeep Wrangler, D.C. plates, license number D-K 4-7-7-4. You might wanna double check the hotel parking garage first."

"Copy, thirty-two. Attention, all units. Be on the lookout for a missing person...."

As the dispatcher rebroadcast the information, Officer Gwynn dug a cell phone out of the front pocket of his trousers. His first call was to the D.C. Medical Examiner's office.

I gulped and held my breath as he asked if the bodies of any unidentified men had turned up at the morgue. I let out a relieved sigh when the answer finally came back negative.

He then called several of the hospitals in the area, but came up empty each time.

"You'll want to make daily calls to the M.E.'s office and the hospitals," Gwynn said to me.

"Okay," I said sadly. "Now what?"

"Now I have to check with my supervisor."

Gwynn dialed another number. I tried to listen patiently as, once again, he rattled off Doug's basic information. The cop paused for a moment to listen, said "no" a couple times, then said into the phone, "Yes, sir. Thank you, sir."

Gwynn put his phone back into his pocket and turned to me. "Here's the deal: As you know, we've issued a be-on-the-lookout to all units, so a lot of people are looking for him now, but–"

"But?"

"But that's as far as I can go. I'll turn my report over to the detectives and someone will be assigned the case on Monday."

"Monday? Why not right now?" I asked, alarm rising in my voice. "Aren't you guys going to set up a command center?" I leaned toward Officer Gwynn. "Doug is *missing*. Time is of the *essence!"*

Gwynn breathed a sympathetic sigh. "I'm sorry, but your loved one is not a minor child, nor is he an elderly person who wandered away. He doesn't have a weapon and is not considered to be a threat to himself or others. Therefore, his case is officially categorized as 'non-critical.'"

I gave him what I hoped was the most menacing look I could muster and leaned closer so that my face was only about a foot away from his.

"He's critical to *me*," I hissed, my teeth bared.

I tried to look tough and determined, but my voice caught in my throat and I began to cry.

ങ ൽ

CHAPTER 27

I spent Saturday night at Doug's apartment, sleeping in his bed. Or *trying*.

By four o'clock in the morning, I gave up. I had to *do* something.

Even though I loathe coffee, I brewed myself a pot and drank the bitter brew while sitting where Officer Gwynn sat just a few hours earlier.

I stared blankly out the window, still expecting that at any minute I'd see Doug returning home.

About six, while it was still dark, I began roaming through his apartment. On the desk in his den, I came across several black-and-white glossy photos Doug took of me on my first day at the White House just five days earlier. It looked as though he was in the process of putting together a collage of my pictures beginning on the day we met in Columbia, Georgia, as I was interviewing the grieving parents of a teenage girl who'd been strangled to death.

Doug had written in neat calligraphy at the top, *A Valentine for my Valentine.* It looked as though he was putting the finishing touches on the poster but the events of the week got in the way and he wasn't able to finish it.

I was touched by his thoughtfulness, but as I ran a finger across Doug's calligraphy, I realized, sadly, I only had a few pictures of him – mostly selfies we'd taken of the two of us.

I checked my phone for the millionth time, but there were still no messages from him. I called his cell, yet again, and listened once more to his soothing voice asking me to leave a message.

I navigated to my phone's photo albums and accessed the short clip I recorded of Doug doing his *Reeeeal Cooool* impersonation of the jive hipster.

"Where *are* you, Doug?" I whispered to his impishly smiling image.

Then I got an idea. Obviously, the pot of coffee I'd been nursing had finally kicked in and I felt suddenly *wired.*

I put my coffee cup in the sink, raced up the stairs to Doug's bedroom, and scrawled a quick note to him: *Doug! I'm worried about you. Call me ASAP!!!!!* Below the message, I drew an enormous heart, signed my name beneath it, and put it on his pillow.

The Metro trains had just begun running, so I caught one of the first ones to Silver Spring. I wanted to run to my apartment, but I was still wearing the four-inch heels I'd worn to the dinner the night before.

When I got home, I tore off my clothes, showered, and dressed in a cozy-warm hooded gray sweatshirt and matching warm-up pants. Then I fired up my computer and spent the next several hours creating a *Find Doug Mitchell* page on Facebook.

I cropped myself out of a photo I had of Doug and used it as the cover picture for the page. I then wrote what I hoped would be an effective blurb that would mobilize people to begin looking for him:

MISSING!

Associated Press White House Photographer Douglas Grant Mitchell, 38, went missing Saturday night, February 19, during the annual White House Correspondents' Association Dinner at the Washington Hilton Hotel, Connecticut and T Streets N.W. in Washington, D.C.

Mitchell was last seen wearing a black tuxedo with a red bow tie.

Also missing is his dark green Jeep Wrangler, D.C. license plate number DK 4774.

Mitchell is 6'2" and 200 pounds. A veteran of the war in Iraq, Mitchell was severely wounded when the lower part of his right leg was severed in a bomb explosion. He wears a titanium prosthesis.

If you've seen him or know where he is, please contact me, or the District of Columbia Metropolitan Police Department.

I added my contact information at the bottom, then took the page live on Facebook at noon. I put a link to it on my own Facebook page, and posted it on Doug's page, too, with a note pleading with his friends to pray, search, and share the page more widely. I also tweeted a link to it on my Twitter account.

By three in the afternoon, the website *MediaBistro.com* posted the story on its *FishbowlDC* page which has as its slogan *Where Politics and DC Media Mesh.*

Within the next hour, I got phone calls from a reporter at WTOP – the all-news radio station in D.C., and from Leon Harris, a well-known, highly respected anchor at WJLA the local ABC affiliate. By the end of the day, the other two D.C. television stations had made contact with me, as did a reporter for the *Washington Post.*

As far as I knew, Doug had no living relatives. His parents had been dead for five years – I'd never met them. Doug's older brother was killed on 9/11. Doug told me it was 9/11 that prompted him to enlist.

Normally by this time I would have reached out to Lionel. He'd always been my champion – a Rock of Gibraltar. But the longer we went without talking, the stronger I began feeling inside. I realized that Lionel had become a sort of emotional and psychological crutch for me. Mentally, I gave myself a pat on the back for not needing him to prop me up.

Or was I just petulantly hardening my heart against him?

Late in the afternoon I got a call from Muriel.

"Lark, you poor dear. Paul told me your friend is missing. How are you holding up?" she asked when I answered.

"I'm trying to be strong, Muriel, but it's not easy. Thank you for your call."

"I know you and Lionel are having a little tiff. Every time I bring you up, he huffs and puffs and changes the subject. If you don't mind my asking, what's going on?"

"The same thing that was going on between him and Holly before she died." Holly, Lionel and Muriel's daughter, died four years earlier while hiking the Inca Trail in Peru.

"Oh dear me," Muriel said, "He's trying to control your life?"

"Pretty much. I know he means well, but it was getting a little overwhelming. I had to take a break."

"Is there anything I can do to help?" Muriel asked.

"How good are you at talking sense into him?"

She laughed. "Not the greatest, but I'll give it a try."

"Thank you, Muriel. I don't want to lose Lionel as a friend and mentor, but he overstepped some boundaries with me."

"I'll see what I can do, Lark. In the meantime, you stay strong. You're in my prayers, dear."

After we hung up, I returned to stewing about Doug's disappearance. Haunting me was the deep conversation Doug was having with Rochelle Grigsby just before he disappeared. When he'd excused himself to go to the bathroom, Grigsby had stayed at the table and talked with Paul Stone who'd been sitting to her left. I also remembered seeing her during the commotion when Rose Gannon collapsed.

Several times during the day I thought about reaching out to Rochelle to see what she and Doug had been discussing. Perhaps there was a nugget of a clue embedded in something he'd said to her, but my relationship with her was so strained that I felt it would be futile to try to contact her.

So, imagine my surprise when, about six o'clock, she called me on my cell.

"It's Grigsby," she said in her no-nonsense tone when I picked up.

"Hi," I said warily.

"How you doing?"

"Not great."

"I saw the Facebook page about Doug. Are you planning to come in tomorrow?"

So, I thought, this really isn't about sympathy, it's about scheduling.

"I haven't even thought that far ahead, but yeah, I guess. I'd go crazy just sitting around. Plus Nathan Mann told me at the dinner last night that I could interview him tomorrow. He said he'd have his secretary get back to me first thing in the morning to nail down a time."

"Good. It's probably a good idea to keep busy."

"Okay then."

"One more thing."

"Sure." I felt myself tense.

"Where are you now?"

"Home. Why?"

"Good. I'm parked outside your building. We need to talk. May I come up?"

I was so shocked I don't remember saying yes, but a moment later I opened the door to a very distraught Rochelle Grigsby.

CB ℬℭ

CHAPTER 28

I stood in the doorway gawking at Rochelle Grigsby. She wore a Navy blue overcoat and a white scarf around her neck. Her eyes were bloodshot and glistening and her nose was running.

"May I come in?" she asked.

"You're the last person I would have expected to see–"

She finished the sentence for me. "Darkening your door?"

"That's one way of putting it." I stepped out of the way and let her come in. "Will you be staying? Can I take your coat?"

She looked uncertain for a moment, but then took off her coat and handed it to me. "Thanks. Do you have a snot rag?"

"Yeah." I put her coat on the doorknob and then found a box of tissues in the bathroom and brought it out to her. "Here." I was trying to maintain a neutral, but wary tone because I did not trust this woman and found her presence in my living room to be extremely awkward and uncomfortable.

She blew her nose with a huge honk. It took at least three tissues to do the job. She must've known there was no way I was going to take them from her and throw them away, so she stuffed them in the front pocket of her jeans.

"May I sit down?" she asked.

"Have a seat." I wasn't going to be mean, but she had long ago exhausted my supply of good will and hospitality.

Grigsby sat on my sofa. I sat primly in a chair across from her. And waited.

She placed the box of tissues on the coffee table, pulled out two more and sat with them balled in her hands resting in her lap.

"I suppose you're wondering why I'm here," she said finally.

"The thought certainly crossed my mind."

"I'm here about Doug."

My blood turned to ice. "What about him?"

"He's missing."

"I *know* that."

"I think I know why."

I inched my chair closer and leaned toward her. "Why?"

She bit her lip as if deciding what – and how much – to say. Finally she said, "Heroin."

I flinched.

"I'm sorry to be so blunt," she said.

"What about heroin?" I was trying mightily to maintain a poker face as my insides were roiling with alarm.

"He was using."

"How do you know?"

Suddenly Rochelle Grigsby began to cry. Deep wracking sobs.

I was too stunned to do anything but sit and wait her out. And it took at least two minutes for the storm of emotion to subside. She grabbed a bunch more tissues, dabbed her eyes, and blew her nose a couple more honking times.

Finally, when it looked as though she'd be able to talk, I asked in a voice devoid of emotion, "How do you know he was using heroin?"

"Because," she began, then stopped. "Because . . ." she looked down. "Because I used to shoot up with him." She glanced up briefly to check my response.

I lost it. "You *what?*"

She stood and took a step toward the door. "I knew it was a mistake to come here."

"Sit down!" It was a command.

She sat.

I pulled my chair closer. "Tell me everything, Rochelle. *Every*thing. Start from the beginning."

"Okay." She took a deep breath. "Doug and I started using heroin together not long after he came to D.C. from Georgia."

"Are you *kidding* me?" I wanted to take her by the scruff of the neck and physically throw her out the door, but I resisted the urge because I needed to know more about what might have happened to Doug. "That was more than eight months ago."

She nodded. "He was already using long before he got here."

So many questions were fighting for attention that I had to pause, take a deep breath, and decide what to ask first. If what she was telling me was true – a big *if* because this was Rochelle Grigsby speaking, after all – Doug had been lying to me about doing heroin only a couple times. Was he also banging Grigsby? Her revelation had also stoked in me a white-hot anger toward Doug. But I needed to stay calm and not jump to any conclusions.

"So how did you start using together?" I spoke in a steely-soft whisper that required Grigsby to lean closer so she could hear.

"It was almost right away after we met. One junkie can spot another a mile away. He was in a new place and didn't have connections. I did."

"What happened?"

"I introduced him to my dealer. Then we'd go somewhere and shoot up."

"Is that *all* you'd do?"

Grigsby nodded. "Pretty much. I wanted to do more, but he didn't. Said he was seeing someone." She looked me in the eye. "You."

"So you've been treating me like shit because you're *jealous?*"

She looked down. "Pretty lame, huh?"

"A *lot* lame. So, why come here? Why now?"

"I want to help."

"Oh, *now* you want to help." My voice dripped with sarcasm. "What's changed?"

"I want to make amends."

"What do you mean?"

"I want to make up for the harm I've done to Doug – and to you."

"Why?"

"It's part of the twelve-step program I'm in."

"How long have you been in it?"

"Four months. I've been clean exactly 120 days."

"Good for you," I sneered. "And you've made my life hell for every one of them."

"I know. And I'm sorry."

I stood. "You're gonna have to do a *lot* better than that."

"I know. That's what it says in the Big Book, too."

"What's that?"

"That's the bible of the twelve-step program. Making amends is step nine: 'Make direct amends to such people wherever possible except when to do so would injure them or others.' I memorized it," she smiled proudly.

"Good for you."

Grigsby's smile faded and she stood. "Actually, Lark, I think I can do more than apologize."

"What do you mean?"

"I think I know where Doug is. Do you want me to show you?"

She didn't have to ask twice.

Cଓ ଔ

CHAPTER 29

It was already dark as we headed south on Colesville Road out of Silver Spring, Maryland, back toward D.C. Grigsby drove, I rode shotgun. She drives a hot, red Mazda Miata. Must be nice.

"So where do you think he is?" I asked, fighting to keep my voice level. My emotions were a churning jumble. *Where's Doug? Why's Grigsby helping me? Am I being kidnapped?*

"Doug could be any number of places, but Rock Creek is my first choice," Grigsby said.

"Why?"

"That's where we usually shot up."

"Why there?"

"It's pretty. And secluded. It enhances the high."

Soon we were in Rock Creek Park, a swath of forest a couple miles wide that cuts the District of Columbia in two from north to south. Technically, it's a National Park with miles and miles of trails for hiking, biking, and horseback riding.

I've been running regularly in Rock Creek ever since I moved to the D.C. area more than six months ago. I love to jog near the Peirce Mill, a well-preserved and operational mill dating back to the 1820s. It's just upstream from the D.C. Zoo, built on the site of a mill once owned by former president John Quincy Adams.

A historical marker along Rock Creek near Tilden Street notes that more than a hundred years ago President Teddy Roosevelt used to take his friend Jean Jules Jusserand, the French Ambassador, on exhausting hikes along the ridges that line the banks of the boulder-strewn stream.

Times have certainly changed, I thought to myself. Now we're looking for a heroin addict in here. Adding to the creepiness, it was dark now and we were driving by the Peirce Mill. It's near where Congressional intern Chandra Levy was murdered while jogging in 2001.

"Keep your eyes peeled," Grigsby said. "Doug could be parked in any one of these parking lots."

We were on a narrow, two-lane road pockmarked with potholes.

"You think he's dead, don't you?" I asked softly.

"I don't know."

"What does your gut tell you?"

She hesitated. "My gut tells me to be...optimistic."

"Bullshit," I hissed. I was feeling increasingly glum about how this would turn out.

"*Guardedly* optimistic," Grigsby amended.

"How did things usually go down when you two would get together?" I asked.

"We'd meet our dealer parked at a gas station on Fourteenth Street. He owns a shoe repair place near there. Drives a fancy black Lincoln. We'd pull up alongside his car and make the exchange. Sometimes there were so many cars lined up it was like the drive-through window at McDonald's."

"Where would you go after you got the heroin?"

"We'd take our squirt guns someplace secluded. Like in here."

"Squirt guns?"

"Syringes. Doug kept his stuff in a toilet kit."

"What stuff?"

"Shooting heroin is all very ritualistic. It involves syringes, a spoon, some water, a lighter, a rubber strap, and cotton balls."

"Why cotton balls?"

"To filter out the impurities and air bubbles. You put the powder in a spoon, add a few drops of water, put a flame under the spoon to cook it, then put a cotton ball in it to sop up the bad stuff. After that, you stick the needle through the cotton ball and suck the good stuff into the syringe."

I laughed derisively. "It's not *good* stuff, Rochelle. It's *poison.*"

"Yeah. I know. But it seemed like good stuff at the time," she said.

I urged her on with another question. "Then you put the strap around the base of your bicep to make the vein in the crook of your arm stand out, right?"

"Exactly, but before you do that, it's a good idea to tap or flick the needle to pop any air bubbles that might have gotten inside the syringe."

"As if any of this is a 'good idea,'" I sneered. I was getting tired of her poor word choices, especially egregious because she often edits my copy.

"Good point," she said.

"Would the two of you shoot up simultaneously?" I asked.

"No. Doug's habit was to just go for it. He was reckless. Often when he'd shoot up, he'd fall off."

"What do you mean?"

"He'd nod off. Pass out. I'd wait to make sure he was okay before I took my hit because I was more cautious and only took a little at a time. He told me that once, when he shot up alone, he passed out sitting in his Jeep in one of the parking lots along here. Someone called an ambulance, but Doug told me he came to when the EMTs rapped on his window. He said to them he'd been taking a nap, then quickly got the hell outta there."

I found myself warming up to Grigsby, at least a little. As emotionally painful as this drive was for me, I appreciated her willingness to "make amends" by telling me about the Doug I didn't know. She'd taken a risk by being vulnerable with me. I began thinking of her as a real person rather than as my enemy and nemesis.

"How hard was it for you to quit?" I asked.

Grigsby shrugged. "I won't kid you. It's been tough. But subbies have helped."

"Subbies?"

"Subutex. It's a prescription pill I got from my doctor."

"Did Doug try to quit?"

"Oh yeah. Over and over. We were actually support buddies for a while, encouraging each other. But then one of us would relapse." She fished her phone out of her pocket and punched a few buttons. "About a month ago I got this message from him on my voicemail." She shot me a glance. "You sure you want to hear this? It's pretty rough."

I nodded. And braced myself. "Play it."

She pressed another button and Doug's voice filled the car. But I'd never heard him speaking like this. He sounded, for lack of a better word, drugged.

"Yo! Grigs!" Doug's voice was slow and lugubrious with lots of pauses. "I just got the best shit from our friend Ray. It's awesome, yo. I'm in Rock Creek. C'mon by. I'll share."

I was crying softly by the time Grigsby hit the *stop* button.

"I was so pissed at him when I got this message," she said. "We didn't speak for weeks. In fact, last night at the dinner was our first talk since then."

"I was wondering about that," I said, wiping away the tears and regaining my composure. "What did you talk about? Did you get a sense that he'd stopped using?"

"He seemed normal. Told me about the emergency room experience last week and how he was trying to quit." She looked at me again. "He said he was trying to quit for *you*, Lark. But I could see in his eyes that the more he talked about it, the hungrier he was getting for another fix."

Most of the parking lots we'd been passing were empty and the ones that weren't held no Jeep Wranglers.

"Who's the guy Doug mentioned on the voicemail? Ray. Is he your dealer?" I asked.

"Uh huh. Ray Barber. He owns a shoe repair place near the bus barns on fourteenth."

"Show me."

Grigsby palmed the wheel, made a few turns, and soon we were whizzing up 14th Street in Columbia Heights. The street was fairly wide as we headed north. We passed barbershops, palm readers, drycleaners, pawnshops, a pizza place, liquor stores, gas stations, storefront churches, neighborhood markets, and a few ethnic restaurants.

She pulled over to the curb in the 4500 block of 14th Street just south of Buchanan. A block to the north on our right was the main garage for the D.C. Metro buses. Across the street to our left stood a row of one-story, white, brick buildings – small businesses. One was a deli. The sign above the door of another read *Ray's Shoe Repair.*

"That's Ray's," Grigsby said. "Looks innocent enough, but believe me – it's not. I get the creeps just sitting here. And the itch. Let's get outta here."

As Grigsby edged her Miata back into traffic, I vowed I'd be back.

$$\text{\Large ঙ ৵}$$

CHAPTER 30

By the time Grigsby dropped me off back at my Silver Spring apartment, my attitude toward her had changed. Time would tell if she could be trusted, but her tone toward me as we searched for Doug had been conciliatory and sympathetic. For that, I was grateful. It was the one ray of hope in an otherwise dismal psychological and emotional landscape.

As soon as I got inside, I packed a suitcase with a week's worth of clothes because I'd decided to camp out at Doug's so I'd be there when he resurfaced. I say "when" knowing all too well I might be totally delusional.

Public transportation in D.C. is great, but this time, rather than take the Metro, I got Pearlie out of the basement parking garage of my apartment and drove to Doug's place. Pearlie's my car. She's a yellow VW Beetle. We've been through a lot together, so it felt good to get behind her wheel again. And talk. She's a good listener.

"I'll be honest with ya, Pearl," I told my car as we headed south toward D.C., "the sobering conversation with Grigsby made me realize there's a strong likelihood that Doug's overdosed somewhere. But I've still got hope. It's possible that he relapsed and is simply too ashamed to face me. Maybe he's just gone off the grid and is holed up somewhere going cold turkey."

That's the thing I like about Pearlie. She doesn't talk back and tell me that I'm probably dead wrong.

On Monday morning – exactly one week after the drone attack on the White House – Paul and I arrived at the Jackson Place briefing center at the same time – about 6:45 a.m. He was long-faced and empathetic, his characteristic exclamation points gone. He seemed to be able to sense my feeling of futility.

When he and I went to Ron McClain's office for the gaggle, the other reporters also seemed sympathetic. On Friday, Gannon had officially named McClain to be his press secretary. I was touched when Ron said to me, "The president is aware that your friend is missing and wants you to know that he and Rose are praying for you – and Doug."

My voice caught when I replied in barely a whisper, "Thank you."

"Speaking of Rose," someone said to Ron, "how is the first lady?"

McClain, all business now, answered, "The latest is she's okay and will be released from the hospital this morning."

Later, about nine, I got a call on my cell from a number I didn't recognize.

"This is Lark," I answered.

"Ms. Chadwick. This is Detective Elena Kerrigan with the D.C. Metropolitan Police Department. I've been assigned to the missing person investigation you launched over the weekend. Is there a good time and place for us to meet?"

"Now's great."

It was an uncharacteristically warm and sunny day, so we agreed to meet on the front steps of St. John's Episcopal Church. It's a block from Jackson Place and across H Street from Lafayette Square. Kerrigan was coming from the 13th and E area of Northwest D.C., so the historic yellow church where Abraham Lincoln used to pray during the Civil War was between our two locations.

I was sitting on a stone bench near the front steps of the church appreciating the sunshine when Kerrigan drove up in a white unmarked Crown Victoria and parked on 16th Street in front of the church in a no parking zone.

I took her measure as she walked toward me. She's in her mid-thirties and looked fit in spite of being at least eight months pregnant. She had on sunglasses, a gray pantsuit, and wore her dirty blonde hair in a ponytail.

She held her hand out to me when she was still several steps away. As she did, she flipped her sunglasses to the top of her head so I could see her eyes.

"Ms. Chadwick? I'm Detective Kerrigan."

We shook hands.

I liked her right away. She had a solid grip and intelligent hazel eyes that made me think she didn't miss much. We agreed to walk and talk across the street in Lafayette Square.

The warm weather had brought a lot of people out of their offices. A few die-hard anti-drone protesters sat cross-legged in a cluster at the edge of the park in front of the White House, steadily beating a big, booming war drum beneath an enormous hand-painted sign with green lettering that declared *NO MORE DRONES!!*

Kerrigan seemed impressed that Doug and I covered the White House for A.P.

"I studied journalism in college," Kerrigan said. "Wanted to be the next Woodward and Bernstein, but then police work got my attention. In a lot of ways, being a detective is like being a reporter."

I really wanted to cut to the chase and talk about Doug, but I knew what the detective was doing: trying to build rapport with me to get a sense of who I am before digging into the nitty-gritty, so I went along with it. I wanted to scope her out, too.

"I've thought about leaving journalism and going into psychology," I told her.

"Hmmmm," Kerrigan said. "Did you know there's a huge need for psychologists in law enforcement?"

"I hadn't really thought about it," I said, "but it makes perfect sense. What's the need?"

"Hostage negotiation, profiling, training cops on how to defuse potentially violent situations. If there'd been an effective shrink heading up a program in Ferguson, Missouri, Michael Brown might still be alive and maybe racial tensions wouldn't be as divisive in this country as they became after Brown was shot and killed by that cop."

I was surprised. "You mean you're on *Brown's* side?"

"Not entirely. I think the kid was kind of a thug, but I believe Wilson, the cop, made some poor choices that caused things to escalate when they didn't have to."

"Interesting. You've definitely got me thinking," I said.

We came to a bench and sat in the sun by the statue of Andrew Jackson on horseback at the center of Lafayette Square.

"I just got your file this morning," Kerrigan began. "I haven't had a chance to study it in depth, so tell me more about your friend Doug."

I summarized for her what I'd told Officer Gwynn on Saturday night when I first reported Doug missing. Without mentioning Rochelle Grigsby by name, I told Kerrigan about the night before when Grigsby revealed during our drive through Rock Creek Park that she and Doug used to shoot up together. I also told Kerrigan about Ray Barber.

Kerrigan watched me at first, but pulled a notebook from her jacket and started writing when I told her about Grigsby and Barber.

"Who's the person who told you all this?" Kerrigan asked casually.

"I'd rather not say."

"Why not?"

"I don't want to get her in trouble."

Kerrigan let it go. "Okay," she said simply.

"Were you able to find out anything about Anne-Marie Gustofsen?" I asked.

"I saw her name in the file," Kerrigan answered. "Virginia isn't in our jurisdiction, but I can make some phone calls to see if the cops over there have anything about her being missing."

"Thanks," I said.

"I should probably tell you," Kerrigan said, "I'm a homicide detective. I'm only on this case for the next few days because the missing persons detective is on maternity leave." She patted her tummy. "I'm next. I'll probably have to turn Doug's case over to her when she gets back this week. But, between you and me, she's not that great, so I'll do my best to keep helping you for as long as I can."

"Good to know. Thanks."

"I've already given Doug's picture – the one you posted on Facebook – to the unit that makes missing persons posters, so maybe later today I'll be able to drop some off for you to pass out and put up," Kerrigan said.

"Okay. Thanks."

"We've been monitoring Doug's bank account, but there's been no activity. Also, his car has not been ticketed or found abandoned."

"What do you make of those two things?" I asked.

"If he's on the move, he's using cash."

"What about his phone?"

"I'm trying to get a warrant so I can get his cell phone records to see who he was texting and calling."

"Isn't there a chip in his phone or something that allows you guys to pinpoint *exactly* where he is?"

"You've been watching too many cop shows on TV," Kerrigan laughed indulgently. "We can't really *pinpoint* where he is, but, if his phone is turned on, we might be able to triangulate his *approximate* location by finding the cell phone towers nearest his phone. But his phone has to be turned on in order for that to happen. By now, even if he had his phone turned on when he disappeared, it's possible he's either turned it off, or his battery is dead."

"I'm afraid to ask this, but I will: Do you think *he's* dead?" I asked, my voice trembling slightly.

"I'll be honest." Kerrigan looked me directly in the eyes. "It's *possible* he's dead, but by no means a certainty. Oftentimes, drug users – especially people addicted to heroin or crack – go off the grid and hide out somewhere to get clean before they resurface."

"That's my hope." I bit my lip to keep from bursting into tears. "It's good to hear it's not false hope."

Kerrigan gently gripped my forearm. "It's not false hope at all." She waited a minute to let me savor the feeling – before demolishing it. "But I don't want you to get your hopes *too* high, because it's still possible this won't end well. He may, indeed, have suffered a fatal overdose, or he was carjacked when a drug deal went south and his Jeep is now what we call a 'crack rental.'"

"What's that?"

"If he didn't have enough money to buy drugs – or if he owed money to his dealer – his car could have been taken from him forcefully and then chopped up for parts."

"What would happen to Doug if that kind of scenario went down?"

Detective Kerrigan squeezed my forearm a little more tightly and her voice became gentle. "He might have been chopped up, too."

03 80

CHAPTER 31

Detective Kerrigan and I talked for about half an hour. Just as I was re-entering the Jackson Place press center, I got a call on my cell from Nathan Mann's secretary. She told me my interview with him was set for five p.m. in his office in the Eisenhower Executive Office Building next to the White House.

At noon, after Ron McClain's eleven o'clock briefing, press office aides took us to the south side of the White House to get a shot of Rose Gannon returning to the residence after being released from the hospital.

The presidential motorcade pulled into the semi-circular drive and came to a stop by the Truman Balcony. The conga line that makes up a presidential motorcade is a thing to behold. A parade of dark blue SUVs and sedans – plus an ambulance, and even a fire truck – stretched beyond the Southwest gate. As far as I could tell, it went all the way back to G.W. Hospital.

President Gannon emerged first from the right rear of the enormous presidential limo. He scooted behind the car, getting to Rose just as an agent opened the left rear door for her.

The first lady, looking grim, wore sunglasses and a bright red scarf pulled tightly around her head.

Press office aides kept us at least thirty yards from the first couple – not conducive to a verbal give-and-take. But I tried anyway.

"How are you feeling, Mrs. Gannon?" I shouted.

Rose Gannon ignored the question – and us – but the president smiled and waved.

"I'm glad she's back home where she belongs," Gannon called jauntily. He didn't walk over to talk with us. Instead, he took his wife by the hand and they walked briskly toward the White House. The two of them were only visible for less than a minute.

After writing up a short piece on Rose Gannon's release from the hospital, I spent the rest of the day reading up on China, drones, and Nathan Mann. Paul helped me brainstorm questions. I was thankful for his help, but it didn't entirely succeed in taking my mind off Doug.

Doug was always lurking just below my consciousness. Every now and then, he'd burst vividly into my head and I'd be caught up in a full-on daydream. More than once Paul commented, "Earth to Lark. Come in, please."

I also found myself wondering and worrying about Anne-Marie Gustofsen. I tried sending her another cryptic email asking for an interview, but it bounced back as *undeliverable* – not a good sign.

That got me thinking about Doug – again. Doug was the only other person who knew that Gustofsen tipped me off that Rogan was blackmailing Mann in order to influence the president. So, it was now entirely up to me to figure out what it was that Rogan had on Mann.

I thought about calling Lionel to get his take, but we still weren't talking. And the longer the silence lasted, the more convinced I was that I'd burned a bridge by hanging up on him. Yet, I reasoned, maybe this friend break will teach him a lesson that I'm not a "kid" and that I don't need him to mansplain things to me. If he really wants to hit the reset button, I stubbornly said to myself, then *he* needs to take the initiative.

I also thought about discussing the Mann/Rogan relationship with my new friend Rochelle Grigsby, but I still wasn't sure how much I could trust her – even though I appreciated her gesture of support the night before.

I suppose I could've turned to Paul, but he'd stepped out of the office, so instead, I tried some deductive reasoning.

Question: What kind of information do people use to blackmail someone?

Answer: A character defect that no one else knows about.

Question: What kind of character defects do people try to cover up?

Answer: Immoral behavior, usually of a sexual nature.

Question: What, specifically, in Mann's life is immoral enough to put him at risk of being blackmailed?

Answer: Dunno.

Question: Is Mann a closeted homosexual or having an affair?

Answer: Dunno.

Question: Does Mann have money problems?

Answer: Dunno.

This was getting me nowhere.

I thought about calling Dolph Rogan under the guise of doing background research for my upcoming interview with Mann. Maybe Rogan would let something slip. Fat chance. I'd rebuffed his romantic advances and left him stuck with the bill. He probably would've paid it anyway, but I was sure my abrupt departure didn't win me any points.

I decided, instead, to do more browsing online about Nathan Mann – the man.

I was intrigued by the Mann/Gannon/Tong connection at Vanderbilt. But that was something that a lot of reporters were already writing about following the coup in China. I found some Google images of Mann running in various marathons, but that was no help, so I decided to try to find out more about Mann's family. But the guy was such an enigma that I decided to include a few questions about his family in my interview. I put them under the heading *PERSONAL STUFF*.

Normally, Doug would have been my photographer. Instead, the desk assigned me to a pleasant woman in her late twenties named Bethany. I'd never worked with her before, but we bonded right away. Her husband teaches economics at the University of Maryland in College Park. Bethany told me she had a three-year-old son at home, "and another on the way," she said, placing a hand on her just-emerging baby bump.

Two pregnant women in one day. What are you trying to tell me, Lord?

For an instant, I felt the same sting of panic when Doug was in the emergency room and I'd thought he'd given me AIDS. I shoved aside this new pregnancy fear.

Bethany and I got to Mann's office fifteen minutes early. His secretary told me he was running a few minutes behind schedule, so I used the delay to go over my questions. Twenty minutes had been set aside for the interview. The secretary assured me I'd still get the full twenty minutes, no matter how late Mann ended up being.

At about 5:20, Mann swept into the reception area of his office with so much energy I wondered if he'd been mainlining caffeine.

"Hi, Lark. C'mon in," he called, barely stopping.

I followed him into his spacious office and introduced him to Bethany as he swung around the back of his desk. He picked up a stack of pink phone messages, scowled, then tossed them onto the mahogany credenza behind him.

"Let's sit over there where it's more comfortable," he said, pointing us to a love seat flanked by two easy chairs.

He was about to sit in one of the chairs when Bethany stopped him. "Sir, you'll be backlit there. Would you mind sitting in the love seat, instead? The background is better there and your face won't be shadowed by the light from the window behind you."

"Sure. No problem," Mann said, shuttling over to the love seat.

"Lark, you sit here." Bethany pointed to the chair facing the window.

As Bethany fiddled with her camera, I took out my iPhone and started recording, then I got out my notebook and list of questions.

Lionel taught me long ago that the key to doing a good interview is to know the ground I want to cover so well that I don't get stuck reading my questions off a piece of paper. He taught me the importance of listening carefully to the answers so that I can adjust quickly and follow up on any unclear or unexpected statement.

I'd already gone over my questions so many times that my list of key words was there just in case I drew a blank.

I started with a bit of chitchat to establish rapport. "Thanks again for making time for this, sir. I really enjoyed meeting you at the dinner the other night."

"You're entirely welcome." Then he leaned forward and touched my hand gently with his delicate one. "I enjoyed meeting your friend at the dinner Saturday night. I'm sorry to hear he's missing. I saw the piece in today's Post."

"Thank you, sir."

A brief story about Doug's disappearance was in the Metro section of that morning's *Washington Post*, including a quote from me.

"Is there anything I can do to help?" Mann asked.

His question took me by surprise. I thought about the scourge of heroin. I considered that Ray Barber needed to be busted. But Mann was a busy guy, trying to keep the world from blowing up. The last thing he needed was for some grieving ninny like me to get him to bring some small-fry, two-bit drug dealer to justice.

"I'm touched by your gesture, sir. Thank you. I'm working with the D.C. police and I'm confident we'll find him."

"I hope it's nothing serious."

"It's *very* serious."

"Oh?"

"Heroin."

He winced and his face fell. "Oh dear."

"I already told the cops the name of the guy who might have sold him the heroin."

"Who is it?"

"Ray Barber. He runs a shoe repair shop by the bus barns."

"Well, I hope your friend turns up okay very soon. Don't lose hope." Mann patted my hand again.

"Thank you, sir."

"I'm ready when you are, Lark," Bethany said. "Pretend I'm not here, Mr. Mann," she said to the president's national security adviser.

I'd divided my interview into four parts: The nuts and bolts of the drone attack; the behind-the-scenes contact with Tong, focusing on the days twenty years earlier when Tong and Gannon had been Mann's students at Vanderbilt; the thorny national security issues that the current détente with China would involve; and the issue of drones.

I hoped I'd be able to squeeze in the "personal stuff" questions. I knew time would be an issue, so I decided to keep Mann engaged and talking even beyond the twenty-minute limit.

My first question was about the drone attack and its immediate aftermath, but when I saw that Mann's answers were going back over the same ground President Gannon had covered on Friday during his Oval Office interview with pool reporters, I quickly moved on.

"Take me back to those days at Vanderbilt when Tong Ji Hui and Will Gannon were in your class," I began. The question I'd composed was, "Did you have a sense that both of them would become great men?" But I modified it on the fly because it was essentially a leading yes/no question that would produce an expected answer.

Instead, I asked, "What were some of the qualities you saw in Tong and Gannon back then?"

Still, I wasn't thrilled with that question, either – a hunch confirmed when Mann talked glowingly about their "shared sense of moral integrity, indignity about injustice, and strong interpersonal skills."

I was getting a letter-of-recommendation answer, and chided myself for wasting my time – and Mann's – on softball questions producing answers that wouldn't make news.

I tried again. "A week ago today, you and President Gannon were about to unveil the administration's stance on the privatization of drones. Reports at the time indicated the president was about to unveil an Open Skies Initiative. Is that true?"

Mann smiled. "Whatever was about to be announced a week ago is being studied carefully now."

"Why?"

"In light of the drone attack on the White House, we're revisiting the entire issue."

"Does it now look like President Gannon is going to reverse his support for loosening restrictions?"

"We're discussing a wide range of options," Mann said. "I'll let the president announce his own decision when he's ready."

"And when might that be?"

"Soon," Mann smiled.

"How soon?"

"Soon."

"Days? Weeks? Months?"

"Sooner rather than later, but the specific timing is up to him."

I glanced at my iPhone to see if it was still recording – and to check the time. We'd been talking for fifteen minutes. So far, he'd barely made any news. I knew I'd be able to build something around the drone angle, but not much.

Mann's secretary popped her head into the room. "I don't mean to rush you, Ms. Chadwick, but, as you know, Nathan's a bit behind schedule. Do you think you can be done in five minutes?"

My heart sank. "Sure," I said. In that instant, a plan formed in my head. "I've got just a couple more quick questions."

The secretary left the room and I turned back to Mann. "As I was deciding what questions to ask you, I tried to find out more about you The Person, especially your family, but there's really not much out there that I could find. So, tell me: How did you meet your wife?"

I had a big smile on my face because, in my experience, politicians get tired of talking about public policy and love to have the opportunity to talk about their families.

I was surprised when Mann suddenly seemed to flinch, apparently not expecting the curve ball I'd just thrown him.

When he began to answer, the smile on his face was sardonic, not warm, or happy. "Joyce and I were high school sweethearts. Met her on the first day of school. She was in my homeroom. And, as they say, 'the rest is history.'"

I laughed. "Oh, not so fast," I said, my tone teasing. "Surely there's more to the story than that. Was it love at first sight? Did you have to woo her?"

A distant look came over him, as if remembering better days. "For *me* it was first sight. For her – not so much." He chuckled. "Really? Do you really want to go here when there are so many more important issues in the world?"

"Ah, but family is important, wouldn't you agree?"

"Yes. I suppose that's true."

"Tell me about your daughters."

"We try very hard to keep them out of the limelight."

"Sure. I understand. They're both in college now, right?"

"That's right."

I knew my next question was bordering on the inappropriate, but I decided to take a risk. "If they're only now of college age, then you and Joyce got started late in life having babies. If you don't mind my asking, why did you wait?"

His face darkened and he stiffened. "Actually, I *do* mind," he said sternly, "but I'll indulge you. There are two reasons: we were completing our own educations, plus Joyce had trouble conceiving. Now, if you'll excuse me–" He made a move to stand.

"Just one more quick one, sir. What's Dolph Rogan's role in the drone policy discussions you've been having with the president?"

Mann stood, a you're-dead-to-me look on his face. "No role. None whatsoever." He then gave Bethany and me perfunctory, dead-fish handshakes and dismissed us with a curt, "Ladies, a pleasure."

"Whoa. You really got under his skin," Bethany said to me as we walked away from Mann's office and down the black and white checkered tile hallway.

"I know," I said. "That was my plan. But now I'm beginning to wonder if it was such a smart one."

CB EO

CHAPTER 32

I got back to my desk about six p.m. after interviewing Nathan Mann. Paul had already gone home, so I had the place pretty much to myself. I sat down and began putting together a short 250-word story based on the interview I'd just done.

Not long after I'd gotten started writing, Elena Kerrigan called.

"I've got the missing person flyers," the detective told me. "Can I drop them off to you on my way home?"

"Sure." I gave her the address of the press office on Jackson Place. "Let me know if they don't let you through the gate on H Street and I'll come out to meet you."

"There've also been a couple new developments," she said. "I'll update you when I get there. Will you still be there around seven?"

"Yeah. I'm writing a story now. I should be just finishing it up when you get here. Can you give me a hint? Do I have good reason to continue to be hopeful?"

"Yes," Kerrigan said. "I strongly advise that you keep your hopes alive. I'll see you soon."

I dove back into writing my story with a renewed sense of exhilaration and optimism. I wrote a so-called "umbrella" lead that mentioned China and drones in the first graph, then expanded on each of those two points. It wasn't as "newsie" as I'd hoped when I'd first landed the interview on the heels of President Gannon's Oval Office interview with Paul and the rest of the pool.

Detective Kerrigan arrived just as I was putting the finishing touches on my story. I saw her pull up in front and got up to open the door for her.

"I'm just about done," I said, leading her back to my desk.

"So this is where all the magic happens?" Kerrigan asked, looking around.

I laughed. "It's where the sausage gets made."

I sat down at my computer and silently read through my story while Kerrigan sat across from me in Paul's chair.

Satisfied that my piece was as good as I could make it, I hit *send.*

"Boom!" I said.

"Done?" Kerrigan asked.

"Done. It's now filed with ELVIS."

"Elvis?"

I laughed. "It's the acronym for our newsroom software: ELVIS - Everyone Loves a Very Integrated System. It pulls everything together into one place – audio, video, pictures, text. An editor at our nerve center in New York will take it from here."

"Then what happens?"

"If New York has any questions or concerns, they'll get back to me. Otherwise, it should be on the wire within the next half hour."

"On the wire?"

"A.P. will publish it and it will then be available in newsrooms and mobile apps around the world."

"Amazing. How many people will see it?"

I shrugged. "Not sure exactly, but I've been told about half the world's population might see it, eventually – give or take a billion."

Her eyes widened. "Whoa! I'm impressed. It's a real high-wire act, but you seem to handle it in stride, Lark."

"You're right," I chuckled. "It's all an act."

Kerrigan laughed and handed me a sheaf of papers she'd been carrying. "Here are the missing person flyers."

It took my breath away to see Doug's face smiling back at me from near the top of the page. I had to fight my emotions before I could concentrate on what was written.

Centered above his picture, in bold red capital letters, were the words *MISSING PERSON*. Above that, in smaller all-caps lettering was the banner *METROPOLITAN POLICE DEPARTMENT – Washington, D.C.* To the right of Doug's impish grin were the basics:

Name:	DOUGLAS GRANT MITCHELL
Location:	CONNECTICUT & T STREETS N.W.
	WASHINGTON, DC 20009
Date/Time:	Saturday, February 19, 7:00 PM
Contact:	Detective Elena Kerrigan or Officer Sarah Johnson
	Command Information Center (202) 727-9099

"Who's Sarah Johnson?" I asked, pointing at the name next to Kerrigan's on the flyer.

"She's the woman in Missing Persons who's on maternity leave."

"So, you're a homicide detective and she's a missing persons officer. Does that mean you outrank her?"

"Something like that," Kerrigan said.

"You were telling me you have some new information about Doug?"

"I do. The most tangible thing is that a traffic camera took a picture of Doug's Jeep going north on Connecticut near Chevy Chase Circle about forty-five minutes after you last saw him at the Hilton."

"Does it show who's driving?"

"Unfortunately, no."

I frowned. "That means Doug's Wrangler might have been a crack rental by then."

"Could be, but that's a nice part of town. Crack rental carjackings are virtually nonexistent there. We're going on the assumption that Doug was driving."

"Anything else?"

"Still no activity on his bank account. And his car hasn't been impounded or ticketed."

"What about his cell?" I asked.

"Ah. His cell." Kerrigan took out a sheet of paper and handed it to me. "These are the numbers he was texting and/or calling right before and after the dinner. As you can see, the last two numbers were contacted about ten p.m."

"That's long after he told me he was going to the bathroom."

"The first number is a text."

"What did he write?"

"We don't have that information – just the number. Fifteen minutes later he placed a call to this number." She pointed at the sheet.

"Who do the numbers belong to?"

"Same person. The shoe repairman you told me about – Ray Barber."

"The alleged drug dealer."

"Yup."

"Have you been in contact with him?"

She shook her head. "Not yet." Her eyes had an unmistakable glint.

I picked up on it immediately and smiled impishly. "How about you take me to his store so I can ask him to put up one of these missing person flyers? You can be Becket – I'll be Castle." It was a reference I hoped she'd get to the cop show on TV in which a bestselling author rides along with a detective.

Kerrigan laughed. "I thought you'd never ask. And one more thing."

"What's that?"

"Ray Barber's shoe store is open tonight until eight."

I checked my watch: 7:20. "Let's go," I grinned.

ങ ജ

CHAPTER 33

It was just after 7:45 when Detective Becket, um, Detective *Kerrigan* and I pulled up to the curb in front of Ray's Shoe Repair on 14th at Buchanan a block south of the bus barns. A red neon sign in the window announced that Ray's was still open.

On the way over, Kerrigan and I discussed strategy. I got her to agree to let me do the talking first, but she got me to agree to remain calm, nonconfrontational, and to make it clear that my companion is a cop. That way, she said, Barber would be less likely to resort to violence. Plus, if he said anything incriminating, it had a better chance of being admissible in court.

I started to open the car door, then hesitated before getting out. Part of me was eager to eyeball Ray Barber, the man I was convinced sold Doug a dose of heroin that might have ended his life – and altered mine forever. Another part of me was nervous – afraid that Ray would turn violent once he realized he might be in serious trouble. And I also identified a healthy dose of rage deep within me – violent, unthinking rage that would push me to make him hurt and suffer as much as I had these past few days.

"You coming?" Kerrigan asked. She stood on the sidewalk in front of the entrance to Ray's store.

"Let's do this." I shouldered the car door open the rest of the way and stepped onto the sidewalk.

A bell over the weathered entrance to Ray's store tinkled as Kerrigan and I walked in. A handsome African-American man with close-cropped hair and gold wire rim glasses was at work behind the counter. An Oxford shoe was upside down in his hands and he was doing something to the sole.

"Hi," I said more brightly than I felt.

The man looked up. "Evenin'." He looked at the Rolex on his wrist. "You got here just in time. I'm about to close." He stood and smiled. "What can I do for you?"

"I'm Lark Chadwick and this is Detective Elena Kerrigan of the D.C. Metro Police Department."

Kerrigan showed him her badge.

The man didn't flinch.

"I'm wondering if it would be okay if we put up this missing person poster in your window." As I spoke, I slowly began to raise the sheaf of flyers I'd been carrying at my side.

"Sure. I suppose that would be–" The man stopped talking and froze when he saw Doug's picture on the flyer.

"Are you Ray Barber?" I asked.

"Yeah," he said softly, his eyes still glued to the picture.

"Do you know why I'm here?"

He looked at me. "Cuz you want to put up the poster?"

"Yes, but there's more. Do you recognize the man in the picture?"

Ray looked at it again, but started to regain his composure. "Yeah. He kinda looks familiar."

"When did you see him last?"

"I'm not sure I've *ever* seen him before. He just looks familiar." He reached below the counter.

I sensed Kerrigan stiffen.

Ray brought a dispenser of sticky tape into view and placed it on top of the counter. "You can use this to put up the poster."

"One more quick question, Mr. Barber, if you don't mind," I said, my voice even.

"Sure."

"When my friend Doug Mitchell went missing, he was trying to call someone. Any idea who that might have been?"

Ray shrugged and did his best to look impassive. "No."

"He was calling *you*, Mr. Barber. We think he was trying to buy heroin. Any idea why he'd be calling *you*?"

Ray Barber wiped a sudden accumulation of sweat from his upper lip, but remained calm and impassive. "Not in the slightest. Maybe he dialed a wrong number."

Elena Kerrigan spoke for the first time. "The call lasted six minutes, Mr. Barber. That's a pretty long conversation for a wrong number."

"When'd you say this was?" he asked, looking at the flyer.

"Saturday night," I said.

"Nope." He shook his head. "Wasn't me. I-I'd lost my phone Saturday afternoon. Must've been somebody else who answered."

"Do you have your phone now?" Kerrigan asked.

"Yeah. A customer picked it up by accident and brought it back yesterday."

"You were open on a Sunday?" Kerrigan asked.

"Sorry. This morning. She brought it back this morning."

"And who is this customer?" Kerrigan asked.

Ray shrugged. "I forget."

"Don't you keep records? A claim check?" Kerrigan said.

"She waited while I worked," he said. "Paid cash. Never saw her before – or since."

I was trembling with rage. Standing in front of me – this mild-mannered small businessman – was a heroin dealer. He *looks* innocent, but he peddles poison. If Kerrigan hadn't been with me, I probably would have said something belligerent – maybe even taken him by the front of his flannel shirt and gotten into his face. But a lot of good that would have done – other than making me feel good...probably for only a nanosecond.

Kerrigan intervened, saving me from doing anything impulsively counterproductive. "Okay, then," she said, cutting four strips of tape from the dispenser on the counter. "Thank you for your time, Mr. Barber. We'll put one of these up and get out of your way."

After we taped a flyer to the front window of Ray Barber's store, we got back into her car.

"So, are we gonna tail him?" I was so angry I was shaking.

Kerrigan laughed. "Too many cop shows, Lark." She put the car into gear and nosed into traffic.

"Seriously. Aren't we going to tail him?" I asked.

"*I'm* not. And I strongly recommend that *you* don't, either."

"W-why not?" I was incredulous.

"We'll keep an eye on him. And he knows it. He won't be selling any heroin for awhile. And, if he does: *boom!* We'll nail him."

"He won't be selling any more heroin for *awhile.* Meaning, he'll just lie low until he's sure you're not looking and then, *boom,* it'll be the drive-up window of McDonald's again." I was pissed.

"Not here it won't be." Kerrigan pointed at a gas station we were passing – the very same one Rochelle Grigsby showed me – the one where she and Doug had bought heroin from Ray a few months earlier. A police car with two cops inside was parked conspicuously on the pe-riphery – perhaps where Doug's Saturday night drug buy had gone down.

I was seething. "He'll just do business someplace else."

"Trust me, Lark. We're on this. Ray Barber is on our radar now – thanks to you."

I wanted to trust. Really and truly I did. But trust is a hard thing to muster when you've been lied to as much as I have over the years by cops, politicians – and even the man I love.

It was a glum ride home.

CI8 8OC

CHAPTER 34

"Home" for the week was Doug's apartment. It was nearly nine and I hadn't eaten yet, so after Detective Kerrigan dropped me off, I got into Pearlie and decided to get a bite to eat and then go looking for Doug.

I stopped at a Smoothie King off Connecticut near Dupont Circle so that I'd be able to sip and drive as I went north on Connecticut toward Chevy Chase Circle, near where Doug's Jeep was last spotted.

My plan was to go up and down the side streets near the circle to see if Doug's Jeep might be parked there. I looked at the map on my GPS and noticed that the area was just to the west of Rock Creek Park.

As I passed the Washington Hilton, I got a text. I'm paranoid about texting and driving, so I pulled over and read it.

It was from Lionel: *Got a few minutes to talk?*

He must have a sixth sense, I thought to myself. And, I realized, he's not calling presumptuously assuming that I'm available to talk at his whim. He's respecting my boundaries, asking, and giving me the option to respond when I'm ready. I was definitely ready to talk, but I didn't want to seem too eager, so I didn't answer right away. I decided to make him wait for it rather than encouraging him with instant gratification.

I pulled away from the curb and continued sipping and driving.

But, while stuck at a red light, I couldn't wait any longer. *Sure*, I texted. *Call whenev.* I didn't want to sound too eager.

Lionel called immediately.

"Hey," I said cheerfully as if nothing had happened between us. "How's it goin'?"

"It's goin'," he said grumpily. "But, more importantly, how's it goin' with you? Muriel and Paul tell me your boyfriend is missing."

"Yeah. I'm out looking for him now."

"You're driving around?"

"Uh huh."

"Look. Lark. I'm calling to apologize." He paused.

I held my tongue. He needed to say more than that.

He coughed uncomfortably. "Um, I was being a presumptuous ass. I didn't respect your boundaries." It sounded as though he was reading a cue card. "I was being a control freak." He paused again.

"Uh huh. Did you write this, or did Muriel?"

"Muriel. She's a better writer than I am."

"Nonsense. You've got a Pulitzer."

"Yeah, but she's better at this kind of touchy-feely stuff."

I chuckled. It was hard to stay mad at Lionel.

"But, if it's any consolation," he continued, "I believe every word of it. I really am sorry, Lark. I was wrong to get so controlling. I meant well, but I was blind to how you might be feeling. You're an adult and I need to treat you like one."

"Thank you, Lionel. Apology accepted."

"Whew."

"And I need to apologize, too," I said. "As usual, I was petulant and impulsive. I shouldn't have hung up on you. I'm sorry."

"Apology accepted. *Eagerly,*" he replied.

"I've missed you, Lionel," I said, trying as best I could to mask the powerful emotions welling up inside me.

"I miss you too, k–, um, Lark." His voice caught.

"So, how *have* you been?" I asked.

"Awful."

"Really? Why?"

"Because I didn't know if I'd ever talk with you again. You're like a daughter to me, and, well...you know..." His voice trailed off.

Holly. I knew.

"Well, you've been like a father to me, so we're even, I guess."

By this time, I'd gotten to Chevy Chase Circle. I took Western off to the right – the northwest border between D.C. on the right and Maryland on the left. The first right off Western was Quesada. I took that and then began going up and down the side streets, looking for Doug's familiar Jeep Wrangler.

Before long, Lionel and I were chattering like the old friends we are.

"How's Muriel?" I asked.

"She's fine. She enjoyed her talk with you the other day."

"And marriage counseling?"

"Yep. Still doing it. But it's hard to teach an old dog new tricks."

"Old dog meaning *you*, right?"

He laughed. "Oh yes. *Ancient* dog. But I really am learning to communicate better with her about my feelings and, more importantly, learning to listen as she tells me about hers."

"What have you learned the most about feelings?"

"You really should become a shrink, you know that, right?"

"I'm actually thinking about it."

"Really?"

"Just thinking. Too many irons in the fire right now. But back to you, Lionel. What are you learning about emotions?"

"I'm learning that I'm more emotionally nuanced than I thought. Anger has always been my emotional default. But it just builds walls and shuts me off to a wider range of other feelings. That's been a big surprise."

"How come?"

"I've always been suspicious of feelings because, as a journalist, it's my experience that emotions get in the way of rational, objective thought. I hate it when people say, 'Just follow your heart.'"

"Why?"

"Hell, if I just followed my heart, I'd be on death row for murder."

I laughed. "Good point."

"I'm finding that it's okay to feel, Lark. But the ideal is to be able to know *what* I'm feeling, and then to be able to articulate *why* I'm feeling it."

This was definitely a new Lionel and I found myself liking him even more than I loved the old Lionel.

As we talked, I steered Pearlie up and down the darkened residential streets of Quesada, Runnymede, Stephenson, past parked Jettas, Mazdas, and Beamers – and an occasional Jeep Wrangler. Talking with Lionel helped relieve the aimless boredom.

"But enough about me," he said abruptly. "What about *you?* The last time we talked, you'd just interviewed that drone guy. I never did see the piece, by the way."

"It got spiked."

"Really?"

"Yeah." I talked steadily for the next twenty minutes. Once I made it clear that we were in the Cone of Silence, I told him about my three a.m. meeting with Anne-Marie Gustofsen, her fear of Rogan, seeing his SUV after she got spooked and ran off, her disappearance, her allegation that Rogan was blackmailing Mann, and my frustration at not being able to prove it.

"And now, with Doug missing," I concluded, "I've been pulled in an entirely different direction. What do *you* think, Lionel?"

By this time I was heading west on Utah Street, winding my way back to Western. It had just begun to sleet.

"Have you checked with the cops about Gustofsen?" Lionel asked.

"Yup. Got the ball rolling on that Saturday night. I haven't heard back yet from the detective who's handling the case."

I stopped at a stop sign. Rittenhouse Street extended to my left and right. Thirtieth Street went diagonally off to the right. A vehicle parked under a streetlight about a dozen yards up the street caught my eye. I turned right onto 30th and pulled up behind it.

Lionel was talking, but I only caught a few words because my ears were buzzing.

The vehicle was a dark, possibly green, Jeep Wrangler. The license plate number was DK 4774.

Doug's.

I got out of Pearlie and, oblivious to the rain-snow mix dampening my hair, slowly walked toward the driver's door, like a cop making a traffic stop.

Lionel was still talking, but I was no longer listening.

I got to the driver's door and peered inside.

Slumped against the steering wheel was the body of a long-haired man wearing a white dress shirt.

The last thing I remember before passing out was futilely trying to open the locked door, screaming while beating on the window.

I also caught a glimpse of the sign attached to the light pole next to Doug's Jeep: *Warning: Neighborhood Watch Area.*

CS 80

CHAPTER 35

Tuesday morning at nine I was sitting, emotionally numb, in a claustrophobic waiting room at the medical examiner's office at 1910 Massachusetts Avenue in Southeast D.C. Detective Kerrigan sat next to me. I was there to officially identify Doug's body.

I was told that someone in the neighborhood of 30th and Rittenhouse had called 911 after hearing my screams and found me lying unconscious in the street next to Doug's Wrangler. I came to just as the first squad car arrived.

Even though I'd found the body and had a personal connection to it, the cops treated it as a crime scene – and me as a suspect. They strung yellow police tape across both ends of the street and had to struggle to back me away from the vehicle.

Because it was sleeting, they placed me in the rear seat of a police car as if I was under arrest, but when Detective Kerrigan arrived, she rescued me and let me sit in her car up front. She left me alone for a few minutes while she conferred with a handful of other cops gathered around the driver's side door of the Jeep.

"It's Doug, isn't it?" I asked when she got back into the car.

"We don't know yet. We have to wait for the medical examiner before we open the door to get a closer look."

"I'll be able to identify the body as soon as you do that," I said.

"I know, but our protocol doesn't allow for that. I have to keep you away from the Jeep. You'll be able to officially I.D. the body tomorrow at the morgue."

"That makes no sense," I fumed.

"I know."

"I insist on maintaining a vigil here until he's taken away."

"I understand. Okay."

But a few hours later, when they actually removed the body, a couple cops held up a tarp that blocked my view. Kerrigan had to hold me back from rushing to be by Doug's side.

Kerrigan was in and out of the car during my vigil. About midnight I placed a call to Rochelle Grigsby.

"It's Grigsby." She sounded groggy.

"It's Lark. I'm sorry to wake you."

Her voice softened for a change. "Hey. No problem. What's up?"

"The worst."

"Oh, God. They found him. Is he dead?"

"Uh huh."

She began to cry.

So did I.

After a couple minutes of mutual snuffling and wheezing, she said, "It goes without saying, but I'll say it: take tomorrow off – and the rest of the week, if you feel you need to."

"Thanks."

After getting off the phone with Grigsby, I used my cell to update the *Find Doug Mitchell* page on Facebook, which now had about five hundred followers:

The worst. I just found Doug's Jeep parked on a nice residential side street in Northwest D.C. next to a light pole containing a neighborhood watch sign. A dead body was slumped against the steering wheel. Detectives are on the scene now, but it won't be known for sure if it's Doug until tomorrow when I can officially identify the body at the morgue. Please pray.

I attached a picture I took of the Wrangler with cops and detectives clustered around it, then tweeted the link and posted it to my Facebook page – and Doug's. By the next morning, there was a short piece in the Metro section of the *Washington Post. Media Bistro* had an update on its Fishbowl webpage.

As Kerrigan and I sat quietly in the tomb-quiet office at the morgue, a middle-aged man with a friendly smile approached. He told me he was with the Wendt Center for Loss and Healing. He gave me a pamphlet about grief, then backed away.

I paged through it, but my eyes could barely focus.

"This is taking forever. When do I get to see the body?" I asked Kerrigan.

"You don't."

I was incredulous. "What? Why not? I can take it."

"They don't do it here like they do on cop shows."

"Stop with the cop shows."

"Sorry."

"So, what happens?"

"You have to make the I.D. by looking at a photo."

"A *picture?* Why?"

"It's just the way they do it here. Less traumatic, I guess."

This wasn't what I expected. I'd expected I'd have a chance once more to hold Doug's hand – maybe kiss it. But no. Not only was I robbed of Doug, I was about to be denied the opportunity to be with him in death. I suppose some people might think that's creepy, but at my core, I'm a realist. I have to see it to believe it. I wondered if a picture would be good enough.

It wasn't.

It felt like a long time before I actually saw Doug's death picture. First I had to fill out and sign several forms. I cried when I wrote down Doug's name. As I did, a crazy, unbidden thought darted into my mind – I attached my name to his: Lark Mitchell. It would never be, of course. Nor had I ever considered marrying him – our relationship was too fresh and new for my thinking to get that far along. But here I was, sitting in the morgue, imagining my name as his. Crazy.

Am I beginning to lose it?

Finally, it was time to look at the photo of Doug. A tall, lithe woman wearing a long white lab coat came into the room carrying what looked like a closed, thin photo album. She sat beside me and explained what would happen next.

"Your loved one's picture is inside here. You may open the cover whenever you're ready and look at it for as long as you wish. Once you're finished, and you're sure of the identity of the person pictured, I'll ask you to sign the appropriate document."

"How does he look?" I asked.

"At peace," the woman said, adding, "but you should realize that often a person who's dead doesn't look the same as when they were alive."

"Are there any visible injuries?"

She shook her head. "No."

Detective Kerrigan reached over and took my hand.

I took a deep breath, gave the closed cover a laser look, then slowly opened it.

The photo was a black and white glossy showing the left profile of a face. Everything else was shrouded by a white sheet. The eyes were closed. The hair was mussed, matted, and dirty.

It didn't look like Doug, but it didn't *not* look like him, either.

The mouth was closed, but the lower lip protruded slightly. That's how I knew for sure it was Doug – the lip. The lip he'd pressed lightly against mine the first time we'd kissed at a bar in Columbia, Georgia.

I kissed my finger, placed it on his lip – and wept.

I stared intently at the photo, wanting to sear the memory into my mind.

When I finally closed the album, Kerrigan put her arm around me and let me lean against her. As I sobbed, I was grateful that no one was rushing me and that I was treated by the morgue staff with so much dignity, respect, and sensitivity.

"Let's go," I said, finally.

In Kerrigan's car, while we were still parked outside the morgue, I made a speech.

"I'm only going to say this once," I said through gritted teeth as I dabbed at my eyes with a tissue, "so listen close. I *demand* that you arrest Ray Barber and charge him with murder."

"Lark–"

"*Wait!*" I turned and snarled at her, "I'm not done."

Kerrigan closed her mouth, folded her hands primly on her lap, and waited for me to finish.

"It's my solemn belief that whoever sells heroin to a person who overdoses and dies is guilty of murder. Maybe not first-degree murder, but at least manslaughter. To me, it's like selling a pistol with one bullet in the chamber to a person the seller knows is going to play Russian roulette – and doesn't give a shit. The heroin dealer is peddling poison. He might not *intend* to kill the buyer, but that could happen and they don't give a *fuck*."

I leaned back against the seat, spent.

"Now it's *my* turn," Kerrigan said. "I hear you about charging Ray with murder, but it's easier said than done."

"But–"

"Wait. You hear *me* out. I listened to you."

"Okay."

"In order to justify arresting Barber, I have to be able to prove in court – beyond a reasonable doubt – that Ray actually sold heroin to Doug."

I said, "I have a witness who was with Doug when he bought heroin from Barber in the past. And the last call Doug made was to Barber just before Doug died of a fatal overdose."

"That's not proof."

"Sure it is."

"No. It's not. It's *evidence*, but it's not *proof*."

I scowled and squinted my eyes at Kerrigan, but she wouldn't budge.

"Look. Lark. I would love nothing more than to bust Ray Barber – and *his* supplier – and send them both away for a very long time. But convicting Barber of murder is no slam dunk."

My scowl deepened.

"Right now, all I have is circumstantial evidence. I have to be able to put them at the same place at the same time as the drug deal. Or maybe get Barber to confess."

"Fat chance of either of those things happening," I grumped.

"You never know. I have my ways."

When I turned to look at Kerrigan, she was smiling.

ೞ ೦

CHAPTER 36

I followed Grigsby's advice and took the rest of the day off. I went to Doug's place, turned off my phone, poured myself a stiff drink, downed it fast, and went to bed. I slept all afternoon.

Around six, I turned on my phone and ordered a pizza. While asleep, I'd gotten a blizzard of texts and phone messages – all of condolence. So, as I waited for the pizza, I slowly scrolled through the texts and listened to the voicemails. But I didn't have the heart, or the energy, to answer any of them. I just wanted to be alone with my thoughts.

I got online. The outpouring of grief for Doug from our friends was touching, but I had no physical or emotional energy to respond to any of the social media messages, either. I was quickly discovering just how exhausting grief can be.

When the pizza arrived, I gave the delivery guy a generous tip, popped open a beer, and began eating – not heartily, but automatically because I knew I should keep up my strength.

I sat by the bay window and watched life go by. I still hoped it was all a mistake and Doug would drive up at any moment.

About seven-thirty my cell phone buzzed. I recognized the number as the White House switchboard because I call that number several times a day trying to track down information.

"This is Lark," I answered.

"Is this Lark Chadwick?" asked the voice of an official-sounding woman."

"It is."

"This is the White House operator. Standby please for a call from the president."

"Um, okayyyy..."

There was a click, a brief delay, another click and then President Gannon's familiar voice came on the line.

"Lark? It's Will Gannon."

"Good evening, Mr. President. What a surprise."

"I won't take much of your time, but I just wanted to let you know – actually, Rose and I *both* want you to know – just how sorry we are about the death of your dear friend Doug."

"Thank you, Mr. President. It's kind of you to call."

"I won't put you on the spot and ask you how you're doing, because I can only imagine how difficult this time is."

"Yes, but your call is certainly helping, sir. And, if I may ask, how's Rose?"

"It's nice of you to ask. In fact, she's right here and would like to speak with you, if you don't mind."

"That would be wonderful. Thank you, Mr. President."

There was a brief pause, then Rose got on the line.

"Hello, Lark."

"Hello, um . . ." I laughed self-consciously. "I don't know what to call you. Is it Madam First Lady?"

She laughed. "It's Rose. You call me Rose, Lark Chadwick." Her voice had a no-nonsense Lauren Bacall quality.

"Yes, ma'am."

"Will and I are both heartbroken for you, Lark. I can only imagine how hard this must be."

"Thank you. You're right, it is hard, but your call is so comforting. And how are *you?* You gave us all quite a scare the other night."

"Yes. I feel terrible about that. It ruined what had been such a wonderful evening."

"Are you feeling better now? Do they know what caused it?"

"I am feeling better, thank you. And they *do* know what caused it. In fact, I'm wondering if you'll let me speak with you confidentially."

"You mean off the record?"

"Yes."

"Well, I'm not entirely opposed to that, but I'm uncomfortable with it because it's gotten me in trouble before."

"Oh? How so?"

"The first time I went off the record, I was a rookie reporter. I got in trouble with Lionel Stone, my boss at the time, because I'd just been given a bombshell story that I couldn't use because I wasn't able to get independent confirmation that it was true. So, going off the record kind of puts me in handcuffs."

"Yes. I understand that. What if I give you permission to use the information and name me as the source, but I embargo the story for release at a later date? Embargoes are customary in journalism, isn't that right?"

"Yes."

"So, you'll agree to go off the record with me now and release the story at a later date?"

"What's the date? How long do I need to sit on the story?"

"Until..." She hesitated, then started over. "Actually, I can't tell you the release date until we're off the record."

"Why?"

"Because that's part of the story."

I laughed. "This is all very cloak and daggery. Let's back up. I suppose I shouldn't look a gift horse in the mouth – no offense – but why is it that you want to tell this story to *me?*"

She laughed. "Your sassiness is helping confirm exactly why I think you're the perfect person to talk with about this."

"Really?"

"Yes. I was impressed with you the day we met. Do you remember?"

"I do. It was in a sweltering convention center in Columbia, Georgia, last spring during the campaign."

"Right. And you asked my husband some very tough questions. Questions he wasn't able to answer very smoothly."

"And you consider that to be impressive? Thank you, but why?"

"Because most women fawn all over my husband. You didn't. After that short interview, I Googled you. I'm very impressed with your personal story. And your ability to write clearly. And your personal integrity. It's why I want to tell this story to *you*. I think I can trust you."

"That's very encouraging. Overwhelming, actually. You certainly have me intrigued."

"But do I have your word that you're willing to abide by my embargo?"

"Is there a date certain when the embargo will be lifted? I don't want to agree to an open-ended embargo."

"You sure are driving a hard bargain. I like that." Rose Gannon paused – to think, I assumed. "No," she said. "I can't promise a date *certain*, but I'm sure the embargo will be able to be lifted sooner rather than later."

"That's still kind of vague. Are we talking years?"

"No. More like weeks. A couple months at most."

"Okay, then. That doesn't seem unreasonable. Thank you for letting me haggle. And for understanding my hesitancy."

"Not at all. I respect that. So, do we have a deal?"

"Yes, but with the understanding that I'm still uncomfortable about the relatively open-ended embargo. I'd like the option of being able to renegotiate the release date once I have a better understanding of what the story is."

"Hold on for just a moment, Lark. I'm going to put you on hold while I run that by my husband."

"That's fine. I'll hold."

As I waited, I wondered and worried that I might have just outmaneuvered myself and that she was going to peddle her bombshell to CNN or the *New York Times*. But, before I had time to talk myself into total self-doubt, the first lady was back on the phone.

"Lark? Are you still there?"

"Yes, ma'am. I'm here."

"I ran it by Will and he's fine with your desire to revisit the release date later."

I was extremely relieved and tried to exhale as silently as I could. "That's great." I dug in my messenger bag and found a reporter's notebook. "I'm ready."

"I'd rather tell you in person," she said. "Would it be inconvenient for you to meet me now in the residence? I can send a car for you."

When the First Lady of the United States of America, after running the idea past her husband, the President of the United States of America, asks that you drop everything and go to her house – the White House – where she will then drop the biggest bombshell story of your career on you – even if you're grieving the loss of your boyfriend, you go.

Besides, I'd just be wallowing in self-pity, anyway.

"No problem," I heard myself say. I gave her Doug's address where I was, hung up, took the fastest shower I've ever taken in my life, and then chose something tasteful to wear to the White House.

ߢ ߤ

CHAPTER 37

It was about nine p.m. when the dark blue Chrysler shuttled me through the Southwest gate of the White House, up the curving drive, and deposited me at the south entrance. First Lady Rose Gannon, accompanied by a Secret Service agent, stepped outside, walked briskly to my door, and greeted me with a hug when I got out of the car.

She was extremely gracious, but I kept nursing the suspicion I was being love bombed – a technique cults use to groom converts so they're receptive to brainwashing indoctrination.

"I'm so glad you were able to come on such short notice, Lark. Thank you," she gushed, her breath turning into a white cloud and blowing away in the frigid breeze.

"You're welcome. Thank *you* for your vote of confidence."

She wasn't wearing a topcoat, so she was eager to get us inside and out of the cold. She thanked the driver by name, then took me by the arm and gently guided us through a double door.

It was like entering a museum. We walked through a small foyer and into a larger oval room with a fireplace on the right and a portrait of George Washington over it.

"This is called The Diplomatic Reception Room," she said. "It's where heads of state arrive – and other Very Important People." She flashed me a big smile.

We passed through the Diplomatic Reception Room and into a vaulted central hallway with plush, deep red carpets. The hall extended to our left and right to both ends of the building.

"Have you ever been inside the White House before, Lark?"

"Only the briefing room last week on the day of the drone attack and the Oval Office for just a couple of minutes just before the president made his joint address with the new president of China.

"Well, then. Let me give you a quick tour before we go upstairs to the residence."

"That would be wonderful. Thank you."

I'm sure I must've looked like a wide-eyed tourist as I walked with the first lady up a marble staircase to the main floor, my mouth agape at what I would call the tasteful opulence that is the Executive Mansion.

"John Adams was the first president to live here," Rose said as we entered the ornate East Room with its massive chandelier. The parquet floor gleamed.

When we walked into the Blue Room, Rose Gannon said, "The entire White House was gutted and renovated between 1950 and 1952."

"Why?" I asked.

"It was so rickety there was a serious concern it would literally implode. According to one story, President Truman was taking a bath upstairs," she pointed above a glittering and stately chandelier dangling from the ceiling, "while First Lady Bess Truman was having a tea down here for the Daughters of the American Revolution. The chandelier began to sway precariously. President Truman later joked that the entire tub could have fallen through the ceiling and onto the gathering, with him only wearing his reading glasses."

I joined her in laughing as I tried to imagine the scene.

Rose continued, "The Trumans lived across the street in Blair House during the renovations."

"Wasn't there an assassination attempt while the Trumans were living there?" I asked, then immediately regretted the indelicate question, remembering too late that assassination is not an abstraction to someone whose husband has just been in the crosshairs of a weaponized drone.

Rose didn't flinch. "That's right. Two Puerto Rican nationalists tried to shoot their way into Blair House in the fall of 1950. President Truman had been taking a nap, but was awakened by the gunfire and actually went to the second-floor window above the front steps and looked out to see what was going on. One of the gunmen was shot and killed by White House policeman Leslie Coffelt, who also died in the shootout."

"I shouldn't have brought that up," I said, "I'm sorry. I'm sure something awful like that is never far from your mind."

"That's alright. I'm a realist. Only now," she said ruefully, "the weapon of choice seems to be a drone, not a gun."

After we'd walked through all the downstairs rooms, shadowed discreetly by her Secret Service agent, we circled back to the elevator and went up to the private quarters of the president and first lady.

President Gannon was standing in front of the elevator when it opened.

"Hello, Lark. Welcome to the White House," he said, a big smile on his face.

I reached out my hand to shake his, but he gently pulled me into an embrace. "I hope you don't mind being hugged by a strange man," he laughed, "but I'm grateful for the opportunity to give you my condolences in person."

He was wearing a dark business suit, light blue shirt, and muted tie. He smelled of Old Spice. Physically the president is a big man with a barrel chest. Up close and in his arms, I felt completely engulfed by his masculinity. I could definitely see – and feel – how women are drawn to him.

The first time I'd seen him in person back in Georgia, I, too, had realized I was attracted to him. I'd never expected to meet him in person that day – any more than I'd expected to be hugged by him on this day, one of the lowest of my life.

Perhaps, because I was still so emotionally wrung out by the shock of finding Doug's body and then having to identify it that morning at the morgue, I was still a bit numb and distracted, and didn't fully appreciate this moment with the president.

The hug was brief and appropriate. But even in the midst of the numbness, I found myself powerfully moved by Will Gannon's warmth.

Gannon must have felt me shudder because he pulled back and gave me a concerned look.

"Are you okay?" he asked gently.

I nodded dumbly, barely able to speak. "It's been a rough couple of days," I managed to croak.

He reached out and rubbed the side of my shoulder. "Yes. I can only imagine." His voice was soft. He backed away and turned to Rose. "I'll leave you two alone now. It's good to see you, Lark."

"Thank you, Mr. President."

Gannon kissed his wife on the cheek, turned and entered the room at our end of the hallway through a large double door.

Rose took me by the elbow. "Let's sit at the far end in the East Sitting Room," she said.

I'd never even seen pictures of the second floor of the White House where the first family lives, so everything was new to me. I felt like I was in a swank hotel with a suite of rooms, not a home, but it was cozier than I expected. The high ceilings made it feel roomy, spacious.

"You'll get a kick out of this," Rose said as she opened a door on the right. "This is the famous Lincoln Bedroom." She stepped across the threshold and walked to the center of the room.

I stuck my head inside.

"Don't be shy. Come on in," she gestured, smiling.

I took a couple steps into the room then stopped to survey it. The room was sizeable and handsomely appointed with diamond-patterned wallpaper of dark brown and beige, lush gold curtains, two seating areas with Victorian furnishings, a white marble fireplace on the wall to my right, and a massive, ornate bed extending into the room from the east wall to my left.

"Is it mahogany?" I asked, pointing at the dark wood of the bed and its intricate carvings of grapevines and birds.

"Rosewood. It's not believed that President Lincoln ever slept in it, but he did have an office in here. Mary Todd Lincoln bought the bed and the Lincoln's son, Willie, died in it in 1862."

"That's so sad."

"Yes. He was only eleven."

Rose led me out the door and turned to her right. We entered a high-ceilinged room decorated in various shades of yellow and gold with a stunning fan window that took up almost the entire east wall at the far end. She directed me to sit on a cream-colored sofa that backed up against the window. I sat at the end and she chose to sit in a low-backed armchair adjacent to my end of the sofa.

She wore a deep purple dress with a high neckline and long sleeves. When she sat I was aware of her fabulous legs. She'd ballroom danced competitively when she was in college and, when I'd first seen her and her husband, they'd done an impromptu foxtrot at a campaign rally.

As soon as we sat down, an usher swept in unobtrusively, set a silver tray with a teapot and cups on the coffee table, poured the tea, and handed each of us a cup and saucer.

"Will there be anything else, ma'am?" he asked.

"No. Thank you, Stephen."

"To your health," I said, holding my teacup out to her.

"An interesting and ironic choice of words." She smiled ruefully and we clicked cups.

"Why is that?" I asked, taking a sip.

"Because it's my health that brings us together tonight. I'll give it to you straight, Lark. I have stage four pancreatic cancer. In just a few weeks, I'll be dead."

At that moment, I was leaning forward to set down my cup and saucer. The teacup clattered onto the coffee table.

ଓଃ ଃଠ

CHAPTER 38

"Oh, how clumsy of me," I said as the tea spilled onto the coffee table.

In a flash, Stephen, the usher, was in the room and dabbing up the spill. He then refilled my cup and withdrew.

Rose waited until we were alone before she spoke again. "Guess I was a little blunt, but there you have it: I'm dying."

"I'm stunned," I said. "And I'm *so* sorry." I reached for her hand, touching it gently, but ever so briefly.

"Thank you." There were tears in her eyes and she gripped a balled up napkin tightly in her hands. So tightly, her knuckles were white.

"Who else knows?" I asked, my hand at my mouth.

"My doctors, me, my husband, and now you."

"Not your children?"

"Oh my no. Not yet. They're still too young. We're taking it a day at a time, but the sicker I get, the harder it will be to hide it from them."

"How will you be able to hide it from the rest of the country?"

"I'll gradually cut back on my public duties. This is going to go very fast, Lark. We want to hold off as long as we can before going public. I don't want my illness to be a distraction to the important issues facing Will."

I felt I should be taking notes, but the information was so stunning it was already being indelibly engraved in my brain. The time would come for note taking, but I decided this wasn't it. Not yet.

"When you say it's going to go fast, what's supposed to happen?" I asked.

"The list is long: pain, lack of appetite, *pain*, puking, drastic weight loss, *pain*, drowsiness, short attention span, confusion, restlessness, *pain*. Those are the things I can remember off the top of my head. Oh! Did I mention pain?"

"Have you gotten a second opinion?"

She nodded. "And a third. Same prognosis each time."

Dumbstruck, I could only shake my head.

She sighed. "At this point, we've decided not to do chemo because chemo can be worse than the disease."

"When you say 'we've decided,' who's the 'we'?"

"My husband, my doctors, and me – but, in the end, it's my call."

"Can anything be done to delay the inevitable?"

"There are some drug therapies which could buy me some time, but only months, at best." She put her hand flat against her stomach and held it there. "Abdominal pain could become a big deal, so there are some treatments that deaden nerves."

I could barely speak. "How are you able to hold up so well under this devastating news?"

"That's a very good question, Lark. I'm wondering the same thing myself. But don't get me wrong. I've had a good cry, or two, plus I journal like a fiend – and that helps. I'm very self-aware and matter-of-fact about life – and death."

I rummaged around in my messenger bag for my phone and a notebook. "Forgive me. I need to come to my senses and get this written down."

"Before you do that," she said, "let's talk about the best way to proceed."

"Okay." I brought out my notebook and phone, but didn't start recording. I merely opened the notebook.

"I want you to help me write my autobiography," Rose said.

I shook my head. "I wouldn't be able to do that and still be working for a news organization. That would be a breach of journalistic ethics."

"Why?" She seemed genuinely surprised.

"It's a conflict of interest. As a journalist, I need to retain editorial control of the story."

Rose scowled. "But it's *my* story." She was beginning to sound a tad peeved.

"Yes. Absolutely. And there's certainly overlap between our two roles." I tried to choose my words carefully so that I could explain my position without alienating her in the process. "We agree that you have things you want to say, and I want to quote you accurately and share it with a wider audience. But, as a journalist, I also have to check out what you say with other sources to put your story in a wider context. And I need to be able to check out the veracity– um, the *accuracy* of your statements. It's a big undertaking."

"Do you think I'd lie to you?"

"I have no reason to believe you would lie, or are lying now. But there's an axiom in journalism: 'If your mother tells you she loves you, check it out.'"

She threw her head back and laughed, deep and throaty. "That's a good one. Hadn't heard that one before. I see what you mean." She turned serious. "So what do I do? I want to tell my story, but I'm not a writer."

"You still can tell your story. I see several options."

"Okay. I'm listening." She rested her right elbow on the arm of the chair, cupped her chin in her hand, and looked at me intensely.

"Here's what I suggest: Since you journal already, keep doing that. Do as much as you can now to write regularly to get down on paper the things you want to say. I'm sure that any publisher would jump at the chance to help mold it into a bestselling book."

As I spoke, the first lady pressed her thumb against her pursed lips as she took in what I was saying.

"In the meantime," I continued, "I could meet with you on a regular basis and interview you. The only difference is that *you'd* be writing an autobiography and *I'd* be writing a news story, and perhaps your biography. The books would be about the same subject – you – but there'd be a different emphasis."

Rose nodded. "I'd be writing – and talking to you – from the heart, saying all I want to say."

"Yes," I said. "My job would be harder. I'd have to corroborate the story and give it a wider perspective by interviewing people who know you."

"You could also quit your job and work directly for me," she said.

I laughed. "I suppose I could if I were independently wealthy."

"Actually, I *am*."

"I think I'm too feisty and independent to allow myself to be, um, constrained in what I'm allowed to pursue."

"Oh, you'd be free to check out my story in whatever way you choose."

I laughed again.

She looked at me, surprised. "What?"

"It reminds me of another axiom."

She smiled, expecting to laugh again.

"It's the golden rule," I said.

She chuckled. "This one I know: 'He who has the gold, makes the rules.'"

"Exactly. Where'd you hear that one?"

"Lee Sherman Dreyfus, the former Governor of Wisconsin. Will told me Dreyfus used to say it all the time."

"So you understand why I need to retain my editorial independence?" I asked.

"Yes. And what you suggest makes perfect sense. Sounds like a very workable compromise."

I was extremely relieved. I liked Rose Gannon. A *lot*. And I admired her, too. I sensed that we'd be able to work well with each other, yet I was grateful that I'd have access without ceding the freedom to follow the truth wherever it led.

I hit the *record* button on my iPhone memo app. "Now that we've got the nutsy-boltsy details out of the way, let me ask you a few questions now for my story. To be clear, we're on the record, but the story is embargoed for release."

"Okay," she said.

"And just so we're clear: the embargo will be lifted when you or the president give the green light, *or* if word somehow leaks out – or is about to leak out."

Rose pursed her lips again. "Not sure I'm comfortable with the 'about to leak out' clause. That seems kind of vague. How can you know if the story is about to leak?"

"I'm not sure, either, but I certainly don't want to be scooped. I'd like to be able to break the story. It's explosive and has wide-ranging geopolitical consequences."

"Geopolitical? Aren't you being a little dramatic?"

"Not really. It's obvious to me that the president loves you very much. Losing you will be an emotional body blow to him. Believe me. I know a little bit about grief. He's about to lose the love of his life, the person who knows him best, the person who is a profound and powerful source of his emotional and psychological stability. That's going to affect him *deeply*."

"Oh, you're being too kind, Lark. I think you're overemphasizing my impact on Will."

"Maybe, but I doubt it. The full force of this hasn't hit either of you yet. That's my guess. When it becomes known that you're dying, he'll be scrutinized like never before to see how he's holding up. Questions will be asked by friend *and* foe about how well he's doing his job. So, yes, the release of the story has *geopolitical* implications."

"All the more reason why I'm opposed to you doing a pre-emptive release just because you think you *might* be scooped. If you're wrong, you prematurely detonate an explosive distraction to his presidency."

I thought a moment. "Yes. Good point. Maybe there's a compromise in here somewhere."

She laughed. "Have you ever thought about running for office, Lark?"

I held up both of my index fingers in front of me in the sign of a cross as if to ward off a vampire. "Oh my *God* no!"

We both laughed.

"Here's what I propose," I said, my iPhone still recording. "If I come across credible evidence that another news organization has gotten wind of the story and is about to break it, then I will come to you and we can discuss what I will do. If, on the other hand, I'm scooped, I will then go public with the story *and* reveal that you and I have been having ongoing discussions."

She nodded slowly, apparently liking what she was hearing. "Okay. I think that will work. Even though you will have gotten 'scooped,' as you call it, you will still establish your credibility because it will be clear your information is coming directly from me."

"Right. Exactly."

"One more thing–" Rose began.

"Have *you* ever considered going into politics?" I teased, eyebrow raised.

She laughed and mimicked my anti-vampire cross. "Oh *God* no!"

As we were sharing a laugh over that, the door opened and President Gannon, now wearing faded jeans, a dark blue crewneck cashmere sweater, and moccasins walked in.

I shot to my feet.

He motioned for me to sit down. "Please. Lark. I'm off duty," he chuckled.

As I sat, I looked at Rose and asked, "Are presidents *ever* off duty?"

She grinned and slowly shook her head. "I wish."

"So, how are you two getting along?" the president asked.

"Fine, dear," Rose said. "I've dropped the bomb. We're now discussing the process."

"Any decisions?" He pulled up an easy chair and placed it next to the one Rose sat in.

"We've agreed that the conversations we'll be having will be embargoed for release at a time when you and I agree."

The president nodded as he listened to his wife.

Rose continued, "And Lark says that if she feels she's about to be scooped, she'll come to me and we'll talk about lifting the embargo."

The president turned to me. "Thank you for your trust, Lark. I'm glad Rose has found someone she feels comfortable talking with."

"You're welcome, Mr. President. And, if I may be so bold–"

He laughed. "Why stop *now?* I still have nightmares about our interview back in Columbia, Georgia, during the campaign. Go ahead. Be *bold.*"

"I'd like to ask you for two things: One – I hope you'll be able to join my conversations with the first lady from time to time as your schedule permits." I glanced at Rose Gannon and she nodded. "Two – after the first lady," I paused, groping for the appropriate word, "succumbs to her illness–"

"She means dies, Will," Rose said.

"Yes. God forbid – dies." I turned from Rose to the president. "Two – I'd like to do an on-the-record interview with you a month or so after Rose dies so that you can talk about how you're doing and what you're learning from the grief process."

President Gannon exhaled – an explosive sigh. "Boy, I don't even want to think about that now. But, yes. I'll join you two when I can and when," he turned to Rose, "when I'm welcome." He turned to me, "And I accept your kind invitation to talk, ah, afterward. But, I'll be honest, I'm not looking forward to that conversation."

Rose reached over to her husband with her left hand and took his right hand in hers. He brought her hand to his lips and kissed it. Their eyes locked in a glistening gaze.

α β

CHAPTER 39

Before I left the private quarters of the president and first lady Tuesday night, Rose and I agreed to meet again late the next afternoon. And she suggested that the president take a couple of pictures of us with my iPhone.

He snapped one of Rose talking with me and another of the two of us looking and smiling at the camera. Then I took a selfie of the three of us.

Rose thanked me profusely for my willingness to meet with her at a time of such pain in my own personal life. She added, "Your friend Doug was a photographer, wasn't he, Lark?"

"That's right."

"Maybe you should consider taking up photography as a hobby. It can be your way of keeping his memory alive."

"That's an excellent idea," I replied. "I think I will."

The same car and driver who brought me to the White House drove me "home" again to Doug's apartment. I hadn't, yet, been able to bring myself to leave it behind and go back to my Silver Spring place.

It was after eleven o'clock when I got to Doug's. The place felt acutely empty without him. I wanted to tell him all about the events of the day. So I did. And something tells me he was listening.

Even though it had been a long, emotionally grueling day, I was wired after my time with Rose Gannon and the president. Before I went to bed, I wrote up an account of the meeting while everything was still fresh in my mind. I knew that I couldn't afford to get behind in my note taking because soon I'd be buried in a blizzard of information as Rose and I began our talks.

I also needed to come up with a way to stay organized. I decided to keep a daily journal of our conversations. In addition, I resolved to faithfully transfer the recording of every interview promptly into my laptop so that'd I'd have a backup in case my iPhone ran out of storage space, or – God forbid – I lost it.

I felt it was too soon to decide if I'd undertake writing Rose Gannon's biography. I could cross that bridge later. For now, I decided, I'd concentrate on our interviews.

Because it was late, I didn't want to awaken Rochelle Grigsby, so I sent her an email to let her know I was going to follow her suggestion to take the rest of the week off.

I debated whether or not to alert Grigsby and my other superiors at A.P. that I would be conducting a series of interviews with the first lady. It was close to midnight, so I decided to put off that decision until my head was clearer.

I'm not a sleeping-pill person – I've heard too many stories of people becoming dependent on pills – but, for emergencies, I always have a bottle of Melatonin with me because it's natural and non-addictive. Doug's death qualified as an emergency. I popped a Melatonin and fell asleep easily.

I had a vividly erotic dream about Doug. I'm shy and squeamish about sharing the details of something so personal, so let's just say it was orgasmic. I woke up crying Wednesday morning. The hollowness I felt after losing Doug made me ache inside.

Grateful for the decompression time I had, I poured myself some orange juice and had a couple pieces of toast. I sat sipping, munching and, from time to time, weeping by the bay window of Doug's living room looking out at Florida Avenue, but seeing nothing. The world went on spinning as everyone else kept living their lives while mine stood still. At least for the moment.

About ten o'clock, I placed a call to Elena Kerrigan.

"I was just about to call you," the detective said.

"Have there been new developments?" I asked.

"Yes and no."

"Ohhh kayyyy."

"Which do you want first, Lark, the yes or the no?

"The no. It gives me something to look forward to."

She chuckled. "We brought Ray Barber in for questioning yester-day."

"You consider that *not* a new development?"

"It is, I guess, but the bad news is that he's got an alibi for the time when Doug was missing. We can't put the two of them at the same place at the same time."

I swore.

"It doesn't mean Ray wasn't the dealer," Kerrigan continued. "He could have used a low-level runner to make the transaction, but so far we can't prove that. But, on the positive side, as I think I mentioned before, we didn't know about Ray at all until you brought him to our attention. Now he's on our radar – and he knows it."

"How would you describe his demeanor when you brought him in?" I asked.

"He's a smooth one, but we put the squeeze on him. Made him squirm."

"Did he have a lawyer with him?"

"No. He came willingly."

"Risky."

"Yeah, unless you know you're innocent, or you know you're insulated and safe."

"What's his alibi?"

"His wife says he was at home in bed with her."

"Yeah. Right."

"I know."

"So, what's the *new* development?" I asked.

"It's unrelated to Doug's death, but remember that person you told me about who went missing after you met secretly with her in Rosslyn?"

"Anne-Marie Gustofsen?"

"Right. She's turned up."

"Is she okay?" I felt a surge of hope.

"Not any more. Her body was fished out of the Potomac south of Chain Bridge on Friday. Her death's been ruled a suicide."

I felt like I'd been sucker-punched in the stomach.

How much more death do I have to endure? I asked the Universe.

"Why a suicide?" I asked Kerrigan.

"Gustofsen had big, heavy rocks stuffed into her overcoat pockets. She drowned. There were no visible injuries on her body."

"How long had she been dead?"

"Six hours or so. Maybe twelve."

"Could she have been poisoned and then her body dumped?"

"The only drug in her system was an over-the-counter sleep aid. The coroner apparently didn't consider that to be poisonous or suspicious."

"Was alcohol in her system?"

"A trace amount. She wasn't intoxicated."

"But Dolph Rogan could've slipped something into that flask Doug saw in Rogan's hand when he picked up Gustofsen. The spiked drink could've put her to sleep. Then Rogan could've put rocks in her pockets before dumping her."

"That's certainly plausible, but you'll need to take it up with the sheriff of Fairfax County, Virginia. It's his jurisdiction."

"Okay."

"Have you decided what you want to do about Doug's body?" Kerrigan asked.

Her question caught me off guard and was another body blow. "I didn't know I had to."

"He's got no known living relatives. So, either his body will be released to you, or to a funeral home of your choosing, or the city will have him cremated and buried in a pauper's grave."

"Wow. I hadn't even thought about that."

"How do you want to proceed?"

"Lemme think." I gnawed at a cuticle. "How about you have him cremated and released to me. Then, if I decide to have some kind of memorial service, I can decide on that later."

"Okay. You'll be getting a bill from the District for the cremation, but it'll probably only be a couple hundred bucks."

"Will I be able to see him again?"

"Only if he's released to a funeral home prior to cremation, but that starts to get pricey."

"How pricey?"

"Thousands. At least a few."

"Ugh."

While I was still absorbing that news, Kerrigan went on: "If it's any consolation – and it probably isn't – you can formally request a copy of the photo of Doug you saw at the morgue, but my guess is you already have pictures of him taken in happier times."

"Yes. I have some. I certainly can't afford to go the funeral home route."

All of a sudden I felt exhausted, weighted down and overwhelmed by pesky details I hadn't anticipated.

I thanked Detective Kerrigan and gave her the go-ahead to have Doug's remains cremated. Then, even though it was the middle of the day, I went upstairs, crawled into Doug's bed, and cried myself to sleep.

03 80

CHAPTER 40

The buzzing of my phone awakened me about three in the after-noon. It was Lionel. The call went to voicemail before I could pick up, so I phoned him right back.

"Hey," he said. "I was just about to leave you a message."

"I'm sorry I haven't called, Lionel. Things have been crazy."

"I know. Paul's been keeping us in the loop."

"What's up?"

"Muriel and I just got to town."

"You're in D.C.?"

"Uh huh."

"That's great. It'll be so good to see you and Muriel again." I tried to choke back the tears, but was having no success. "I-I..." I tried to say more, but couldn't.

"Don't try to talk. I know this is a tough time. We just wanted to be here for you."

"Where are you staying?"

"We're at a hotel near the Capitol, The Liaison. Paul's got a dinky place on Capitol Hill, so we found someplace nice near him."

"How long will you be in town?"

"Dunno yet. We're playing it by ear."

"We need to get together."

"Ya think?"

I laughed.

"It's good to hear you laugh," Lionel said.

"I need to, but it's not easy."

"How 'bout dinner tonight? You, Paul, Muriel, and me. Is eight good?"

I looked at my watch. "Yikes! It's three-ten. Good thing you called because I forgot to set my alarm."

The White House car was going to pick me up at four and I still needed to take a shower.

"Eight *might* work, Lionel. Not sure when I'll be done tonight. Can I give you a definite 'maybe' for now, then check back about seven-thirty?"

"Yeah. That should be good."

We agreed I'd text him later with an update, then we hung up and I jumped into the shower. Usually, I try to savor my time under the soothing running water, but this wasn't one of those times.

I was ready just as the White House Chrysler pulled up out front.

When it comes to interviews, I'm a master planner, but today I felt like an idiot, winging it going into my first in-depth interview with Rose Gannon.

Once again, she met the car when it pulled to a stop on the south driveway beneath the Truman Balcony, an entrance out of sight from the press corps.

Her hair was in a ponytail and she wore a gray sweat suit – definitely nothing fancy. I felt overdressed, but comfortable.

Now that I knew Rose Gannon was dying, I looked closer than usual at her, but she seemed the picture of good health as she greeted me warmly with a hug then hustled me inside and up the elevator to the room where we'd sat the night before. This time, President Gannon was nowhere around.

I'd checked the A.P. wire on my iPhone app on the way over. Gannon's poll numbers were sky-high following the rapprochement with China. His Gallup Poll approval rating was 71% – stratospheric, plus he was still in the honeymoon phase that all presidents seem to enjoy, at least for their first hundred days, or so. There was talk about a U.S.-China summit, but both presidents said they wanted first to methodically lay the groundwork for talks rather than simply go forward on the basis of euphoria alone.

A trial date had been set six months from now for Joseph Fan, the Air Force officer accused of piloting the drone that attacked and destroyed the briefing room. Renovations were well under way, but weren't going to be completed for another six to nine months, "and maybe more," according to Ron McClain in today's briefing.

Normally, I'd be thrilled with the exclusive conversations I'd be having with the first lady – and perhaps the president, as well – but grief is exhausting and I found myself constantly distracted and brought low by Doug's death – and the trauma of being the one to find his body. If it weren't for the distraction of the Rose Gannon project, I'd probably be staring slack-jawed out the bay window of Doug's apartment, or lying in the fetal position bawling.

Rose must have sensed my inner turmoil. She quickly turned the spotlight onto me.

"Thank you again, Lark, for meeting with me, especially at a time that must be so difficult for you. How are you holding up?"

"I'm doing the best I can, but it's not easy. Frankly, I'm grateful for the opportunity to work with you. It reminds me that even though grief is personal and feels unique, I realize so many other people – including you and the president – have much pain of their own to bear."

She nodded knowingly. "Shall we begin?"

"Yes." I got out my notebook and my iPhone and began recording.

"I've been journaling for a big chunk of the day, so I think I'm pretty focused," she said.

"What kind of ground did you cover? Did you get any insights?"

We talked – or I should say *she* talked – steadily for the next three hours.

"There's nothing like one's own impending death to focus the mind," she began, "so that's what I wrote about first this morning."

"Any conclusions? Insights?"

She leaned back, crossed her hands behind her head and looked at the ceiling. "I realized two things: I don't want to die, but I've had a good life."

"In your writing, did you find yourself speculating about what comes next?"

She shook her head slowly. "No. Not yet. That will come later. For now, I find myself looking back. Remembering. Assessing."

"Assessing. What's your preliminary assessment?"

She flashed a far off smile. "That I've done pretty well. No major regrets. But I suppose that's to be expected."

"But so many people *do* have regrets. Why not you, too?"

"Ah, Lark. You ask such good questions. Did you ever consider going into psychology?"

"Actually, I have."

She sat up and leaned toward me. "Really?"

"Yes, but this conversation isn't about me, it's about *you*."

She chuckled. "I keep forgetting."

"Now lean back," I said, in a mock Freudian accent. "Relax. Tell me *everything*."

She laughed again. "I'll have to think more about *why* I don't have more regrets, so let's hold that for next time."

"Okay. Let's turn to remembering. Looking back on your life, what memories stand out?"

"My children and my husband."

"In that order?"

"Apparently." She gave me a look. "You're good, Lark."

I blushed. "Thank you. But I'm really just a backboard. You hit the tennis ball and it bounces off the wall and returns to you. Or maybe I'm a mirror. You look at me, but it's your image that reflects back."

"Yes. Good analogies."

"Your children and *then* your husband," I prompted. "Explain. Use both sides of the page, if necessary," I grinned.

She flashed me an amused smile. "I guess I list Grace and Thomas first because as tiny, helpless beings – at least at first – they required *constant* attention. Will, of course, was thrilled when Grace was born, but he became a little disconcerted by the new family tableaux."

"Tableaux?"

"Yes. Think of the picture this way: At first, husband and wife are facing each other." She held up her hands in front of her, palms facing each other. "But when Grace came along, my attention was diverted to her. It was as if I'd turned my back on Will." She swiveled one of her hands so that its back faced the other hand's palm.

"Turning your back. Are those the words he used to describe how he felt about the new dynamic?"

"Not exactly, but he moped a bit because I wasn't paying as much attention to him any more."

"Did he get over it?"

She nodded vigorously. "He did – once I set him straight."

I chuckled. "What did you say?"

"I said, 'Look here, Mister' – or words to that effect. 'This little baby is totally helpless. She needs me. You're a big boy. You can take care of yourself.'"

"He got it?"

She snapped her fingers. "Instantly."

"When was this?"

"Let's see. Grace was born eight years ago, so it would be just before his first campaign for governor. I was thirty. Will was pushing forty."

"How old were you when you got married?"

"Twenty-eight."

"Many young women at that age are fretting about their biological clock, worrying that if they don't marry soon, it'll be too late to have children. Did that concern you, too?"

"Not really."

"Why not?"

"As I've said before – and as perhaps you'll see throughout our conversations – I'm a realist. Like many women, I looked forward to *possibly* having children. But I didn't want a man as merely a means to that end. If I did, then I'd just be marrying a sperm donor.

"In my gut I knew that before I could seriously think about having children, I first had to find a good man. And, if I couldn't, then I'd either be single for a very long time – perhaps forever – or, if still single and in my forties, then probably childless – and I'd have to be okay with that."

As she talked, I checked my iPhone. It was still recording. I made quick scribbles in my notebook of topics I wanted to explore based on what Rose was saying. I jotted down the words *dating* and *mom* and *meeting Will* as memory prompts.

"You're raising lots of questions and topics I want to get into – your relationship with your mother, and how you and Will met and decided to marry – but first I want to explore something you just brought up."

"This is better than therapy," she laughed giddily. "I *love* this. Thank you, Lark. You're such a good interviewer."

Again, I blushed. "Thank you. I learned from the best."

"Lionel Stone?"

I nodded. "Let's go back to your thinking about children *before* you became a mother."

"Okay."

"This is a shot in the dark, but I'll give it a try anyway. One thing I've noticed about people is that they often allow their heart to get out of alignment with their head. They let their feelings rule. You don't seem to be like that. Why not?"

She nodded vigorously as I was asking my question and couldn't seem to wait to begin answering.

"You are *absolutely* correct. And thank you for the opportunity to try to put my thinking into words because I've thought about this very thing a *lot.* Here's what I think: Feelings are very powerful. But they're fickle. They exaggerate and they contradict. They're like waves in a stormy sea. And we often feel as if we're at their mercy."

As I listened, I realized she could be describing me.

"So, how did you learn to tame your emotions?" I asked.

"Oh, I don't think I have. It's not that I believe emotions are bad. They're wonderful. They add spice and depth to the human experience."

"But?"

"But there comes a time when the head needs to intervene."

"And when is that?"

"That involves some discernment. I think women, especially, understand how healthy it is to give in to our emotions and just have a good cry. I don't know about you, but I feel great after I've cried."

I nodded.

"It's like I've opened a safety valve and allowed the build-up of emotional energy to be siphoned off," Rose said. "It's very cleansing, at least for me."

"So what role does the head play?"

"Ah. The head. That's where journaling works for me. I think I was ten when I started to journal seriously. That's where I examine – with my head – the emotions I'm feeling. I try to figure out *why* I'm feeling a certain way. And then, I try to determine if I need to change the way I'm behaving."

"Why? What's the connection between behavior and feelings?"

"I'll give you an example from my life. I was twenty-six when I met Will – and we'll go into that later."

"And he was thirty-six?"

"Yes. I've never had any doubt at all about my love for Will. But not long after we married, I – for lack of a better way to describe it – fell in love with one of his . . ." she paused, seeming to choose the next word with extreme care, "...friends."

"Who?"

She waved me off. "The who isn't important. What's important is the head-heart balance we're talking about. Here's my point: I loved my husband, but then I met someone who I was also attracted to and came to love, as well. Big dilemma."

"How did you handle it?"

"I journaled about it. The man was a mutual friend. He was considerably older and I was entirely enthralled by him."

"How did you keep your behavior in check – or did you?"

"I did keep it in check. I suppose a lot of people have affairs. But we didn't. Based on my journaling, I think the reason we didn't have an affair is because I realized that no one person – not even a husband – would be able to meet all my needs.

"But, as I thought about it, I also realized that while many people have an affair – and then become miserable and guilt-ridden – there was a better way. He and I chose friendship, instead. An out-in-the-open friendship.

"We could talk about so many things on so many levels. But my head kept my behavior in check and, once I found myself resisting the temptation to have a fling, gradually my feelings fell in line. That's the relationship between feelings and behavior. Making the right choices brought the feelings into line."

"Did Will know?"

"He knew I was attracted to the guy – and vice versa – but Will trusted me."

"That's hard to believe. Wasn't he jealous?"

"Maybe a little. Will knows that I adore this person, but he's also come to realize that I've never allowed myself to act on my emotions. And neither did our friend."

"But it takes two to get into trouble – or to stay out of it. How was this other person also able to toe the line?"

She laughed. "The short answer is guilt. He's a devout Roman Catholic. So, we've been able to maintain an appropriate, above-board friendship all these years."

I took a risk. "I know your husband's bio pretty well. Could the person you're describing be Nathan Mann?"

Suddenly, Rose looked stricken. She didn't say anything, but blushed a deep crimson.

☙ ❧

CHAPTER 41

Later that evening I sat with Lionel, Muriel, and Paul in the restaurant of the Liaison Hotel near the Capitol. Everyone was laughing at something Lionel had just said, but I realized my mind had been drifting. It was their laughter that suddenly brought me back to the present.

I joined in the laughter, but late. I could tell that Lionel sensed something was wrong. And, indeed, something was.

"You two run along ahead," Lionel said to his wife and son. "Lark and I are going to have a catch-up nightcap." He signed the credit card receipt and Paul and Muriel bade me a goodnight.

After they left, Lionel leaned across the table and said, "Look. I know I'm being presumptuous, but I can tell you've not only got a lot of pain, but something's eating at you. Feel free to pass up my offer of a nightcap, but I'm willing to listen, if you're willing to talk."

"Let's talk."

"Good."

"Do you want a change of scenery, or should we stay here?" he asked.

"I'm comfortable here. How 'bout I get the first round?"

"Or we could split a bottle of wine – in the long run, it's cheaper than by the glass."

I checked my watch: 9:50 p.m. "I don't have to be up early tomorrow, but I'm not sure I can handle half the bottle."

"That's okay. I'm a charter member of The Clean Plate Club, so I'll tackle whatever's left over. White or red?" Lionel asked me when the waiter came to pick up the check.

"Red. Maybe a Cab?"

"Works for me." Lionel pointed to the wine list and said to the waiter, "A bottle of this, please."

"Yes, sir."

"Okay," Lionel said to me after the waiter had retreated, "Talk to me."

I put both hands to my face and took a deep breath to collect my thoughts. "First, thank you for being here. I really need to think things through. I've missed having you as a sounding board."

"Especially because I never sound bored?"

I laughed. "*Especially* that."

"Is it Doug?"

"Yes. But it's *way* more than that."

"Where do you want to start?"

For the next half hour, between sips and sobs, I brought Lionel up to date on all that was vexing me – from Anne-Marie's tips to look more closely at Dolph Rogan and his relationship to Nathan Mann, to Anne-Marie's death – and Doug's.

After I'd finished, Lionel asked, "Do you think Rogan had Doug bumped off?"

"I really don't think so. I think Doug's death is separate from Rogan."

"Why?"

"By all indications, it's simply an all-too-common heroin overdose. *I'm* probably more at risk of getting bumped off by Rogan than Doug was."

"But Doug was with you when you interviewed Rogan and he gave you the drone demonstration, so, as far as Anne-Marie's killer is concerned – and let's assume for the moment Rogan killed Gustofsen, or had her killed – Doug would know what you know about the Rogan-Mann blackmail."

I thought a moment about what he was saying and slowly shook my head. "Geez, Lionel, I don't see it. I'm not saying you're wrong, but it just doesn't feel connected to Rogan. I respect your insights, though, so I'm willing to keep an open mind about it."

We both took simultaneous sips of our wine. As I did, I debated how much, if anything, about my talks with Rose Gannon I should reveal to Lionel.

"However..." I said coyly.

"Uh oh. There's more?"

I nodded.

"What's his name?"

I scowled and squinted at him menacingly.

"Okay. Too soon. I get it."

"There's one other thing that happened earlier this evening that I need your take on."

"Shoot."

"We're in the Cone of Silence, right?"

"Always."

"I was talking with Rose Gannon today."

His eyes widened. "Name dropper."

I smiled.

"I'll bite. How is it that you just happened to be talking with the First Lady of the United States of America?"

"She likes me."

"Uh huh." He was skeptical.

"I've managed to land a series of in-depth interviews with Rose–"

"Oh. So now you're on a first-name basis with her?"

"Actually, yeah."

He scowled.

"I know what you're thinking," I said.

"What am I thinking?"

"You're afraid–"

"I'm not afraid of *any*thing. Or any*one*. Although there is one person I'm afraid to turn my back to." Lionel smiled playfully.

"Oh? Who?" I took a sip.

"A proctologist."

I nearly snorted my wine.

"Okay," I said when I'd regained my composure. "You're *concerned.*"

"Better word."

"You're concerned that I'm getting too chummy with Rose Gannon and that I'm in danger of losing my objectivity."

"You're right. I am concerned. But go on. What's the nature of your conversations?"

"Right now I'm not allowed to reveal the reason why we're talking."

"Even to me?"

"To anyone."

"Even your editor?"

"I haven't thought that one through yet."

He scowled again.

"Let's set aside the reason Rose, um, Rose *Gannon* and I are talking because it's something she said that's eating at me."

"Go on."

"Remember I mentioned that Dolph Rogan is allegedly blackmailing Nathan Mann about something?"

"Right, but you don't know what."

"Tonight Rose revealed that she has a connection with Mann that's deeper than I thought."

Lionel leaned in closer and whispered, "Is she having an affair with Mann?"

I shook my head. "But Rogan might think so. Maybe he's trying to control Mann by holding even the appearance of an affair over his head."

"Yeah. That makes sense. So, what're you going to do?"

"What would *you* do?" I asked.

"Well, as salacious as it sounds, I'm not sure there's really a story there."

"Why not?"

"She's not an office-holder, therefore, she's not accountable in the same way the president is. As you know, when I was covering the

White House when Kennedy was president, we knew he was messing around, but we mostly looked the other way. That is until we got wind that he might be cavorting with a mobster's girlfriend and an East German spy. That got our attention, but his assassination rendered our investigation moot."

"But times have changed and something like that would be big news now – and justifiably so, right?"

"Maybe yes, maybe no. I'm old school. As far as I'm concerned, it's a story only if there's a public policy angle. If someone's just getting something on the side, I don't think that's strong enough for a reputable news organization to care about."

"So, if a public official is lying to his wife, you don't consider that to be a character flaw that could result in him also lying to the public?"

Lionel scowled and took a drink – his way of losing the argument without having to admit it.

I pressed my case. "But, as far as the Rose Gannon-Nathan Mann relationship is concerned, doesn't that rise to the level of a public policy issue if Mann is being blackmailed so that Rogan influences the president's decision-making?"

Lionel nodded slowly. "Yes. But you need to make the link."

"Maybe Rose Gannon is my link."

"How so?"

I began to gnaw my cuticle. "Not sure."

"It seems to me," Lionel said, "the link is to show that somehow Rogan's hold on Mann is so strong that Rogan's able to use Mann to get to the president."

I thought for a moment and took a sip, trying to find a hole in Lionel's reasoning. "But even if the president decides to forcefully back an open skies initiative that gives free rein to the commercialization of drones, that doesn't mean that the president arrived at his decision through Rogan's coercion."

"You're right. But that's not the point."

"What *is* the point?"

"You already know."

I snapped my fingers. "The point is not that Rogan *succeeded* in changing the president's mind, it's that he blackmailed one of his top officials to *try* to influence a presidential decision."

"Bingo."

"So I'm back where I started – trying to figure out what it is Rogan has on Mann."

"Enter Rose Gannon," Lionel smiled.

"Indeed. But will she tell me? For that matter, does she even *know* about Rogan's blackmail attempt?"

Lionel shrugged. "Ya got me."

"But..." I was thinking out loud.

"But what?" Lionel prodded.

"But if Rogan thinks Anne-Marie spilled the beans to me, then maybe I'm next on his list."

"When did she die?"

"Friday."

Lionel counted on his fingers. "Saturday, Sunday, Monday, Tuesday, Wednesday. Five days. That's a long time to wait before making a move against you."

"Maybe he's waiting to see what happens."

"Nah. If he's that desperate, then he can't afford to wait. Has anyone been following you?"

"Not that I know of, but you're making me more paranoid than I already was."

"Maybe he's just waiting for the right opportunity."

"Or maybe Anne-Marie really did kill herself."

"Or not," Lionel grinned.

I didn't.

CB BO

CHAPTER 42

It was after eleven when Lionel and I finished talking. I'd come directly from my interview with Rose to the restaurant in the White House Chrysler, so I ordered an Uber and was back at Doug's place before midnight.

As I walked up the steps and fumbled for the house key, the tune from Gilbert O'Sullivan's "Alone Again (Naturally)" began playing unbidden in my head.

My legs got increasingly leaden with every step until all I could do when I got inside was to plop down in the chair by the bay window and stare outside without even bothering to turn on the lights.

Maybe it was all the wine I'd had at dinner, and then afterward with Lionel, but I suddenly felt incredibly morose. All the losses I'd endured over the past several years came washing over me like a psychological tsunami.

The string of losses began with Annie, the aunt who was mother and sister combined in my formative and young adult years. Finding her dead on the floor of carbon monoxide poisoning was a trauma I still hadn't gotten over, much less processed.

And then there was Jason. Kind, gentle Jason. He was a television reporter in Madison, Wisconsin when I worked for Lionel at his paper in nearby Pine Bluff. I touched my lips, remembering when Jason and I were on Granddad's Bluff and he kissed me for the first time. It seemed so long ago. One of our last conversations had been an argument. And then I found his broken body in a heap at the foot of Table Rock.

I was sobbing by the time my thoughts turned to Doug. Dangerous Doug, a Casanova who had me convinced he was willing to break the cycle of constant one-night stands because, in me, he claimed he'd found someone he truly loved. Yet sadly, tragically, infuriatingly, heroin had him by the throat and wouldn't let him go.

Yet again, I pulled out my cell phone and accessed the video clip of Doug impishly dodging, weaving, and bouncing as he delivered his "reeeeal-coool" standup routine, ironically in the same space where I was right now.

By midnight, I was seething with anger at Ray Barber. He was able to hide behind the thin patina of respectability as a supposedly humble businessman when in reality he was peddling a highly addictive poison that ravaged body and soul, ruined and ended lives, and resulted in extended waves of pain as other lives were left wrecked in its wake.

Did he care?

Would he care?

Could he care?

Maybe, I thought. Maybe he would. Maybe I could get through to him.

As I drifted off to sleep, still sitting in front of the bay window, I hatched a wild plan. I would confront Ray Barber and show him my rage and the depth of my pain. By confronting him, maybe I could get him to see and realize the awful consequences of his cynical and uncaring behavior. Even though he was beyond the reach of the justice system, maybe I could put the fear of God into him.

I resolved that by this time tomorrow I would make an indelible impression on Ray Barber and his pathetic life.

ᘓ ᘔ

CHAPTER 43

I dozed in my clothes and awoke with a start at seven Thursday morning with a crick in my neck. I thought about going upstairs and collapsing into Doug's bed, but figured if I did that, I'd stay there the rest of the day.

Instead, I showered and changed out of the clothes I'd slept in. As I showered, I heard myself actually groan out loud as I realized that the burden had fallen on me, by default, to clean out Doug's apartment. I had to sort through his stuff, save a few mementos for myself, donate the rest to Goodwill or the Salvation Army, and then vacate by the end of the month.

And Doug's ashes. I'd need to get them from the morgue soon. Would I have a memorial service for him? Had he been here in D.C. even long enough to have forged any friendships? I decided to give Rochelle Grigsby a call to get her thoughts. But not now.

There was a voicemail on my phone when I got out of the shower. I hit *play* and heard Muriel's comforting voice: "Hello, Lark. Muriel here. I'm checking to see if you'd like to join me for lunch later today. Lionel and Paul will be hanging out in the pressroom." She chuckled to herself. "I think Lionel wants to relive his glory days. Anyway, it would be wonderful to spend some time with you today – that is, if you're able... and willing."

She gave her cell number, but it really wasn't necessary because I'd be able to press the *call back* button – which I did.

"It's so nice of you to call, Muriel," I said to her when she answered. "You've just given me something to look forward to."

"Are things that bad?" she asked.

"Worse, I think."

"How can I help?"

"Oh, Muriel, I really don't want to trouble you."

"It's no trouble at all, dear. That's why we came."

I swallowed the lump in my throat and told her all the things I needed to do.

"Do you know what Winnie the Pooh says about this?" she asked.

"Um, no I don't, Muriel," I smiled into the phone.

"Winnie the Pooh says, 'It's always friendlier with two.'"

I laughed. "Perfect."

"Tell me where you are, I'll catch a cab and be there before you know it. Is now good?"

"It is. It'll be so good to be with you. *My* quote is, 'Misery loves company.' I don't know who coined it, but it's just as apt as your Winnie the Pooh sentiment."

I gave her Doug's address and she was there within the hour. It gave me time to do a quick read-in online of the day's news. Even though I was off duty and grieving, I told myself sternly that I still needed to stay up to date with what's going on in the world – and at the White House.

I already knew that Rose Gannon would be on the road giving a speech in Chicago, perhaps one of her last forays out of Washington before she began to pull back on her public appearances. Our next appointment to talk wasn't until late the next afternoon.

While waiting for Muriel, I took out my reporter's notebook and began making bullet points about things that had been eating at me that I wanted to look into.

Topping the list was talking with the officials in Fairfax County, Virginia who dealt with the so-called suicide of Anne-Marie Gustofsen. I didn't for a minute believe the suicide ruling.

I knew from what Doug told me that Rogan had intercepted Anne-Marie, lured her into his SUV where he had a flask. He'd probably already slipped the over-the-counter sleep aid into her drink. Once incapacitated, it would be easy to drive her to a secluded place – perhaps Chain Bridge in the middle of the night – put heavy stones into her overcoat pockets, and toss her into the Potomac where she'd drown.

I needed to find the right law enforcement official in Virginia – and disclose my clandestine meeting with Anne-Marie in which she voiced her fears about Rogan just before she died.

The more I thought about her death, however, the more I realized that Rogan had probably recognized me as the person he saw Anne-Marie talking with in the parking garage. I assumed he believed I knew more than I actually did. That meant it was highly likely that he would want me out of the way before I put two and two together and went to the Virginia authorities – which I was now on the verge of doing.

Muriel arrived before I could work myself into a full-blown para-noid froth. I was grateful for the distraction – and for her help.

We systematically went through every room and made decisions about everything we found. If I'd been working alone, it would have been too easy for me to get distracted – and then overwhelmed. Muriel was amazing – in fact, by the end of the day I was calling her "Muriel the Marvelous." She helped me focus and make clear-eyed decisions.

The first major decision was to give almost everything to the Salva-tion Army, but Muriel convinced me to keep Doug's camera gear. I re-solved that, once the dust had settled, I'd enroll in a photography class so that I could honor Doug's memory by trying to become as proficient a shooter as he had been.

Muriel was simultaneously impressed and creeped out by the oil-on-velvet nude portraits Doug had painted in the years after he was maimed in Iraq. There were about a dozen and I decided to keep them, at least for now. They were the fruits of Doug's creativity; I wasn't ready to part with them just yet. One painting in particular meant a lot to me – a portrait of a friend and former colleague of ours at the paper where Doug and I had worked back in Georgia.

I also retained – and knew I would always treasure – the unfinished Valentine's Day collage of photos Doug had taken of me throughout our friendship, including the ones he took the day of the Valentine's Day drone attack on the White House briefing room.

Muriel and I took a break at noon and walked to a bistro on DuPont Circle where we caught a quick bite. Muriel is, to me, the mother I nev-er knew, but, thankfully, we've managed to avoid all the mother-daughter friction and angst that I know is so common – especially among unmarried women my age. We can talk with each other about anything – or nothing.

As we sat in the crowded bistro, I was grateful that we were able to keep the conversation light and inconsequential. Unlike Lionel, and his instinct for the journalistic jugular, Muriel sensed I wasn't ready yet to go deep and personal in my grief about Doug. That would come later – and it did by late afternoon when we were ready to quit for the day after we realized we'd done an amazing job getting our arms around the monstrous task of dealing with Doug's belongings.

I made coffee and we sat sipping it on easy chairs at the bay window.

"How do you feel you're holding up, dear?" she asked. "And, let me hasten to add that if you don't want to talk about it right now, that's entirely alright."

I leaned back. "I'm numb, Muriel. You're a Godsend. Working with you today has helped me see that I can move forward."

"I notice you didn't use the phrase 'moving on.' Why not?"

I crinkled my nose as if smelling something unpleasant. "I think it's because 'moving on' means I've buttoned up my grief and sealed it away in a box. To me 'moving *forward*' means that I'm learning to accept that Doug was – and still is – an important part of my life."

"Even at the end?"

She didn't need to use the H-word – we both knew she meant heroin.

"Perhaps *especially* at the end."

"Why especially?"

I found my mind going back to the unfinished business I had with Ray Barber. "Heroin is a scourge, Muriel." I felt my anger intensifying. "The bastards who peddle that poison need to know, in no uncertain terms, that they're murderers."

She nodded soberly. "But what can one person do?"

"Maybe a *lot*, Muriel. Maybe a lot." I felt my pulse quicken and my blood come to a slow boil. And, I thought to myself, maybe I can do a lot tonight.

An hour later, after Muriel and I had said our goodbyes, I was at a gun store in Kensington, Maryland, holding the plastic pistol grip of a 45-caliber handgun.

CR BO

CHAPTER 44

"How can I help you, little lady?" He was about fifty and wore an untucked flannel shirt that did nothing to hide his bulging stomach. A fringe of thick, dirty-gray hair curled out from beneath his baseball cap, which I was pretty sure covered up some major baldness. His pudgy fingers were splayed on top of the glass gun-display case between us.

"I hate guns," I scowled as I hefted the pistol in my hand.

To myself I said, I hate Ray Barber even more than I hate guns.

The man chuckled condescendingly. "But you still need a gun, right? We get you liberal-types in here all the time."

"I never said I'm liberal."

"You hate guns, don'tcha?"

"That doesn't make me a liberal."

"Then what are ya?"

"Last time I checked, it's a secret ballot in this country. No offense, but it's none of your business."

"Just what I thought: liberal," he sneered.

"I'm not anything," I mumbled.

"Sure. Right."

"Do you want to sell a gun or don't you?"

"I thought you hate guns."

"I do, but I need one."

"What fer?"

"Protection."

"Ah! Boyfriend problems."

I grimaced. "You sure do make a lot of assumptions about people."

"It's my job."

"Really?"

"Yup."

"I thought your job is to help me choose a gun."

"Oh, it's that. But there's more to it."

"Really?"

"Yup." He put a finger to his temple. "It's all up here."

I frowned. "I don't get it."

"'Chology," he explained, as if to an addled child.

"Ohhh. Psychology. So you've got me all figured out, huh?"

"Pretty much."

I put the gun down and stood back so he could see me better. "Okay. I'm game. What have you figured out about me so far?"

"You mean in addition to you being liberal?"

I nodded and put my hands on my hips.

He leaned back, stroked his chin stubble and appraised me, a smirk playing on his face. "I'd say your boyfriend had too much to drink and got a little too up-close-and-personal, so you got pissed and kicked him out. Now you need a gun to make sure he stays the hell away." He beamed and puffed out his chest. "How'm I doin' so far, sweetie?"

"You. Are. *Brilliant.*" I stepped to the counter and picked up the gun again.

Even though my voice reeked with sarcasm, he actually blushed. "Thanks. I get that a lot." He nodded at the gun in my hand. "I can tell from the way you're fondling that weapon that you like it."

"Fondling. Really?"

"Sure. It's the word of the week in *Reader's Digest.*

I shook my head in disbelief.

"I'm constantly trying to bolster my . . ." – he paused to make sure I was duly impressed – "my 'cabulary."

"Ah, yes," I agreed. "There's nothing more powerful than a well-chosen word."

"'Cept maybe one o' these honeys." He stroked the gun barrel. "You like?"

I looked at the gleaming metal. "Actually," I smiled, "I do."

Two hours later I was parked on 14th Street directly across from Ray Barber's shoe repair shop. Ray sat at the counter polishing a shoe. He'd be closing in just a few minutes.

It was dark. There were a few cars on the street, but no pedestrian traffic.

My heart began to beat faster as the time inched closer to eight. I knew I was taking a big risk but, if all went according to plan, I'd be able to catch up with Muriel, Lionel, and Paul for dinner at Johnny's Half Shell near the Capitol by nine.

I felt twitchy. My breaths came fast and shallow and my ears began to ring. I was worried I'd be spotted, wouldn't be able to shoot straight – or both.

I rolled down my window and was just about to take aim when, out of the corner of my eye, I saw a man wearing a dark overcoat and fedora walking briskly from my right. His hat was pulled down so I couldn't see his face. His hands were stuffed in his coat pockets.

He got to Ray's store, hesitated, then opened the door with a gloved right hand and barged in. As he burst through the door, he pulled something from his left pocket and raised his arm toward Ray.

Ray looked up from his work, surprised.

Suddenly, a series of staccato flashes lit up the store. A nanosecond later I heard the sound of muffled gunfire.

I watched, stunned and open-mouthed. Ray was thrown backward against the wall then crumpled to the floor behind the counter and out of sight.

The shooter darted behind the counter, opened the cash register, grabbed a handful of money from the till, and stuffed the bills into his coat pocket.

Shocked by the spectacle playing out in front of me, I finally came to my senses. I took aim just as the man was heading out the door toward me, the gun still in his hand. As I began shooting, I saw the guy's face. It was Nathan Mann.

CB 80

CHAPTER 45

An hour later I was still shaking as I drove up to Johnny's Half Shell restaurant between the Capitol and Union Station. Lionel, looking perplexed, stood out front waiting for me. I flashed my lights to get his attention and pulled to the curb.

"Quick! Get in!" I hollered when he opened the door and scrambled into the front seat. I didn't even wait for him to close the door before I squealed away.

"Geez," he exclaimed, struggling with his seatbelt. "I got your text. What the hell's wrong?"

"Something terrible's happened."

"What?"

"Just a minute." I bit my lip and concentrated on not hitting anyone as I tried to maneuver around a double-parked taxi. I zipped around it, made a right onto Louisiana, another right onto D, and a sharp right onto New Jersey, worriedly checking my rear and side mirrors the whole time.

Lionel turned to look over his shoulder. "Are you being followed?"

"I don't know."

"What's going on?" He was getting pissed.

"There's something I have to show you. And then I need your advice like I've never needed it before."

"This isn't like you, Lark. You've got a death grip on that steering wheel. If you're not careful, you're gonna break it."

I found a parking place, pulled in, turned off my lights and cut the engine. Cars continued to pass by, but none seemed particularly interested in me.

I turned to Lionel. "Something terrible's just happened and I don't know what to do." My voice trembled.

"Start from the beginning. What just happened?"

"That's not the beginning."

Lionel sighed, impatient. "Let's start there any way. One step at a time. What just happened? Go."

I took a deep breath. "There's been a shooting."

"Okay. Good start. Who got shot?"

"Ray Barber, the guy who I think sold heroin to Doug."

"Is Barber dead?"

"Dunno, but I'm pretty sure he is. He was shot several times at point-blank range."

"Who shot him?"

I looked at Lionel and slowly shook my head. Our eyes locked.

He turned pale. "Did *you* shoot him? Dear God, Lark. Don't tell me *you* shot him."

"We need to back up."

He looked around, confused. "Why? Your parking job is fine. Don't change the subject."

"No. I mean before I tell you who shot Ray, I need to back up the story and give you some context."

"Talk about burying the lead," he grumped.

"Remember what we were talking about last night?"

"About you being buddy-buddy with the First Lady of the United States?"

I gave him my classic squint-scowl. "Try again."

"Let's see. You were telling me about the allegation that the drone guy..." He snapped his fingers, trying to think of the name.

"Dolph Rogan."

"Yeah. Rogan. That he was blackmailing Nathan Mann into getting Gannon to give a big green light for the commercialization of drones."

"Right."

"Okay. What's that got to do with tonight's shooting of a heroin pusher?"

I pulled out my iPhone, opened up my photo album, found what I was looking for, and swiveled the phone in my hand so that Lionel could see it.

He looked at the picture and frowned. "It's Nathan Mann looking a bit sketchy."

"Look closer."

He leaned in, took off his glasses, and squinted at the screen with one eye.

"Mann's carrying a handgun." Lionel looked up at me, his eyes wide and questioning.

"This is a shot I took of him leaving Ray Barber's store an hour ago. Lionel, I saw Nathan Mann shoot Ray Barber."

Lionel put his glasses back on. "What were *you* doing there? Did Mann beat you to the punch?"

I shook my head slowly.

"Larrrrk?" He drew my name out long, his tone ominous and deeply skeptical.

Ashamed, I looked down.

"Am I right?" he nudged.

"Not exactly."

"Then *what* exactly?" He raised his voice to the same judgy intensity I imagine he used often with his daughter Holly before they became estranged.

"Even though Doug's last calls were placed to a known heroin dealer, the cops weren't able to connect Barber to Doug," I said.

"So you decided to take matters into your own hands?"

"I thought about it," I said softly.

"How *much* did you think about it?"

"It was really eating at me so, earlier today, I went to a gun shop in Kensington."

"Jesus, Lark."

"But I chickened out, okay? Or maybe I just came to my senses. As much as I wanted Ray Barber to pay for Doug's death, I realized that I didn't have it in me to kill him – or even wave a gun in his face to scare him."

"So you didn't buy a gun?"

I shook my head. "No. I hate guns."

"So why were you sitting in front of the heroin dealer's store when he just happened to get shot?"

"Don't use that tone on me. You're making it sound like I planned this."

"Well, that's what the cops will think."

"I know."

"So why *were* you there?"

"I was going to tail Barber after he left work. I thought I might be able to take a picture of him making a drug deal."

Lionel shook his head slowly, dubiously.

"A friend of Doug's who used to go with him to buy drugs from Barber told me the line-up of cars full of people buying from him was like the drive-through window of McDonald's."

"I don't suppose you've gone to the cops to tell them what you just saw and photographed."

"Actually, I tried."

"Really?"

"I called Elena Kerrigan."

"Who's she?"

"She's the detective who'd been handling the case when Doug went missing. And she was with me when I identified his body."

"Were you able to get through to her?"

"No. I got a voice message that she just had her baby and is on maternity leave."

"So now what?"

"That's where *you* come in."

"You want my advice."

I nodded.

"My first instinct is that you should go to the cops," Lionel said.

"Right. Mine too. But–"

"But, it gets complicated because the president's national security adviser is the shooter, right?"

"Exactly. It's bigger than just the shooting death of a shoe repairman."

"Is it being reported on the news yet?"

"Geez. I don't know. Let's check." I gave the key in the ignition a half turn and tuned the radio to WTOP, D.C.'s all-news radio station.

An announcer was reading a weather forecast. While we kept the radio on in the background, I used my phone to get online. There was nothing yet on the *Washington Post* website, but I did find something on the WJLA-TV site.

I put my phone between us so Lionel and I could both read it:

D.C. Metro police are on the scene of a fatal shooting at a shoe repair shop on 14th Street in Northwest Washington. One person is dead. Robbery appears to be the motive, according to police, but so far, no witnesses have come forward.

Lionel gave me a look. "So far."

"So far," I repeated.

"You're gonna have to come forward, Lark."

"I know. But first I need your help thinking this through."

"Okay," Lionel shrugged, "let's think."

"We need to figure out what we know, what we don't know, and what we need to prove."

Lionel smiled incongruously. "That reminds me of a joke."

I gave him a look.

Undaunted and oblivious, Lionel barreled ahead. "The Lone Ranger and his faithful Indian companion Tonto are riding together on their horses in the Wild West."

"Faithful Indian companion?" I scowled.

Lionel frowned slightly. "Hmmmm. I guess I need to update that. The politically-correct version of the joke should identify Tonto as the Lone Ranger's faithful *Native-American* Indian companion."

"Okay. Go on," I said in surrender, crossing my arms and leaning back. "Let's get this over with."

"Anyway, all of a sudden the Lone Ranger and Tonto are surrounded by Ind—um, Native Americans in war paint."

"Uh huh."

"The Lone Ranger looks at Tonto and says, 'Looks like we're surrounded, Tonto.' Tonto turns to the Lone Ranger and says, – wait for it, Lark...wait for it...Tonto says, 'What you mean *we*, Kimosabe?'" Lionel began chortling as if he'd just told the funniest joke ever.

I remained stone-faced. "And you're telling me this joke *now?* Why?"

"What you mean *'we'* have to figure this out, Kimo-Larkee?" His chortle became a full-blown belly laugh.

"Lionel. This isn't funny."

"I know. I know." Lionel tried to force himself to be serious. "I just thought I'd try to loosen the tension a little."

I sighed. "Nice try."

"I'm just relieved you didn't buy a gun." Lionel turned serious. "After what you've already told me, we actually have the beginning of what could turn into a very strong story."

"What you mean, *'we'* Lionel-sabe?" I gave him a gentle nudge.

"Yes. *We*. We're in this together, Lark." He reached over and squeezed my hand.

"Thank you, Lionel," I whispered. My lower lip trembled. "That means...everything."

After a moment, I composed myself, cleared my throat, and continued. "So, here's a possible lead: 'Associated Press White House Correspondent Lark Chadwick witnessed National Security Adviser Nathan Mann shooting and killing a shoe repairman in Washington tonight.'"

"Yeah. It needs a little work. You're not the most important person in the story, Mann is. You're the attribution. But you've got the general idea."

"Even so, you and I both know that the story is way bigger than just a shooting."

"True."

"There are more dots to connect."

"Yes."

I began making a list on my fingers. "We know that, according to police, phone records show that A.P. White House photographer Doug Mitchell was trying to contact Barber right after Mitchell disappeared from the White House Correspondents' Dinner."

"Right."

"We know, based on a statement by A.P. Washington Deputy Bureau Chief Rochelle Grigsby, that Grigsby and Mitchell bought heroin from Barber in the past."

"Wait!" Lionel interrupted. "Grigsby is willing to go on the record with that?"

I frowned. "Not really. Probably not. But we could fudge that."

"Maybe, but *I'm* not convinced. Go on. What else do we *know*?"

"We know that drone entrepreneur Dolph Rogan was blackmailing National Security Adviser Nathan Mann to get President Gannon to lift restrictions on drones."

"And how do we know that again?"

"Because his executive assistant, Anne-Marie Gustofsen, told me that during a clandestine, predawn interview in a northern Virginia parking garage."

"Christ. This is like Watergate," Lionel said under his breath. "We don't *know* that Rogan was blackmailing Mann. All we know is that it's alleged."

"There's more. Gustofsen told me she was afraid Rogan would kill her if he found out she was talking to me. Then our interview was cut short because she heard a noise, got spooked and ran."

"Okay. Go on."

"Right after Gustofsen ran, I saw what looked like Rogan's SUV leaving the garage."

"SUVs are a dime a dozen."

"Rogan's has gold rims. So did the one I saw leaving the garage."

"Did you see Rogan behind the wheel?"

"No. But Doug did. And he saw Rogan lure Gustofsen into the vehicle."

"Lure?"

"That was Doug's impression."

"But Doug can no longer corroborate that statement."

"Maybe not in a court of law, but he was an eyewitness and told me what he saw."

"Go on. What else do we know?"

"One thing we *do* know is that Gustofsen turned up dead twelve hours later."

"Right."

"Officially, her death is a suicide. Drowning. But I'm not buying it."

"Neither am I," Lionel said. "The timing of her death is suspicious. But let's back up. There's a lot of conjecture and innuendo in your story so far. The only two things we know for sure is that Mann shot Barber and that Gustofsen died shortly after accusing her boss of blackmailing Mann. The question all of this raises: Why would Mann kill a heroin pusher? Surely not for a handful of money from the cash register," Lionel said.

"Mann probably took the money to make the shooting look like a robbery. Maybe Mann was running a heroin-smuggling operation out of the White House."

"Whoa. *Major* conjecture, Lark. There's no way you can go with that."

"Maybe not. Yet. But consider: Mann is the former U.S. drug czar. He had the power and was in a position to intercept and redistribute heroin."

"Yeah, but why would he do it? Accusing Mann of running a heroin operation out of the White House is irresponsibly dangerous innuendo of the highest degree, Lark. If you're wrong, your reputation as a journalist is shot to hell."

"Enter First Lady Rose Gannon," I smiled coyly. "Remember, she and Mann are *extremely* close friends."

"Do you think she's involved? Is the president involved? You're her best bud. Why don't you ask?"

"You know why not."

"Why?"

"Because if I ask and she and the prez *are* involved, I'm dead meat."

Lionel looked out the windshield and nodded soberly, then turned to me. "Do you trust them?"

"Trust is a pretty strong word. I *like* them."

"Yeah, no surprise there. That's job number one for any politician – and his wife: to be liked. The Gannons have more than succeeded on that – they're *hugely* attractive. But do you *trust* them?"

"The jury's still out on that. In their favor, Gustofsen told me Rogan decided to blackmail Mann because the president isn't that kind of guy – that he's incorruptible."

Lionel snorted.

"I think that, for now, healthy skepticism is the wisest approach," I said.

"I agree."

I touched Lionel's arm. "Thank you, Lionel. You've been a big help."

"Really? We're done? I thought we were just getting started."

"Oh, believe me, we are. I've got a plan."

"You do?"

"Yes. First, we're going back to the restaurant."

He looked worriedly at his watch. "Geez. Muriel and Paul are probably wondering where I am and what's up."

"Next," I said, "we're going to tell Muriel and Paul."

"Why?"

"You'll see."

"And then?"

"You're gonna buy me dinner," I grinned. "I'm *hungry!*"

ଓ ଈ

CHAPTER 46

Okay, so I really didn't have a plan, but I really was hungry. And talking with Lionel had calmed me down enough so that I could think straight. And eat.

Actually, I sort of had a plan, but it was only half-baked. After talking, Lionel and I returned to the restaurant. Over a late dinner, I brought Paul and Muriel into my confidence. That was step one.

Step two was to work with Paul to begin dummying up a story. My plan was to work on it in tandem with Paul, but the byline would be his. I respected him as a reporter and wanted him to be a part of it because I felt I was too personally involved to be objective. Working with Paul, I reasoned, would insure the story's survival if something happened to me as a result of our investigation.

There was still much reporting to do, and the more digging I did, the more likely it would be that I'd stir up forces beyond my control.

After dinner, the four of us went back to Lionel and Muriel's room around the corner at the Liaison Hotel. We worked until midnight talking and writing the first draft of the story.

Here's what we came up with:

Gannon Aide Nathan Mann Wanted for Murder

By: PAUL STONE

President Gannon's long-time friend and national security adviser Nathan Mann shot and killed a shoe repairman last night in Washington. Associated Press White House Correspondent Lark Chadwick personally witnessed the shooting and snapped a photo of Mann leaving the store with the gun still in his hand.

[INSERT THIS WHEN CONFIRMED:

Chadwick has made a statement to D.C. Metro police who are investigating.]

[INSERT POLICE QUOTE HERE]:

[   ]

The motive for the shooting could be the tip of a much bigger iceberg involving drug dealing and blackmail at the White House.

According to Chadwick, the victim of the shooting, Ray Barber, was a drug dealer who police were investigating for selling a fatal dose of heroin to her boyfriend, A.P. White House Photographer Doug Mitchell.

On Monday, Feb. 21, Chadwick discovered Mitchell's body slumped at the wheel of his vehicle two days after he disappeared from the White House Correspondents' Association Dinner at a Washington Hotel.

[INSERT WHEN CONFIRMED:

District Medical Examiner [insert name here] ruled Mitchell died of [insert correct term here – is it "heroin intoxication."???]

Police confirm that Mitchell's last phone calls were to Ray Barber, but authorities have not been able to prove that Barber sold heroin to Mitchell.

Chadwick said she witnessed Barber's killing as she sat in her car parked across the street from Barber's shoe repair shop.

"I was planning to tail Barber after he closed his store," Chadwick explained. "I hoped I'd be able to get a picture of him selling drugs to someone."

According to Chadwick, just before the store closed, a man wearing a hat and overcoat stormed into the store, shot Barber several times at point-blank range, then took a handful of money from the cash register.

"I took a picture as the man was leaving the store," Chadwick said. "I was stunned when I recognized the assailant as Nathan Mann."

Before Chadwick came forward, police were treating the shooting as a robbery-gone-bad.

[INSERT MANN'S POSSIBLE REAX HERE]:

[   ]

According to Chadwick, Mann was being blackmailed in an attempt to influence President Gannon's policy on the commercialization of drones.

[INSERT POSSIBLE COMMENT FROM MANN HERE]:

[   ]

Chadwick said that on the eve of the Valentine's Day drone attack on the White House, she got an anonymous tip to investigate drone developer Dolph Rogan, founder of Applied Electronics in Reston, Virginia.

According to its website, the company's motto is, "A Drone in Every Garage."

Chadwick interviewed Rogan the day after the drone attack and he gave her a demonstration of how drones operate.

During their interview, Chadwick said Rogan called on President Gannon to lift the current ban on the commercialization of drones.

[INSERT ROGAN QUOTE HERE:]

[   ]

According to Chadwick, the anonymous tipster kept pressing her to look more deeply into Rogan's associates.

"I was getting impatient with the tipster," Chadwick said. "I thought I might be getting spun by Rogan himself, so I insisted on a face-to-face meeting or I'd walk away."

Chadwick said the tipster agreed to a clandestine, middle-of-the-night meeting in the same parking garage in Arlington, Virginia where Washington Post reporter Bob Woodward met with Deep Throat during the Watergate scandal in the 1970s.

"The tipster was Anne-Marie Gustofsen, Rogan's co-founder of Applied Electronics," Chadwick said.

A few hours after their interview, Gustofsen's body was found in the Potomac River just north of D.C.

"In our interview, Gustofsen said she feared Rogan would kill her if he found out about our meeting. She then alleged that Rogan was blackmailing National Security Adviser Nathan Mann to influence President Gannon to lift the ban on the commercialization of drones," Chadwick said.

Chadwick said their interview was cut short before Gustofsen could explain how Rogan was blackmailing Mann.

"She got spooked and ran away," Chadwick said.

Chadwick said she saw a vehicle that looked like Rogan's Lincoln SUV leaving the parking garage.

Chadwick added that Mitchell, who was waiting for her in a parked car just outside the garage, saw Gustofsen get into an SUV driven by Rogan.

Fairfax County, Virginia Coroner [insert name here] ruled Gustofsen's death a suicide.

[INSERT POSSIBLE CORONER QUOTE HERE – ARE THEY REOPENING THE INVESTIGATION?]

[   ]

Nathan Mann is a long-time friend of President Gannon and First Lady Rose Gannon.

Mann was one of Will Gannon's law professors at Vanderbilt University 20 years ago. Gannon has frequently called Mann "my friend and mentor."

Mann left Vanderbilt 10 years ago to become the head of the Drug Enforcement Administration. He later became head of the Federal Aviation Administration.

According to Mann, he was at the F.A.A. when he met Rogan.

[INSERT REAX FROM PREZ AND/OR ROSE GANNON HERE]:

[   ]

A.P. White House Correspondent Lark Chadwick contributed to this story.

We all agreed the story was still riddled with innuendo, speculation, and probably even some libel. But it was a start. A lot still needed to be fleshed out and confirmed.

Step three: I emailed a copy of the still-incomplete story to Paul and Lionel.

Step four: Sleep!!!

Or try.

03 80

CHAPTER 47

Paul Stone and I sat across a conference table from Rochelle Grigsby and her boss, A.P. Washington Bureau Chief Scotty Barrington. It was a little after eight Friday morning, but both Grigsby and Barrington were probably on their third cup of coffee.

Hours earlier, after Paul, Lionel, Muriel and I had drafted the dummy story in Lionel and Muriel's hotel room, we agreed that Paul would send an email to Rochelle and Scotty requesting an "emergency" meeting first thing in the morning. I then went back to Doug's and slept for a couple hours.

I was awakened at six by a text from Paul informing me the meeting with our two immediate supervisors would take place at eight at the A.P.'s D.C. bureau at 13th and L Streets.

As we sat down in the conference room just outside Barrington's office, Scotty, a dapper guy in his mid-forties, spoke first. "So, what's the emergency?" he smiled. "You two not getting along?"

"We're getting along *great!*" Paul said with his typical enthusiasm. "Actually we're getting along so great that–"

"You're getting married?" Grigsby joked.

Paul blushed. "I should be so lucky," he chuckled.

I felt myself trying to sink into my chair.

"Actually," Paul continued, "Lark and I have been getting along so well that we wrote this last night." He slid hard copies of our story across the table to Barrington and Grigsby.

I carefully watched their faces as they each picked up their copy and began to read.

Grigsby visibly blanched when she read the lead.

"Holy *shit!*" Barrington exclaimed a second later. He glared at me. "Where's the picture?"

I already had it open on my iPhone and slid it across the table so they could both have a look at the shot I took of Nathan Mann, gun drawn, leaving Ray Barber's store.

"Holy shit!" Barrington repeated.

As I retrieved my phone, I smiled to myself at how professional wordsmiths sometimes have such a limited vocabulary.

"How did you–? What did you–?" Barrington sputtered, a million questions trying to get out of his mouth at the same time.

"Keep reading. It gets better," I said.

Barrington turned his attention back to the story, but kept muttering expletives as he continued to read.

Grigsby said nothing, but her jaw muscles tightened noticeably. She finished first, her face impassive. She looked at Barrington, waiting for him to get to the end.

"This is incredible. *Explosive,*" he said, looking back and forth between Paul and me.

"That's why it's not in the system yet, sir," Paul explained. "But we wanted to give you two a heads up."

"Have you gone to the authorities yet, Lark?" Barrington asked.

"Not yet, sir. That's next," I said. "I'm going to talk with D.C. and Virginia authorities today, right after our meeting. My thinking is to let them know that our story is locked and loaded, but we're holding off on it for a day to give them a chance to get a head start on their investigations."

Barrington shook his head. "Not sure I like that. Word could get out prematurely and we get scooped."

"Good point," I said, "but it could also tip off Mann and Rogan. They could then hunker down, lawyer up, disappear – or maybe even come after me."

Barrington stroked his chin thoughtfully, then turned to Grigsby. "What do you think, Rochelle?"

"I agree that Lark should go to the authorities, but as soon as she does, I think we should pull the trigger and run with it."

I felt my hands get cold and clammy because as soon as the story became public, my life would be subject to many forces out of my control.

Barrington shook his head. "Before we pull the trigger, Lark and Paul still need to try to reach Mann and..." he looked down at the story, "the other guy–"

"Rogan. Dolph Rogan," I said.

"Right. Rogan. We still need to try to get them on the record." Barrington turned to Paul and me. "I assume you haven't gone to them yet because you didn't want to tip them off?"

"That's right," I said.

"And the president," Barrington said. "We need to give him a chance to respond. It's obviously too explosive to bring it up in a briefing, or filter it through his spokesman."

"I might be able to get a quote from Rose Gannon," I said. "I'll be seeing her later today. And perhaps the president, too."

They all turned to look at me, surprised. I'd said more than I'd intended.

"Oh?" Barrington asked, eyebrows arched.

"I suppose this is as good a time to mention it as any," I said. "I've begun meeting privately with the first lady, doing a series of in-depth interviews with her for release at a later date."

"What kind of interviews?" Grigsby asked. "Does it have anything to do with her collapse at the correspondents' dinner a week ago?"

"It does."

Grigsby shifted uncomfortably in her chair. "Why'd she collapse?"

"I can't reveal that yet."

Barrington and Grigsby exchanged glances. Paul looked quizzical.

"We're your editors, Lark," Barrington said softly. "I think we're entitled to know."

I paused a moment to think. He was right. "Obviously, it stays in this room," I said, looking at all three of them. "Are we in the Cone of Silence?"

They all nodded.

I took a deep breath and said, "Ross Gannon told me she's got pancreatic cancer. She's only got a few weeks to live."

Barrington exhaled as if he'd been punched in the gut. He slumped against the back of his chair. "Whoa. That's rough."

"Big story, though," Grigsby chimed in.

"Have you been able to confirm that beyond her say so?" Barrington asked.

"When I see her today, I'm going to try to get her to have her doctor talk with me. If she doesn't let me talk to her doctor, then we'll just have to let the story play itself out. We'll know if it's true or not in a couple weeks."

"We might get scooped if we wait," Barrington said.

I nodded. "But she wouldn't tell me until I agreed we were off the record."

He scowled.

"But I got her to agree to consider lifting the embargo if I get wind that someone else might break the story first."

His scowl deepened.

"But even if we get scooped," I said, "I'm the one already on the inside. It was the best I could do, but I think it's pretty good." I felt two inches tall.

Barrington nodded. "You've been doing some kick-ass work, Chadwick. Some of us in this room have had our doubts." He shot Grigsby a look, but her eyes avoided his. "We'll sit on it. For now. In the meantime," he continued, "at least we won't be caught flatfooted." He turned to Grigsby. "Let's make sure her obit is up to date, too."

"Whose? Lark's?" Grigsby smirked.

I didn't think it was funny.

Barrington smiled at Grigsby. "Rose Gannon's – just so we're clear. But, now that you mention it..." He laughed, pushed back his chair, and stood. "Good work. Both of you," he nodded at Paul and me. "Keep us posted."

Paul walked out of the room behind Barrington, but Grigsby took me by the arm and stopped me.

"Thanks for keeping me out of your story," she whispered. "I owe you."

 Cʒ ᴈ◌

CHAPTER 48

Paul and I huddled as soon as we left the conference room and were on our way down the elevator to the lobby.

"How about you go to the Virginia authorities?" I suggested. "Show them our story and ask if they intend to reopen the investigation into the death of Anne-Marie Gustofsen?"

"Shouldn't you go there with me?"

"Normally, I would, but I think we need to divide up the job to save time. You can give them my contact information and let them know I'm willing to make a statement about my clandestine meeting with her."

"Okay."

I gave him the contact information for the coroner, for the district attorney, and for the sheriff's department.

"What'll you do?" Paul asked me.

"I'm going to see if I can track down my detective friend. She just had a baby, so if I can't find her, I'll make a cold call and show up at the police department to talk with any homicide detective who'll meet with me."

"Okay." He checked his watch. "It's eight-thirty now. I need to be at the White House briefing at eleven."

"Right. Let's keep in touch. We'll regroup at noon."

"Or before," Paul said, a worried look on his face. "Barrington and Grigsby will be breathing down our necks about touching all the bases so they can release the story."

"Once that happens, things are going to explode and every reporter in the world will start chasing the story," I frowned. "Then it'll be like trying to hang on to American Pharoah's tail in the home stretch of the Kentucky Derby."

By this time we were standing on the sidewalk outside the bureau on L Street.

Paul nodded grimly and gave me a sudden hug. "You stay safe, Lark Chadwick. I'll talk to you soon. May The Force be with you," he smiled.

"And with you, Paul Stone. Are we having fun yet?"

He laughed mirthlessly, hailed a cab, and drove off for Virginia.

I got into another taxi and headed for the D.C. Metropolitan Police Department's homicide division headquarters located on M Street in Southwest about three miles south of the White House not far from Nationals Park.

It was almost nine when I arrived. The homicide division is in the old Anthony Bowen School, a squat three-story red brick building. Before I went inside, I placed another call to Elena Kerrigan. To my surprise – and relief – she picked up.

"Detective Kerrigan. Hi! It's Lark Chadwick. Congratulations on the new baby."

"Hi, Lark. What a great surprise. It's good to hear from you."

"Are you getting any sleep?" I laughed.

"A little," she chuckled. "This mommy thing is exhausting. But at least I've got the energy to take a *few* congratulatory phone calls."

"I won't take much of your time," I said, "I wanted to let you know about something extremely important."

"What's up?"

I quickly told her about the shooting I'd witnessed and that I'd gotten a picture of Nathan Mann leaving Ray Barber's shop holding a gun. I wrapped up my story by saying, "I'm outside the homicide division on M Street getting ready to go inside to make a formal statement."

"That's First District headquarters in Bowen School, right?"

"Right. I just wanted to give you a heads up so if they check with you, you won't be blindsided."

"I appreciate the gesture, Lark. Thank you. You'll be in good hands there. They'll take you seriously, and they'll know what to do."

"You also need to know – and I'll tell this to the detective I speak to – that my bosses want to run with the story as soon as I make my statement to authorities and we touch base with Mann and Rogan to see if we can get a comment."

"Oh, no. I wish they wouldn't."

"I know. But it's out of my control now."

"It could really complicate things, Lark."

"That's what I tried to tell them."

"How much time do we have to make our move?" she asked.

"Only a few hours at most."

"Okay. Don't go inside yet. Lemme make a quick call to grease the skids for you. I'll call you right back to tell you who to talk to."

"That would be great. Thank you. Do you think they'll try to arrest Mann now?"

"Dunno. They might."

"Do you think they'd let me come along with them when they do?"

"You can ask. I'll put in a good word for you."

"Wonderful. Thanks."

"I'll call you right back."

I hung up and paced back and forth shivering on the sidewalk as traffic swished past along the four-lane street with a grassy center divider. Within six minutes, Kerrigan called me back.

"Ask for Detective Triolo," she said. "Nick Triolo. I've talked with him and he's expecting you. He's kind of a cowboy, but he's a good cop."

"Thanks. Did you mention I want to be there when he busts Mann?"

"I did."

"What did he say?"

"Nothing. My guess is it'll be a hard sell."

"I'm used to that. Anyway, thank you so much. And good luck with the new baby."

"Thanks, Lark. Stay safe."

Triolo was waiting for me when I arrived. He looked fit and about forty with a bushy mustache. His jet-black hair was slicked back, his eyes and mouth were hard. He wore a sky-blue shirt, sleeves rolled up halfway, a pistol – butt forward – strapped snugly against his left side in a leather shoulder holster.

The office was nearly deserted.

"Have a seat." He pointed at the chair next to his desk and sat down behind it.

I sat.

"Kerrigan tells me you had some excitement last night," he said, opening a notebook and taking a pen from his top drawer. "Tell me about it."

I told him everything.

Instead of taking notes, he studied me as I talked. I felt I was being judged and dissected. He asked to see the picture I took of Mann leaving the store after the shooting and I showed it to him. That seemed to animate him. He asked me to send it to him in an email, so I did that as we sat talking.

"Why were you outside the store?" he asked.

"I believe Ray Barber is a heroin dealer who sold a fatal dose to my boyfriend. I was going to tail Barber after he closed to see if I could get a picture of him making a drug deal."

"Why a picture?"

"Because I'm a reporter."

"Tell me more."

I wasn't sure how much he knew from Kerrigan's short phone call so, at the risk of being repetitious, I told him where I worked and what I did. I also told him about Dolph Rogan, Anne-Marie's allegation that Rogan was blackmailing Mann, and that Anne-Marie died shortly after she and I met.

I ended my story by telling Triolo, "My colleague Paul Stone is meeting with the authorities in Virginia right now trying to get Gustofsen's suicide-by-drowning case reopened. As you can see, it's far bigger than just the murder of a shopkeeper."

Triolo nodded. He was deep in thought trying to figure out how to handle this. His mind worked fast.

"You're probably right, but first things first. We've got the picture you took, plus you're an eyewitness – that's enough on Mann right now to bring him in and charge him with murder. And it's a D.C. matter, so that makes it easier. Once we have him in hand, then we can get the feds involved and try to sort out the bigger picture."

"Are you gonna pick him up now?"

He nodded. "If I can. Do you know where he might be?"

"He's the president's national security adviser. His office is in the EEOB, but he could be anywhere. He might even be in the Oval Office meeting with Gannon."

"Hmmmm. That sounds complicated," Triolo said out loud, but more to himself than to me. "I've got an idea."

Triolo picked up his phone and speed-dialed a number. "Maybe the uniformed guys at the Secret Service can tell me where he is," he said to me as he waited for someone to answer the phone.

"Hey, Bobby. It's Nick Triolo, D.C. Police." He paused to listen, a slow smile spreading across his face. "I'm good, man. Thanks for asking. It *has* been too long. Say, listen, I need to come over there and pick up someone. Can you check the whereabouts of a guy named Mann – Nathan Mann?" He paused. "Right. The president's national security adviser." There was another pause. "Okay, thanks." He hung up.

"What's the word?"

"You were right. Mann's meeting with the president. I'll slip the cuffs on him when he leaves the Oval Office." Triolo winked at me – he was beginning to enjoy himself.

I winked back at him. "I'd like to be there for that." I opened the photo app on my iPhone. "I could get a picture of Detective Nick Triolo doing his duty to protect the country." I smiled and squeezed off a quick shot of him.

"Well, next time make sure you get my good side," he grinned and stood. "Lemme run this past the captain first. Stay here."

He was gone less than five minutes.

"The captain thinks it's better to take a more low-key approach," Triolo said when he came back. "Because it's such a high-profile and sensitive case, he just wants me to question Mann and see if he'll come in voluntarily."

I scowled.

"C'mon, Chadwick." He took the dark sport coat draped across the back of his chair and put it on with a flourish over his shoulder holster. "Let's make history. It'll be fun."

Fifteen minutes later we were driving through the Southwest gate of the White House and parking in the first available diagonal space on Executive Avenue between the West Wing and the Eisenhower.

As we were getting out of his unmarked car, Triolo's cell bleeped.

Triolo put the phone to his ear. "What's up?" He listened, a scowl etching wrinkles across his brow. "Shit," he said. "Why didn't you guys stop him?" A pause. "Okay. I just got here. I'll watch for him. Thanks."

"What's going on?" I asked as Triolo pocketed his phone.

"Mann's left his meeting with the president and he's heading toward us on his way back to his office." Triolo patted the left side of his sport coat, but didn't draw his weapon.

"How come the Secret Service didn't stop him?" I asked, getting out my iPhone and readying it.

"My buddy said they'd keep an eye on him for me, but if I wanted to arrest him, that would be up to me."

Just then the door to the basement level of the West Wing opened and Mann walked outside.

"There he is," I pointed. I put my iPhone on *video* and began recording.

"Nathan Mann?" Triolo called out.

Mann stopped just outside the door, about thirty yards from us, his face quizzical.

Triolo walked toward him, a grim look on his face. "I'm Detective Nicholas Triolo, D.C. Police." He whipped out his badge and held it up, but he was too far away from Mann for him to see much.

Mann's eyes widened.

Triolo kept walking toward him. "Sir, I'd like to ask you a few questions about the shooting last night of Ray Barber."

A sudden panicked look overcame Mann. He dropped his briefcase, turned, and ran.

03 80

CHAPTER 49

"Halt! Police!" Triolo shouted.

Mann dashed two at a time up a flight of concrete steps that led to the driveway by the West Wing entrance. Before I lost sight of him, Mann was sprinting toward the Northwest gate.

Triolo bolted to the stairs and raced to the top. But he wasn't fast enough.

"Shit," he said.

He stutter-stepped down the stairs and back to me as I stopped recording.

"I forgot to tell you: he's a marathon runner," I said to Triolo as we hustled back to his car.

"He's *fast,*" Triolo said. "He was already at the gate and getting away."

We got in and Triolo threw the car in gear, backed out of the stall, turned on his flashing lights and siren, and squealed down Executive Avenue toward the Pennsylvania Avenue gate.

I caught a glimpse of Mann racing down Jackson Place by Lafayette Square, but he was gone by the time the guards could swing open the gate for us.

Triolo grabbed a dash-mounted microphone, keyed it, and began shouting into his police radio. I wasn't listening to him because at the same time I was pulling up Shotzie's phone number from my contact list and giving him a call.

The gate finally swung open and Triolo gunned the car onto the Pennsylvania Avenue pedestrian mall, scattering a flock of tourists walking in front of Blair House. He palmed the vehicle to the right, but had to hit the brakes to keep from plowing into another mass of people gathered to take pictures of the north portico of the White House.

"Shotzie!" I shouted into my phone when he picked up. "It's Lark Chadwick."

"Hey, Lark. What's up?"

"Are you in your bar?"

"Uh huh."

"I need your help."

"Okay."

Triolo made a quick left turn onto Jackson Place. Mann was nowhere in view.

"Do you know what Nathan Mann looks like?" I asked Shotzie.

"The national security adviser? Sure."

"Look out your window and tell me if you see him."

"Okay. What's going on?"

"He's in a big hurry and I think he's heading your way."

Triolo floored it and his unmarked car shot past the temporary press center on the left, screeching to a halt at the end of Jackson Place which paralleled the west side of Lafayette Square. A guard shack and retractable metal posts blocked our entry onto H Street. There was another delay while the uniformed Secret Service agents began to lower the posts for us.

"Yeah. I see him," Shotzie said after a brief delay. "What's going on?"

"Where is he? What's he doing?"

"He just got into a taxi."

"What's the number on the cab?"

"I didn't get it. Sorry. It's red with a gray streak along the side, heading north on Connecticut."

"Okay. Thanks."

Triolo, his jaw muscles set and tensing, scanned the street in both directions. When the way past the guard shack was clear, he nosed into the one-way traffic on H. Our only option was to go right.

"Turn onto Sixteenth," I said to Triolo as he turned onto H. "My friend saw him get into a cab and head north on Connecticut."

Triolo maneuvered the car to the left lane. At St. John's Church, he turned and rocketed north on 16th Street, made a left at the next corner and hurtled toward Connecticut Avenue.

"What did your friend tell you about the cab?" Triolo asked.

"He didn't get a number, but said the cab is red and gray."

Triolo snorted derisively. "That narrows the field to about seven thousand vehicles. There are about a hundred cab companies in D.C. and *all* of their cabs are red with a gray stripe."

As he turned right onto Connecticut, he retrieved the mic from the dashboard and called dispatch. "Suspect is in a red and gray cab heading north on Connecticut. I do not have him in view, nor do I have a company name or vehicle number. How soon until the U-S-V is on site?"

"Two minutes," a voice crackled from the dashboard.

"Ten-four."

"What's a U-S-V?" I asked Triolo.

"Unmanned Surveillance Vehicle."

"A drone?"

He nodded. "Yeah. In layman's terms."

"Sweet," I pumped a fist.

Triolo gave me a weird look.

"Poetic justice," I explained, smiling.

ᘓ ᘔ

CHAPTER 50

Connecticut Avenue slices diagonally through the Northwest quadrant of Washington, D.C. The three lanes in both directions are almost always clogged with stop-and-go traffic, including lots of cabs.

Even though Triolo had on his lights and siren, it was amazing to me how most people were either oblivious to his presence or, instead of moving over, they simply hit the brakes and froze in place. Not helpful.

Triolo swore as he tried to inch through traffic. Every now and then we'd come to a red and gray cab, but Mann didn't appear to be in any of them.

My phone bleeped. Paul Stone.

"I was just going to give you a call," I said. "Major developments."

"Here, too," he said.

"Whatcha got?"

"I went to the district attorney's office first and told them what we had. They're going to reopen the case of Gustofsen's supposed suicide. Someone's going to be contacting you soon about making a statement. What do you have?"

Quickly, I told him what had just happened. "I'm in a cop car now heading up Connecticut Avenue. We're looking for Mann, but not having much luck."

"Are you thinking what I'm thinking?" Paul asked.

"Yes. It's time to file what we have."

"Give me Rogan's phone number and I'll try to get a quote from him," Paul said.

"Okay. Just a sec." I pulled up Rogan's contact info and read his number over the phone to Paul. "I'm gonna call Grigsby now. I'll let her know you'll be calling her once you call Rogan."

"Sounds like a plan. It's ten-fifteen now. I'm heading for the press center. This could be on the wire before the eleven o'clock briefing."

"I'll make you a bet," I said.

"What's that?"

"If this hits the wire in the next half hour, the briefing's gonna be delayed until they can get their story straight."

"I think it'll happen no matter what."

"Dinner?" I challenged.

"And drinks."

"You get the first round."

"Deal."

We hung up.

As Triolo inched his way northwest on Connecticut, head swiveling as he searched for red and gray cabs, I speed-dialed Grigsby.

"Rochelle," I shouted when she picked up. "It's Lark."

"What's with the siren? Has there been another attack?"

"I'm in a police car chasing after Nathan Mann."

"Oh my God. What happened?"

"I was with a D.C. detective when he tried to question Mann at the White House, but Mann bolted. I got it on video."

"Holy shit. I'm going to loop Scotty in on this. Hold on."

There was a clunk and some clicks and then Barrington was on the line. I told him what I'd just told Grigsby.

"Time to pull the trigger on this puppy," Barrington said.

"Also," I said, "Paul Stone just told me that the district attorney in Virginia is going to reopen the case of Anne-Marie Gustofsen's suicide. Paul's trying to get a reax now from Rogan. You should be hearing from Paul any minute with that part of the story."

"That's great," Grigsby said.

"I'm sending both of you the video clip I shot of Mann bolting when the detective confronted him. I'm also sending you the picture I took of Mann with the gun leaving Ray Barber's after shooting him."

It took a minute for the picture and video to upload and send. While that was going on, I said, "I think we should go with a bulletin that police are looking for Mann, then follow up with leads that dole out the story step by step."

"Agreed," Barrington said. "This will be a double byline, Rochelle – you and Paul Stone. But we make it clear that Lark contributed to the story."

"Gotcha, Scotty," Grigsby said. "No problem."

"So, here's the bulletin," I said. "National Security Adviser Nathan Mann is on the run, wanted by D.C. police for murder."

"Excellent," Grigsby said. I could hear her keyboard clicking as she typed up what I had to say.

I knew that as soon as this story hit the wire, I would no longer have it all to myself. But I was okay with that because the bigger issue for me was not the exclusivity of the story, but putting a stop to what I now believed was Nathan Mann's drug operation.

A moment later, as I continued to dictate additional news alerts to Grigsby, my iPhone vibrated and my Associated Press app displayed the first bulletin.

The cat was now officially out of the bag.

CB ED

CHAPTER 51

We were nearing Chevy Chase Circle where the state of Maryland begins, D.C. ends, and so does Triolo's jurisdiction. We'd passed several red and gray taxis, but none had Nathan Mann as a passenger.

Triolo cut his lights and siren, circled the roundabout and began cruising southwest on Connecticut. While I'd been on the phone with Grigsby filing updates on the Mann escape story, a video feed from the surveillance drone was displaying on Triolo's dashboard-mounted screen.

The drone – smaller than the one Rogan demonstrated for me – hovered about twenty feet above and just ahead of us, scouring Connecticut Ave. for red and gray taxis. The drone was no bigger than a bird.

"I think we lost him," Triolo said.

"I'm not ready to give up yet."

"Well, he's not along here." Triolo swore and hit the steering wheel. "If you were him, where would you go?"

"I think he's going to get his gun."

"Why would he do that? And where's his gun?"

"He probably doesn't have his gun with him."

"Why?"

"Because I doubt very seriously that he would be allowed to carry it into the White House, especially if he meets regularly with the president."

"Good point. Why would he want his gun?"

"Because I think he's a desperate man. He's nearly at the pinnacle of power when suddenly his world begins to unravel. He has so much to lose."

"Like what?"

"He's at the right hand of power. Hell, he helped mold the career of the president. But for some twisted reason – probably money – he becomes a heroin king pin. When one of his clients – my boyfriend – died of a fatal heroin overdose, it was about to become very high profile. I think Mann feared his distributor would blow the whistle on him, so he got rid of him."

"Okay. Makes sense," Triolo said.

"You saw the terror in his eyes when you suddenly showed up."

"Oh yeah. He was totally freaked."

"Right. He panicked. Now there's no turning back for him."

"So, where does he live?"

"You tell me."

Triolo got on the radio and called dispatch. "This is Triolo."

"Go ahead, Triolo," came the disembodied voice from the dash.

"Let's get the drone to check out this guy's crib. Suspect is Nathan Mann, m-a-n-n. Can you track down his address?"

"Ten-four. Hold one."

While Triolo and I had been talking, my phone was vibrating with each news alert that I'd filed with Grigsby.

"Dispatch to Triolo," the dashboard said.

"This is Triolo. Go ahead."

"Suspect's address is 1147 Chain Bridge Road in McLean, Virginia. It's known as Hickory Hill."

"I know that place," I said. "It's where Bobby Kennedy used to live when he was his brother's attorney general."

"Time to get the Fee-bees involved," Triolo said to me, then keyed his mic. "Please notify the FBI, but let's send the drone there and keep the feds in the loop," Triolo instructed.

"Ten-Four."

"We can keep an eye on things from here," Triolo said to me. "I'll swing over to Canal Road and Chain Bridge just in case he comes back into the district at that location."

My phone vibrated again. Paul Stone.

"I'm back at the press center," Paul said. "I tried calling Rogan, but got no answer on his cell. Tried calling his office, too, but the secretary said he's in a meeting and can't be disturbed. For now we're going with 'Rogan can't be reached for comment.' Can you keep trying him, Lark, while I go to the briefing?"

"Is there gonna be one?"

"Right now it looks like it. I take my steak medium rare and my Jameson Irish whiskey neat."

I scowled and sighed. "Okay. I'll keep trying."

I was about to dial Rogan's personal cell when Triolo said, "Hey, Chadwick. Take a look at this."

I leaned closer to the screen. It was an aerial shot of Hickory Hill, the place where Mann lives. The feed showed a sprawling, white, stone mansion with light blue shutters, numerous chimneys and well-manicured, wooded grounds. The body of a woman lay sprawled on the flagstones of a patio just outside the back door, a pool of blood widening from beneath her head.

"Jesus. If my hunch is correct, Mann got home, got his gun, and has just killed his wife. He's coming unglued," I said.

"Jesus indeed," Triolo said, keying his mic and calling in what we were seeing.

08 80

CHAPTER 52

With my iPhone, I snapped a shot of the computer screen on Trio-lo's dash. It showed a wide shot of Hickory Hill and the body of the woman sprawled on the patio.

"We don't know that's his wife," Triolo said. "And we don't know if the guy's still on the premises."

As he spoke, the shot from the drone showed police cars converging on the location.

I got on the phone to Grigsby. "This is not for the wire," I shouted, "but I want to let you know what's going on."

"Do I need to loop Scotty in again?" Grigsby asked.

"Yes!"

In a moment Scotty Barrington came on the line with Grigsby.

"What's the latest, Lark?" Barrington asked.

"This isn't for the wire, Scotty, but I think Mann has just shot and killed his wife."

"Holy shit! How do you know?" he asked.

"I don't know for sure. I'm still in a D.C. police car trying to find Mann. I'm watching a video feed from a police surveillance drone hovering above Mann's house in McLean. Again – this is not for the wire – but the image I'm looking at shows the body of a woman lying on the patio at the rear of Mann's house. I *think* Mann just killed his wife, but that's unconfirmed."

"Understood," Barrington said.

The dashboard radio crackled and the dispatcher instructed Triolo to turn to a "multi-agency tactical frequency." Once he adjusted his radio, I was able to hear the radio transmissions of the cops on the scene at Hickory Hill.

"Do you see Mann?" Grigsby asked.

"I don't, but he might still be there. The cops have just arrived on the scene. It looks like the place is surrounded. They've got their guns drawn. An ambulance just pulled up."

"Where's his place?" Barrington asked.

I gave him the address on Chain Bridge Road. "It's Bobby Kennedy's old Hickory Hill estate."

"Must be nice to be part of the one percent," Barrington said. "You're sure it's Mann's house?"

"Yes. I had a hunch Mann might go home to get his gun, so I had the cop I'm with get his dispatcher to find out where Mann lives. The FBI is on the case now, but it looks like the first responders are Virginia authorities."

"Okay," Barrington said. "Rochelle, we can bulletin that police have surrounded Mann's home and a body of a woman can be seen on the grounds. We can also say it's not known if Mann is inside the home. Are you good with that, Lark? Anything you need to tweak or add?"

"No. I think that's accurate and doesn't go beyond what we know."

"We'll work the phones from here to see if the responding authorities can give us any more," Barrington said.

I could hear Grigsby's keyboard clattering as she banged out the next bulletin. A moment later, my phone vibrated and the bulletin was on my iPhone, almost word-for-word what Barrington had just dictated.

"You've heard from Paul Stone, right?" I asked.

"Yup," Grigsby said. "Rogan can't be reached for comment. We've dropped that into the write-through."

"Okay," I said. "I'm going to keep trying Rogan. Maybe I can get through to him and get a quote." I looked at my watch. "It's eleven. Do you know if the White House briefing is gonna happen?"

"Last we heard from Paul, it's a go," Grigsby said. "All the local TV stations have already gone on the air with a bulletin on the search for Mann. With this latest bulletin of ours, they'll launch their helicopters to get aerial shots of Hickory Hill. Once there are pictures, CNN and the other national cable news nets will probably go wall to wall on this, crowding out coverage of anything else."

"Keep up the good work, Lark," Barrington said.

Triolo turned right off Arizona Avenue and drove north on Canal Road alongside the Potomac River to the D.C. side of the Chain Bridge.

"Has anyone tried calling Mann on his cell?" I asked Triolo.

"Yeah, but they're not having any luck. While you were on the phone, I heard chatter on the radio that there's no answer at the house and they retrieved two cell phones from the briefcase he dropped when he ran away from me at the White House."

"So he's out of touch with the rest of the world?"

"Looks like it, unless the cab's radio is tuned to an all-news station."

Triolo pulled off the road onto the shoulder at the foot of the bridge where it intersects with Canal and the Clara Barton Parkway. From there we could see the cars coming directly toward us on Chain Bridge from Virginia to the D.C. side of the Potomac. If Mann came this way in a red cab, we'd see him.

"Keep watching for those taxis," Triolo said to me. "If he's already left the mansion, it's possible he'll re-enter D.C. here."

"Okay," I said.

Most of the cars coming off the Chain Bridge were turning right to go south into the District, but some were turning north onto Clara Barton.

As I placed a call to Rogan's office, the drone at Hickory Hill had swooped lower and was sending back close-up images, first peering through the open back door, and then looking in the windows, trying to see if Mann was still inside. So far, it appeared the house was empty.

At one point, as the drone swung around briefly, I could see a SWAT team carrying bullet-proof shields. They were protecting two EMTs as they made their way along the side and to the back of the mansion. They got to the body and were checking vital signs.

To my surprise – and delight – Rogan's receptionist put me right through to him.

"Hello, Miss Chadwick." Rogan sounded downright jovial. "I see from the way the Associated Press is blowing up my phone that you've been busy."

"An understatement, sir." I pulled out my pen and opened my reporter's notebook to a fresh page. "Thank you for taking my call."

"A pleasure." Beneath the bluster, Rogan's voice was tense.

"If you've been following our coverage, then you know why I'm calling," I said.

"Actually, I don't. I can see that Nathan Mann is on the run and that the investigation into Anne-Marie's death has been reopened, but I don't see what any of that has to do with me."

"The reason I'm calling is to ask you a few questions about Anne-Marie and about Nathan Mann. And, just so you're clear, we're on the record."

"Very well. But I still don't see why you need a quote from me. Although I can certainly tell you without reservation that Anne-Marie's death is tragic. A devastating loss for me personally."

"Are you denying that you had anything to do with her death?"

He laughed, a hollow bark. "Of course I'm denying it. What a ridiculous thing for you to insinuate. She was brilliant. A trusted friend. A valuable partner. Why would I kill her?"

"Perhaps to keep her quiet – or to punish her?"

"For what? You're making no sense, Miss Chadwick."

"Just hours before she died, she met with me and alleged that you were blackmailing Nathan Mann. I also saw what looked like your SUV near where she and I met."

"The world is full of SUVs, Miss Chadwick."

"Ones with gold wheel rims?"

"I wouldn't know."

"Would you know that you were seen inside that SUV picking up Anne-Marie right after she met with me?"

"So you say. I wouldn't know that, either."

"What about her blackmail allegation?"

"What about it?"

"She alleged you were blackmailing Mann to influence the president to open the skies to commercial drones."

"That's preposterous. I don't deny *lobbying* Nathan – or anyone else who would listen, for that matter. Even you. But blackmail? I hardly think so. But I might be able to provide you with some insight as to why Nathan may have shot that shoe repairman."

"I'm all ears."

He laughed.

"What's so funny?"

"I'm picturing the image."

What an asshole, I thought to myself. To Rogan, I said, "You say you have a theory about Nathan Mann?"

"Oh. It's more than a theory. The man's personal life is a mess."

"How so? And how do you know?"

"He told me so himself."

"When? Where? And what did he tell you?"

"It was a year ago while he was still F.A.A. Administrator. We were on a panel together at a conference at the Hilton in Tysons Corner in northern Virginia. We were having a drink together afterward in the lounge just off the lobby. One drink became several. We were developing a great rapport.

"At one point, when I realized how late it was getting, I apologized for keeping him out so late. 'Your wife is probably worried about you,' I'd said. He replied – and this is an exact quote – 'Oh, she probably passed out hours ago. She's a hopeless lush.' Those are his exact words, Lark."

"Why would he tell you that?" I asked.

"Probably because by that time he was pretty drunk himself. That, plus we'd struck up an excellent rapport."

"So his wife's a drunk and that's why he seems to be cracking up? I find that hard to believe."

"I think it's deeper than that," Rogan said. "As we talked, he told me he was worried about how he'd be able to sustain his lavish lifestyle because his daughters had just been accepted into Ivy League schools, but didn't have scholarships. Nathan had gone from academe into government, so he had the power, but not the wealth to sustain his habit. He told me he was leveraged to the hilt."

"So he turned to selling drugs?"

"Oh, I wouldn't know about that. All I know is that he told me that he was in way over his head financially. But, now that you mention it, I suppose, with his background as drug czar, he could have used his position to intercept heroin and mount his own distribution ring. Sort of 'Breaking Bad' on steroids, so to speak." Another hollow laugh.

I started to ask another question, but I stopped when I heard a commotion in the background coming over the phone line, then Rogan began shouting. "Lark! It's Mann. He's got a gun. Nathan! No – no! Oh, God!"

There were two loud percussive noises followed by a clunk. Then Mann's voice came on the phone. "Lark? Lark Chadwick? Is this you?"

"Mr. Mann? What happened?"

"I've just killed that son of a bitch Rogan. Now I'm coming for you."

There was another clunk and the line went dead.

CHAPTER 53

"Oh my God!" I exclaimed, nearly dropping my phone.

"What's wrong?" Triolo asked, alarmed.

"Oh my God!"

"What? What is it?" he demanded.

"Mann just shot Rogan."

Triolo grabbed the mic from his dash. "Where? Where'd this happen?"

"In Rogan's office near Dulles."

"An address. I need an address, goddammit."

"I've got it. Hold on." I fumbled with my cell and found the address. My hands were shaking so badly I kept bobbling the phone, nearly dropping it.

"Hurry!" Triolo yelled.

"Here it is!" I read it to him.

Triolo keyed his mic. "This is Triolo, D.C. Police."

"Go ahead, Triolo," came the voice of a man who I assumed was handling joint tactical operations.

"Report of shots fired." He gave the address. "I have reason to believe the suspect has shot and possibly killed another person."

As Triolo called in the shooting, I speed-dialed Grigsby.

"Rochelle!" I yelled into the phone when she answered. "I was on the phone with Rogan when Mann barged into his office and shot him."

"Okay. Calm down and back up." Her voice was in The Zone, a steely calm I've experienced myself when on deadline and laser-focused on the story and only the story, blocking out all distractions. "Tell me exactly what happened," Grigsby said.

I kept trying to catch my breath.

"Begin with what you think is the best way to bulletin this," she instructed as I began to get my wits about me.

"Um...um..."

"Steady, Lark. Steady..."

"Okay, okay," I said, gasping for air. "Authorities are responding to shots fired at the northern Virginia firm of drone developer Dolph Rogan." My voice quavered. "Fugitive National Security Adviser Nathan Mann is believed to be the shooter."

"Okay. Just a sec," Grigsby said. I heard her keyboard clatter and a moment later the bulletin caused the phone to vibrate in my hand. "Now, tell me what happened. Just let it out. I'm taking notes. What did Rogan tell you?"

"Rogan expressed sadness at the death of his long-time assistant Anne-Marie Gustofsen, calling it 'tragic,' but denied having anything to do with her death."

"Okay. Good." I could hear her typing. "You're sounding stronger, Lark. Then what happened?"

"Rogan also denied Gustofsen's allegation to me that he's blackmailing Nathan Mann. I'm part of the story, Rochelle, so I'm not sure how you want to handle that."

"I'll make it 'denied Gustofsen's allegation in a telephone conversation with A.P.'s White House Correspondent Lark Chadwick . . .' blah, blah, blah."

"Okay. There's more."

"Shoot."

"Really?"

"Sorry. Go ahead."

"Moments before shots rang out in his office, Rogan told Chadwick Mann was under financial pressures and speculated that may be the reason Mann is on the run. Am I going too fast, Rochelle? Are you getting this?"

"You're doing fine. Keep going."

I spoke slowly and clearly, giving Grigsby more quotes from Rogan including his comments about Mann's financial problems.

I concluded my filing by telling Grigsby, "Chadwick reports that while they were talking, Rogan exclaimed, 'It's Mann. He's got a gun.' Then, 'Nathan. No. No! Oh God!' Chadwick heard what sounded like two gunshots, then Mann got on the line. 'I've just killed Rogan and now I'm coming for you,' Chadwick said Mann told her."

Triolo, who'd been telling the dispatcher to send the drone to Rogan's office, lowered the mic and looked at me. "Did you just say he's gunning for *you?*"

I took the phone away from my mouth. "Uh huh," I nodded.

"Where does he think you are?" Triolo asked, urgently.

"Just a sec, Rochelle," I said into the phone, then, to Triolo I said, "He probably thinks I'm at the White House press center on Jackson Place next to Lafayette Square. We went right past it when you were chasing him toward H Street."

"Okay," Triolo said, throwing his unmarked white Crown Vic into gear, turning on his lights and siren, and whipping a U-turn onto Canal Road. As he floored the accelerator, he keyed his mic again. "This is Triolo."

"Go ahead, Triolo," the dashboard said.

"Suspect is believed to be armed and heading for the White House press center on Jackson Place. I'm heading there now."

"Ten-four, Triolo."

"I just heard that," Grigsby said. "I need to check with Scotty to see if he wants to go with it. If Mann's still in a cab, he might be listening to coverage on a car radio. Not sure it's a good idea to tip him off that he's expected."

"Yes," I said.

"Paul's calling in on the other line. I'll call you back," Grigsby said and hung up.

Triolo, his face tense and both hands on the wheel, was rocketing south on Canal Road toward Georgetown.

Traffic, as usual, congealed at the Key Bridge as cars and trucks coming from Virginia emptied into the District. Canal Road morphed into M Street and was backed up in both directions.

Triolo's flashing lights and yipping siren weren't making much difference, yet somehow we managed to weave through traffic as we inched our way closer to the White House.

From time to time, we'd pass a red and gray cab, but Mann wasn't in any of them.

"How do you think he's getting around?" Triolo asked me.

"My guess is he's still in the cab."

"Wouldn't he be in his own car by now?"

"I doubt it."

"Why?"

"These bigwigs are driven everywhere. He probably hasn't gotten behind the wheel in ten years."

Triolo nodded thoughtfully. "We haven't heard reports of any car-jackings or stolen cabs."

"It could be the cabbie has no clue," I said. "Mann stops at a place, tells the guy to wait, goes inside, kills someone, then tucks the gun away in his belt or a pocket, sashays back to the cab and has the guy drive to the next place, where the process is repeated. The cabbie just thinks his passenger's running errands."

"Or," Triolo said, "Mann's now got a gun to the cabbie's head."

We looked at the video feed on the dashboard monitor from the drone. It was hovering over Rogan's office building. Police had arrived and were taping off the area.

"It looks like the drone's searching for any sign of a man running away," I said, watching the view from the drone swivel aimlessly from side to side.

Triolo keyed his mic. "This is Triolo."

"Go ahead, Triolo."

"Believe suspect might still be using the taxi to get around. I suggest you use the USV to look for him in a red cab between the site of the latest incident and the White House complex."

"Ten-four, Triolo. Thanks."

We watched the screen as the drone turned and pointed in the direction of 16th and Pennsylvania, then began scanning roads leading in that direction. From time to time it would swoop closer to a red cab.

I was amazed as I watched the drone dive and then fly next to the vehicle and peek inside. That's much more effective, I thought, than a helicopter that has to hover hundreds of feet above traffic. But so far, Mann wasn't in any of the cabs the drone found.

I checked the Associated Press app on my phone and saw that the write-through story had just been updated. It featured about a dozen photos including a file picture of Mann in happier days, the shot I took of Mann escaping after shooting Ray Barber, the video clip I shot of Mann running from Triolo, pictures from the scene of the two shootings, a shot Doug took of Rogan and Gustofsen giving me a drone demonstration – and a picture of Doug I'd never seen before. The warm smile on his face took my breath away.

The story also included portions of the initial report Paul and I had written the night before.

Gannon Aide Nathan Mann Wanted for Murder

By: ROCHELLE GRIGSBY and PAUL STONE

Police in the Washington, D.C. area are in a desperate hunt for Nathan Mann, President Gannon's National Security Adviser. Police believe Mann is responsible for three shooting deaths in the past two days.

The most recent shooting took place at 11 a.m. at the office of Applied Electronics in Reston, Virginia. Authorities say one man is dead, but aren't releasing his name.

A.P. White House Correspondent Lark Chadwick was on the phone with the victim at the time of the shooting.

"He said, 'Lark! It's Mann. He's got a gun. Nathan! No - no! Oh, God!' " Chadwick said.

The reporter said she then heard what sounded like two gunshots.

"A voice that sounded like Mann's came on the line and threatened to kill me," Chadwick said.

Presidential Press Secretary Ron McClain's briefing was cut short at 11:15 a.m. The temporary press center near the White House is on lockdown.

McClain expressed surprise that Mann is now a fugitive.

"I informed the president that Nathan is wanted by police and the president is calling on his national security adviser to turn himself in to authorities," McClain said.

Mann is a long-time friend of President Gannon and First Lady Rose Gannon.

President Gannon has frequently called Mann "my friend and mentor."

About an hour before the shooting this morning in Reston, police responded to a disturbance at Mann's home in Northern Virginia where they found the body of an unidentified woman sprawled on the patio at the back of Mann's mansion.

"The victim had been shot multiple times," Matthew Johnson of the Fairfax County Sheriff's Department said.

Police are not releasing the name of the victim until next of kin can be notified.

The manhunt began about 9:30 a.m. when D.C. Metropolitan Police Detective Nicholas Triolo confronted Mann on Executive Drive between the White House and the Eisenhower Executive Office Building.

Mann is wanted for questioning in connection with the shooting death last night of Washington shoe repairman Ray Barber.

The A.P.'s Lark Chadwick witnessed the shooting.

Seconds after Thursday night's shooting, Chadwick took a picture of the escaping gunman who bears a strong resemblance to Mann.

Chadwick was with Detective Triolo when he confronted Mann this morning.

"Mann appeared to panic, dropped his briefcase and ran away through the Northwest gate of the White House," Chadwick reported.

Chadwick filed a video clip of Mann escaping.

Triolo, with Chadwick in the police car, gave chase.

Mann was last seen a few blocks from the White House hailing a taxicab heading north on Connecticut Avenue in Washington.

The motive for the shootings could be the tip of a much bigger iceberg involving drug dealing and blackmail at the White House.

According to Chadwick, Ray Barber, the victim of the first shooting Thursday night, was a drug dealer who Chadwick believes sold a fatal dose of heroin to her boyfriend, A.P. White House Photographer Doug Mitchell.

On Monday, Feb. 21, Chadwick discovered Mitchell's body slumped at the wheel of his vehicle two days after he disappeared from the White House Correspondents' Association Dinner at a Washington Hotel.

Police confirm that Mitchell's last phone calls were to Barber, but authorities have not been able to prove that Barber sold heroin to Mitchell.

Preliminary autopsy results confirm Mitchell died of "heroin intoxication."

Chadwick said she witnessed Mann shoot and kill Barber as she sat in her car parked across the street from Barber's shoe repair shop in Northwest Washington.

"I was planning to tail Barber after he closed his store," Chadwick said. "I hoped I'd be able to get a picture of him selling drugs to someone."

According to Chadwick, just before the store closed, a man wearing a hat and overcoat stormed into the store, shot Barber several times at point-blank range, then took a handful of money from the cash register.

"I took a picture as the man was leaving the store," Chadwick said. "I was stunned when I recognized the assailant as Nathan Mann."

Before Chadwick came forward, police were treating the shooting as a robbery-gone-bad.

If the president's national security adviser did, indeed, kill an alleged drug dealer, it raises the question, why?

"In my opinion, Nathan Mann was desperately trying to silence one of his heroin distributors," Chadwick said.

According to Chadwick, drone mogul Dolph Rogan was blackmailing Mann to influence President Gannon's policy on the commercialization of drones.

Chadwick said Rogan's executive assistant, Anne-Marie Gustofsen, made the blackmail accusation to Chadwick as an anonymous source.

Gustofsen was found dead shortly after speaking with Chadwick.

Chadwick said that on the evening of the Valentine's Day drone attack on the White House, she got an anonymous tip to investigate Rogan, founder of Applied Electronics in Reston, Virginia.

According to its website, the company's motto is, "A Drone in Every Garage."

Chadwick interviewed Rogan the day after the drone attack and he gave her a demonstration of how drones operate.

During their interview, Chadwick said Rogan called on President Gannon to lift the current ban on the commercialization of drones.

In a phone conversation moments before the shooting in his office, Rogan denied blackmailing Mann.

"That's preposterous," Rogan said. "I don't deny lobbying Nathan - or anyone else who would listen...but blackmail? I hardly think so."

According to Chadwick, the anonymous source kept pressing her to look more deeply into Rogan's associates.

"I was getting impatient with the tipster," Chadwick said. "I thought I might be getting spun by Rogan himself, so I insisted on a face-to-face meeting or I'd walk away."

Chadwick said the tipster agreed to a clandestine, middle-of-the-night meeting in the same parking garage in Arlington, Virginia where Washington Post reporter Bob Woodward met with Deep Throat during the Watergate scandal in the 1970s.

"The tipster was Anne-Marie Gustofsen, Rogan's co-founder of Applied Electronics," Chadwick said.

A few hours after their interview, Gustofsen's body was found in the Potomac River just north of D.C.

"In our interview, Gustofsen said she feared Rogan would kill her if he found out about our meeting," Chadwick said.

Chadwick said Gustofsen alleged that Rogan was blackmailing National Security Adviser Nathan Mann to influence President Gannon to lift the ban on the commercialization of drones.

Chadwick said their interview was cut short before Gustofsen could explain how Rogan was blackmailing Mann.

According to Chadwick, "Anne-Marie got spooked and ran away."

Chadwick said she saw a vehicle that looked like Rogan's Lincoln SUV leaving the parking garage.

Chadwick added that Mitchell, who was waiting in a parked car just outside the garage, saw Gustofsen get into an SUV driven by Rogan.

Fairfax County, Virginia, Coroner Lee Chalmers ruled Gustofsen's death a suicide.

But Friday morning authorities reopened the investigation into Gustofsen's death based on new information provided by the Associated Press.

In Chadwick's phone conversation with Rogan, just before the shooting in his office, Rogan expressed sadness at Gustofsen's death, but denied killing her, calling it a "devastating personal loss."

"She was brilliant. A trusted friend, a valuable partner," Rogan said. "Why would I kill her?"

Chadwick suggested Gustofsen might have been murdered to punish or silence her. Rogan called that "ridiculous."

In the telephone interview with Chadwick this morning, Rogan said that Mann was having financial difficulties and suggested that might have triggered the current shooting spree.

"The man's personal life is a mess," Rogan said.

Mann was one of Will Gannon's law professors at Vanderbilt University 20 years ago. Mann left Vanderbilt 10 years ago to become the head of the Drug Enforcement Administration. He later became head of the Federal Aviation Administration.

According to Rogan, he met Mann when Mann headed the F.A.A.

Chadwick said Rogan told her he didn't know if Mann was selling heroin, but Rogan speculated that because of Mann's background as the nation's drug czar, it's possible.

"All I know is that he told me that he was in way over his head financially," Rogan said. "He could have used his position [as drug czar] to intercept heroin and mount his own distribution ring. Sort of 'Breaking Bad' on steroids, so to speak."

According to Chadwick, that's when she heard a commotion over the phone, Rogan pleading with Mann not to shoot, and then gunshots.

A.P. White House Correspondent Lark Chadwick contributed to this story.

I looked up from my iPhone to see that we'd finally passed through Georgetown and had turned off M Street onto Pennsylvania that led diagonally to 17th Street and the White House complex.

The street was wider here and Triolo was able to pick up speed.

Just then my phone bleeped. I looked at the screen: *Rose Gannon.*

ଔ ଙ

CHAPTER 54

I answered my phone. "Hello, Mrs. Gannon."

Triolo shot me a look. "What the–" *Rose Gannon?* he mouthed.

I nodded at him – and smiled.

"Lark. Are you all right?" Rose's voice was urgent. "Everyone's carrying your reporting. Where are you?"

"In a police car heading back to the press center on Jackson Place. Where are you?"

"I'm at a luncheon in Blair House across from the White House." She sounded exasperated. "My Secret Service detail has locked down the building. They've got me cooped up in the basement like some kind of prisoner. This is maddening."

"Have you been in touch with Nathan Mann?" I asked.

"I've been trying, but he's not picking up. Is it true that he's threatened to kill you?"

"Yes. He probably assumes I'm at the press center, so we're on our way there to head him off. "

"It's suicide. He must know that," she said, more to herself than to me.

"Are you still close friends?" I asked.

"We're still close. Always have been."

"Did you see this coming?"

"Are we off the record?"

"No. We are *on* the record. And it's not negotiable."

She sighed and was silent a long moment. Finally, she spoke. "I knew that he was unhappy in his marriage. I knew he was worried about money. I had *no* idea about the heroin."

I was scribbling notes. "Does the heroin allegation surprise you?"

"It does. A little. But the more I think about it, the more I realize he was certainly in a position to make it happen."

"When was the last time you spoke with him?"

"Monday night. On the phone. It was the day I got out of the hospital. We try to talk regularly."

"That would have been within hours after I interviewed him," I said.

"Yes. He mentioned that."

"What did he say?"

"What did *you* say during the interview?" she asked. "It really seemed to set him off."

"In what way?"

"He was annoyed when you tried to press him about his family. He's very sensitive about that."

"I also nudged him about Dolph Rogan," I said.

"He didn't mention it."

"And I do remember him expressing sympathy about Doug," I said.

"Yes. That sounds like him."

"I wasn't going to burden him, but when his concern seemed more than perfunctory, I told him I was working with the cops to bust Ray Barber, the guy who sold the heroin to Doug."

"Oh my," Rose said, surprised. "That certainly explains how we got to where we are now."

"Did you tell him about–" I stopped, realizing that Triolo was eavesdropping. "Did you tell Nathan about what you revealed to me the other day?"

"About my illness?"

"Yes."

"No. I was still processing it then."

"Did you notice anything different about Mann during your last conversation with him Monday night? Anything that alarmed or worried you?"

"Yes. He seemed more agitated than usual. Agitated and morose. I was becoming concerned."

"About what?"

"I thought he was starting to fall in love with me again."

"Again?"

"Oh, he had a thing for me a long time ago when we first met. I think I alluded to it when you and I spoke the other day. But I'd made it clear to him back then that he was a friend and nothing more. And he seemed to accept that."

"Until Monday?"

"Yes. I really wish we could go off the record, Lark."

"I'm sorry. I can't do that. It's a fluid, breaking story. Nathan Mann is at the center of it and you're one of his closest and long-term friends."

Triolo and I had just zoomed past 20th Street, closing in fast on 17th and Pennsylvania. I noticed the drone flying just ahead of us, its video feed displaying on the dashboard screen. The drone swooped alongside a red cab. Sitting in the right rear seat was Nathan Mann.

"There he is!" I shouted at Triolo.

Triolo picked up his mic. "This is Triolo."

"Go ahead, Triolo."

"Suspect is in the right rear of a red cab that's approaching Seventeenth and Pennsylvania Northwest. The USV has him in view."

"Copy that, Triolo."

"Oh my God," Rose Gannon said. "He must be just down the block from where I am right now. I'm going out there. Maybe I can talk some sense into him."

"Wait!" I shouted.

The line went dead.

CΒ ΒϿ

CHAPTER 55

Triolo and I were still a few blocks behind the cab carrying Nathan Mann. The drone continued to hover to the side and just above the car, keeping Mann in view, but out of his line of sight.

I immediately called back Rose Gannon. To my amazement, she picked up.

"Don't try to talk me out of this, Lark. My mind is made up." Her breathing was labored as if she was climbing stairs, or walking fast.

I heard a man's voice in the background, probably the lead agent of her detail. "Ma'am! Ma'am! I can't let you go outside. It's too dangerous."

"Mr. Blake," Rose said, "I'm dying anyway. I *am* going out there. He is my best friend and if anyone can stop him – *peacefully* – it's *me!*"

I kept listening, wanting to see how this would play out.

"What do you mean you're dying?" the agent asked.

"I've got cancer. And it's spreading fast. The only people who know this are my doctor, my husband, my friend here on the phone – and now you. I'm willing to take the risk."

"But, ma'am–"

"No!" she yelled, cutting him off. "You're welcome to tag along. Bring the rest of your team, if you must – and your guns – but this is my *friend* we're talking about."

"But–"

"I *mean* it, Mr. Blake." Her voice was steel-strong. I could hear the click-click of her high heels echoing on a marble floor. She was walking fast, and kept talking to her bodyguard. "When Ronald Reagan was shot, Nancy Reagan defied her agents and told them she was ready to *walk* to the hospital, if necessary, to be with her husband. Nathan Mann is one of my husband's best friends. And mine. He may be losing his marbles, Mr. Blake, but I firmly believe that as long as there's life, there's hope."

"Yes, ma'am," the agent said. I heard a rustling sound and then he spoke again, presumably into one of his cuff links. "Dancer is on the move. Repeat: Dancer is on the move. She plans to confront the suspect outside Blair House."

"Are you still with me, Lark?" Rose Gannon asked.

"Yes, ma'am."

"Pretty cheeky, huh?" she chuckled.

"Very impressive, but very scary. You know Mann's probably killed at least three people in cold blood, don't you?"

"Oh, I'm aware. But maybe I can stop him."

"I'm going to put you on hold, ma'am, but please keep this line open so I can hear, okay?"

"Think you can use it in the book?" she laughed. "Sure. I'll hold."

The cab was pulling to a stop at a red light. I put the first lady on hold and speed-dialed Grigsby.

"Whatcha got?" she asked.

"Mann and the cab are stopping at Seventeenth and Pennsylvania."

"How do you know?"

"I'm watching the video feed from the drone on the dashboard of the cop car I'm in."

"Is he holding the cabbie hostage?"

"Not that I can tell. Also, I'm on the phone with Rose Gannon. She's at Blair House. Even though the place is locked down, she's defying her agents and is on her way out to try to – in her words – 'talk some sense' – into Mann."

"Holy shit!" I could hear the tension in Grigsby's voice as she pounded the keyboard. "Hold on, Lark. Lemme get this out."

A moment later, the typing stopped and my phone vibrated with the latest bulletin: *Fugitive National Security Adviser Nathan Mann spotted near White House. First Lady Rose Gannon defies agents in at-*

tempt to confront and "talk some sense" into Mann. A.P.'s Chadwick on the scene.

"I'm going to patch you through to radio, Lark, just like during the drone attack the other day."

"Really?" I gulped.

"You're probably the only reporter on the scene right now. The press center is on lockdown, it's a no-fly zone for the news choppers, and until the locals and other crews mobilize and get there, you're the nation's eyes and ears."

"Okay..." I said with not a lot of conviction. Quickly, I merged the call with Rose Gannon's line, took her off hold and said urgently into the phone, "Rose, are you still there?"

"I am, Lark. I'm almost to the front door of Blair House. I'm followed by every Secret Service agent in the world – or so it would seem. Guns drawn, I might add."

"I'm about to go live on A.P. radio. I've patched you in. Please stay on the line, okay?"

"Ah! My legacy. Charming." She let out a long sigh. "Sure. Okay. I'll put you on speaker."

I put my phone on speaker, as well. There were a few clicks and then, before I had time to panic – or to compose anything articulate or meaningful – I heard the strident tones of A.P.'s news-bulletin sounder, followed by an urgent, stentorian voice.

"This is a breaking-news bulletin from the Associated Press. I'm James Macateere in New York.

"A dramatic scene is taking place just outside the White House near where fugitive National Security Adviser Nathan Mann has been spotted. He's wanted for the shooting deaths of three people over the past two days.

"A.P. White House Correspondent Lark Chadwick is on the scene for us. Lark, tell us what's happening."

I took a deep breath, released a silent prayer, and began speaking. I decided it would be less stressful to simply make it a conversation with Macateere.

"James, a dramatic scene indeed. I apologize for the sound of the loud siren, but I'm speaking to you from inside a police car pursuing Nathan Mann. We're at Eighteenth and Pennsylvania, about to pull up behind a taxicab carrying the president's national security adviser. The cab is a block away from me and has just arrived at Seventeenth Street and Pennsylvania Avenue.

"As you said, Mann is wanted by police for three shooting deaths. He's believed to be armed and heading for the temporary filing center of the White House Press corps located adjacent to Lafayette Square across from the executive mansion.

"James, before I go any further, I should tell you that I'm also on the phone with First Lady Rose Gannon. She is a close friend of Mann's. She's inside Blair House – just a few dozen yards from where Mann is right now.

"Even though Blair House is on lockdown in anticipation of Mann's arrival in the area, Mrs. Gannon is defying her Secret Service detail and is planning to confront Mann and try to talk him into giving himself up.

"Mrs. Gannon, can you hear me?" I asked.

"I can, Lark." Rose Gannon sounded strong and serene.

"Why are you taking this risk, ma'am?"

"Because Nathan Mann is my friend. It's the least I can do. And I ask anyone who's listening right now to pray for Nathan and for the families left behind in his wake."

I thought ruefully that, as far as I was concerned, two of Mann's victims were murderers themselves and that a special place in hell belonged to Ray Barber for selling a fatal dose of heroin to Doug.

"I'm heading outside now, Lark, but I'll keep the line open," Rose said.

"James," I said to Macateere, "as we're speaking, I'm using my iPhone to make a video of what I'm seeing. I'm watching a real-time video feed from a D.C. Police drone that just moments ago located Mann in the backseat of one of Washington's red and gray taxicabs.

"I'm with D.C. Detective Nicholas Triolo who alerted his superiors that Mann was nearing and about to arrive at the White House complex.

"The video feed coming from the drone is showing the taxi carrying Mann stopped at a red light at the southwest corner of Seventeenth and Pennsylvania. Amazingly, Mann seems to be calm and unrushed. And the cab driver appears to be unaware that the person paying for his fare right now is at the center of a major, if you'll excuse the term, manhunt."

"So, this is not a hostage situation, correct?" Macateere asked.

"Yes. You're correct. It's not a hostage situation. In fact, Mann has just gotten out of the cab and it's pulling away and turning south onto Seventeenth Street, the driver apparently oblivious to the danger he was in or the drama that appears about to unfold here."

"What's happening now?" Macateere asked. "Is there a police presence in the area?"

"There's a guardhouse at this end of the pedestrian mall, but access to the area is not restricted to someone on foot. Mann's walking briskly across Seventeenth Street. He's wearing a dark blue overcoat and a fedora hat pulled down to obscure his face. He's going wide of the guardhouse and staying close to the high fence that fronts the Eisenhower Executive Office Building. The guards didn't see him."

"Is he carrying a gun? Do you see a weapon?" Macateere asked.

"No. His hands are empty and are swinging at his sides as he walks. He appears to be blending in quite well with all the tourists and pedestrians out for a noontime stroll along the pedestrian mall by the Eisenhower and the red brick Renwick Museum of Art.

"Mann appears to be unfazed by our approaching siren," I said, "perhaps because in D.C. and many large cities, sirens are nothing more than white noise."

Triolo pulled to the curb at 17th Street at a perpendicular angle facing Mann as he continued walking nonchalantly. No one seemed to notice him.

Triolo killed his siren, but kept his flashers on.

"The police car I'm in has just pulled up to the Seventeenth Street end of the Pennsylvania Avenue pedestrian mall, James." I reported.

"Stay here," Triolo barked at me. He got out of the car and hustled toward the guard shack.

I ignored Triolo and got out, too, and ran behind him, steadying my iPhone sideways and in front of me with both hands.

"James, I'm following Detective Triolo as he pursues Mann on foot. There are quite a few people here on the pedestrian mall. Triolo is at the guardhouse now, James. Let's listen."

Triolo, dressed in civilian clothes – a sport coat – flashed his badge to the three uniformed agents manning the guardhouse. He spoke in authoritative rapid-fire bursts. "Triolo. D.C. Police. Man with a gun. Follow me. This way."

Two of the guards unholstered their weapons and followed Triolo who also whipped his pistol from inside his sport coat as he trotted after Mann, now nearly half a block away.

"James, I'm a little out of breath because I'm trying to keep up with Detective Triolo and two uniformed Secret Service agents. They're running after Mann who is now nearing Blair House." I paused and took a deep breath, then continued. "The front door to Blair House is opening. First Lady Rose Gannon is stepping through the doorway."

ଓ ଞ

CHAPTER 56

The first lady, wearing a bright red overcoat and black high heels, held her cell phone waist high in her left hand.

Mann, walking on the far side of the Pennsylvania Avenue pedestrian mall, hadn't noticed her yet.

As I ran, I tried to hold my iPhone in front of me as steadily as I could and continued to video the scene while also talking live with A.P. Radio's James Macateere in New York.

"James, Mrs. Gannon appears to be poised and calm as she makes her way slowly and deliberately down the front steps of Blair House. She is swarmed by her Secret Service detail. I count at least four men and two women – all but two have their guns drawn."

"Are they pointing their weapons at Mann?" Macateere asked.

"No. Their guns are at the ready, but pointed toward the ground. A few of the agents have gone ahead of the first lady and are keeping pedestrians out of the way. Another agent is gesturing at Detective Triolo and the two uniformed agents. He's trying to get them to keep their distance. Two agents, both men, are standing on either side of the first lady, but their guns are not drawn."

"Triolo and the two guards have now slowed to a walk. They're about twenty yards behind Mann – and I'm about twenty yards behind them."

"Nathan!" the first lady called out, her voice strong. A nanosecond later the sound of her voice came through the speaker of the cell phone I held in my hand.

I lowered my voice and spoke more softly into the phone, "Mann's stopped walking and has turned to look at Rose Gannon."

For a fleeting second I had this wildly incongruous thought that my hushed voice made it sound as though I was narrating a dramatic moment at the Masters golf tournament: *And here's Tiger Woods at Augusta on the eighteenth hole putting for an eagle – and the green jacket.*

I pushed the thought from my mind and continued my reporting. "Mrs. Gannon has come to a stop at the curb in front of Blair House. Mann sees the first lady. He just stopped and is standing across the street at the far curb. A clear space of about twenty-five yards separates them.

"Detective Triolo and the two uniformed Secret Service agents are now standing about ten yards from Mann. Their guns are out and they're pointing them at the national security adviser. I'm hovering another ten yards or so back from them. From my vantage point at the curb across from Blair House, I can see everything. This moment is electric, James," I stage whispered.

"Nathan," Rose repeated, a little more gently. "What do you think you're trying to prove?"

"Nothing, Rose. Just trying to even the score." His voice was tired, flat.

"What do you mean?"

He held out his hands, palms up. "My life is over. It's over." He let his hands drop to his sides.

"No it's not, Nathan. Don't talk like that."

He gave her a helpless shrug and hung his head.

"You need help, Nathan," she said gently. "Turn yourself in."

He kept his head down. "It's too late for that, Rose."

"No it's not." She stepped off the curb.

All the Secret Service agents standing near the first lady tensed and the one to her left put a firm hand on her shoulder, stopping her. "We believe he's armed, ma'am," he said to her.

"Turn yourself in, Nathan," Rose repeated. She held out a hand to him. "I'm still your friend."

Mann looked up at her. From where I stood, I could only see the left side of his face. His jaw muscles were tensing. The turmoil going on inside him at that moment must have been incredible.

Even though I'd been able to hear him when he spoke, apparently the iPhone microphone wasn't strong enough to pick up what Mann was saying. So, James Macateere in New York, apparently uneasy with all the dead air, chose this moment to jump in.

"Lark? Lark Chadwick?" His powerful voice boomed from my phone's speaker. "Are you still with us? We're only able to hear one side of the conversation. What's Mann saying?"

Until that moment, Mann hadn't seen me, but when he heard my name coming from behind and to his left, he spun toward the sound. Our eyes locked and his face flushed with rage.

"Chadwick!" he bellowed. "There you are, you bitch. You've ruined my life."

Before I had a chance to react, Mann jammed his hand into the pocket of his overcoat and whipped out his pistol.

"Gun!" several of the agents yelled simultaneously.

In one smooth motion, the two agents flanking Rose Gannon pivoted and literally carried her, screaming angrily, up the steps, their bodies shielding her from Mann. The other agents leveled their weapons directly at him.

Mann's face was a contorted snarl of diabolical hatred. He began to raise his gun to shoot me.

I didn't flinch, not because I'm brave. I simply froze.

Triolo's gun was the first to flash and roar, followed in rapid succession by several other big booms that echoed off the stone façades of the buildings lining both sides of the street.

The force of the bullets striking him in the chest blew Mann backward. As he hit the pavement, sprawled on his back, his gun clattered to the street and his hat rolled harmlessly off to the side.

As soon as the shooting stopped, Triolo and the others ran to Nathan Mann, now lying motionless, eyes open, staring at the gray February sky.

"Lark! Lark! What's happening?" Macateere asked urgently.

I heard myself telling him that shots were fired.

I heard myself telling him that Mann appeared to be dead and First Lady Rose Gannon had been carried to safety.

I heard myself describing the conversation between Rose and Mann before the shooting.

I heard myself describing the moment Mann turned and focused his wrath on me.

I heard myself describing the aftermath of the shooting.

And then, I suddenly realized I was sick of hearing myself describe anything more. I'd had enough. I was spent. Exhausted. There was nothing more to describe.

There was nothing more that could be done to bring back Doug.

Was this justice? Would the violent deaths of Ray Barber and Nathan Mann stop others from selling – or using – heroin?

"James," I said simply, "that's all from here. Back to you."

I ended the call, turned off my phone, sat down on the curb, buried my face in my hands – and wept.

CB ☙

EPILOGUE

Two Weeks Later

The Nathan Mann story was big news for several days because it took a while for law enforcement authorities and reporters to put together all the pieces of the puzzle. Mann's heroin-dealing operation had managed to fly under the radar undetected for so long because he'd kept it small and he held the reins tightly.

It began when he was the nation's drug czar. He'd managed to find a vulnerable and corruptible Coast Guard officer stationed in Annapolis, Maryland who, in exchange for cash, was willing to provide Mann with a portion of heroin the Coast Guard intercepted and seized in busts from time to time along the Atlantic coast and in Chesapeake Bay.

The Coast Guard officer has been court-martialed. His trial is pending.

Ray Barber was one of what officials believe are only a few of Nathan Mann's heroin dealers. No arrests have been made, but Detective Elena Kerrigan tells me that police are watching a couple people very carefully and suspect they may have been part of Mann's small distribution network.

Police theorize that Mann panicked when he learned from me that the cops were looking at Ray Barber as the possible source of Doug's fatal heroin overdose. Mann then lost it completely when Triolo confronted him outside the White House.

Police were able to track down the Ethiopian immigrant who'd been Mann's cab driver. They questioned him for several hours.

The cabbie told police he was unaware of the identity of the man he picked up by Shotzie's Pub and was also unaware his rider was being sought by police.

While Triolo and I were searching in vain for Mann in a cab going north on Connecticut Avenue, Mann had instructed the cabbie to take a side street and head south over the Memorial Bridge into Virginia, so we were going in opposite directions.

According to the scenario of events reconstructed by police, Mann, as I suspected, then went home to retrieve his gun. He was becoming increasingly hopeless and unglued as his world unraveled.

The cab driver told police Mann instructed him to wait out front of the Hickory Hill mansion. Mann then shot and killed his wife as she tried to flee out the back door. The cabbie told police he was unaware of the shooting because it happened out of his view on the back patio and he didn't hear any shots because his car windows were closed due to the cold weather.

But Mann still had more scores to settle.

The cab driver reported that Mann seemed agitated when he got back in the car, but the cabbie thought nothing of it because, he said, often his riders are impatient and upset when they're running late for something.

Mann told the cabbie he had a plane to catch at Dulles, but when they got near the airport, Mann instructed the cab driver to go to Dolph Rogan's office.

Once again, Mann asked the driver to wait, then "calmly" went inside where he shot and killed Rogan while Rogan was on the phone with me. Police say Mann barely gave a second thought to the terrified receptionist who hid under a desk during the shooting.

When Mann returned to the cab, sweating profusely, he told the driver he'd forgotten something and instructed him to return to the White House.

The cab driver had been listening to a CD and not the radio. Consequently, he told police, he remained unaware of the search and the trail of death Nathan Mann was leaving in his wake. It was only after police pulled over the taxi shortly after it dropped Mann off near the White House that the cabbie realized how close he came to being taken hostage or being killed in the crossfire during the shooting.

Police finally released the cab driver when he was able to show that Mann used his credit card to pay the more than $500 tab he racked up. Before leaving the cab, Mann left the driver a generous thirty percent tip.

Police confirmed that the Mann-Rogan connection began on the day the two men appeared together on a panel discussion when Mann was F.A.A. Administrator. Authorities theorize that Rogan, in addition to learning of Mann's financial troubles, also learned of Mann's heroin-dealing activities – dirt that gave the greedy and narcissistic Rogan added leverage in his blackmail of Mann.

Police were able to confirm that Rogan killed Anne-Marie Gustofsen when they found video from a surveillance camera on Chain Bridge showing a grainy image of Rogan – his Lincoln SUV parked at the railing – tossing Gustofsen's unconscious body from the bridge into the Potomac at approximately four a.m., about an hour after she'd met with me in the Arlington, Virginia, parking garage.

Authorities agree with my theory that Rogan incapacitated Gustofsen by putting two ground-up tablets of a legal, natural, over-the-counter sleep aid into the booze that was in the flask Doug saw when Anne-Marie got into Rogan's SUV with him. Once she lost consciousness, police believe he placed heavy rocks into her pockets and dumped her into the water, making her drowning look like a suicide.

The video clip I took of the Mann shooting outside Blair House went viral and, I'm told, has been seen by at least four million people worldwide. After I filed it, I never looked at it again. But I frequently watch the reeeal coool clip I shot of Doug's standup routine in his living room the night we made love for the first – and only – time.

The White House Correspondents' Association gave me the Merriman Smith Award for Breaking News Coverage. It's named after the UPI reporter who was first to tell the world that shots were fired at President Kennedy's motorcade in Dallas in 1963. I share the prize with Rochelle Grigsby and Paul Stone.

I'd much rather have Doug Mitchell back in my life.

The White House News Photographers Association posthumously honored Doug for his still picture of the snarling soldier guarding the White House moments before the drone attack and the dramatic shot he took of Ernie Crandall holding back Stallings Ridgeway at the front of the briefing room just before they were killed.

I'm looking into the possibility of having Doug's cremains buried in Arlington National Cemetery.

Rochelle Grigsby relapsed shortly after the Mann shooting. She is currently in rehab at a Hazelden Betty Ford Foundation treatment center in Minnesota.

On the Monday following the shooting of Nathan Mann outside Blair House, I began meeting once a week with a grief counselor at the Wendt Center for Loss and Healing – the same organization that gave me literature at the morgue the day I identified Doug's body.

I'm no stranger to grief, but Doug's death threw me. I'd fallen hard for him. And I fell hard against my better judgment. So now, in addition to coming to grips with missing him, I'm trying to understand myself better so that I won't fall for another bad boy who'll end up breaking my heart.

Right now it feels like my heart's on Novocain. Will I ever be able to love again? I wonder and worry about that a lot.

But maybe I'm making progress.

For a week after the shooting, Nick Triolo was blowing up my phone with texts asking me out for dinner. I kept putting him off, while he not-so-subtly kept reminding me of how he saved my life.

I talked it over with my grief counselor, telling her I felt like a mean person for giving Triolo the brush-off. But talking with her helped give me the clarity I needed.

I gave Triolo a definite no. His wedding band, wife, and four-year-old son helped factor into my decision. He's finally stopped pestering me.

I think Paul Stone still has a crush on me, but he seems to accept that I have him firmly in the Friend Zone. Perhaps he's so accepting because I've made it clear to him that I treasure friendship and don't consider him to be "just" a friend. We talk regularly.

I continue to give serious thought to the idea of getting a Masters in psychology so that I can either write about psychological issues and/or become licensed to counsel others who've been vexed like me.

The news of Rose Gannon's terminal cancer is still a state secret. She gave me permission to talk with her physician who confirmed she only has a matter of weeks to live. She and I meet almost daily to discuss her life for our respective books. At times, President Gannon joins us – as he did during this session, which took place, as usual, in the private family quarters on the second floor of the White House two weeks after the Mann shooting.

Rose sat on a couch next to the president, her legs tucked beneath her, a brightly-colored afghan pulled up almost to her neck, her raven hair pulled back in a ponytail. She'd clearly lost weight since a news conference she gave right after the Mann shooting. She hasn't been seen in public since, but the time is coming when she'll have to go public with the news she's dying.

President Gannon's poll numbers dipped slightly in the aftermath of the Mann shooting. Guilt by association. They might have dropped precipitously had it not been for Rose's courage in being willing to confront Mann and try to talk him into giving up. Her approval rating far exceeds her husband's.

In the days following the shooting, the Gannon Administration rolled out an aggressive program that partners with the private sector and nonprofits to tackle the scourge of heroin addiction on six fronts. The program not only focuses on law enforcement, but also funds mental health programs that help addicts get treatment and rehabilitation, while also focusing on prevention and grief counseling for people, like me, devastated by the loss of a loved one to heroin's stranglehold.

Amazingly, there is bipartisan support for the initiative in Congress, perhaps because lawmakers are coming to realize that the tentacles of heroin reach everywhere and can affect *any* family. Perhaps the Congressional good will is also because President Gannon unveiled an Open Skies Initiative that significantly scales back the policy on drones that he'd been about to announce on the day the White House was attacked. The revised policy allows for the commercialization of drones, but with strict licensing requirements, limits on where and how high they can be piloted, and civil liberties protections that require law enforcement to get a court order to, in effect, window-peek.

Today's session with the first lady was devoted to discussing the Mann shooting. I placed my iPhone on the coffee table in front of Will and Rose Gannon and hit *record.*

"Mister President, where were you when Nathan Mann arrived on the Pennsylvania Avenue pedestrian mall?" I asked.

"My Secret Service detail had whisked me from the Oval Office where I'd been working and took me to that now legendary 'undisclosed location.'"

"Were you aware that Mrs. Gannon had decided to defy her agents and was going outside to confront Mann?"

"I was only aware at the last minute. I was actually in the process of defying my own detail and was on the way out there myself to see what I could do."

"Were you upset with your wife?"

"Initially, yes. I was. But I was more worried than upset. Rose is a very courageous person. She always has been. It's one of the many reasons–" His voice caught and he had to stop for a moment. "It's one of the many reasons I fell in love with her."

"Mrs. Gannon," I asked, turning to the first lady, "were you at all worried about your safety?"

"No. Not at all. I don't mean to sound like I'm bragging, but I really wasn't. I honestly thought I had a chance to get through to Nathan."

"You've had a couple weeks to think about the events of that day. What have you learned?" I asked her.

She let out a huge sigh and studied the ceiling for a long minute. "Lark, I've learned there's a big difference between love and control."

"What do you mean?" I asked, noticing that the president was nodding his head vigorously.

"When we love someone," she said, "the feeling of wanting what's best for that person can be so strong that you literally try to control things so that it all turns out the way *you* want. The problem is, love isn't love without the freedom to choose. And, all too often, the people we love make choices that aren't good for them – or aren't what *we'd* choose for them."

The president added, "Yes," he said to Rose, "but in some cases, it's not an unwise choice that your loved one is making." He turned to look at me. "Sometimes, as is the case with Rose, something entirely outside of our control intervenes. I'm supposedly the most powerful person in the free world, but I can't stop cancer from snatching her away from me. Love is powerful, but it has its limits."

An hour later I was sitting in Pearlie by the light pole on 30th Street just off Utah Avenue where Doug died. I come here regularly now to sit, and ponder – and sometimes to cry.

And there are times I do all that, plus talk with Lionel on the phone – which is what I did after my conversation with the Gannons at the White House.

As I listened to Lionel, I studied the asphalt patch next to the curb where Doug's Wrangler was parked for two days, his body slumped against the steering wheel. As I sat in my darkened car, light from the streetlamp spilled like a spotlight, illuminating the place where Doug died.

Cars regularly passed by, and every now and then a person – alone or with someone else – would walk or jog past. At one point, a man walking his dog paused to wait while Fido peed on the light pole. Then they walked on, oblivious to the stranger sitting alone crying in her car parked at the curb.

Where were all these people when Doug needed them?

Suddenly, I pushed open my car door, opened the trunk and got a wrench out of the toolbox I always carry with me.

"Uh huh, uh huh," I said into the phone to Lionel, but I was only half listening. My mind was focused on a job I felt I had to do.

I walked to the light pole and in less than a minute I'd taken down the sign attached to it that I found so offensive because of its hollow ominousness:

Warning:

Neighborhood Watch Area

This neighborhood reports all suspicious activity to the Metropolitan Police.

Or not.

"You're breathing hard, Lark. Are you all right? Are you crying?" Lionel asked, his voice softening uncharacteristically.

"I am crying, Lionel," I sniffed. "But I'm all right."

I put the wrench back into the toolbox and placed the neighbor-hood watch sign next to it, then slammed the lid of the trunk.

"Yes," I said more to myself than to Lionel. "I think I'm going to be all right."

ଔ ଓ ଔ ଓ